Rank

Visit us at www.boldstrokesbooks.com

RANK

by

Richard Compson Sater

LiBERTY
-- EDITION --

A Division of Bold Strokes Books

2016

RANK

ISBN 13: 978-1-62639-845-0

This Trade Paperback Original Is Published By
Bold Strokes Books, Inc.
P.O. Box 249
Valley Falls, NY 12185

First Edition: November 2016

Credits
Editor: Jerry L. Wheeler
Production Design: Stacia Seaman
Cover Photo of Airman by Wayne R. Comer
Cover Design by Melody Pond

Acknowledgments

Rank stands as a testament to those I worked with, for, and against during twenty-four years in the U.S. Air Force. Thanks to my spouse, Wayne Comer, for his patience and understanding—and for giving me time to write. Thanks in particular to my friends Leland Bard and Bob Burt for their detailed constructive criticism of this manuscript in draft form, and in general to everyone who took the time to read and comment on earlier drafts of *Rank*. Their honest feedback was invaluable during the writing and revision process. Finally, thanks to an old friend and longtime mentor, Dr. Robert Gale, for his inspiration and encouragement.

For Wayne Comer,
and in memory of my mother, Dolores J. (Kline) Sater

CHAPTER ONE

A week of leave at Christmas had done little to reverse my impression that I was not aiming as high as the U.S. Air Force intended.

I arrived at the personnel building a few minutes after seven on the second day of the new year. As I walked through the lobby, I barely noticed the mural on the wall spelling out the mission: FLY, FIGHT, WIN.

That to-do list would have to wait.

More immediate were sixteen messages scrawled on pink slips, most marked "urgent," taped to my office door. Inside, the phone answering machine blinked on and off, informing me of forty-one new voice mails. A stack of airman performance evaluations to complete and award nomination packages to revise and submit sat where I'd left it on my desk.

I hung up my coat and hat and sank into the chair. Out of habit, I logged onto the computer. My inbox contained two hundred and thirty-five unread emails, over half of them red-flagged as important. According to my appointment book, the morning was already shot, reenlistments and retirement counseling from eight until noon. Four dreary meetings, back to back, would likewise kill the afternoon. Tomorrow was similarly full, and the next day. How had the Air Force gotten along without me for an entire week?

I affixed a fresh calendar to the wall with dull certainty that the new year would be just like the old one. Not for the first time, I brooded about my decision to seek a commission in the Air Force as a solution to a post-graduate school career going nowhere. After high school, I'd tried the enlisted route, and that little adventure hadn't panned out as promised, either. What made me think the officer recruiter would be any more trustworthy than the enlisted one?

The military personnel field was hardly the target I'd had in mind, and my position as deputy chief of personnel was as impressive and interesting as its name suggests. The glamour-and-excitement quotient registered zero, but I suppose the Air Force can only do so much with a recruit holding a master's degree in American literature.

I still owed three and a half years against my four-year commitment. Would I ever reach the flying, fighting, and winning part?

Certainly not today. I headed for the break room in search of motivation. Perhaps our chief master sergeant had brought doughnuts, but no luck. And no coffee either, an ongoing stalemate. Everyone drank it, but it was never anyone's turn to make it. Maybe I could brew a pot and start the new year with an unselfish gesture of goodwill toward my fellow airmen and colleagues.

Right.

I boiled a mug of water in the microwave and stirred in a spoonful of dark-roast instant. Back at my desk, I sipped carefully and wondered if enough caffeine could somehow dispel my winter's discontent. I surveyed the pile on my desk, uncertain where to begin. Get organized, I told myself, stern. Buckle down. Eliminate the most tedious tasks first. Get them out of the way so they aren't hanging over your head all week.

That resolution cooled as quickly as my coffee.

At half past seven, the chief unlocked the waiting-room door, and we were open for business. At the same moment, the phone rang. Inwardly, I recoiled, and very nearly let the answering machine pick up instead. Regardless of my frame of mind, I wouldn't be able to ignore it indefinitely, however. I picked up the receiver.

"Air Base Wing Office of Personnel. Good morning. Lieutenant Mitchell speaking. How may I help you?"

I'd answered the phone that way too many times to muster even a spark of enthusiasm. Quite possibly, I did not actually *want* to be of assistance.

"Second Lieutenant Harris Mitchell?" a deep voice barked. I detected a hint of a Southern drawl. Where had I heard that voice before?

"Speaking."

"General O'Neill here."

I drew a blank, offering a tentative "Um, who?" Clearly an unsatisfactory response.

First, a noisy, impatient exhale, then he said, "U.S. Air Force

Brigadier General Seamus O'Neill. Your boss's boss's boss, Lieutenant."

Rudeness was not a habit with me, but I was in no mood for jokes. Why would the commander of Sixth Air Force call me?

"Oh, come on," I said. "It's too early in the day for prank calls."

The blowback from the other end of the line nearly singed my hair. Making any more assumptions would not be smart, particularly if he *was* in fact the Sixth Air Force commander. I apologized profusely.

"I want you in my office at 0745 hours, sharp," he said.

I glanced at the clock. I had thirteen minutes. At least the headquarters building was close by.

"Yes, sir. Is there anything else I can do for you, sir?"

"Be on time," he said, hanging up before I could ask any of the questions that immediately crowded my mind. What did he want? Was I in trouble? Had I been guilty of some breach of courtesy, or worse? How was it possible, when I'd never met the man?

I'd seen him but once, six months back, at the newcomer's briefing required of all personnel assigned to the base. I recollected a tall, rangy man in dress blues with an impressive mustache that clearly exceeded the Air Force regulation size limit. He'd welcomed us to the unit with a short speech delivered in a countrified accent, his deep voice weaving together a string of clichés about duty, honor, and patriotism with complete and mesmerizing conviction. He was in and out of the room in ten minutes.

I had been sufficiently intrigued to make a detailed examination of his official photo, part of the portrait gallery in the main hallway of the headquarters building. Each framed eight-by-ten had a brass plate identifying the name and position of our leaders, from the wing commanders all the way to the President of the United States, Commander in Chief. I noted General O'Neill was a handsome man up close, and then I'd promptly forgotten about him.

An unexpected directive from a one-star general could certainly shake off one's new-year lethargy, at least temporarily. The clock reminded me three more minutes had ticked away. I grabbed my jacket and hat and stopped by my supervisor's office.

"What's up, L.T.?"

"I'm not sure, Major Beckett. I've just been summoned to General O'Neill's office."

"What kind of mischief have you gotten yourself into now, L.T.?"

This stereotype about second lieutenants surfaces at the least provocation. As a breed, we couldn't possibly be as inept and ignorant as we are often painted, nor as guilty. I'd developed a thin skin about the kidding, so naturally, I was a frequent target.

"He doesn't even know me! I saw him once, at the newcomer's orientation briefing last year when he gave us a pep talk."

"He's famous for that."

"Why would he want to see me? I don't get it."

"You will, especially if you're late." He checked his watch. "You got, like, seven minutes."

"I have a senior master sergeant coming in at eight to process her retirement paperwork, and three reenlistments after that," I said.

"We'll cover," Major Beckett said. As I headed out the door, he yelled "L.T.! Wait!"

I backtracked, a little alarmed. "What is it?"

He grinned. "Happy New Year, L.T." Really? I tried to formulate a suitable retort. "Run," he said.

❖

I felt like an errant student being called in to see the principal as I raced to the headquarters building. I stopped in the restroom briefly to make sure my tie was straight, thankful I'd worn a clean and pressed shirt that morning. I also took a moment to catch my breath and reinspect General O'Neill's official photo.

Under different circumstances, he might have made a fine pin-up.

I marched into the staff suite with a minute to spare and found him in the outer office, talking with a secretary. I came to attention as I waited for him to acknowledge me, close enough so he could see me but distant enough to get a good look at him.

My ill humor vanished, and even the dread subsided a bit.

The portrait in the hall didn't half do him justice. He wore the standard haircut, cropped short, his hair still mostly jet-black but streaked haphazardly with gray. Only his bushy eyebrows and even bushier mustache remained stubbornly true to their original color. Under the black push broom, in his teeth, he clamped the stem of a pipe. It wasn't currently lit, although a faint and pleasant rum-and-maple aroma in the air suggested he did not strictly heed the base's no-smoking indoors policy. Given his clearly robust constitution, one would never guess smoking could be detrimental to good health.

I noticed immediately how well the flight suit hung on his lanky six-foot-plus frame. I also noted idly he wore no wedding band, only an ostentatious ring on his right hand that announced an Air Force Academy pedigree. The south stretched across his loping drawl like a warm blanket covering a bed. A voice like his could lull me to sleep or arouse me fully.

His pieces fit in a most pleasing assemblage.

The general turned to me abruptly, short-circuiting my reverie, and extended his right hand. I returned his firm grip. I liked the way his brown eyes looked into mine, and the approval reflected in his when I refused to look away. I found no censure in his gaze, and that eased my mind as well.

"My aide position is vacant. I need to fill it immediately, Lieutenant Mitchell," he said.

"Yes, sir."

That was it? I was an aide-de-camp candidate? He might have warned me. It would have saved me a little sweat, if not exactly tears and blood. I wondered immediately why he had singled me out, less than a year after my commission, since a one-star general usually rated a first lieutenant or even a captain as his aide. Besides, the position was not only subservient by definition but also very conspicuous, with a high potential for blundering, the last thing a second lieutenant needed.

Would I be given the option to decline?

He walked all the way around me, inspecting. I stood up a little straighter and held my breath. He came to a stop in front of me again and crossed his arms. "This isn't an interrogation," he said. "Stand at ease."

I exhaled and relaxed my posture a little. "Yes, sir."

"Who's your boss?" he demanded.

"Major Beckett. Dan Beckett, commander of the personnel flight."

"Who's *his* boss?"

So actually it *was* an interrogation. The personnel flight fell under the support group, and I'd interacted with the commander frequently: "Lieutenant Colonel Margaret Corelli."

"Her boss?"

The support group came under the wing. "That's Colonel... Abrahms." His first name escaped me.

"His?"

Our wing, and three others, fell under the Numbered Air Force, in our case, Sixth. "That's you, sir." If he went any farther, I would run out of answers.

He did. "Mine?"

I wished immediately I'd paid more attention to the other photos in the leadership portrait gallery. I couldn't even picture the man who was one step above General O'Neill, let alone recall his name. My silence prompted the next logical question. "My boss's boss?" A heavy, sad sigh came before he asked, "Who's the Secretary of the Air Force?" Silence. "Jesus. Can you at least name the Commander in Chief?"

"Oh, yes, sir. Of course. The President of the United States." If every prospective aide underwent similar grilling, how many fared well enough to be hired?

"How can you work for an organization when you don't even know who's in charge?"

He had a valid point. However, we all take some things for granted. A framed poster on the wall behind the secretary's desk reminded me of the Air Force core values, which I *had* committed to memory and which did matter to me: integrity, service before self, excellence in all things.

I indicated the poster. "Right there, sir. The core values make sense to me. They're good practices, no matter what you do for a living. That's a code of conduct I can respect, and the kind of organization I'm proud to serve."

The general nodded. "Good save, Lieutenant." He cleared his throat. "I'm sure you know what a Numbered Air Force is, and why the NAFs are critical to the mission of the United States Air Force."

"Oh, yes. Certainly, sir."

"Mmm-hmm," the general said. "A NAF is a tactical organization with an operational focus consisting of two or more air wings, grouped with smaller auxiliary units, forming a large striking organization to provide one major aspect of air strength—either airlift, with cargo planes, or refueling capability with tankers, or tactical defense, with bombers and fighters."

"Yes, sir." I was not, in fact, up to speed on the finer points of the NAF structure and mission. I was grateful he chose to lecture rather than ask more questions I couldn't have answered to his satisfaction.

"The NAFs, running consecutively from First Air Force through Twenty-Fifth Air Force, form the senior war-fighting echelon of the U.S. Air Force. As commander of Sixth Air Force, I oversee nine active-duty air wings spread out across nine installations," he said. "That's nearly one hundred twenty-eight thousand acres of real estate, incidentally. Each wing consists of four or five groups. There are sixty-seven squadrons under those groups, comprised of eighteen thousand six hundred forty-three airmen. In addition to y'all, I'm responsible for seven hundred thirty-nine civilians, including my invaluable secretary, Linda Swanson here."

The invaluable Linda Swanson rolled her eyes. I suspected she'd heard this before.

"Our mission is to facilitate the training, equipping, and deployment of assigned units in support of Air Mobility Command," he said. "I own three hundred fifty-two cargo aircraft, the C-5 Galaxy, the C-130 Hercules, and the C-17 Globemaster. Currently, eighty-one of my airframes are involved in one way or another with the Global War on Terrorism. I've got two hundred seventy-seven airmen deployed to various points around the globe, including ninety-eight on the ground in Afghanistan. I have a lot on my plate."

I didn't doubt it.

"A general casts a long shadow," he said. "A good general casts a longer one. I make every effort to be the best general I can be. I accept my responsibilities wholeheartedly. I take them seriously, and I expect y'all to do the same. I set high but attainable standards. I'm quick to praise a job well done and equally ready to criticize when I see a problem. I make the best decisions I can, based on the facts tempered with judicial opinion and honed by thirty years of service in the United States Air Force."

His decisions weren't the only thing honed by thirty years of service. I suspect he'd given this speech numerous times before. It was too detailed, too practiced, to be extemporaneous, and his performance was flawless.

"I need an aide who can manage a general with that much responsibility. Are you the man, Lieutenant Mitchell?"

"I am, sir." I sounded much more confident than I felt. I had no idea what an aide actually did, but suddenly I wanted the job very much.

"Very good." He steered me into his office, offered me a chair, and sat down himself. My personnel file was spread out on his desk. He picked up the pile of documents and then set it down again, clearly dissatisfied.

"Where the hell are my glasses?"

Linda entered the office, murmuring with apparent disapproval under her breath as she handed him a pair of reading glasses and then left us alone again. He shuffled through my file, reviewing each page before setting the stack of paper aside.

"Second Lieutenant Harris Alfred Langdon Mitchell," he said. "That offers nearly endless possibilities."

"Yes, sir," I said. "That was my mom's idea, one middle name from each of my grandfathers."

"What a stirring tribute," he said, his tone suggesting nothing of the sort. "You're prior enlisted."

"Yes, sir. Four years, just after high school."

"What brought you into the service?"

I could hardly implicate my high school trigonometry teacher, upon whom I had a deep and serious crush during my senior year. A reservist himself, he regularly told us tales of his adventures on deployment during Operation Desert Storm a decade earlier. Up to that point, I'd never even considered the military, but he encouraged me when I showed interest. The attacks of September 11, 2001—which occurred during my senior year—actually convinced me to take the big step. When I brought up the subject of military service with my friends, however, most of them jeered, convinced that I'd never survive the rigors of basic training, particularly since I'd come out very publicly that same year.

My bluff having been called, I talked with a local recruiter, and he offered me a slot as a photographer. I liked the job description; at that time, the recruiter couldn't ask and I didn't tell, so I signed on the dotted line for a four-year commitment. A month later, I was on a plane from Columbus to San Antonio and Lackland Air Force Base, Texas. Basic training lasted six weeks and proved moderately strenuous but not particularly difficult, even for an airman prohibited from telling. I'd even earned the designation of honor graduate as well as the Small Arms Expert Marksmanship ribbon.

I completed my bachelor's degree concurrent with my four-year enlistment, working as a reservist one weekend a month and two weeks in the summer, eager to do my bit for the Global War on Terrorism, camera in hand. I discovered I had some talent and a good eye for composition, too.

Unfortunately, digital photography completely overtook the career field early in my term of service. We no longer processed film in a darkroom, and all photo editing and printing were done via computer. I took little satisfaction in it; by my estimation, the art and craft were gone. I missed spending hours in the "soup" to achieve the perfect print.

"Old-school," the general said. "Very good. Is that why you didn't reenlist?"

My decision had been based primarily on the fact that my unit, a fighter wing, was never called to serve in Afghanistan or Iraq, though we trained accordingly. I waited for the promised deployment but it never came, and my patriotic fervor cooled rather quickly. The breakup of a year-long relationship with one of my college English professors coincided with the arrival of my reenlistment papers in the mail. All things considered, I chose not to re-up and enrolled in graduate school instead, concluding my unexceptional enlisted career at the rank of senior airman. I didn't feel obligated to share *all* this information with the general, however, so I sketched only the relevant facts.

Several years of teaching four literature courses per semester at a community college dimmed my fervor for academia as well. Desperate for a change of pace and scenery, I'd visited the Air Force officer recruiter and applied for officer training when school let out for the summer. One thing had changed about the military since my enlisted days, and it made all the difference. I could accept a commission only because "Don't Ask, Don't Tell" was about to fall and I'd be able to serve out in the open.

General O'Neill would find out anyway, if he didn't already know, and I preferred that he'd hear it from me. When he asked what had brought me back to the service after six years' absence, I told him. "The repeal of 'Don't Ask, Don't Tell.'"

He made direct eye contact on that, and his eyebrows went up, too. So there was at least one thing he couldn't extract about me from my personnel file.

"In theory or in practice?" he said.

"Both, sir."

He may have been shocked or at least startled, but he gave nothing away. I hoped my being out would not hurt my chances. He continued leafing through the pages in my file until he reached the last one, then straightened the stack and closed the folder.

"Tell me what a deputy director for personnel does all day to improve quality of life for my airmen."

I outlined my routine for General O'Neill: the endless paperwork, phone calls, emails, meetings. I stayed busy all day, but the actual quality-of-life impact seemed questionable. The general agreed.

"Sounds like you're bored stupid," he said. "Do you like the service?"

"Yes, sir." It was true, regardless of my new-year crisis not an hour earlier. "I just don't feel as if I'm exactly flying, fighting, or winning right now."

He nodded. "That'll do, Lieutenant Mitchell," he said. I stood to leave. "Should I check your teeth and thump your belly?" An easy grin lurked beneath the mustache.

He could put his hands on me anytime. "Maybe you'd better, sir," I said. "Just in case."

He arched an eyebrow. "I'll take a rain check."

As soon as the interview was over, I steered past the chain-of-command photo gallery and made note of the general's boss and the rest of the group under the President. I jotted down the names and put the paper in my back pocket. The information might come in handy at some point.

My next stop was Julia Waterston's office. She was the general's chief of public affairs as well as my best friend. We'd even dated briefly when I'd first been assigned to the base the previous summer, before she let on that she'd known all along about my preferences. We grew even closer after that, sharing every confidence and even comparing notes about our dream date. Mine was older, mustached, and furry-chested in addition to the requisite tall, dark, and handsome. She'd immediately suggested, jokingly, I'd assumed, that her boss met all my specifications.

And now I might be working for the very man. Perhaps Julia would have the lowdown regarding my mysterious summons to his office.

"You'll never guess where I've been," I told her.

She was grinning. "How did your interview go?"

Ah. It all made sense. How else would the general have known about me? "You might have asked me if I had any interest in being a general's aide," I said. "Or at least given me a warning."

"You would have said no, Harris." I moved to protest, but she shook her head. "You need a challenge. The personnel office is crushing your soul."

True, perhaps, but even so. "He called me this morning and ordered me to show up at his office in fifteen minutes with no explanation. I was sure I'd done something wrong, but didn't have any idea what it was."

"General O'Neill asked for my recommendation, and you were the only one who came to mind," she said.

Julia's word would carry some weight. Part of the reason she got along so well with the general was that they had both graduated from the Air Force Academy, though twenty-five years apart. Still, it gave them some common ground. Few around the NAF had a similar pedigree.

"I'll bet he interviews a dozen guys for the job," I said. "Why would he pick me?"

"I'd say you have a very good chance, Harris."

"In other words, if I get the job, it'll be your fault."

"Don't look at it that way," she said. "Think of it as a lottery ticket. You just might win the grand prize."

Years ago, I discovered the curious fact that straight men flirt with each other all the time, subconsciously, a game they play with a kind of I-dare-you subtext. I'm always amused to see a presumably straight man behave so damnably queer, but I can't say I haven't gotten my hopes up on occasion. I couldn't shake the impression General O'Neill had been flirting with me during the interview, and it was a pleasant sensation alongside the physical proximity of a handsome man. I wondered for the rest of that day and all of the next if I'd pass muster. Imagine working alongside such a boss!

From the Air Force Link website, I downloaded General O'Neill's military biography. It contained little beyond the facts, nothing about the man behind them. I learned that he was a native of Tennessee and that he'd started his military career thirty years earlier with his graduation from the U.S. Air Force Academy in Colorado Springs— first in his class, no less. He'd been flying cargo aircraft throughout his career, racking up more than ten thousand hours in the air. He'd held a number of command positions and accumulated an impressive rack of campaign ribbons, including tours of duty in Saudi Arabia, Afghanistan, and Iraq, as well as medals for various achievements.

Anything else I would have to learn firsthand.

Two days later, General O'Neill made an unannounced visit to the personnel office. Someone shouted "Attention!" so he had a good-sized audience. He was, he said, sorry to report that I was apparently the best he could do on short notice. He warned me that the position would be mine for a single year, as general's aide was not a career but only a career-broadening tour. Afterward, I could return to the personnel office or opt to retrain into a different career field. In spite of Julia's confidence, I was astonished and thrilled he chose me.

After the handshaking, Major Beckett sent everyone back to work and pulled the general aside. "Can I talk to you for a minute, sir?"

The general nodded and followed the major into his office. The door closed and some earnest conversation went on behind it. I could guess the gist, although I couldn't hear the words, only the rise and fall of their voices and some apparently sharp words from the general. At least I'd beaten Major Beckett to the draw. I had a good idea what he was telling the general.

The door opened abruptly, and the general strode out alone. "You've got until Friday to conclude your business here, Lieutenant Mitchell," he said. "I'll see you at 0715 sharp next Monday."

"Yes, sir. Thank you, sir." And he was gone.

My first thought was to contact his secretary and find out if she had any good advice for a new aide. All she would tell me, however, was "be on time." After a little research, I located my predecessor, one Thomas Drake, a new captain, settling into a deputy position in our security police unit. I tracked him down and told him I'd been selected as the new aide.

"Man, who did *you* piss off?" he said.

Uh-oh.

He needed no urging to continue. "General O'Neill is a total asshole. He'll ask you to do anything he can think of. One time he sent me all over hell and back because he ran out of pipe tobacco. I had to drive to the mall on my lunch hour to get the kind he wanted," he said. "I was in trouble, like, all the time. Usually it wasn't even my fault, but he'd pile on the shit anyway. In front of other staff officers! Over two months I worked for the son of a bitch, and he couldn't even remember my name. Called me 'Dickweed' or 'Meathead' or some stupid thing."

Captain Drake detailed the general's quirks and weaknesses at length: his demanding nature, his insistence on punctuality, his attention to detail, the long hours, even his fondness for opera.

The captain rolled his eyes after outlining that particular addiction. "It's *so gay*," he said.

With effort, I kept my mouth shut, but he didn't even notice. I was beginning to rethink the strategy of pumping him for insight. A good twenty minutes passed, filled with colorful illustrations, before the captain wrapped up his diatribe with "Good luck, man."

"Thanks, Captain Drake. I think." We shook hands.

"When do you pin on first lieutenant, Mitchell?"

"I'm eligible in six months, but probably not until next year."

He shook his head. "You'll be eaten alive."

So my new boss was unreasonable. At least, I told myself, he was a good-looking man, although I wondered—not for the first time—if showing my pink wouldn't get me in trouble one of these days.

I headed next for Julia's office, just as I had after my initial interview. I got right to the point. "What kind of boss is General O'Neill?"

"You got hired? Harris, that's fantastic! Congratulations!"

"Maybe," I said. "What's the real lowdown?"

"Harris, I've been telling tales about General O'Neill ever since we met!"

"I know. But I never thought I'd be working for him five days a week, all day long."

She laughed. "You got a couple of hours?" She invited me into her office, offered me a chair and a soda, and we settled in for a chat.

"He's spoiled," she said. "What do you expect? He's a general. He's used to getting his own way. When colonels become generals, they become more and more isolated. The layers of protection around them get thicker. Generals get removed even further from reality because no one ever says 'no' to them anymore. But he's got a lot of responsibility. Did you get the Grand Recitation?"

"You mean the one about the nine hundred aircraft and forty thousand people and fifty million acres of land he's responsible for?"

Julia laughed. "I guess you did. Everyone on his staff hears it at some point. In spite of the chest-thumping, there's a lot of truth to what he says. He needs good people around him who can help him get the job done."

From a public affairs standpoint, he was perfect, she said, fully aware of the value of good community relations and willing to do his part. "He's a terrific speaker in front of any audience. Very media-savvy, too. Reporters love him because he's sincere and straightforward and well-spoken. And photogenic. He comes across fantastic on TV," she said. "He makes my job that much easier."

She continued. "He's smart. He listens when you talk to him, but you better get right to the point. Once you prove you know your job, you earn his respect and keep it. I like that. But he's a general, and generals get to be difficult if they want. I get tired of hearing 'because I'm a general' when someone asks him for a reason about anything. But I think he's a good commander and a genuinely nice guy under all the bluster. I couldn't ask for a better boss."

"His last aide would disagree with you," I said. "I just talked to him. He thinks the general is a real…um…asshole."

Julia snorted. "Tom Drake is an idiot. He barely lasted two months on the job," she said.

"Maybe I should talk to the guy before him," I said. "Who was that?"

"I can't even remember," Julia said. "There's been a revolving door on the aide position for the last two years. Did you know you're the fifth one since General O'Neill became commander?"

I gulped. What kind of boss goes through five aides in two years? Was it too late for me to retract my acceptance? "Why do you think I've got a better chance than any of the other ones?"

"Trust me, Harris. It will be a great fit for you," she said. "This place is like a carnival that never ends, complete with freak show and a midway full of rigged games. The general runs the roller coaster himself, and you're in for the ride of your life."

If I could hang on.

CHAPTER TWO

I admit I'm not the best time manager. I mean well but too often, my best intentions get sideswiped. As a concession to my new job, I determined to develop better habits in that regard, particularly since I'd been warned to be prompt. Over the weekend, I readied myself. Got a haircut and trimmed my mustache carefully. Starched and pressed my best blue shirt and aligned my nametag and ribbons evenly. On Sunday night, I set my alarm clock half an hour earlier than usual and put it across the bedroom so I couldn't reach over and hit the snooze button. I had little else to do Monday morning besides shave and shower and eat my cornflakes over the sink.

As I knotted my tie and surveyed my appearance in the bathroom mirror, I was confident I'd make a good impression. I hopped into my old Toyota a half hour earlier than usual, on track to make my 0715 appointment in front of the general's desk with many minutes to spare. Instead of the morning news, my usual companion on the daily commute, I slipped a club-mix CD into the player, a little high-energy dance music to put me in good spirits. Until I had to hit the brakes.

A jackknifed semi-truck on the highway blocked traffic in both directions. My upbeat mood evaporated and twenty minutes ticked by before I could extricate myself from the mess. With no other option, I detoured several miles along back roads at unsafe speeds to reach the base. I skidded into the office about five minutes late. At least I had the satisfaction of a solid excuse. Or so I thought.

The general was speaking with Linda. I came to attention a respectful distance away. Finally, he turned to me.

"My instructions specified 0715."

"I apologize, sir. I left home in plenty of time, but—"

"My instructions specified 0715. Did they not?" He spoke each word more distinctly and louder, as if perhaps I hadn't heard him before.

"Yes, sir."

He pulled a watch from his pocket, an old silver timepiece ticking audibly, hanging on a chain. He snapped the case open and consulted it. "It's now 0723."

"I'm sorry, sir. There was an accident—"

"I don't give a damn!" he thundered. "You're late!"

"Yes, sir. I'm sorry, sir." My antiperspirant would earn its money this morning.

"You may set a land-speed record for the fastest trip in and out of the aide position. Is that your intent?" I'm sure he could be heard halfway down the hall.

"No, sir." Underneath the general's admonishment, I was faintly aware of Linda clucking her tongue. I couldn't tell if she was expressing sympathy or disgust. She had warned me, after all.

He sighed and pointed to his office, its door wide open. "In there."

I went in and stood at attention in front of his desk, awaiting his entrance. He kept me standing there for a good ten minutes. My confidence wilted as the seconds ticked by, and my T-shirt was soggy under the arms by the time the general came in and took his seat.

Finally, he motioned for me to do the same.

"I'd rather be an hour early than a minute late," he said.

"Yes, sir."

"I'm not angry at you, but when I say 0715 and you agree, we've made a pact. Your word is your bond, Timepiece."

"Yes, sir." I vowed to myself never to be late again, even if it meant leaving home the night before to ensure I'd have plenty of time for contingency routing if necessary.

"Who's my boss?" he said.

Relief washed over me. I'd committed the names to memory over the weekend, just in case. "General Raymond E. Johns Jr. at Air Mobility Command Headquarters."

"And his boss?"

"Air Force Chief of Staff General Norman Schwartz, who reports directly to the President."

"Consider your ass saved. Coffee?"

Whew. What could go wrong with serving coffee? I stood again. "Yes, sir. Cream or sugar?"

He waved me back into the chair. "Do you *drink* it?"

Oh. Hmm… "Yes, sir."

"Good. I don't trust a man who can't enjoy a good cup of coffee. How do you take it?"

"Cream," I said. "No sugar."

He disappeared. In his absence, I took my first good look around his office. An elegant walnut desk and credenza reflected good taste as well as his high position. Shelves crowded with books and memorabilia of a long career—model airplanes, trophies, insignia and other small souvenirs—were nonetheless exceptionally well ordered. A leather couch and matching chairs surrounded a coffee table with ornate carved legs. On its top were a neatly fanned selection of military and aviation magazines and an oversize Air Force history picture book. On the wall, instead of the usual aircraft prints and proof of military accomplishment, the general had opted for handsomely framed Monet and Van Gogh reproductions instead.

I could hear music playing low, a soprano expressing her fervent opinion about something or other. The tune sounded familiar. I located the stereo, a top-of-the-line brand, and a rack next to it crammed with compact discs. From my seat, I could make out some of the names on the CD spines: Mozart, Bizet, Wagner, Verdi, Puccini. The general returned a moment later with two steaming mugs, and he handed one to me.

"That's quite a music library you have there, sir."

He arched an eyebrow. "And Maria Callas is your favorite singer," he said.

"Well, sir, I don't know much about the performers, but my mom is a big opera fan, so I heard a lot of it at home," I said. "That sounds like it could be Puccini."

"It is. *Turandot*. Very good." He sounded equally pleased and incredulous. "I'd like to meet your mom someday. None of the heathens around this place appreciate good music."

He rummaged in his desk drawers for something, muttering under his breath until he produced a crumpled pouch of tobacco. He dug into his pocket for a pipe, tamped it full, lit it carefully with a wooden match, and then he directed his full attention to my aide lessons.

"I drink coffee all day long," he said. "One cube of sugar per cup. The box is next to the coffee pot." I gathered he would not be bringing me coffee hereafter. We sipped in silence for a minute, eyeing each other over the rims of the mugs. As on our first meeting, I refused to look away. His eyebrows went up, and he finally grinned.

"You talked to your immediate predecessor?" he said.

"I did, sir."

"Did he tell you I'm a prick?" He smirked.

"Oh, no, sir. Of course not."

He grinned. "Liar. But I'll give you points for loyalty to a brother officer. What's your impression?"

I answered honestly. "Too soon to tell, sir."

"Good answer. Caution is a virtue. First impressions can kick your ass. Are you a quick study?"

"Yes, sir, if the subject interests me."

"Does it?"

I suspected it would, but caution being a virtue, I gave him the same too-soon-to-tell answer, and he liked it just as well the second time.

"Do you learn from your mistakes?"

"Yes, sir. Mistakes are good teachers," I said. "If you don't make mistakes, how much time are you going to spend examining your process to see how you can improve it?"

He liked that, too. "You'll do, Sparkplug. Major Beckett didn't think you would be a good candidate for this job."

"Yes, sir. And I'll bet I know why."

"You do, eh?"

"He wanted to make sure you knew I was gay, didn't he?"

"He did. But I already knew that."

"Yes, sir. But I'm sure Major Beckett thought you wouldn't want your aide to be gay."

"He was most insistent about it," he said.

"Thank you for giving me a chance, sir."

"Don't thank me yet. Speak your mind and be straight with me— er, so to speak," he said. "We'll get along fine."

We stood and shook hands. He appeared to harbor no lingering ill will for my tardiness, for which I was truly thankful. He seemed like a different man from the one who'd dressed me down so thoroughly for being five minutes late.

"One more thing," he said. I waited, expectant. "What kind of softball player are you?"

I knew the general was first baseman on the NAF team. Its last-place rank in the base league was a standing joke, in fact. As for me, I hadn't played softball since high school as part of the mandatory physical education program. I'd been useless then, with no opportunity or desire to improve.

"I suck, sir."

"You're on the team anyway, Electrolux."

"Yes, sir."

Being a general's aide might be more complicated than I'd realized. But with snow on the ground and spring three months away, I wouldn't concern myself with softball. He sat down again and turned his attention to a report on his desk, annotating it with a red pen. Left-handed, too. I stood before him, awaiting instruction, and a full minute passed before he seemed to notice.

"Are you still here?" he barked. "What the hell are you waiting for, Sawbuck? Get to work!" The ghost of a smile lurked beneath his mustache.

The carnival had begun.

CHAPTER THREE

In spite of the warning I'd received about first impressions, I didn't need a week to discover that Seamus Edwards O'Neill interested me tremendously. Complicating the matter was the fact that he may not have been the Wyatt-Earp-crossed-with-Lincoln-and-Jesus of my dreams, but he was as close as I'd found. I liked him immediately, which set off all kinds of warning signals in my head. How long before liking crossed the line into its much more troublesome follow-up? I made a conscious effort to keep such thoughts away, however. A crush would be as painful as its name and uselessly doomed. Besides, I was sure I'd be fired any time, so the split would be easier for me if I wasn't *too* fond of him.

My predecessor in the aide position was right about one thing. The general ignored my name as well as my rank or even its commonly accepted shortcut, L.T. His peculiar habit was to call me some hardware or kitchen appliance or other inanimate object that made no sense in context except it crossed his mind at the moment. It took me more than one missed summons before I realized he meant me when he hollered "Domino!" or some other randomly generated term. Only his increased volume suggested I had better see what he wanted. At first, I just assumed he was too busy to be bothered with something as mundane as a name, or perhaps he thought little enough of me to remember mine. But I quickly realized that he didn't subject anyone else to it. I assumed he was simply staking his claim to me, a sort of unspoken "your ass is mine."

And it certainly was. An aide's primary responsibility is to serve as a kind of consultant to a single client, the assigned general, removing all possible obstacles from the general's military life. To do so efficiently, the aide must be intimately familiar with his boss's habits and preferences. Mind reading is a useful skill, as is the ability to predict the future. A general's job does not include endearing himself to his aide, and mine didn't even try. Imagine working for a man who will not always tell you what he wants—but will not hesitate to tell you when you get it wrong.

Years of practice allowed him to perfect the fine art of the glare. His brown eyes telegraphed a full range of injury and outrage in direct proportion to the gravity of the issue at hand. A single raised eyebrow conveyed a dozen shades of meaning, and his mustache surely had its own posse.

When the general was really bothered or intrigued, his mustache quietly mobilized the forces, as if it could worry through a solution all by itself. The bristle was so subtle I doubt he was even aware of it, but it proved to be a seismograph for his depth of concentration as well as a transom into his subconscious. Once his mustache was activated, short-circuiting him was impossible. The fuse was lit, and he would have his way or his mischief.

My small office was located right next to his, well within earshot, in a suite shared by the vice commander, executive officer, protocol officer, and secretary. The general never used the intercoms to summon any of us, preferring to yell. In addition to a desk and chair, my office housed a hardwood armoire that actually belonged to the boss, stocked with an extra flight suit and cap, blue shirt, tie, belt, pair of boots and other spare parts. I called it the general store, and I added to it regularly as I learned his habits of work as well as play.

Early in my tenure, I purchased a sturdy backpack with a lot of zippered pockets and pouches, and it became my constant companion, sort of the general's aide's aide. Since he refused to carry anything that would not fit into his pockets, the backpack served as a mobile office as well as dispensary and convenience store. I added to it regularly as I grew more familiar with the general's routine—reading glasses, appointment book, the newspaper, a couple of the ceremonial coins he handed out sparingly as a souvenir of a job well done, a pouch of tobacco, a handful of red-and-white pinwheel peppermints, a bottle of water. I grew accustomed to lugging the pack around every time we left the office.

General O'Neill's normal operating mode seemed to be "crisis." He came to depend on those of us who kept his life on track in big and little ways. That dependence naturally rankled him. Subconsciously, at least, he fought back.

"Have you thought about carrying a cell phone, sir?" I asked him after my first week, which included two instances of my having to chase him down in the staff car to deliver an urgent message and one occasion when I'd been unable to reach him in time regarding a change of plans and had to bear his wrath. "I talked with our I.T. guys. They can issue you a phone, and it won't cost you anything."

"I don't want one."

I hadn't yet learned not to ask why.

"I'm a general. I don't have to be available twenty-four seven for anyone's convenience. That's *y'all's* responsibility!"

There was, apparently, *nothing* he detested more than cell phones. As he warmed to his subject, his volume increased until Linda, sitting at her desk, covered her ears. No other single device played such a critical role in the undermining of polite society and civil discourse, he said. He hated hearing the private conversations of others in restaurants and banks and the commissary and the club and the gym and even the men's room. He refused to be part of the problem.

As soon as I had a minute to myself, I set my own cell phone to vibrate so he couldn't hear it ring. I also decided the safest course of action would be never to answer it in his presence, no matter where we might be. He underscored his opinion by issuing me an actual pager. I hadn't seen one in so long, it took me a moment to identify it when he handed it to me. I didn't have the faintest idea how it worked.

"If you can call the pager, couldn't you just…um…call my cell phone, sir?"

He seemed thunderstruck that I would even have the temerity to suggest such a thing. I found instructions online for using the pager and clipped it to my pocket. To my surprise, the general actually used it now and then to contact me, though he must have guessed how I returned those calls.

He wasn't above reinforcing his point of view with truly vigorous action when the situation called for it. A few days after our cell phone conversation, I attended my first staff meeting in my capacity as his aide. Per Linda's instruction, I made the requisite announcement about turning off all electronic devices beforehand. Incredibly, halfway through the meeting, someone's phone rang anyway, its obnoxious electronic beep spitting out "Off We Go into the Wild Blue Yonder" as the unfortunate owner, our vice commander, Colonel Dave Blankenship, frantically retrieved it from his pocket.

The staff was aghast at this breach of clearly defined policy.

Everyone present knew the general's position on the subject of cellular phone technology.

"Let me get that," the general said, evenly. He reached for the phone, and the colonel, sheepish, handed over the offending instrument, still declaiming the Air Force's theme song. "How do I answer it?" the general said. The colonel tapped the screen. "Now what? I just talk?" The colonel nodded.

"Hello?" A pause. "No, ma'am, he can't take the call. He's in a very important meeting. He was told to turn this thing off, and he didn't. It's plain insubordination. Maybe demotion to the rank of major would be suitable punishment. What do you think?"

Colonel Blankenship buried his head in his hands. He could, I suspect, see his career disintegrating before his eyes. There was a longer pause as the woman at the other end of the line offered an explanation or apology. "You'd like to leave a message?" the general said, when she was finished. "Hold on, let me find a pencil." He got up and stepped into the hall and heaved the phone to the other end of it. We heard it clattering down the tiled floor.

"Hey, Sodbuster," the general said after he sat down again. I knew he was addressing me. "You think I'm a prick yet?"

He *had* told me to be straight with him.

"Well, since you asked, sir, you certainly *can* be a prick when you put your mind to it." Julia, sitting to my left, kicked me under the table, but it was too late. The rest of the staff gasped, but once the general broke into laughter, so did everyone else. When the uproar subsided, the meeting continued, but he wore a self-satisfied grin for the rest of the hour.

At the end of the meeting, the general gave everyone a last chance to bring up any other topic of interest before dismissing the group.

"Any alibis?" he said. No one offered. He cleared his throat. "By the way, I'm well aware of the office pool y'all have been running this past year against my aide position. Knock it off."

There was faint laughter, but the general didn't seem to be kidding. My sense of goodwill evaporated in an instant. So they were already betting on how long I'd last. I wondered if Julia knew anything about it.

After the meeting, I tidied the conference room and turned out the lights. The executive officer, Lieutenant Colonel Jennifer Cartwright, pounced as soon as I stepped into the hallway. "Lieutenant Mitchell, report to my office. *Now.*"

"Yes, ma'am."

I followed her. She sat behind her desk, stern and unsmiling—her usual demeanor. She did not offer me a chair. I wondered if I should come to attention.

"Lieutenant Mitchell, what were you even *thinking?*"

"Ma'am?"

"One does *not* speak like that to a general officer under *any* circumstances."

"But, ma'am, General O'Neill asked me to be straight with him. On my first day of work—"

She shook her head. "No," she said. "No. *No.*" The fact that General O'Neill had asked me to be frank in no way tempered the reality that I had been disrespectful, not just to his face but in front of his entire staff. My recollection of the meeting suggested he'd been thoroughly pleased with my remark, but I guess we see what we want to see. And if Lieutenant Colonel Cartwright was predisposed not to like me, I might never be able to change her opinion.

"Didn't you learn anything about customs and courtesies when you were enlisted?" she said.

"Yes, ma'am. I'm sorry, ma'am."

"It's not me you should apologize to. It's General O'Neill." I half expected her to grab me by the ear and march me into the office to beg his forgiveness. She put me in mind of the nuns from my elementary years in parochial school. I would not have been surprised to hear her say my infractions would go down in my permanent record and follow me for life, or at least into my next officer performance report. I could do little except look repentant and repeat, "Yes, ma'am. No, ma'am. It won't happen again, ma'am."

"I'll bet," she said. She kept me standing there, maybe trying to think of some additional humiliation, but she finally dismissed me with one parting shot. "You won't last any longer than the rest of them, Lieutenant Mitchell," she said. In a fierce whisper, she added, "And I'll put my money where my mouth is."

I wondered if she might be right. And Julia later corroborated my suspicion about who was behind the betting pool.

CHAPTER FOUR

After the first-day scolding I received for being late, I really did intend to be punctual. I started getting up an hour earlier on work days and usually arrived at the office at least thirty minutes before the general. But the planets and stars sometimes conspired against my best intentions, and all day long, opportunities for tardiness were plentiful. The second time I arrived late, the general gave me another thorough dressing-down. I'm sure his rant could be heard in the next state, not to mention Lieutenant Colonel Cartwright. Once again, he had no interest in my perfectly legitimate excuse.

When I arrived belatedly for some staff function, my third offense, the general laid down the law like some old gunslinger. "From now on, you're docked a dollar for every late minute or portion thereof," he said, clearly enjoying himself. And why not? He had a rapt audience, representatives from half a dozen agencies in the NAF.

"The fine is payable at the time of the infraction," the general said. "No exceptions. Exact change, or the amount is doubled. Understood?"

I was embarrassed as well as outraged. Could he do that? Charge me for being late? I looked to the others, frozen in their chairs, but no one came to my defense. I bit my lip. "Understood, sir."

After the general established the policy, he found every excuse to enforce it. At first, I didn't much mind paying out a few dollars, even though I'm sure he deliberately set me up to be late on more than one occasion. When I didn't improve quickly enough to satisfy his impatience, he upped the rate to two dollars a minute and then three. By the time the stakes increased to five dollars, I had made a real effort to reduce my tardiness, in part because I was angry as hell. Gradually, punctuality became a habit, or else I hit a lucky streak.

I lost count of how much it cost me. I didn't want to know.

A good aide remains virtually invisible, but my boss took perverse pleasure in aiming the spotlight directly at me. He reminded me daily that any junior airman currently serving in the U.S. Air Force could do my job better than I. As one week followed the next, I continued to assume the axe was imminent. But it never came. Perhaps he felt disconcerted by his significant failure in the aide department thus far and was determined to succeed with me, molding me into the perfect sidekick. Perhaps he wanted to set an example of tolerance in our newly gay-friendly Air Force. Perhaps the extortionist liked the extra income.

Perhaps, although I didn't consider this angle until later, he simply liked me, and he wanted to be sure I noticed.

My relationship with Lieutenant Colonel Cartwright would never thaw. After our first run-in, she seemed distrustful of me, possibly because I served by default as a sort of sentry, a filter. I know she resented having to ask an aide for an appointment to see the general, but that's what he wanted, as he made clear the first time she went directly to him in spite of my protest. As long as the general was at my back, she had little recourse except to seethe in silence.

Thankfully, I enjoyed more congenial relationships with others on the staff. I could not have navigated the first month without the assistance of Julia, Colonel Blankenship, who remained grateful to me for helping him dodge the general's bullets after the cell phone incident, and Mark Sinclair, the civilian budget chief and a retired officer himself, who, I discovered, was gay as well. They offered useful pointers and endless encouragement.

After some preliminary misgivings on her part, I also persuaded Linda to join my team. As the general's secretary, she drafted all his correspondence, kept the files, answered the telephone, kept track of his calendar, and so on. She was in a unique position to know how demanding the general could be. A good aide deflected a lot of the heat from her, but since none of my predecessors had lasted more than a few months, I didn't blame her for being skeptical at first.

The federal repository for NAF scuttlebutt, Linda had been secretary under six commanders in her twenty-three years, but even she couldn't shed any light on the general's conspicuous consumption of aides before me. I figured I'd find out for myself soon enough when he fired me too, but I kept that thought to myself. After six weeks on the job, in a burst of confidence, I offered to relieve her of coffee-brewing duty. She was especially pleased, since she didn't even drink the stuff.

The general congratulated me for my initiative. I didn't realize what I'd gotten myself into.

Fixing coffee sounds easy enough, but not so fast. A drip coffee-maker? Barbaric. Instant? The downfall of empires. Only an electric percolator could deliver appropriate brew. General O'Neill spent forty minutes with me one morning to instruct me of its proper use, an indicator that it was as critical as jet fuel around here. He'd concocted a precise blend of French roast and Columbian with a scoop of plain Maxwell House thrown in. I wondered how long he'd worked to devise the recipe, like some alchemist. Could he actually discern the various ingredients when he tasted the viscous, sturdy broth, or was he simply exerting his right to be a general, to establish rules and demand that others follow?

My final exam was to brew a pot. Happily, I made the grade. Later in the morning, I noticed that his mug was half empty, so I brought in the pot and a single sugar cube for a refill. As I was leaving, he cleared his throat. Uh-oh.

"Sir?"

He sighed. "Goddamn it, Mainspring. You've thrown my coffee-to-sugar proportion out of balance," he said. I wasn't sure if he were truly angry or not, but I apologized, dumped the offending brew and brought him a fresh cup. After that, I never refilled his mug until it was empty. And since he drank coffee all day long, I developed the habit of peering into his mug, always kept on a leather coaster in the same place on his desk, without being too obvious about it.

❖

My gaffes were usually more spectacular than upsetting the general's coffee-to-sugar ratio, and he never conserved volume when informing me of his displeasure. February included breakfast with the recently elected governor, which provided my baptism of fire. The assignment seemed simple enough at the outset. I called the governor's office and verified the place, the date, and the time. I emailed a biography of the general to the governor's secretary and received one in return. Checked with the club to reserve a suitably elegant table. Called the front gate and requested a welcome message to run on the electric signboard. Talked with the governor's driver, gave him specific directions, and assigned an escort to meet them at the gate and bring them onto the base. I was proud of myself for having figured out that all these things needed to be done.

On the morning of the breakfast, General O'Neill sat in the waiting area outside his office and had a cup of coffee with Mark Sinclair and Lieutenant Colonel Cartwright.

"Have a seat, Lawnchair," the general said. I sat, a little nervous at the attention. "Ever met a governor?" he asked.

"No, sir."

"This is your lucky day. Tell me about the guy."

Confident, I rattled off the relevant facts from the official biography.

"He sounds dull," the general said. "Military service?"

"There's none listed in his biography, sir."

"What are his politics?"

"He's a Republican, sir."

"Yes, but what are his politics? How does he vote?"

I was mystified. "On what?"

The general's exasperation brought out his sarcasm. "Agricultural issues impacting local farmers. What else? What's his position on military base realignment and closure?"

Ah. I didn't know.

"How does he feel about units shutting down?" the general said. "Is he in favor of expanding the base? There's talk of an Air National Guard unit relocating here. What does he think about that?"

I didn't know.

"Was he supportive of homosexuals being able to serve openly in the military?" he said. "You should be able to tell me that, at least."

I flushed, and my temper rose, but I could say or do nothing. The general knew it, but he forged on with his point. "Damn it, Lawnchair, I'm not asking just for the hell of it. I've got to spend an hour and a half with this man, and it's bad business for me to be stupid about what he stands for. You think I put up with these damn things because I like soggy French toast?"

He raged, warming to his task as if he'd rehearsed it thoroughly beforehand, and I perspired accordingly. Lieutenant Colonel Cartwright enjoyed watching me squirm, as usual. Mr. Sinclair seemed a bit embarrassed to be caught in the middle of it.

"This is my chance to put in a good word for the NAF and this base," the general said. "We've got another round of closures coming up next year. We're not guaranteed to make the cut. Our asses might be on the line. If I'm not prepared, I'm wasting my time and his, too. When I was at the Academy..."

He railed at me until it was time for us to head over to the club. I was relieved to have any kind of respite, though I expected the diatribe to continue en route. To my surprise, he was well behaved, even genial during the ride in the car, and the breakfast itself went surprisingly well. You'd never have guessed that he wasn't intimately informed about the governor's politics, but I suspect the general had done the necessary homework himself. After breakfast, back in the car, we made more small talk until we reached the office again—where he picked up his rant with a new and predictably petrified audience.

I was sure I'd be dismissed that same afternoon, but all the same, I was angry at him for not being more specific in his instructions. I could easily have accomplished the required research, if he'd only hinted it needed to be done. Perhaps I should have thought to ask if he required any preparation, but I still believed his wrath was far out of proportion to the perceived infraction. I fumed for the rest of the day, and I'm sure he knew it. And I could not give voice my resentment, which seemed to amuse him all the more.

At the end of the day, he called me into his office. I assumed the worst. As I stood there, sullen, he looked up from his paperwork and grinned. "Sit, Horsethief."

I sat.

He gave me his full attention. "I know you think I'm a prick. Admit it."

"All right, sir, if you insist. You can be a prick sometimes." I resisted the urge to embellish with more colorful analogies.

He beamed. "You're the first one who's ever been willing to own up to it," he said. "I work hard at being a prick, and damn it, I want people to notice." Leisurely, he set his papers aside, found his pipe, tamped tobacco into it, and lit it. After a contented puff, he looked at me again. "You're doing a great job, you know, but you screwed up today."

"Yes, sir." His remark about my doing a great job intrigued me most. He had never indicated as much before, and my outlook brightened considerably, though I did wish for other witnesses to my moment of triumph.

"It won't happen again?"

"It won't, sir." At least that particular mistake wouldn't. I knew there would be others, but I was relieved that he seemed to have forgiven me.

He grinned. "Get the hell out of here. See you on Monday."

I was more than ready for the weekend.

CHAPTER FIVE

After winter comes the spring. We awake from hibernation. Green appears. We reach for the sun and grow. In spite of his very public displeasure, General O'Neill came to trust me, and my duties expanded accordingly. He complained sometimes that his job was three-quarters decorative and one-quarter actual work. An outsider might think so, but I knew better. Like a good social secretary, I spent half of my day on the phone, working closely with our protocol staff and Julia in the public affairs office to engineer his appearance at various events, changes of command, important promotion ceremonies, official dinners, and so on. The rest of the time I spent with the general, shadowing him, catering to his mercurial nature. At the end of every work day, I synchronized my calendar with Linda's to make sure the schedules were identical.

Three times a week, his schedule included a rigorous workout of stretching, calisthenics, and distance running. With all his nervous energy, he would never be overweight, but he firmly believed in the health benefits of regular exercise, preferably outdoors. In the dead of winter, he frequented the gym, and I was left to pursue my own workouts beyond his watchful eye. By late February, he was restless to escape the confinement of the walls and the monotony of the treadmill and determined to hit the streets on the first day of March, with me by his side.

Despite sun on that day, the thermometer read thirty-one degrees, which deterred the general not in the least. Though my track-star past was some years behind me, I fell into that groove again easily, silently grateful his sport of choice wasn't fencing or weight-lifting. On the road, I matched his speed with ease, but after five miles, I was barely winded and he was whipped, much to my satisfaction and his annoyance.

We fell into a routine. We'd begin at the gym, changing into our running togs, stretching, and then hitting the road. We'd return damp and thoroughly exercised. Alas, he received the key to the distinguished visitors' locker room, while I had to content myself with the cattle barn reserved for the rest of the lowly others. It was just as well. I'd reprimand myself sternly every time my thoughts strayed to the unexplored territory under the general's T-shirt and baggy shorts. Lusting for Seamus O'Neill could only lead me in every wrong direction.

❖

For all the tedious aspects to the workday, there were perks I didn't expect. My favorite came in the form of travel. As the NAF commander, the general routinely made one or two brief trips a month. From the start, he insisted I accompany him, primarily because it relieved him of having to bother with any of the details like meals, lodging, and ground transportation. My favorite trips were those from base to base, when he'd visit the various wings attached to our NAF and under his command. He'd pilot one of our C-5s and put me in the jump seat next to him. Plugged into a headset, I could listen to the soundtrack for the flight as he explained the various aspects of maneuvering an airframe. Someone who is enthusiastic about his job takes great delight in showing it to the uninitiated, and I found such learning opportunities rewarding and fascinating, though I had no interest in becoming a pilot myself.

Under the general's critical eye, I reluctantly became a better officer as well, though I was not the most apt pupil. Being a second lieutenant is like singing along with the radio. No matter how good you are at the job, no one's going to pay attention. I found much about military ritual to be a little absurd, with no practical application, though I didn't dare breathe a word to suggest that my opinion differed from his.

"You have every right to be proud. Act like it. You're serving in the United States Air Force. Stand up straight. Don't slouch," he barked at me regularly when we walked together. "Keep up with me. Don't follow."

He began hauling me outside during his official smoke breaks so he could continue instructing me or, more often, telling stories of his own experiences. And there we were, twice a day for twenty minutes, himself parked on the front stoop of the NAF headquarters, puffing contentedly in all weather, and myself sitting awkwardly next to him, much to the consternation and unease of those coming and going from the building. How does one greet a general sitting on the step in a cloud of blue smoke? Most people chose to err on the side of caution and snapped a salute. He'd grin and return the salute with a wave of his pipe and a terse greeting. It unsettled everyone, which is certainly why he chose to do it.

Anyone passing by could learn a thing or two from one of the general's monologues if he was in the mood to hold forth on the subject of customs and courtesies, traditionally a big part of day-to-day life in the Air Force. The general was a strong advocate of insisting upon on all he was due, but he also insisted I receive my share as well. I hated being saluted as much as most people disliked saluting a lieutenant. I went out of my way to avoid it if possible. Nor could I ever bring myself to upbraid anyone who failed to salute. We all had better things to do. But the general had no use for lack of professionalism from any rank.

"You look sharp," he said, "so *be* sharp. Salute with pride, like you mean it. They're not saluting Harris Mitchell, the lieutenant. They're showing respect for centuries of military tradition. As you advance in rank and become more experienced at your job, the word will get around. You'll be saluted for who you are, because they'll respect you for being a good officer and a good leader."

Easy for him to say. He virtually never had to salute first. I had no aspirations to be a leader. I preferred to follow. It was less complicated. I was not merely passive, I just liked to watch. At the end of his break, the general knocked his pipe against the railing, emptying it of sparks and ash. He concluded this ritual with a pinwheel peppermint, a sort of dessert, as we headed back inside.

❖

After a relatively calm month, during which General O'Neill earned not a single dollar from me for being late, he summoned me into his office at the end of the workday.

"Stopwatch, what are your plans tonight?"

Hmm…laundry, a microwavable pizza, a little mindless internet surfing, and a good book. "Nothing worth mentioning, sir."

"We're going out to dinner to celebrate," he said. "It's been thirty-four days since you were late, and I think we can safely assume you've learned your lesson."

"Yes, sir."

"There will be no more late fees, but I reserve the right to reinstate the program at the first sign of slacking."

"Agreed, sir."

"Meet me in the parking lot at eighteen-hundred hours," he said.

"On the dot," I said.

"Exactly. Dress appropriately, Shirttail. We won't be going to a burger joint."

At home, as I showered and chose suitable attire, I couldn't help but think that the general had made a dinner date with me, however one chose to look at the situation. Even as that thought crossed my mind, however, I immediately pushed it out and sternly lectured myself about backing wrong horses of different color in midstream. Regardless, I felt a rush of excitement as I drove back to the base.

I arrived a good thirty minutes early, just to be safe, leaving me thirty minutes to pace, check my watch, and worry before the general pulled into the lot precisely at six in a stylish dark-blue hybrid, immaculately kept. I'd never seen him in civilian clothes before. He wore dark slacks, a charcoal sport jacket, white shirt, and maroon tie as elegantly as his dress blues, and great God! He was even more handsome. For once, he chauffeured me, and I was surprised when he parked at one of the fanciest restaurants in town.

Our meal began with appetizers and a bottle of white wine, and after one glass, I'd never felt so relaxed in his presence. In civilian clothes, we might have been mistaken for two friends enjoying an evening out. As effortlessly as the general could make me shake in my boots under his frown, he could put me entirely at ease, as if anything were open to consideration. I felt confident enough at last to compliment him about his accent, which I'd come to love.

"Awwww, shucks. That ain't nothin'," he said, stretching his words like molasses taffy.

We both laughed.

"My dad's job relocated him from Boston to Knoxville just after he married my mother. That's where my sister and I were born and raised. I made an effort to lose the twang when I started college," he said. "I didn't want my fellow cadets at the Academy to think I *really* was a hillbilly. I worked at it hard for a while but I got bored. It's too easy to get lazy when you're self-improving."

What was left mixed his old Southern with just a salting of nondescript Midwestern. It was peculiarly and endearingly his own, its timbre as deep as Christmas and as insinuating as a bribe, promising twice as much loot in exchange for the right kind of cookies and milk under the tree. He could talk all night, and I would be content to listen.

He shared some family history about all four of his grandparents being first-generation Americans, right off the boat from Ireland in the early years of the twentieth century. How his mother insisted on a traditional name for him, even if most people mispronounced it. "Nowadays," he said, "I get a kick out of it when somebody calls me 'SEE-mus,' but when I was a kid in east Tennessee, it drove me crazy."

Over chicken Kiev with rice pilaf and roasted vegetables, our conversational well never ran dry, ranging broad, far, deep, and easy, through literature (I urged him to read *Moby Dick*, my choice for the greatest American novel) and music (he insisted that Tchaikovsky's Fifth was the pinnacle of symphonic achievement) and movies (we both liked old westerns) and travel (he'd visited all seven continents yet had never been to Paris, one of my favorite cities), even sports (he loved listening to baseball games on the radio, a habit he'd learned as a boy from his grandfather).

I asked when his mustache had made its first appearance.

"I started cultivating it in high school," he said. "My senior portrait is proof that it wasn't much, but I was certainly proud of it at the time."

"They let you keep it at the Air Force Academy?"

"Not until I'd completed Basic Cadet Training. After that, it was tolerated but not encouraged. I had to trim it nearly every day. It was tedious business. I don't have to worry about it anymore."

"Why is that?"

He arched an eyebrow. "I'm a general." His all-purpose excuse again. I had to laugh. "If I trim the damn thing to conform with the Air Force regulation, I'd look like Hitler," he said. "That's not going to happen."

"So your mustache will remain disobedient, sir?"

"Wayward and threatening mutiny. I wouldn't be surprised if it didn't bail out and set off on its own with no warning. One day, I'll wake up and find it gone."

"There is much head-shaking and disapproval wasted on your mustache, sir."

"I'm well aware. My command chief master sergeant has a fit every time he's in the same room with it. You would think our whole air and space force is in danger of collapse because of my black haystack."

"I imagine you chop it down a little when it gets too threatening."

"Occasionally," he said. "With a scythe."

"You don't think flaunting the regulation sets a bad example?"

He beamed. "Everyone should aspire to attain a position in life where he can flaunt the rules without consequence."

"Someday, maybe I'll earn the right to wear one like yours," I said.

He chuckled. "Could you handle that much responsibility?"

"I have none of your firepower at my disposal right now," I said, "so I am forced to landscape my mustache according to regulations. But don't let this well-manicured evidence fool you. My mustache yearns to mimic Mark Twain's, and it will not be denied forever."

I'd never seen him laugh so heartily.

When our leisurely three-hour meal ended with coffee and dessert, I felt as if we'd really gotten to know each other. I couldn't even guess at his intent, but I was grateful just the same. I thanked him for his generosity, and he merely wagged his eyebrows at me. When the waiter brought the check, the general paid in cash, all ones and fives.

"Don't thank me, Bankroll. It's your treat."

I was learning him by heart.

By mid-April, softball season was in sight. The general marked our first practice on the calendar and reminded me that I would be on the team. Reluctantly, I purchased a mitt at the base exchange, though I was annoyed that the cheapest one available cost nearly thirty dollars. I turned out for the first practice, my stiff new glove conspicuous among everyone else's well-worn ones, veterans of hundreds of games.

At least I'd get out of the office an hour early once a week.

Attired in sweatpants, ball cap with NAF patch, team shirt, and cleats, the general was the most committed player on the team. He'd played at the Academy, as he reminded us repeatedly, though his mere presence ensured at least minimal concentration from the other players. The general was not the actual coach, but he might as well have been.

He spent a lot of time in the batting box discussing strategies and substitutions with the poor major who nominally held the position. The general leaned hard on the coach, who usually caved in, much to the derision of the rest of the team.

Our boss proved reasonably adept at first base, being a good catcher with quick reflexes, though, on more than one occasion, he'd been guilty of more enthusiasm than skill. I recall him crouched next to the base, glaring from under his ball cap, with all the potential energy of a cocked trigger. Batting was another story. A lefty, he was unreliable and knew it. He'd rarely strike out, but someone in the field usually caught his graceful pop flies. "Damn it, not again," he'd mutter. "At least I'm consistent!" he'd yell in response to the catcalls. "That's more than I can say for most of y'all sons-o'-bitches."

Practice was useful to me, as I'd had little experience. No one had ever instructed me on the finer points of the game. Simple things like keeping an eye on the ball. How to hold the bat. How and when to swing it. How to throw hard and fast and far without spraining one's arm. I kept my dad informed of every detail of our practice and our games, and I knew he was equally proud and mystified at my sudden interest. I didn't admit I hadn't been given a choice.

The general was as hard on me at the diamond as he was in the office, and he had a mostly new audience to watch the show. To be fair, he refused to let up on anyone who didn't give one hundred percent, but everyone else on the team was a veteran of seasons past and knew how to behave. When the gap between my enthusiasm and my skill level proved too wide to ignore, the general spent a good half hour in his office with me one afternoon, the door closed, a rolled newspaper in my fists, attempting to follow his instructions as he explained the logistics of gripping and swinging a bat.

"Damn it, Strikeout. Do it again. Line up your knuckles. Like that. Swing it level. Bring the bat all the way around and shift your weight onto your right foot." I tried. He watched and railed. "Shift your *weight*, damn it, and follow through. Swing level! Do it again." He grabbed the rolled newspaper from me and demonstrated. "See? That's half your power right there. You get it right, and the ball will go twice as far, but you want it to feel natural." He handed the newspaper back to me. "Do it again." He sighed, deep. "*Level* swing, I said. Jesus. You're not even trying!"

Finally, frustrated at my inability to follow his instructions, he moved behind me. In a moment, he folded himself around me, his body molding to mine. The unexpectedness of the motion startled me. As we stood with our arms twisted around each other in an odd embrace, I looked around and up at him, curious. He merely grinned, and his eyebrows shot up and then down in a fraction of a second that spoke volumes.

"Easy, Sandbagger," he said. "My intentions are honorable. I'm just trying to make you into a ballplayer. Now move with me."

He was close enough to me that I could smell his aftershave, just a hint of it, so subtle I don't think I'd noticed it before. It suited him. And he suited me at that moment; his confident physicality, his body pressed firmly against me, and his strong hands covering mine, were enough to give me an erection, the first time I'd ever connected those particular dots with him. I was grateful he was behind me and didn't notice. But I didn't have the time to worry too much about it, because he got right down to business, reducing bat-swinging to basic principles of physics and geometry.

I moved with him. Willingly. He did the best he could in this single instance where I could not accommodate his being left-handed.

At the end of our batting session, he said, "Be careful, Sandbagger." I felt that he wanted to say more, but I wasn't sure what he was chasing. He fumbled with his pipe and finally, he just said, "Watch out for yourself. Don't get yourself hurt. Promise, now."

I couldn't imagine how his curious remarks related to softball. But I promised.

I could smell the faint, exotic musk of his aftershave on my shirt all afternoon. And I wonder if we are all left-handed in our various ways, trying to make our way in a right-handed world.

❖

Not long after that, I visited the local batting cage to see if I had learned anything. The unrelenting machine shagged its balls at me, and I tried to recall everything the general had told me about stance, grip, swing, and following through. Without the inconvenience of having to run each time I connected with the ball, I settled into a groove. Before long, my bat slammed against the ball consistently with solid contact. At the end of a hundred balls, I was tired but satisfied. Even if my arm and shoulder muscles were stiff and sore for a few days afterward, I felt somewhat more accomplished.

To the surprise of everyone except the general, who took full credit, I became a reliable hitter. Near the end of the season, one of the other players would point out to me that I had the highest batting average of anyone on the team. Though I rarely parlayed those hits into more than a single, at least I'd never struck out or popped out.

The offset was my lack of skill in the field. If I'd been even inconsistently useful out there, life would have been perfect, but I never got the hang of catching balls lobbed at me. The team could count on me to drop those crucial flies when they headed in my direction. The coach put me in the outfield as a rover, wandering between right and center field, where I could do the least damage with a decent player in the primary positions.

So I prowled across my assigned territory, but I kept an eye on the general. Watching him was my favorite part of those afternoons. I didn't even mind when he hollered specifically at me as he stood at the fence, occasionally encouraging but usually berating, chastising, and beseeching, his mustache working furiously, reaching absently under his shirt to scratch some itch.

Our team was hardly well-prepared for our weekly games. Faced with an actual opponent, we usually fell apart regardless of the strategies we'd built up during practice. Before the games, the general tossed grounders, flies, and curves my way in a valiant effort to kick-start my fielding instincts. He yelled himself hoarse at each of the games, trying to pump some spirit into the lot of us.

Julia attended occasionally to cheer us on, and I appreciated her support. She was there during our third game when I managed to pull off my single instance of better-than-adequate fielding. We were losing by a run or two, and we had one more at-bat as soon as we struck out our opponents. I was parked between center and right field, and the batter socked the ball right to me. I could not pretend it was anyone else's responsibility. Not feeling particularly hopeful, I nonetheless stuck my gloved hand into the air.

Now and then, we get one of those spectacular moments as a reward for other hell in our lives: the perfect ice-cream catch, a scoop of dirty vanilla plopped perfectly into the leather cone of a mitt stretched up to the blue sky. Maybe it was simply an accident, a bonus meant for someone else. I don't know. But it didn't matter. The batter was out, and we were up.

As our team trotted off the field, the general grabbed my hand and pumped my arm. "You've been holding out on us, Pipeliner," he said. "Good work!" It made the whole effort worthwhile, as far as I was concerned. We didn't win the game, but I felt like a hero that night anyway.

Afterward, we drank beer in the parking lot, provided by those who had struck out during the previous game. The general put an arm around my shoulder. His mustache brushed against my ear as he whispered, "You're getting better all the time, Dodger. You're my greatest success story. I'm proud of you." That's all I needed to hear. I only wish he'd said it loud enough for the rest of the team to appreciate as well.

"My dad wants you canonized for getting me interested in softball, sir," I told him. "He thinks you're some kind of miracle worker."

He chuckled. "I am."

CHAPTER SIX

M y dad has a vested interest in softball and such things. He's managed a sporting goods store in our Ohio hometown for years. It's a great fit for him. He'd been hired as a clerk at the same store when he was still in high school, and in the years since, he'd worked his way up to being a half owner in addition to manager. The place does great business, supports the home teams, keeps up with the trends, and gives him some flexibility with his time.

I was more interested in academic pursuits as a kid. I preferred to spend a sunny Saturday with a book rather than a ball, and my dad never pushed too hard. In high school, I tried out for the track-and-field team because he insisted I get involved in an activity that required physical exertion outdoors. I had the build for running, so it was the logical choice. Once I overcame my initial reluctance, I rather enjoyed it. Longer distances proved to be my forte. I picked up a first-place trophy for the mile run at a regional track meet and pulled off the same feat at the state level as well.

My dad and I have come a long way since then. We've traveled some rough terrain, mostly mapped by my refusal to budge once I'd announced unequivocally that I was queer. I used to wonder if we'd come through the woods alive, but we did. We don't talk much. We've never needed to.

He'd been drafted into the Army at eighteen, sent to Vietnam for combat duty in the waning days of the war, and sent home at twenty. He rarely mentions his hellacious, harrowing tour, but after I was commissioned, I asked him if he would consider telling me about his experience. He looked at me for a long time, thought about it, and nodded. We will find the right time.

He has been a passionate fisherman since his own father began taking him to rivers when he was four or five years old. Dad tried to do the same with me, but fishing bored me as a kid. I didn't realize how important the sport was to him until I was in college. By then, I wanted us to spend more time together, and the easiest way was to find activities we could share.

He was frankly amazed the first time I asked him if he'd take me fishing, and he had the pleasure of showing me how all over again. I paid close attention, and I learned how satisfying it could be, getting up at four a.m. for the drive in his old Ford pickup to one or another of the lakes within a short distance of home, launching the skiff just before dawn, and catching our limit if we were lucky.

The night before any of our fishing trips, he generally spends hours preparing, choosing the proper accessories for the tackle box, testing the reels, tying off extra hooks. We could, I think, catch anything from a goldfish to a blue whale with the gear he loads into the pickup, though we're unlikely to find anything but good-sized rainbow trout, bass, walleye, pike, depending on the season. It's his passion, and I would not interrupt it or criticize. He's the most talented angler I know, and I will never stop learning from him.

We've grown closer through our fishing trips, but that bond has absolutely nothing to do with pouring our souls out to each other in conversation. We hardly say a word. The silence is its own generous instructor, as it can be anytime two people share a task that both enjoy.

❖

I am likewise close to my mom. Our relationship has always been solid. We've never had to work at it, but I certainly have never taken it for granted. She was always home when I was growing up. When I entered Ohio State as a freshman, she enrolled at the local community college, ultimately earning her associate's degree in medical administration.

I was as proud of Mom's straight-A report cards as she was. After graduation, she hired on with a physician in town, but she quit after five or six years because she decided she hated the work. She's found greater personal reward and a fuller schedule volunteering at the hospital, Meals-on-Wheels, a local food bank, and the library. She has her own interests and her own circle of friends, and my dad has his, but they intersect enough that they are content.

Their only battle zone is the stereo.

My mother chooses to listen to *Madame Butterfly* or *Aida*. Mom inherited her appreciation for the trained voice from her dad, my late grandfather, who sang in a beautiful tenor himself. Her extensive knowledge of opera, of plots and characters and arias, grew from no particular schooling, simply a love for the drama and music. Puccini is a favorite of hers, and Mozart and Verdi, too.

My dad, however, prefers the classic country style of Hank Williams, Johnny Cash, Willie Nelson, and Patsy Cline and their twangy, uncomplicated songs about complicated emotions. My dad claims to be a simple man and prefers music he can understand. Three or four chords are generally sufficient. Privately, my dad thinks all opera sounds like yowling cats. Privately, my mom thinks country music celebrates an ignorant redneck sensibility with a little too much enthusiasm.

When I was growing up, the soundtrack for my life was a splendid train wreck of grand opera and Grand Ole Opry. I refused to pick a side, maintaining a foot in each camp. In no way can I mine an unhappy childhood for excuses of any sort. I've genuinely enjoyed being part of our small family. Years ago, I hoped for a brother or sister to relieve some of the pressure of being an only child. But I grew out of it. My parents seem to be satisfied with me, and I certainly am with them.

The general's experience, however, was quite different. Although he'd speak on occasion of the Great Smoky Mountains and the Little Tennessee River—beautiful country, he'd tell me, and I must see it one of these days—he rarely shared any details about his family. I don't think he deliberately withheld anything. He just didn't want to talk about it much.

The general's mother died from cancer when he was in his early twenties, not long after he'd graduated from the Academy. His dad sold the suburban family home and bought a condominium in the city. The general's younger sister is married with five children in Virginia. No one else in his family chose a military career. I wondered why he was so close with the details. Doesn't everyone talk about family?

❖

I re-upped in the spring of 2011, not long after the President had signed legislation to eliminate the damnable "Don't Ask, Don't Tell" policy across the whole Department of Defense. The ban was still in place, however. It would not be officially dropped until the military services were "ready," due to the projected risk that homosexuals posed to combat readiness.

Whatever.

Perhaps some of the other estimated sixty-five thousand gay servicemembers were as surprised as I was when the policy was abruptly eliminated at midnight as Tuesday, September 19th, became Wednesday the 20th. For the first time, gay soldiers, sailors, airmen, and marines could serve openly, as if years of gay-baiting and witch-hunting and homophobia had never happened.

I remember the anxiety and exhilaration I felt that morning as I dressed and ate my breakfast and drove to work. But I also knew I would not remain silent. As I showed my ID to the security-forces airman at the front gate, I announced a bit breathlessly, "I'm gay!"

The moment was liberating for me but lost on the gate guard.

I parked my car and walked into the building, eagerly scanning the faces of the people surging toward the doors, looking for a sign of the new times. Airmen rushed past me, anxious to get inside before the base loudspeaker system started broadcasting "The Star-Spangled Banner" at half past seven, for which they'd have to come to attention and salute until it concluded, and thus be late to work.

At the end of our morning briefing, when Major Beckett asked if anyone had any final announcements notes for the group, I raised my hand. "I just wanted to let everyone know that I'm gay."

"Well, *duh*," someone said. Everyone laughed.

"Okay, thanks for sharing," the major said. "Anything else?" And we were dismissed to start our work day, sent out to deal with the customer-service complaints of an endless line of airmen with urgent personnel issues to discuss. A typical day, full of standard vexations and tiny victories.

In the days that followed, I continued to search for something tangible on our base as witness to the change. For me and others like me, serving openly was radical, groundbreaking, deserving of speeches and brass bands, parties and proclamations, if not a rainbow banner flying on the mast next to the Air Force flag and the stars and stripes.

It was not cause for celebration in every quarter, however. I came to realize the best way to commemorate the revolution was to ensure that business continued as usual. After all, we had an air and space force to run and a nation to protect, and we had insisted for years that allowing gay people to serve openly would not be disruptive.

When I saw the flyer posted at the gym in late April, four months into my tenure as the general's aide, I couldn't help feeling supremely pleased. It was an advertisement for airmen interested in marching in the gay pride parade in June. It would be the first occasion when actively serving military personnel could march without doing so undercover, and I didn't want to miss it. I jotted down the phone number and called later. To my surprise, the guy who'd posted the flyer was one of my old colleagues from the personnel office.

"Sergeant Forester! So you came out, too."

He laughed. "You set a great example, Lieutenant Mitchell. Are you marching with us?"

"Wouldn't miss it. Sign me up."

"Great!" he said. "So far, you're the only officer who's called. I'd like to get a few more. There are plenty out there. Except most of them aren't actually out." He laughed. "Hey! Maybe we should ask Beemis!"

That would be Lieutenant Colonel Matthew Beemis, commander of our security forces unit, for whom I'd developed an immediate dislike. Once I'd overheard him tell a truly offensive gay joke when he knew I was in earshot, as if he dared me to say anything about it. I didn't. I suspected his intense homophobia was a protective posture, that he was gay and in full denial. This topic generated some gossip around the NAF. Perhaps he hated himself as much as he claimed to hate the rest of us "fags," but I couldn't summon much sympathy for him.

"You think he'd be interested?" Sergeant Forester said. "Of course, he'd have to drop that charismatic 'gay-baiting asshole' pose long enough to reveal the true rainbow within." Without missing a beat, he added, "Did I say that? Oops. Sorry."

"Except you're right," I said. "Beemis *is* a gay-baiting asshole. I wouldn't want to claim him even if he did come out."

"You got that right, sir. Still, it would be nice to get another officer or two. Maybe a captain or major."

"Good luck with that. Somehow, I don't think being out and proud would look good to a promotion board. Maybe someday, but not yet," I said. "It would help just as much if a couple of the chiefs would join us. How many senior-enlisted guys do you have on your list?"

"Let's see," he said. "That would be zero."

"Not even the maintenance superintendent?"

He laughed. "Chief Jordan? Nope. I bet he still thinks people haven't figured him out, but I know a couple of guys who can give you the real lowdown on Fairy Gary. He's as bad as Beemis, except that the chief *isn't* a homophobic asshole. He's just scared."

I agreed. "It's a shame. He's got nothing to lose. No more promotion boards to meet. Chiefs carry a lot of weight. It would set a great example, not just for the junior guys, but the officers, too."

"Yeah," he said. "I think there's hope for him, but he hasn't met the right guy."

"Go for it."

"No, thanks. I'm not interested in a science project just now. Anyway, we've got about thirty signed up so far. We're getting T-shirts with 'serving out loud' on the front with the NAF patch on the back. The shirts cost twelve bucks apiece if we order in quantity, but I'll have to get the money in advance."

"No problem," I said. "What's the plan for the march? Drill formation?"

"Nothing like that. We're making a big banner to carry in front, but otherwise it will be kind of informal. I grabbed a big stack of the recruiting brochures for the NAF, and we can hand those out, too. Maybe we can drum up some interest in the unit."

"Sounds like you've thought of everything."

"I just hope a lot of guys show up to march," he said. "Spread the word, okay? And bring your boyfriend, too, Lieutenant Mitchell. The more the merrier."

Hmm. If only I had a boyfriend to bring. "I'll stop by later today with the T-shirt money, Sergeant Forester." We traded good-byes.

I decided not tell General O'Neill about my plans. I figured it was none of his business how I spent my off-duty Saturdays. Even if he found out, what could he say to me that wouldn't get him into trouble with the Office of Equal Opportunity, our own Gatekeeper of Political Correctness?

❖

The day of the parade dawned, gloriously perfect, warm sun and cloudless blue, like optimism come alive. I had been attending pride parades for years as a spectator. For the first time, my colleagues and I could proudly announce our identities as a gays and lesbians serving in the U.S. armed forces. I was looking forward to it.

In spite of the fact that we were free to be as out as we chose,

I'd come across few people on the base who were eager to identify as openly gay. Beemis and Jordan were hardly isolated cases. New worlds aren't necessarily easy to explore, and the knowledge that one is a trailblazer isn't necessarily a comfort. One day, being gay was a crime punishable through the Uniform Code of Military Justice. The next day, being gay was fine, and all military personnel were ordered to accept it, pretend it was no big deal, and not be troubled by it at all.

On base, still a little unsure, we trod cautiously. But the pride parade was different. The mere act of participating meant you probably had at least one thing in common with others who came to march. And on the day of the parade, about twenty-five airmen and a few civilians were brave enough to show. I can't say for certain how many chose to take part out of mere curiosity—who *else* from our base was gay or lesbian?—but I admit I was among them. Indeed, most of us were giving each other a friendly once-over. Who knows? If you're looking for a partner or even a friendly hook-up, you might as well hang out in places that draw like-minded people.

As the senior-ranked person and the lone officer in attendance, I became the default leader of our little group, checking people in and handing out the T-shirts according to the list provided by Sergeant Forester.

"Forty-six signed up, Lieutenant Mitchell," he said. "I kind of figured some of them would get cold feet."

Participants were mostly unfamiliar to me. Nearly all of them were junior enlisted guys and gals, the ones with nothing to risk, who'd grown up feeling comfortable in their own skin, confident that they had nothing to hide or be ashamed of. But I was still a little disappointed the group wasn't more diverse in terms of age and experience.

Following instructions shouted by a woman with a bullhorn, our little faction lined up behind a high-school marching band and in front of a church group on a bus inscribed "God sends a rainbow sign." I took one end of our banner and Sergeant Forester took the other. When our turn came, we stepped out with purpose.

It was a good day for confidence. We were greeted with cheers and applause all along the parade route and had no trouble handing out our recruiting brochures. When we reached the end, after friendly hugs and handshakes all around, the group scattered to enjoy the rest of the weekend. I rolled up the banner and was heading to my car with it when a man wearing a professional camera around his neck stopped me.

"Excuse me. I'm Ron Gilbert, from the *Times*." He offered his hand and a friendly smile. "I cover the military beat. Last time I was on base, I saw the flyer. I wanted to check out the parade to see if any airmen would actually march. Got a minute?"

"Sure. Beautiful day to be out and proud, isn't it?"

"The best. I got a couple of photos of your Air Force group marching, and you in particular with the banner, but I need to get your name and make sure you won't get any grief if your photo appears in the paper. Okay?"

I gave him my name and unit of assignment, and he jotted it down in his notebook.

"You got time for a couple of questions?"

"Sure."

"How does it feel? To march in the parade as an openly gay serviceman?"

I thought for a moment. "It's been a long time coming," I said. "The old policy had its place, I guess. It was a good transition, but it outlasted its usefulness. This is the twenty-first century, and it's about time we can serve openly and proudly. I'm glad I don't have to stay in the closet anymore."

"So you're out at work, then?"

"Yup."

"What does that mean for you?"

"Well," I said, "for one thing, I don't have to pretend to my coworkers that I'm dating a woman. I can put a picture of my boyfriend on my desk at last." The reporter laughed as I'd hoped, and thankfully didn't press the issue.

"And how do your coworkers feel about your coming out? Were they surprised?"

"Not really. I haven't noticed much difference in the way people treat me in the unit." That wasn't entirely truthful. There would always be those who didn't want anyone to be openly gay.

"How is the Air Force adjusting to the new policy?"

I couldn't speak for the whole Air Force and told him so. "But I think any time there's a big change, there will be a period of adjustment. It will be a while before the prejudice is entirely gone. It's not a big deal for the younger airmen. They don't think being gay is anything to hide or be ashamed of."

I was warming up. No one had asked my opinion thus far, and I was as eager to share it as Mr. Gilbert was to hear it. "In twenty years, the young airmen who were marching in the parade today will be the chief master sergeants and generals who are in charge. They'll be the senior-enlisted advisors and wing commanders. That's when the real change is going to happen, when the old ideas are gone."

The reporter scribbled furiously in his notebook. "Old ideas such as—?"

"For one, there's the idea that being gay and serving in the military are incompatible," I said.

"Hmm. I see. So you think it's going to be twenty years before there's a real cultural change?"

"That seems about right. In the meantime, we'll keep doing what we can to change their minds."

"Do you still find a lot of prejudice toward gay people now that you can serve openly?"

"There's some, naturally," I said. "You find it anywhere, not just in the military. The tone is set by the senior leaders, and sometimes they can be slow to change."

He nodded. "Uh-huh. And what's your line of work?"

My telling him I was a general's aide didn't impress him, but he certainly perked up when he found out my boss's name.

"The commander of Sixth Air Force? *That* General O'Neill?"

"You know him?"

"Tall, skinny guy with the oversize black mustache and pipe. Handsome like a movie star. Very opinionated," he said. "So he has an aide who's gay, huh? That's a great hook for the story."

It finally dawned on me that talking at length to a newspaper reporter on this particular topic was perhaps not in my best interest. But it was too late to extricate myself. Inwardly, though, I shrugged. I didn't believe I'd done anything wrong. I hadn't said anything untrue or revealed any of the NAF's trade secrets. I did, however, remind the reporter once again that I was speaking for myself, not the NAF or the Air Force.

We shook hands and parted. I put the banner in the trunk of my car and spent the rest of the afternoon at the festival that followed the parade. My T-shirt got quite a bit of notice. Dozens of people shook my hand and thanked me for serving—openly.

❖

On Monday morning, the Sunday newspaper was waiting for me on my desk, the local news section folded open to show a prominent color photo of a grinning lieutenant carrying a "Serving out loud" banner in the gay pride parade. The name under the photo was mine, of course, and I quickly scanned the article that appeared alongside it. I'd meant to pick up the paper yesterday morning but had actually forgotten about it.

The article itself was well-written and fair. If I'd been the reporter and an eager, articulate, and talkative gay airman had crossed my path, I would certainly have taken advantage of the opportunity. I groaned when I read the line about the boyfriend's picture on the desk. I also wondered if I'd been perhaps a bit too forward with my observations about the climate and culture for gay servicemembers, considering my own limited perspective.

I measured the coffee, filled the percolator with water, and plugged in the pot. As it gurgled and chugged, I stood by, lost in thought until I heard someone speak up. "Hey, Harris! You're standing between me and my caffeine fix, and that could be dangerous!"

I turned to find Mark Sinclair, the budget officer, smiling, mug in hand.

"Oh. Good morning, Mr. Sinclair. Sorry." I picked up the pot. He extended the mug and I filled it. "Cream or sugar?"

He shook his head. "Black. Thanks."

I filled my own mug and stirred in some cream.

"Have a good weekend?" he said.

"Yes, sir." I didn't have to call him sir, I guess, but many retired officers are reluctant to surrender the respect they commanded when in uniform. I knew several people around the headquarters who still called him Colonel Sinclair, and he didn't correct them.

He blew on his coffee to cool it and took a cautious sip. "Certainly was beautiful. Finest weekend we've seen for a while."

"Yes, sir."

I waited. He seemed to want something, but when no more words came, I excused myself until he rested a hand on my arm.

"Harris, have you…um…got a couple of minutes?"

"I guess so. What can I do for you?"

"Just wanted to talk with you about something," he said. "Could you come to my office?"

I'd never been called to the budget office before for any reason. I checked my watch. "Can it wait, sir? General O'Neill expects me to be here when he arrives. Actually, he should be here by now. It's not like him to be late. When he gets in, I can ask—"

"It's okay. General O'Neill asked me particularly to speak with you, so he won't mind," he said.

My curiosity piqued, I followed him down the hall to his office. He closed the door and offered me a chair. I noticed the Sunday paper on his credenza, open to the picture of me, and I suspected our impending chat would have some connection to the coverage.

I didn't know much about Mark Sinclair apart from his job title and the fact that he was gay. There was little about his manner to suggest he was, probably the result of a military career spent in the closet. For him to have reached the rank of full colonel without detection would have required a very dedicated single-mindedness. By now, discretion was probably a habit with him. Impeccable in his grooming, he dressed conservatively in a tie and sport coat but still wore a military haircut. I'd place him around fifty, near the general's age.

Sinclair's office was as businesslike as his demeanor, with only a few personal photos and an aircraft lithograph framed on one wall and the standard military "I love me" stuff on another. The retired colonel had always been friendly toward me and encouraging as I grew into my aide position, but I'd had little reason to seek his company beyond professional courtesy.

He offered me a chair and sat down across from me, rather than behind his desk, which I appreciated. He offered a plate.

"Raisin bran muffin? Homemade and delicious too, I must say," he said.

I accepted. "Thanks."

He cleared his throat. "So, Harris, General O'Neill wanted me to talk with you."

"You mentioned that, Mr. Sinclair."

"Mark. Please."

"Okay, Mark."

"How was the parade?"

"Good fun. A terrific day for it. Were you there?"

"No. My partner Lou and I usually go, but we were out of town this weekend and didn't get back until last evening."

"It was quite an event."

"I'm sorry we missed it." He cleared his throat again. "I suppose you've seen Sunday's *Times*."

"Not until this morning. Someone left a copy on my desk." My defenses assumed their position. "Is there a problem with the article?"

He sighed. "Well, there's nothing exactly wrong with it, Harris.

It's just that General O'Neill isn't too happy about being featured in a story about the gay pride parade."

"It's not really about him." Something inside me—not quite anger, but close—began an ascent, like the temperature climbing on a warm afternoon.

"But he's prominently mentioned, alongside your comment about the fact that senior leaders have to set the course for the new gay-friendly military." Mark scanned the article again. "And although you never say that General O'Neill isn't on board with the new policy, the implication is that he's part of the old guard that doesn't like gay troops to serve openly."

"I didn't say anything of the kind. The reporter was a little liberal with his interpretation there."

"Maybe so," he said. "But whether you actually said it or not is beside the point now. It's in print, and even if it's inaccurate, you can't undo it. You can't offer a clarification or retraction."

I felt myself begin to perspire, a combination of nervousness and irritation. "How would it look if I refused to give my name to the reporter? All I said is that I worked here as General O'Neill's aide. It's no secret. The point is that we don't have to be anonymous anymore."

"I agree completely, Harris. Believe me, I'm on your side all the way. But sometimes discretion is the better part of valor."

I thought my boss a bit of a coward for not speaking to me himself if he was so concerned about the article in the paper, but if he had, I knew he would not reprimand me gently over coffee and a muffin. But, still. "So, General O'Neill asked you to tell me to put a lid on it, huh?"

"Absolutely not. He just wanted me to share some personal experiences with you. Maybe provide a little mentoring from one gay man to another. Okay?"

I nodded.

"Good." He cleared his throat again. "I don't mind mentioning to you that the old man was pretty steamed when he called me yesterday."

"Is he going to fire me? I keep waiting for the axe."

"Don't worry about that. I talked him out of it."

"Mark, I didn't say anything to that reporter that isn't true. And I made sure to tell him it was my own point of view, not the Air Force's and not the NAF's. I'm entitled to my own opinion." I could hear my voice rising with my exasperation. "If General O'Neill doesn't like gay airmen, he shouldn't have hired me to begin with."

"Come on, Harris. Be fair. Give him a little credit. He's trying."

"Does he know about your partner?"

"Of course he does. General O'Neill has been to our place several times. And he invited us over to his house for dinner to celebrate my civilian promotion last year. Most people on the staff have met Lou at one function or another."

The news surprised me. Perhaps the general was more open-minded than I thought.

"How long have you guys been together?"

"About a hundred years." His grin sparkled. "Actually, we celebrated our twenty-fifth anniversary a couple of weeks ago." He pointed to a small framed photo on the wall of two men in baseball caps, their arms around each other's shoulders. "That's us."

He told me that Lou ran the Chamber of Commerce in town, that he'd never served in the military, that they'd staked a claim to their partnership in spite of the service.

"For years, I had to pretend Lou was my girlfriend. I had to modify the pronouns anytime I swapped stories with colleagues about our weekend activities. It got old fast, and I resented having to do it," he said. "'Don't Ask, Don't Tell' didn't help guys like me who were in committed relationships. I still couldn't invite Lou to pin on my eagles when I was promoted to colonel, and that hurt."

"After you retired, when did you come out?"

He laughed. "Immediately. At the ceremony, in fact. Lou was front and center, and I thanked him for his love and support and told the crowd he was at least as much of a patriot as I was. I also went into detail about how hard it was for a gay man to serve with honor and integrity. My boss—who was General O'Neill's predecessor—was visibly uncomfortable, but he remained civil."

"I didn't know you retired from our NAF."

"About five years ago. We wanted to stay in the area, so I applied for a civilian slot as a budget analyst. A month after I retired from the Air Force, I came back to the same office and the same coworkers—only I wore different clothes."

"And you could hang a picture of Lou on your wall."

"Yes. I haven't exactly played the flaming queen, but everyone knows. I think it's important to show the staff that we're just like everyone else. We're team players. We conduct ourselves professionally and get the job done. I'm a damn good budget officer, and I'm willing to bet most people think of me first as the money guy, and second or third or fifth or sixth as the gay guy—if they even think about it at all."

"That's how it should be."

"I agree. The closet is a lonely place to live, Harris. I know for a fact. Under 'Don't Ask, Don't Tell,' we learned how to keep secrets," he said. "It was necessary for survival if you were gay and you wanted to serve."

"But we don't have to keep secrets anymore," I said. "I don't know why anyone stays in the closet now. I mean, we're not the only gay guys on the general's staff. There's the medical-squadron deputy, and the maintenance chief. I'd lay money on the security-forces commander too, even though he hides it well. Why haven't they come out? I don't get it."

"How long have you been in the service?"

"About five years altogether. Four years enlisted in the Reserve just out of high school. I re-upped and took a commission when they announced 'Don't Ask, Don't Tell' would be dumped."

"You're young yet, Harris, and you're lucky. But some people are very comfortable in the closet. I can't see why anyone would want to stay there, but we have no right to disturb them if that's their choice. I guess some guys just don't want to deal with the drama, and I can understand that, too," he said. "This new climate is unexplored territory, like you said to that reporter."

Suppose you had a gay commander, and he showed up at a formal dining-out with his boyfriend? Seeing them as a couple holding hands and dancing together would make a lot of people uncomfortable. The Department of Defense may be able to make a new law that says the military has to accept the new reality, but the government can't dictate the gut reaction of someone who sees it up close for the first time.

"There's still a lot of homophobia out there," I said.

"Yes. There will be for a long while," Mark said. "I doubt if it will ever disappear entirely. For some people, this whole thing is an open wound. They don't like being told they have to tolerate something that runs against their grain. It will be easier for us in the long run if we keep it low-key. It's okay to be out. It's okay to remind people that you're gay, but you need to have a little situational awareness about it. The Air Force says 'Service before self,' and that means putting the best interests of the unit ahead of our own, whether we're gay or straight. We have to remain aware at all times of the consequences of what we say and do. 'Don't Ask, Don't Tell' was eliminated because we argued that gay servicemembers are no different than straight ones and being gay would not interfere in any way with accomplishing the military mission."

"That's true."

"Of course it is. So we don't want to draw attention to being gay if it's going to overshadow the mission. There's a time and place. Choose your battles carefully. That's all I'm suggesting. What do you think?"

"I guess it makes sense."

He breathed a relieved sigh. "Good. I was a little apprehensive about bringing up the subject with you. Thanks for making it so easy."

Our coffee had long since gone cold. I happened to glance at the clock and was horrified to notice that it was nearing eight fifteen. "Uh-oh. Even if General O'Neill wanted us to talk, I doubt if he wanted the conversation to last for an hour."

"Don't worry. I'll have a word with him."

We walked back down the hall toward the general's office. "I've certainly enjoyed getting to know you a little better, Harris. I think we could be great friends."

I agreed.

He surveyed my desk. "So where's this picture of your boyfriend?"

I shook my head. "That was a little poetic license, I admit. It seemed like a good sound bite for the reporter, but I don't actually have a boyfriend at the moment."

"No? Well, don't worry. You'll meet the right guy. He's out there, and he's worth waiting for."

We shook hands. "Thanks, Mark."

"My pleasure, Harris. Any time."

"Tailgate!" A familiar voice, exercising its maximum volume, interrupted us. "Get the hell in here."

I sighed. "The master awaits."

Mark slapped me on the back and smiled. "You better get the hell in there, Tailgate. Guess I'll talk with him later."

And so we were back to work. To my surprise, the general never mentioned the article in the *Times*. He had delegated that little chore, it had been handled appropriately, and it did not need to be brought up again.

CHAPTER SEVEN

If my job was occasionally tedious, it kept me extremely busy. After six months or so, I realized that I was good at it and took some satisfaction in giving the general substantially fewer reasons to yell. I appreciated the encouragement of the staff as I navigated this foreign land, and gratefully accepted any suggestion in my quest to avoid the mistakes made by my predecessors. More than once, Linda and Julia and Mark saved me some embarrassment or a good dressing-down.

I was learning. But why did he always criticize me so roundly when others were present? Though most of my coworkers might have agreed in principle that his lessons had a point, I'm sure they translated them into more evidence of his dislike for me, proof of my failure to meet his expectations.

In return, I dutifully insisted to my friends and my folks I disliked him just as thoroughly as ever. It was the safest and easiest façade, particularly since the general's gruffness toward me always intensified when anyone was around to watch. Yet when we were alone, he always spoke in a normal conversational tone, at which times I found him most amiable, even damnably charming.

My resistance was eroding.

He didn't help matters when he took leave for a week to visit his dad in Tennessee. A few days after his departure, I found in my mailbox a postcard, a picturesque view of the Smoky Mountains. On the back, in his curious slanted scrawl, he'd written: *Linedrive—Having fine time, wish you were here, etc. Behave yourself while I'm gone. Yours, SEO.*

Mine?

Stunned, I stood at the mailbox and read it over and over, examining the picture and the Knoxville postmark and the words scratched on the back as if they would suddenly reveal secrets, establish motive, eliminate doubt, quench a growing thirst. I taped the postcard to my refrigerator, as if I needed a regular reminder of him. I marveled over the fact that he had gone to the trouble of taking my address with him, not to mention buying the card and mailing it.

Many weeks before, I had looked up his address, too, in the base phone directory, but I'd resisted the impulse to go there, perhaps for fear he'd see me and demand an explanation. And what would I tell him? In his absence, however, I took advantage one evening and went looking. I found his home in the most exclusive neighborhood of the base housing area. I stopped in front, idling for a minute as I examined the place, a stately two-story colonial with an immaculate yard, carefully landscaped. There were no surprises, and I couldn't learn anything from looking at the exterior, its white blinds shut tight. I wanted to park in the driveway, sit on the porch, walk around to the backyard, peep into a window to see what I could discover.

I did none of these, of course.

The staff spent a quiet, relaxing week at the headquarters while the general was gone, and the days passed uneventfully at low volume. But I yearned for his return, even if no one else did.

❖

"You've been working as General O'Neill's aide for half a year, Harris. That's a record," Julia said. "What's your opinion? Gay or not?"

We had stopped by Julia's apartment after our customary Friday dinner-and-movie date to change before heading over to the club for a little late-night dancing. We had an hour to kill before the DJ would start his set, and we'd settled down with beer and a bag of pretzels when Julia popped her question.

I laughed. "Where did that come from?"

"You're in the best position to know. You spend more time with him than anyone."

I groaned. "Please. I'm off duty. Give me a break. I don't even want to think about General O'Neill again until Monday."

Julia laughed. "You can drop it anytime," she said.

"Drop what?"

"You might just as well quit pretending you don't like him," she said. "I see right through your act, even if you have everyone else fooled. General O'Neill is certainly your type."

"He is not!"

"Oh, come on, Harris. Who are you trying to kid? You go for older guys, the skinny, dark ones with the mustaches. The intellectual-cowboy types. You told me so yourself last year, when you came out to me. Remember?"

"He's no cowboy."

"Put him in a Stetson hat, and you'd never know the difference." She giggled. "You know you'd be interested if you had the chance."

"I never said anything like that!" At least I'd never said it aloud, although it had crossed my mind a little too often. On that long-ago dinner date, Julia and I had joked about whether or not the general might be gay, but that was before I even knew him. Now I knew him almost too well.

"So," Julia said. "Your opinion, please. Gay or not?"

"I honestly don't know, Julia. I suppose he might be gay, but even if he is, you'll never catch him coming out. So what difference does it make?"

Julia nodded. "I suppose you're right. Generals don't do such things, at least not yet. It'll be a few years before any senior leader has the courage to come out while he's still wearing the uniform. Somehow I don't expect General O'Neill to lead the way, even if he *is* gay. But I can tell he really likes you, even if he has the rest of the staff fooled into thinking he's the boss from hell."

I didn't let on I'd already figured that out, too. I pretended surprise. "He's a good actor, then." I gulped down the rest of my beer and busied myself with the pretzels.

"Did you know he was married once?"

That was startling news. Such a thing had never even occurred to me. I assumed he'd always been single. I bit down an immediate and irrational feeling of jealousy. Where had *that* come from?

"Did you know her?"

"No. They divorced a couple of years before he was assigned here. He was still a colonel, but he'd already been selected for promotion to brigadier general," Julia said. "Linda told me about it. Said the wife was very attractive and quite a bit younger than him. They were married for ten years. I guess everyone was pretty surprised when they split up."

"I can imagine," I said. "But it sounds a little fishy to me if he didn't get married until he was nearly forty. Not to mention that he got divorced only *after* the promotion was announced."

Julia nodded. "Like he didn't need her anymore."

"Exactly." I almost hesitated to ask. "Any kids?"

"No. It's kind of hard for me to imagine General O'Neill as a dad."

"Me, too." I was significantly relieved. Perhaps I feared competition.

"So he gets a check mark in the 'maybe straight' column for marrying a woman, but a check mark in the 'maybe gay' column for waiting until he was almost forty to do it. Not to mention the sketchy timing of the divorce. I think the odds may still be in your favor, Harris."

Enough. "*I* think you should get changed so we can head over to the club."

She giggled. "Just wait until you see what I picked up last week. It's fantastic!"

Left to my unquiet thoughts, I wondered what Julia would say about the general's postcards. I'd received four, so far, one from each out-of-town trip he'd made without me. I'd never told her about them. Each was signed "yours, SEO," and while I'm sure he regarded me as his private property, I would hardly dare consider him mine. I knew no straight man who would go to such trouble if his only aim was to frustrate a gay man.

And what would Julia say regarding a certain incident involving the general and myself in the men's room? He'd walked in on me standing at the urinal and chosen the one right next to mine, even though there were four unoccupied. When he looked over the partition to see what I held in my hand, my mouth dropped open from surprise, if not shock.

I half expected him to make a joke of some sort. But he merely raised his eyebrows and grinned. Or was that a smirk under his galloping mustache? He zipped up, flushed his urinal, washed his hands, offered me an exaggerated wink and a rakish salute, and was gone. I stood there, too startled even to move. When I regained my composure and returned to the office, he acted as if nothing out of the ordinary had taken place at all. I knew no straight man who would have the nerve to indulge so obviously in such sport.

Such evidence led me to only one conclusion, but I could be a genius at misinterpreting signs. Maybe it was wishful thinking on my part. Besides, what good would it do for a second lieutenant if the general actually were gay? We could never have any kind of satisfactory relationship.

Julia cut short my reverie when she emerged from the bedroom to show off her attire for our adventure in Clubland—short white skirt flavored with Day-Glo lemon, tangerine, and lime, accessorized with a wide blue belt, platform shoes, and geometric costume jewelry—all recent thrift-shop purchases, she told me, and straight out of the 1970s, a decade before we were born. My black trousers and white shirt and skinny tie were likewise behind the times but fully a decade beyond her on the fashion timeline. I certainly couldn't match her flair.

A warm night stretched before us. I was relieved to leave the gay-or-not discussion behind us as we hiked to the club, holding hands, gossiping, laughing, as if we'd made some unconscious decision to be lovers. It was part of the game, and the playing of it seemed natural enough. Besides, as games are supposed to be, it was fun.

The base club tended to be a staid and stuffy place, designed to appeal to middle-aged officers and chief master sergeants rather than junior personnel. But on Friday and Saturday nights, the club featured popular guest DJs and remained open until one o'clock, so we'd have a few hours to enjoy ourselves and blow off a little steam. I did *not* want to talk about the general anymore.

The floor was packed. Usually, I'm a little self-conscious about dancing. I'm not very good. I've never learned any formal steps, and I've got a limited repertoire otherwise. It's only the kinetic energy of movement and the persuasion of the beat that coerces me to the floor. And the fact that Julia is actually a terrific dancer.

I enjoy watching her and mimicking her stylized movements to the best of my ability. Mostly, she makes us look good, and I let her lead. She isn't afraid to put her hands on me and navigate us around the floor, whether the tempo is fast or slow. Her steps always have some method to them. They aren't simply aimless, and that in itself sets us apart from everyone else there.

We pester the DJ to spin old songs we remember from a decade ago or more and shout along with the choruses while the mirrorball shimmers and spins from the ceiling, turning everything kaleidoscopic and reflecting back our true colors. Is this what dating is like in the straight world? I think sometimes I could grow accustomed to such things.

I wonder if I would ever have the nerve to bring a man here.

After an invigorating session on the crowded floor, my sleeves rolled up, my shirt already soggy from perspiration, my face flushed, I waited in line at the bar, tapping my foot to the beat thudding from the speakers and looking around in the dim light for some familiar faces. And at the end of the bar, looking straight at me as I turned his way, sat the general.

He still wore his flight suit, making him even more conspicuous in the place. I wondered if he'd come to the club directly from the office, or if he simply wanted to stick out. You can put nothing past a general, certainly not any opportunity to be the center of attention. He nursed a glass of some dark brew, and he nodded at me.

I couldn't pretend I hadn't seen him. After I paid for two bottles of beer, I went over to say hello.

"Evening, Matchbox," he said loud, over the din. "Looks as if you've been cutting quite a rug."

I ran my fingers through my damp hair. "Hey, sir. Yup. It's a little crowded on the floor. It feels like a sauna in here. Enjoying the music?"

He shook his head. "Too monotonous for my taste. And too loud."

He emptied his glass.

"Can I buy you another one, sir?"

"I might be persuaded." He noticed the two bottles of beer in my hands. "Looks like you already have a date, Budweiser. Maybe another time."

As if on cue, Julia joined us, breathless. "I wondered if you got lost. Hi, General O'Neill. Checking up on us?"

"There was a line at the bar. Sorry." I handed her a bottle. We clicked the necks together in a wordless toast, and took a swallow.

The general seemed surprised to see her, or at least to see us together.

"I assumed your date would be of a slightly different gender," he said to me.

Julia giggled.

"I like to keep people guessing," I said. "Sorry if you're disappointed, sir."

I was wondering what we could talk about next, or at least how to make a graceful exit, but the DJ solved the problem for me. Sweeping strings eased into a seductive beat that grew more and more irresistible as a familiar, nagging synthesized riff spilled from the monitors, a song from our elementary school days. Julia squealed. "There it is! Come on, Harris. We asked for this one, so we'd better get out there. Good night, sir," she said to the general as she pulled me away, toward the dance floor.

Madonna's music was as much a part of my youth and my coming out as anything I might name. Her songs were titillating, edgy, and propulsive, but above all confident. This one in particular spoke to me and probably many thousands of other young and uncertain gay kids.

Life could be painful and uncertain; why not escape to the dance floor, lose yourself in the rhythm and melody, pretend for a while that you are someone you might otherwise envy, assume the pose of Marilyn Monroe, or Lana Turner, or James Dean, Bette Davis, Rita Hayworth, Fred Astaire? All it took, Madonna insisted, was imagination and unconditional surrender to the music and the mood. And the beat.

You, I, anyone could be beautiful. There was nothing to it, and no special skills required.

As Julia and I bounced and swooped and struck angular poses, I knew we were being watched. I could see that the general had shifted his seat to get a better view of us on the floor, and he was craning his neck to see. He was all the audience I needed. My performance became frantic, manic, as I stepped and twisted and froze, stepped and twisted and froze again.

As the song ended, the exuberant crowd of dancers clapped and cheered. Without thinking, I pulled Julia to me and gave her a kiss that was long and wide and deep and tall enough that she stared at me for a second after I let go. I knew the general had been watching intently from his seat at the end of the bar, the voyeur. But by the time we were finished, he was gone.

"Why did you do that?" Julia said.

I was a little embarrassed. "I don't know. I'm sorry, Julia. Are you mad at me?"

"Well, I guess not," she said. "It's a little weird, though. Sometimes I can't figure you out, Harris."

Sometimes I couldn't figure myself out, either. I apologized again, and we went back to our seats.

"You want another beer? Maybe a soda?" I said.

She didn't. Nor did I, and when she suggested that we call it a night, I didn't argue. We walked back to her place in silence. After a quick, awkward embrace, we said good night and she said she would see me on Monday. Instead of driving back to my apartment, I took a long walk, a couple of miles at least, because it took me past the club, past the base hospital, into the housing area to the general's home. Behind a drawn blind, a light shone in a second-story window, perhaps the general's bedroom.

I hoped fervently, selfishly, uselessly, that he slept alone. The walk back to the car seemed to take twice as long, and an endless, empty weekend yawned before me. On Monday, the general was so irritable with me that I couldn't help but feel as if he were extracting some sort of revenge, as if he had caught me in some shameful adulterous act. As if I had somehow been unfaithful.

❖

My six months as the aide may have set a record, but I didn't feel much like celebrating. Publicly, General O'Neill still voiced his dissatisfaction with me for the headquarters staff and the world to hear. Privately, he continued to either surprise or confound me in unexpected ways. I won't forget chatting with a coworker in the hallway one afternoon when the general came by and smacked me playfully on the seat of my pants with a hefty paperback book.

"Great American novel, hell!" he said, but I could hear the chuckle in his voice. He didn't stop, just walked past us. I pretended to be as mystified about the general's behavior as my colleague, but I knew precisely what had happened. So the general didn't care for *Moby Dick* as much as I did. By then, I knew I cared for the general. I'd pushed away such feelings for as long as I could, but if my strict and unsympathetic inner voice of reason was still functioning, I paid little attention.

What prompted my complete and unequivocal surrender to the inevitable was a much more public moment in front of the entire NAF. We were required to receive yearly training on sexual-harassment awareness. In past years, it had been coupled with a review of the Air Force's homosexual-conduct policy, the damnable "Don't Ask, Don't Tell" farce. I wasn't sure what to expect this year, but I knew the fact that gay servicemembers could serve openly had created a huge headache for the Military Equal Opportunity Office, and I was sure the topic would be addressed.

Because the refresher course was required for everyone, military and civilian alike, the Sixth Air Force leadership made an effort to get it over with as efficiently as possible. That meant crowding into the base theater one afternoon to knock out the training all at once. I grimly waited for the interminable slides and video clips projected dimly on a screen in a dark auditorium.

Such stuff makes me squirm.

Even if I have chosen to be out of the closet at work, many other gay men and women at our base have stayed in. I see them at the gym and at the exchange and the commissary and in the NAF headquarters. We recognize each other. Pick up the vibe. Tune into each other's wavelength, but we keep many secrets to ourselves out of respect for privacy. It's comforting to know that so many gay men and women are in uniform, but I rage at the culture that seems to prefer their silence. I wonder sometimes how smart I was to come out. But as long as the Air Force insists on integrity first, I had no choice.

On a hot summer day, we filed into the theater at the appointed time. The air conditioning wasn't working, which made the situation even more unpleasant. I didn't sit with the general, who was usually front and center, but I sat close enough so I could keep an eye on him without being too noticeable, in case he needed anything.

I could summarize the training in one sentence along the lines of "Do unto others as you would have them do unto you." It would be considerably less painful, but the Air Force chooses a traditional route for ancillary training: bludgeoning its constituents with the obvious.

The sexual harassment portion opened with a video illustrating various concocted scenarios, badly acted and not particularly realistic. Most provoked laughter. Can anyone imagine a drooling old chief saying, "Hey, honey, looking good in that tight sweater!" to a young female airman? I howled along with everyone else, and even the Military Equal Opportunity major who helmed the proceedings seemed a little apologetic and embarrassed about presenting such materials in the guise of required training. The unfortunate part is that the ludicrous trappings obscured information about a serious issue.

In the old days, the "Don't Ask, Don't Tell" homosexual-conduct policy briefing led to nasty catcalls yelled out from the safety of a dark auditorium, but no one ever filed a complaint. To whom could we complain? The audience response, as well as the fact that no senior leader saw fit to quell it, served as more proof that the military work environment was downright hostile to the idea of gay airmen being able to serve, openly or not. I wondered what sort of training we would get this year under the new policy. I shuddered to think it might include video of scripted scenarios and was relieved that it didn't, only dozens of slides full of words projected on the big screen, dutifully read aloud by the major.

I'm sure someone had agonized over the information presented. Terms were defined and policies spelled out carefully and clinically, so as not to offend. The Department of Defense maintains a zero-tolerance policy for harassment, violence, or discrimination of any kind based on sexual orientation. Sexual orientation is no longer a bar to military service, nor is it a factor to be considered in recruiting and retention. The Air Force cannot discharge any airman based on sexual orientation. All airmen will be evaluated based on individual merit, fitness, and capability, not sexual preference.

Sexual misconduct of any kind by an airman—homosexual or heterosexual—is grounds for administrative or legal action. The policy will be enforced under the Uniform Code of Military Justice. If you have moral or religious concerns regarding homosexuality, you are free to maintain your beliefs and free to exercise religious expression within the law and policy. Discuss concerns with your commander or chaplain, but continue to treat all airmen with dignity and respect and follow all lawful orders. In the context of their ministry, Air Force chaplains are not required to take actions inconsistent with their religious beliefs.

There is no policy in effect to grant you a discharge if you are opposed to the repeal of "Don't Ask, Don't Tell" or if you are opposed to serving or living with homosexual or bisexual servicemembers. There will be no segregation of facilities or quarters based on sexual orientation. If you have complaints, use existing mechanisms for redress, including your chain of command and the Office of the Inspector General. Homosexual airmen who feel that they are victims of harassment or unfair treatment because of their sexual preference are encouraged to use the same existing mechanisms to remedy the situation.

The major reiterated the policy, standing at a lectern onstage and reading the slides one by one as the crowd perspired and grew more restless. Occasional snickers and rude remarks punctuated the briefing, growing more frequent and daring as she droned on, doing nothing to stop them. As I tried to build up enough nerve to stand up and protest, I happened to look toward the general. Even in the dim light, I could see he wasn't watching the screen, but he was clearly listening, scowling, impatient. He chewed his mustache absently until he could stand no more.

He stood up, sudden, and turned into the beam of the projector in the dark, lighting him up like some devil, and he blazed like hell's fire. "Enough, damn it!" After a collective, hushed gasp, the place grew instantly, carefully quiet, and suspense hung in the air like fog on a cold morning. "I've had all I can stand of y'all's immature outbursts. I won't tolerate any more. It took a long damn time for the United States military to do the right thing and allow everyone to serve, straight or gay or in between. If any of y'all have a problem with it, then *get the hell out*. The way y'all are behaving would insult the Army and the Marines and the Navy, but we're airmen in the United States Air Force, for God's sake, and I expect y'all to act like it. The major is required to deliver this briefing, and y'all are required to hear it, so give her the courtesy of your attention and *listen up*. You might learn something. Keep your ignorant opinions to yourself and sit quiet, or I'll file a harassment complaint against every single one of y'all!"

Abruptly, he took his seat.

Even the major on stage was startled by the length and depth of General O'Neill's eruption, but she recovered quickly and resumed her presentation, the crowd now raptly attentive. Without the distraction of an unruly audience, she finished within minutes. The briefing concluded with a reminder of the core values and the importance of diversity in establishing unit cohesion. The auditorium was called to attention for General O'Neill's departure. Still scowling, he strode up the center aisle and out the door. The crowd filed silently out of the stuffy auditorium, into the bright intolerant sun of the afternoon.

I searched the lobby, the restroom, and parking lot twice each, but the general had vanished. At last, reluctantly, I drove the staff car back toward the headquarters, but I didn't pass him anywhere along the route. Just to make sure, I looped around again, searched the parking lot once more, and took an alternate road back to the office. No luck. I worried, but all I could do was wait. I returned to the office.

"Where's General O'Neill?" demanded Lieutenant Colonel Cartwright, the moment I entered the door.

I hated to admit I'd lost him. I knew how she would take that news.

"I don't exactly know, ma'am."

"What do you mean, you don't *know*?"

"After the briefing, I went out to the lobby, but I couldn't find him. I looked everywhere around the auditorium, even the restrooms—"

"I can't believe what I'm hearing!" I'd never seen her so livid. She pointed at the door. "You get out there and *find* him! Don't you dare come back here until you do." She had plenty more to say, and at a volume on par with the general at his most pompous. To my tremendous relief, he strode in at that moment and caught her in mid-tirade. His color was up, as was his temper. His unlit pipe was clamped in his teeth hard enough that he could have bitten off the stem.

"That'll do, Jenny," he barked. I knew how she felt about being called Jenny. The general only did it when he wanted to annoy her.

"Where have you been, sir?" she said, meek. "I was getting concerned."

He cut her off. "I walked back. No reason for anyone to be concerned. Y'all aren't my keepers. I can take care of myself." Under his defiance, Lieutenant Colonel Cartwright slunk away to her desk.

I fumbled with an apology, assuming I was to blame for his irritation, but he shook his head. "It's not your fault, Schoolyard. For once."

That stung a bit.

From his office a few minutes later, he yelled for coffee. I hustled in with the percolator and a sugar cube. He remained sullen and testy all afternoon and didn't even bother to open the window as he puffed away on his pipe.

At twenty minutes past four, as usual, I stood in his doorway and waited for him to acknowledge me. I was proud of him for what he'd done at the briefing and wasn't sure how he would respond if I told him, but I couldn't resist. When he finally looked up, over the top of his eyeglasses, he barked again, impatient. "Well? What?"

"Thanks for speaking up at the theater this afternoon, sir. That was a good call." He stared at me for a moment, and his face softened.

"Thanks, Arkansas." He sighed. "I should apologize for being so short-tempered today."

"It's okay, sir. I know I'm not your keeper, as you pointed out, but it *is* my job to know where you are during the duty day, and I get worried when I can't find you."

"Understood," he said. "I *am* genuinely sorry, but nothing gets my dander up more than ignorant people showing off their ignorance like they're proud of it. I had to blow off a little steam afterward, and it was best for me to do it by myself."

"I don't blame you, sir," I said. "I was angry, too. The briefing was hard enough to sit through without all the catcalls making it worse. It was so clinical. Kind of dehumanizing. Speaking up was a brave thing to do."

He shook his head. "No. It was the *right* thing to do. And I should be the one thanking you instead. Trailblazing is never easy. I admire your courage."

He could talk that way all afternoon, and I'd be content to listen.

But he waved me away. "Out," he said. "I promise to behave myself from now on, but I have work to finish now, and you're always distracting me."

Hmm. And I thought I was the only one being distracted.

As I pondered this conundrum, he roared, "Git!"

I got. And spent that night, and some of the nights and days after that, uselessly and hopelessly in love.

CHAPTER EIGHT

The trouble started innocently enough, with the kind of out-of-the-ordinary tasking I dreaded. It amounted to little more than babysitting after hours on a Friday night in mid-July. The occasion was a formal retirement dinner for another general whom I'd never met. The actual ceremony had taken place earlier in the day, with the celebratory dinner the same evening at the base club, the usual venue for such doings. I was to meet my boss there at six o'clock sharp, and I'd arrived in plenty of time.

When I saw him walking toward the club from the parking lot, my mouth dropped open. In keeping with the note on the invitation for formal civilian attire, he'd chosen an elegant black suit, Italian by the cut of it. The fabric bore a faint sheen that, in the falling sunlight, looked as if it were shot through with sparkling colors. He wore suspenders (real ones that buttoned to the pants, rather than the clip-on sort), gleaming wingtip shoes, a perfectly starched white shirt, and for distinctive accessorizing, a neon stoplight-red tie.

I was shocked at how arrestingly handsome he looked. How sexy. The suit had clearly been tailored to fit his lean frame. He was quite at home in it, and he cut a sharp, elegant figure. He would certainly outshine the nominal "star" of the evening and everyone else on hand, too. I knew I was staring. I couldn't help myself.

He walked up to me and grinned and said, "What's the matter, Telescope? See something you like or something you're scared of?" My answer, had he stopped to listen, would have been "both." But he paused only long enough to drop his car keys into my trouser pocket and tell me, "You're the designated driver tonight. I'm having myself a good time, and consequence be damned."

Consequence be damned. Hmm...

The event kicked off with cocktails, then dinner, followed by interminable speeches and testimonials. The night would conclude with music for dancing, courtesy of an Air Force band ensemble. The general, per his rank, had a place of honor at the head table, while I sat quite far back. I kept in his line of sight, discreetly, in case he wanted anything from me, but I figured he could take care of himself. He remained seated until after the speeches, when the dancing commenced.

The band leader was a friendly sort, tall and blond, rather handsome—a senior master sergeant, probably ten years older than I. It didn't take either of us long to figure out we both belonged to the same club. Some eye contact, a smile, an unspoken signal, and we knew as soon as we introduced ourselves.

"Your band sounds fantastic," I said.

"Thanks. We play a lot of events like this. Do you know the guy who's retiring?"

"Nope," I said. "I'm only here to chaperone General O'Neill so he can have a good time tonight. I'm his aide. He likes his champagne, but he doesn't want to drive home later. I can think of better ways to spend a Friday night."

"Yeah. Most of our gigs are Friday and Saturday nights, so I don't get much of a social life myself," he said. "Do you get stuck very often?"

"Not much. He leaves me alone on the weekends, usually."

"Which one's General O'Neill?"

I pointed.

The band director's eyebrows went up. "Wow," he said. "Mr. Red Tie is a general, eh? I noticed him the second he came in. You can't miss him, and he obviously knows it. And he's your boss, huh?"

"Yup."

The band director shook his head. "Damn. Bet you enjoy working around him every day. What kind of boss is he?"

"He can be a prick sometimes, as he's well aware. When I do something dumb, he's not shy about pointing it out. But overall, we get along pretty well," I said. "It's interesting work, except I could do without some of the fringe benefits. Like having to waste a perfectly good Friday night at a retirement dinner for someone I don't even know."

"Oh, come on, sir," the band leader said. "Don't tell me you really mind."

For once, I think, someone had guessed my secret. I enjoyed

fringe benefits that had nothing to do with being a general's aide and everything to do with being the close companion and confidant of a very attractive man. I grinned. The director and I understood each other.

When the dancing kicked off, my general truly came into his own. Somewhere along the line, he'd gotten the lessons, or maybe he was just naturally talented. I was amazed to discover how graceful he was, and how much he enjoyed himself. It's a pleasure watching a good dancer dance, and dance he did, with all of the officers' wives and anyone else who was interested.

Clearly, he was without peer. And without anyone planning it, a contest ensued. The band threw down a foxtrot as its first challenge. Easy. A waltz? Small stuff. The floor gradually cleared, the crowd circling at its edge to watch. A samba. He called it and danced it. Next? A tango, a mambo, a rumba, a western two-step, even the Charleston. And there he was, slicing up the floor with one lucky female partner after another, none of whom matched his flair. It was all they could do to keep up, but by the time they were finished, they were flushed with pleasure.

The band director waved his baton, but he wasn't watching the musicians. His eyes were fixed on the general. After a beguine, the director conceded. He bowed to the general amid much laughter and applause, and the general bowed in return, a huge grin on his face. Someone brought him a bottle of champagne. "Compliments of the band," the director said into the microphone. The general popped it open, toasted the crowd, and took a long swig, directly from the bottle. More laughter.

"Y'all can have the floor back now," he said. "I've done enough showing off for three generals." More applause. The band took a break after that, with the director promising to return for one last set. The general nursed his bottle of champagne by himself, as graceful as ever, and even more handsome, if such a thing were possible. I let him be.

The director caught my eye, and I gravitated to the bandstand to chat.

"Your general is a damn good dancer," he said.

"He is. I didn't know that."

The director gave me a suggestive leer. "I'll bet there's a lot you don't know. He looks like he's keeping some big secrets to me."

"You think so?"

"Most definitely. I'm tracking on him, big time. Don't tell me you haven't already figured him out."

If I could be honest with anyone, the band director was the man. "Actually, I've been thinking the same thing for a long time. But even if he is, what good will it do me?"

He nodded and smiled, a little sadly. "What a waste," he muttered, and I agreed with that, too. I understood precisely what he meant. From any perspective, a queer serviceman has his work cut out for him whether he chooses to come out or stay in the closet. It isn't easy. So much fear. So many regrets and so many potential opportunities lost. I didn't know what to say. I complimented him on the band's chops and his direction, thanked him for the music, and wished him luck.

"Good luck yourself, sir," he said as we shook hands. He whispered to me, "He's pretty well lubricated, if you ask me. You'll never have a better opportunity to make your move, if you have a mind to!" The break ended as the band regrouped for its last set, and I drifted back to my chair. My move? The mechanics of what might constitute such a maneuver kept me lost in thought for a while.

The floor filled up once again with couples, and my general continued to listen to the music, tapping his foot, restless. Before long, he was out there again, cutting in on various couples, being very gracious. And when the night was nearly over, the company thinned considerably, and the waiters discreetly clearing the tables, he found me.

"You're next, Rugcutter."

"Sir?"

"This is your dance. There's no one left worth interfering with, and you haven't had a turn all evening." His face was flushed. His grin, in the hushed light of the ballroom, seemed quite devilish. I was more than a little unsettled.

"Um, thank you, sir, but if it's all the same to you, no, thanks. I don't know the first thing about ballroom dancing."

He would have none of it. "I'm an equal-opportunity employer, and this is your dance, damn it."

What could I do? The sooner I gave in, the sooner it would be over. He led me to the floor as the band began its last number, a waltz. I even picked out the tune, "Beautiful Ohio," my home state's official song.

"By special request," he said. "The waltz is the easiest kind of dance. Just follow me. *One*-two-three, *one*-two-three," and he folded me into the music and rhythm as if we had been dancing together for our whole lives. "Good, good," he said as we skirted the floor. "Move

with me. Just follow. Let me lead. Pay attention to the clues, and you'll
know what to do."

Good advice for a long life, I thought.

The other dancers were amused. Who could help but notice the
general's latest stunt? From the good-natured laughter, I assumed no
one minded. But perhaps they thought they knew the general well
enough to recognize he was just kidding around, sparked by a little
extra champagne. Even though it was now perfectly legal for one man
to dance with another at a military function, no one expected to see
such a thing. And certainly not with a general participating, unless he
were having his little joke. None of this was lost on the band director,
either, who caught my eye and gave me a wink and a thumbs-up.

The general held my right hand in his left. He pressed the fingers
of his right hand lightly against the small of my back, and I had my
left arm around his shoulder. We were close enough that I could feel
his breathing, inhale the scent of his pipe tobacco and peppermints. I
hadn't drunk anything stronger than coffee all night, but dancing with
the general went to my head like a double shot of whiskey swallowed
neat, the warmth spreading through me like fire in short, dry grass.

He held me a little too close for my comfort. His proximity
gave me an erection, that lazy arousal that builds like a slow elevator
climbing to the top of a tall building. Pressed against me, he could
very well have felt my excitement through my trousers, and the more I
concentrated on ignoring it, the more trouble it gave me. That would be
the final indignity, for he would surely make some remark that would
embarrass me even more.

But he did not.

Instead, did I hear him whisper into my ear? "If you're not careful,
you're never going to shake this trouble, Foxtrot."

The waltz reached its end too soon. The general bowed to me
formally, and said, "You'll make a fair Ginger Rogers with the right
partner." And that was all. He went over to shake hands with the band as
the musicians packed up their music and dismantled their instruments.
I'm sure his compliments made the director happy.

I waited by the door with the general's half-empty bottle of
champagne, and he found me when he'd bid his good nights. He fished
his watch from his pocket and checked the time. "Damn," he said. "It's
already tomorrow. You ready to go, Cabdriver?"

"Yes, sir."

"Take me home."

Sometime during the warm evening, the rain had come, slow and sufficient enough to dampen any weekend plans. I parked the general's car in his garage and helped him to the front porch without incident, but before we could go inside, he remembered he'd missed his evening pipe. He would not be persuaded against it, so I could do little but watch and wait as he tamped tobacco into the bowl. In quick succession followed the scritch of the match against the box, the sudden flame illuminating his face in the dark as he puffed, shaking the match out. He seemed quite content to stand on the porch, enjoying an unhurried smoke as I paced nervously behind him.

After the last draw, he knocked the pipe against the railing, unwrapped a peppermint for himself, and declared he was finished. I unlocked the door and escorted him inside. So far, so good. Perhaps I could be on my way shortly. I groped for a light switch and faced the general. The wicked grin he wore suggested he would not continue to be cooperative.

"How are you feeling, sir?"

He laughed. "Damned fine, Foxtrot." Much to my surprise, he wrapped his arms around me in a vigorous bear hug, squeezing tight in a most familiar way. When we separated, he laughed as I stared at him. "Something the matter, Foxtrot?"

"Nothing at all, sir." Everything under the sun and moon and stars, sir.

I was inside his house. I'd long wanted to see it, to get some sense of how he lived his life outside the office. I had imagined getting a tour under different circumstances, however. I retrieved a hanger from the hall closet and helped him out of his jacket. "Come on, sir," I told him. "Let's get you upstairs." But he seemed intent on more dancing. He turned on a lamp in his expansive living room and wrapped his arms around me as I attempted to loosen his tie, but he was more interested in doing a samba. Or was it a mambo? I didn't know the difference. He was laughing, and I had to join in.

"We need some music," he said. He showed off an old Magnavox stereo record player, probably forty years old, its wooden cabinet polished and gleaming, a piece of furniture worthy of its elegant name and clearly a source of pride for him.

"And all these?" he said, indicating the ornate cabinets lining the walls. He opened one. "Full of records. Thousands of 'em." He selected a particular LP, slid it out of its cover and protective sleeve. Handling the vinyl carefully by its edges, he placed it on the turntable.

The music started, bright and up-tempo and vaguely familiar. Against my protests, he took me in his arms again and navigated me expertly around the floor. We finally collapsed onto the couch, perspiring from the exertion and the warmth of the night in spite of the cool air-conditioned hum inside the house.

"Enough?" he said.

"Yes, sir. Enough to last me for some time."

"When you dance with me, you stay danced with," he said.

I certainly felt danced with. But I needed to put him to bed and get out of this place. He started humming along with the record and tapping his foot, and I knew we were in for more fox-trotting if I didn't short-circuit his choreography. I was losing patience as he got to his feet and pulled me into his arms again.

"That's enough, sir!" I said, more firmly than I should have, perhaps. It stopped him cold. I suspect he hadn't been scolded in years.

"What?"

"It's time for bed, sir."

"Says who?"

"Aren't you tired, sir?"

"No," he replied. "I want to finish off that champagne before it goes flat. Uncork it, please, and pour two glasses. One for me, and one for yourself."

"Are you sure you want more of that, sir?" I said, dubious.

That stopped him again. "Damn it, Corkscrew. Will you quit trying to be my mother? A glass of champagne now!"

The best choice at the moment was to humor him. I figured another glass or two would make him docile, if it didn't knock him out cold, and then I could deposit him in bed and go. I'd still have a two-mile walk in the rain back to the club to retrieve my own car, and I wasn't looking forward to the trek. I retrieved the bottle from the backseat of the car.

Meanwhile, he'd set two glasses on the counter in the kitchen. He had also dropped his suspenders, though they were still attached to his trousers, and unbuttoned his shirt halfway as I poured. He polished off his glass quickly and emptied the bottle into his glass. I wasn't alarmed yet, just a bit concerned about putting the general to bed and getting myself as far away from his house as possible. He would have the whole weekend to recover, and I could relax miles away from him. I took a sip of champagne.

"Drink up like a man," he said, stern.

Reluctantly, I emptied my glass, and he followed suit.

"That's more like it," he said. He unbuttoned his dangling suspenders and draped them across my shoulders. "What now, Snowplow?"

What indeed? "I think it's time for bed, sir."

He grinned. "All right, but remember it was your idea."

Even if he was drunk, I didn't want him to talk like that. I didn't want him talking like that at all.

CHAPTER NINE

S hall we go up then, sir?"
He agreed. I followed him up the stairs and into the bedroom. He turned on the bedside light, and I pulled down the spread as he looked on. He emptied his pockets onto the nightstand: a white handkerchief, some coins, his pipe, a peppermint, the watch.

"That's quite a timepiece, sir."

He handed it to me, and I examined it up close, an elegant thing, spring-wound, weighty as a pendulum, in an engraved nickel case with a snap cover. "My granddad's," he said. I set it down on the wooden nightstand and its ticking resonated throughout the room, the only sound for a moment.

"I like the rhythm," he said at last. "Good company for a lonely man."

I didn't want to know he was a lonely man. I would want to change all that, and I couldn't. I couldn't do a single thing. When he made no move to undress, I initiated the process, helping him out of his shirt. Underneath it, he wore a sleeveless undershirt that barely managed to contain a generous carpet of black fur.

Next, I helped extract him from the undershirt. He got tangled in it and we both laughed again. The lamp on the nightstand cast a warm, friendly glow, extremely generous with its soft luminescence, spreading intriguing, enticing shadows across the wall.

As the general weaved in and out of the light, I watched the dark hair on his chest. It was the first time I had seen him this undressed, and I had to stop and catch my breath in wonder. He was almost gaunt, and as tense as the coiled spring inside his watch. He breathed in and out as if our dancing had either exhausted or energized him. I could count his ribs, under their furry blanket, with every breath he took in. And I could detect the faint scent of his aftershave, that suited him so perfectly.

"What's the matter?" he said. I was, I guess, staring, mesmerized. He looked down at himself as if he were surprised to discover that the terrain was densely populated with thick, coarse hair, spreading in a neat pattern against the hard, dinner-plate concavity of his belly. "Pretty crowded down there, isn't it?" he said.

I had to admit he was pretty crowded down there.

He scratched the deep pile. "Looks like I could use a good mowing, doesn't it?"

Well, there is no answer for such a question.

"Itches like hell sometimes," he said. "Don't know why. You'd think I'd be used to it by now, but it still itches like hell sometimes. I might have to keep you on standby to scratch in case of emergency."

He could add that to my job description any time. I would not complain. I wondered, briefly, about the consequences of seducing a slightly soused general. If such a thing were even possible. I doubted it. But here was this clueless, fuzzy general saying he'd let me scratch his itch, and surely he must be kidding. But I stood three feet and six ranks away from him wishing he weren't kidding.

Nothing will feed that hunger.

"Sit down, sir."

He did, heavily. I suspected he would not be long awake. I untied his shoes and removed them and started on his socks, but he stood up.

"I am perfectly capable of undressing myself." Belligerent.

"Yes, sir. You just finish up and climb into bed, and I'll be on my way."

He sat down again. "So soon?" he said, penitent.

"It's late, sir. Don't you think it's time for bed?"

He grinned again, the spark glowing to life. "You keep saying that, Kingsize. Just what do you have in mind?"

Would he just stop? My frustration was growing in proportion to something in my pants. "Nothing at all, sir. You must be tired. It's been a long day, and you were quite active tonight," I said. "Where are your pajamas, sir?"

He snorted. "Pajamas are for sissies."

Okay, no pajamas. I wondered if he might want a shower after his exertion earlier in the evening, but it would complicate things even more, so I didn't even make the suggestion. He managed his socks, and then he stood, a little unsteady.

"Help me with my trousers, will you?"

I knew I stood at the edge of a mined field, dangerous ground I'd never hike if I were smart. But there was himself, bidding me forward. He asked again. I took a deep breath and reached for the buttons. As our fingers fumbled with the buttons, his eyes, quizzical, locked onto mine, and we were caught suspended for a moment, as if we were strapped into the front car of a rollercoaster at the top of the steepest grade, after all the clattering and clanking of this carnival night, poised for the eternal second before hurtling down into the thrilling fear.

To my surprise, he wore no undershorts. Perhaps he also felt they too were only for sissies. And as I wrestled him loose from his pants, I was even more startled to find evidence that he had grown aroused.

Quite clearly. And quite aroused.

I was momentarily puzzled. Was it merely his excitement after the triumph this night? Just some reflex? Had his proximity to me brought him to this state? He stood in front of me, trousers heaped at his feet, breathing hard as if he'd just run a marathon, his furry chest rising and falling as he gulped in air. And neither of us could ignore the glorious, obvious reality of his erection, full and proud, pointing directly at me.

For a moment, he was speechless. I was, too, though cacophony filled my head, a thousand voices hollering like a stadium full of riled fans after a spectacular play. I couldn't sort out any of it; the noise deafened me. The general's eyes found mine again, and he wondered for a moment, I think, how to proceed. Should he be embarrassed, should he make a joke, ignore it? A thousand years or a second could have passed before he spoke. I don't know. And when he finally did speak, he was guarded. Even uncertain.

"I believe, Harris," the general said, flat, "you are being saluted."

"Yes, sir?" My answer was its own question, barely whispered. I couldn't remember the last time he'd used my name. Possibly never. His use of it now made me cold and hot all at once, and his analogy to the salute was certainly apt. I had already snapped to full attention inside my trousers, returning the greeting in kind.

"Tell me, Harris," he said, still as evenly as if he were dictating a memo, "what does your military training tell you to do when you receive such a greeting?"

A pause. I had more at stake here than I cared to think about at the moment, but my heart won over my head. Perspiring freely, I swallowed and took a deep breath before answering: "Salute back, sir. Proudly, the way you taught me."

His brow furrowed, as if he needed concentration to process my reply. He requested clarification, I think, and registered utter disbelief when I merely repeated myself.

"What?" he whispered. In that one word, I suspect he questioned his whole life up to that time, putting an entire career, an entire way of thinking, of living, on the line. It hung there for a second before he repeated it, agonized. *"What?"*

"I think you heard me correctly, sir," I said, but for a second I wavered. Perhaps I was the one who misunderstood.

"Do you realize what you're saying?" he whispered.

I listened for any shade of cruelty, of taunt in his voice, but I heard none. In my momentary uncertainty, I half expected him to renege on his offer, to call me names, to admit he had set this trap to poke fun, or to curse me for tempting him and chase me out of the house, but I could not give him time to consider any of these options. "I do. Absolutely, sir."

He groped for me with clumsy, unpracticed hands, and if he doubted what I'd said, he certainly couldn't doubt the hard evidence that proved otherwise. The shock in his eyes lasted only a second, and he gave me no time to consider my options, either.

He ripped three buttons from my shirt as he extricated me from it, and he nearly did similar disservice to my trousers. Inside a minute, he was on his back on the bed, and I above him on my hands and knees, staring down at him framed against the sheet, frightened, grateful, awed, curious, and genuinely excited in a way I'd never felt before, with the general's lanky form stretched out under me. He trembled, perhaps from the coolness of the air in the room, perhaps from anxiety or eagerness himself.

His chest still rose and fell with the heavy breath of exertion and anticipation. Black hair swirled against his chest like some unruly crop grown wild and windblown. In the dark pit of his crotch stood the proof that his own urgency was as undeniable as mine. I couldn't quite believe I was on hand to testify, convinced I'd never seen anything as magnificent as Seamus Edwards O'Neill in his splendid nakedness. Quite possibly I would still be there, my eyes full of wonder, if he hadn't interrupted my reverie.

"Harris," he barked, hoarse. "I'm not some damned national monument. For God's sake, quit behaving like a tourist, and put your hands on me."

He didn't have to ask twice. When my fingers first made contact with his belly, the jolt was electric, like the perfect blue arc of a welder who knows his machine. With his urgent fury finally given release, the general roared as we fused. His mouth, flavored with tobacco and peppermint and champagne, plumbed mine and down we went, diving headfirst into each other. I had never tasted such hunger in a man, and I had never been so hungry myself.

I lowered my mouth to the plane of his chest. There was no time for grace, no time for leisure. Urgently, he pushed himself at me and willingly, I obliged him. He needed no words to pledge his approval. He rose to meet me with every stroke, the perfect counterpoint. From time to time, I came up for air but never stopped exploring. And he was in no way shy about communicating his desires. When he would no longer be denied, I sensed his impatience and concentrated my persuasion where he most needed it.

As we moved together, I became aware that he was muttering to himself, "Oh, damn. Damn. Damn." But it didn't sound like swearing. It sounded instead like a prayer. Our passion was the same, and we loped after it urgently. I could almost feel the champagne coursing in his veins, as if someone had shaken up his bottle and popped his cork. He stiffened as he tumbled from the edge, uttering a long, low, lustful animal growl as his satisfaction bubbled over, spurting and fizzing.

Afterward, he pulled me up to him, gently. In the warm light from the night table, he focused his eyes on mine and held me there, close, as if he were looking for the solution to some puzzle. I was uncertain how he would respond, how I should respond. Having come down to earth after his spectacular flight, how he would feel about me? About himself? About us, if I could dare to refer to him and me collectively? My head as well as my heart knew that nothing would ever be the same. Whether this was for better or worse, I did not know then.

"Damn, Shooter," he murmured.

"Did I do something wrong, sir?" I asked, uncertain. A little scared, I admit. And he stared at me for a moment until, I guess, he decided I expected an answer to my question. He shook his head slowly.

"You couldn't," he said. "Ever. Not one wrong thing." When the shadow of an uncertain smile crossed his mouth, I believed him, but I had other pressing concerns that required attention. I've never been shy about expressing my appreciation for a handsome man, and under the thin shelter of the covers, I could not easily hide the effect of his proximity. Upon noticing my condition, he raised his dark eyebrows—a row of exclamation points—and grinned. His mustache was running its own fifty-yard dash as he lifted the sheet.

He let out a low whistle. "Let me state for the record that I am impressed. You didn't get that at Officer Training School."

"No, sir. Standard equipment."

"Hardly standard." He ran his fingers up and down the skin of my chest and I shivered. His touch launched me a thousand miles up, and before I had time to collect my thoughts or say a word, I found our positions reversed. I was on my back with him above, his talented mustache exploring my belly first and then brushing the inside of my thighs.

I could tell he enjoyed his task, and he liked what he found. I still wasn't certain of the protocol, but no propriety could stop me from enjoying myself, too. In the next quarter of an hour, his mustache swept everywhere except where I most wanted him to, and his tongue explored as if he'd never tasted such exotic flavor. He could feel the desperate ache in me, too, and he paused just long enough to tell me to relax.

"Easy, now, Stagecoach. I know where you want to go, and we will get there. But I'm in the pilot seat, and I'll set the course and fly this jet. Half the pleasure of any trip is the journey. Understood?"

Easy for him to say. "Yes, sir. Sorry, sir."

Please hurry, sir.

We glided deep into valleys and soared high above sharp peaks, up and up and up, until I touched the sky at its sharpest blue. I didn't have to tell him when I could stand no more. I guess he could sense it. When he lowered his hungry mouth against my impatience, I simply couldn't be polite anymore. I lunged against his heat and the bristle of his mustache, and he inched me toward the precipice until I tumbled willingly over the edge, headlong, lost.

I felt wrung out and happier than I'd ever been in my life. The general reached over and turned out the lamp, and then he slid next to me in the dark, wrapping his arms around me, my back against his matted chest. I had never imagined such pleasure, and I couldn't envision anything outside of this bed.

"Well, Firecracker," he murmured in my ear as we settled down. I could hear him grin. "Suitable bottle rockets, even if the fourth of July is already past. How was it for you?"

"You did good," I told him.

"I know," he said.

"Because you're a general?"

"Why not?" He pulled me even closer to him, but I couldn't relax at all. After a minute, I struggled to free myself from his embrace.

"What's the matter?" he said.

I couldn't even begin to answer his question, so I didn't try. The bedsheets were as tangled as my mixed emotions, and I couldn't stand the suspense. It had to be a dream, and I made up my mind the first move would have to be mine, much as it would hurt. "I guess you'll want me to be going now, sir?"

He sat up. "Why?" He seemed honestly mystified.

"Well," I said, rather doubtful. "Don't you think I should?" He would hardly want to wake up tomorrow morning, naked, uncertain, possibly hung over but unquestionably next to a second lieutenant twenty-plus years his junior? And his aide, no less? I wasn't sure *I* wanted to be there in the morning when he put these pieces together. If he chose to invoke the "I was so drunk last night I don't remember a thing" cliché, I would be crushed. I'd heard it before and had always considered it the coward's last ditch.

As I tried to build a suitable response, he said, "Where will you go?"

I'd forgotten that particular detail. "I guess I'll hike back to the club and get my car and go home," I said.

"The club is a couple of miles from here," he said. He glanced at the clock on the night table. "It's raining, and it's past two. If the base cops discover you walking around here at this hour of the morning, they'll stop you."

He was probably right. And what would I tell them? The truth?

"You'll stay put, Boxcar," he said. "I want you to be here in the morning."

He did? "Why?"

"You think I'm drunk, don't you?"

I did, but this was probably not the time to accuse. "Well, sir, maybe I wouldn't go that far. But you might not be at your most clearheaded right now, sir. It's pretty late."

"And you think I've consumed enough for three," he said. "All right. I drank more champagne than usual. But believe me. I am stone-cold sober now. I didn't plan for this to happen. I'm as surprised as you are."

"If you say so, sir." But I remained unconvinced of his sobriety or his innocence. He'd known I was gay from the first day we met, which gave him the upper hand. Yet I wondered how much of the blame belonged to me.

He sighed. "You have every right to be upset. What I've done is inexcusable, and I'm sorry. Forgive me?"

In retrospect, all the sudden passion, the eruption between us, seemed so overwhelmingly wrong. I should have nipped the bud before it flowered, however much I may have yearned for the bloom. I knew better, I told myself, yet I let it happen. Stupid, stupid, stupid. I found myself saying, "I should ask you to forgive me."

"None of that," he said, stern. "This isn't something we can fix tonight. Let's get some sleep, and we'll sort it out in the morning."

He sounded very sure of himself, but I didn't believe him for a second. "How?"

He had the perfect response to counter my personal chastisement. "I'm a general," he said, as if that would solve the whole problem. This time, however, rank *was* the problem.

"That's fine for you, but I'm a second lieutenant," I said.

"It doesn't have the same ring of authority, does it?"

"It doesn't have *any* ring of authority!"

"Then you're overruled because I outrank you," he said. "You'll stay. Understood?"

"Is that an order, sir?"

He sighed again. "No. It's not an order. It's my humble request. Please?"

I swung my legs over the edge of the bed, and he crawled from under the covers and sat next to me. And damn him for being so attractive. When he placed a hand on my shoulder, the touch made me recoil, tense, defensive. "Easy, there," he whispered. "Easy," as if he were soothing a skittish horse. "Believe this," he said, his deep growl surprisingly gentle. "I would never hurt you. I couldn't."

We stood up and faced each other, two lean figures, naked, in the middle of a room, in the warm shaded light of the single bulb of the lamp on his bedside table. His furry chest rose and fell with his breathing, and time might have stopped again.

"But—" I started.

He put a finger to my lips. "Let me show you something better you can do with your mouth than talk," he said. He demonstrated, pressing his own against mine, and we could have swallowed each other whole. I felt myself going under, down for the third time, and I never knew

drowning could be so easy. He stood back from me a minute later, and his eminence front seemed to have retreated. He shook his head. "I'm sorry. I'm out of my league," he said. "I have no right to insist—"
"Sir, don't you think it would be best for me to go?"
He shook his head. "No. It would *not* be the best thing."
I wanted him to reach for me, to take hold and never let go. How could I ask? But maybe he read my mind, because he moved. He moved toward me, and I reached out and took hold of the fuzz on his belly. He engulfed me in his arms, and any reservations I had melted against his warmth.

He whispered to me. "You're staying put, Buckshot. Understood?"
I nodded. "Thank you, sir. For insisting." That caught him off guard. I was startled to see his eyes well up, but out of habit or a triumph of will, he never spilled over. He kept himself under control, at least until we climbed into the tangled sheets again and put out the light. He folded himself around me, soft and comfortable as a flannel blanket. The fearful violence in my heart stilled, and I felt as content and safe as I ever had in my whole life.

Once I was settled against him, breathing in tandem with him, and he realized I was content to stay there, he let his tears wash my neck. Why he should sob perhaps I was too young to understand. When he tried to apologize, I pressed my hand over his mouth and told him "Shhh." There was nothing to be sorry for, and he held on even more tightly.

Anything that could happen the next day—his wrath or his diffidence, I didn't care—would have been worth the dark of that night as we fell asleep, as he held me against him and I lost myself in his intoxicating warmth. There might be other nights when the tick of his watch would lull me to sleep with its insistence, its tireless attention to detail, keeping time for us in one-second increments, each with its own name spoken aloud and thus marked.

But I would always remember this first night.

CHAPTER TEN

Several hours later, I found myself wide-awake. We had separated at some point as we slept, and I didn't want to move for fear the general would awaken also. But my mind raced, and I just couldn't close my eyes again. Finally, I climbed out of bed as carefully as I could. He didn't even stir.

I turned on the bedside lamp and surveyed the room, finding evidence of our urgency everywhere. I found hangers in the closet and hung his clothes up. His closet was neat, not overfilled, his uniforms arranged in some order—trousers first, then short-and long-sleeved blue shirts, then flight suits, then several sets of the dusty-colored airman's camouflage uniform, and, finally, the desert-brown battle dress uniforms, proof that he'd served in Afghanistan in the early days of the war. Half a dozen civilian suits, sport coats, elegant dress shirts in muted colors. A rack full of ties, a whole paintbox of shades. Button-down sport shirts. Blue jeans and sweatshirts folded neatly on the shelf. I couldn't picture him wearing denim, but I knew so little about his private life.

How or where could I possibly fit?

What could there ever be between a brigadier general and his second-lieutenant aide? I didn't want to think about it, but I couldn't push it away. I collected his socks and undershirt and deposited them into the laundry hamper I'd seen in the hallway. I folded my own clothes as neatly as I could.

I found his wallet on the dresser. There wasn't much in it, apart from some folding money and a couple of credit cards. No photos except for the pictures on his driver's license and military ID. I examined his dog tags, too, stamped with his full name, Social Security number, blood type and, on the last line, reserved for religious preference, one word: "infidel." That almost made me laugh out loud. So he was the last of the old reprobates after all.

While I had the opportunity, and since the chance might never present itself again, I started scouting. I don't know what I was looking for. Clues, perhaps, even the most mundane evidence that would expose the secrets of his personal life. I started with the big bathroom, white and spotless. The fixtures gleamed. The medicine cabinet held nothing more extraordinary than aspirin, shaving cream, razor blades, toothpaste, and some first-aid basics. White, luxurious towels were neatly folded on the rack, as if he were living in a four-star hotel.

One of the other bedrooms was furnished as a guest room, with a double bed and chest of drawers, the closet empty except for hangers. He'd fixed up a third bedroom as a den or office, with a laptop computer on the desk, a filing cabinet, shelves filled with old textbooks and reference manuals, and an ancient manual typewriter. A framed photo of a beautiful young woman, black-and-white but painstakingly hand-tinted, had a place of honor on one wall, with a dried red rose positioned behind it. The picture might have been taken in the fifties. From the family resemblance, I assumed she was his mother. It was the only solid evidence I'd found of his family, of a life lived outside the Air Force.

A fourth bedroom held nothing but large cardboard moving boxes, twenty-five or thirty of them, taped shut, stacked and cryptically labeled with his scrawl and packed full of—what? His past or his future? What would I learn if I were to dig through the stuff?

I examined the large rooms, impressed by their curious impersonality and neat sparseness. Everything was in order. I had thought myself perhaps overly tidy, but this man took it to an extreme, by expedience or habit or compulsion. Appearances, however, can deceive. Sometimes order on the outside reflects inner order as well, but sometimes a neat façade masks chaos. Up until this night, I would have sworn every aspect of the general's life was as straightened underneath as it appeared on the surface.

Downstairs in the kitchen, I rinsed our champagne glasses and left them to drain on the rack in the sink. I even peered into his pantry to see what kind of groceries he kept on hand. The most startling artifact I found inside was a box of Cap'n Crunch cereal, which I couldn't even stomach as a kid for its cloying sweetness. That made me laugh out loud. We are most human when measured by our idiosyncrasies.

And no bran flakes in sight. Good for him.

A small bathroom adjoined the kitchen and a laundry room. An ironing board, steam iron, and can of spray starch suggested he pressed his own shirts. It dawned on me that the general's life between 5 p.m. and 7 a.m. was probably much like that of any single man, myself included. He washed dishes and scrubbed the toilet and fixed supper for himself and mowed the yard. Rank aside, the distance between us suddenly seemed minimal. Certainly no insurmountable obstacle.

Thus cheered, I continued my tour. I wandered through the impressive dining room, its oval table roomy enough for ten and its cabinet with glass doors containing a beautiful, austere set of white china and crystal glassware. I wondered how often he used such things. Did he throw dinner parties? Host important military or civic leaders?

Only in the living room could I find any real sense of what he considered important. The phonograph and all those records certainly took up the most space. I opened several of the cabinets and glanced at the albums, neatly alphabetical, mostly classical music, boxed sets of operas and symphonies and string quartets. And a couple shelves of jazz and swing, from Louis Armstrong and Chet Baker to Weather Report and Lester Young.

Imagine having the patience to listen to records in the twenty-first century. I knew no one else who did. My parents had scrapped their LPs in favor of the less labor-intensive compact discs years ago. Although the general opted for the convenience of CDs at the office, I was not surprised he'd refused to surrender his records at home.

I picked up the sleeve of the album we'd been dancing to only hours before, a collection from the late 1950s entitled *Arthur Murray Favorites*, its stylish artwork depicting men coupled with women. Mr. Murray would no doubt have been scandalized by the use to which we had put his favorites that night.

The living room even had a fireplace. I assumed it would hold a fake log with a propane jet flame underneath, but the log in the grate was real, and the ashes underneath it were evidence enough that he liked his fire, at least in season. The ornate wood box was not merely decorative; it was full, ready for a change in the weather.

Bookshelves, built into the wall on either side of the fireplace, had been systematically arranged with dozens of volumes. The military history and biography didn't surprise me, but I was pleased to discover a handsomely bound set of Shakespeare's complete works and novels by Twain and Hemingway, two favorites of mine. I found an old Cub Scout manual, a stack of popular espionage thrillers, Civil War histories and photo books, Walt Whitman's *Leaves of Grass*, and an Oxford English Dictionary. I counted nearly three dozen volumes about opera, classical music and jazz, and the arts.

I realized after a minute that the room was missing a television. The TV was the centerpiece of most family living rooms, my own parents included. He might have had a set hidden somewhere, but maybe not. Perhaps he watched programs online—or not at all. Could he possibly spend his evenings reading books and listening to records?

We would get along famously, if he would let me spend some of those evenings with him.

Apart from the photo of his mother hanging in his upstairs office, I found no other pictures and no personal memorabilia, which struck me as odd and a little sad. In fact, little about the house made it seem truly lived in. The furniture was solid, plain, functional, obviously of the highest quality, but not warmly inviting, however comfortable the cushions on the couch and chairs might be. The framed art and other decorative objects were smart but impersonal. For all its stylishness, it was a sad, lonely house, and after my hour's exploration, I felt a little guilty, as if I were spying on its ghosts. I went back upstairs to his bedroom.

A clock somewhere downstairs struck five in solemn tones. For a minute, I watched the general sleep, unaware. He stretched, turned, restless, his mustache quivering. What dreams were his companions? I noticed the streamlined angles and lines under the crop of fuzz that patterned his belly so invitingly. I was unaccustomed to seeing him so still. He was possibly the most attractive man I'd ever known, and he'd endeared himself to me completely, however fragile or shaky this encounter might render our future. I was not a little overwhelmed by this newfound awareness. I'd gotten to know him better in the last six hours than I had in the previous six months.

I was suddenly exhausted, and I turned out the bedside lamp and crawled carefully back under the covers. As I let out a deep breath and settled down as close to the edge of the bed as I could, he stirred again. He reached out and found me.

"I wondered where you got off to, Locksmith," he murmured, matter-of-fact. His voice startled me, coming as it did from the pitch-blackness before my eyes had adjusted to the dark. After a second he said, "I missed you." As if he had been waiting for me his whole life, he pulled me in close, and before I knew it, I was nestled against his chest, drowning in him again, and off to some deep and pleasant sleep.

❖

"Hey, you."

My eyes popped open, and I sat bolt upright, disoriented and a little fearful in those first seconds of waking up in an unfamiliar room to a voice I couldn't immediately place. But it was my own general, sitting on the edge of the bed, unself-consciously naked, holding out a cup of steaming coffee.

"You planning to sleep all day, Jackknife?" he said.

"Sorry, sir." I wondered if I should be embarrassed. "What time is it?"

"Nearly eleven. I've been prowling about for a couple hours already."

Wow. "Good morning, sir." I wondered what had he been doing since rising. And how long he had been sitting there, watching me?

He offered the cup and saucer.

"Thank you, sir."

He left the bedroom abruptly and returned a moment later with his own cup and sat down next to me. In silence, we blew on the hot liquid to cool it down and sipped cautiously. I waited for him to say something, but perhaps he was waiting for me to speak, so we were silent. I was far from comfortable, though relieved that today was Saturday. I could get home, somehow, and still have Sunday to sort things out. I half expected him to throw me out, as if our coffee was the calm before some storm. I, if not we, might have to face a world of trouble and hurt as a result of last night's turn of events.

I emptied my cup and carefully set it down on the nightstand.

"A refill?" he said.

"Not just now. Thank you, sir." He set his empty cup next to mine and then turned his attention back to me.

"You mind if I sit here?"

"It's your bed, sir. You can sit where you like. Um…should I mind?"

"I wouldn't like to wake up with a naked old guy in my bed," he said, gruff.

"I would," I said. "Every single day." He seemed surprised, but he was as attractive a sight as I am ever likely to see upon waking. "Your scenery is truly magnificent. Certainly worthy of a national monument."

When he laughed, it came from somewhere deep within him. It

surged up from his bedrock and took hold of his whole self. I could hear it and feel it, and it was contagious. What else was there to do? He stood up and made an exaggerated turn, three hundred and sixty degrees.

"Get your eyes full," he said. "Although at my age, I should think twice about parading naked in front of someone I want to impress."

"Well, *don't* think twice," I said. "I'm already impressed, but thanks for the tour. Where can I buy the postcards?"

He shook his head. "I don't understand you. But I'm not immune to flattery." He sat down on the edge of the bed next to me and just let me look. I could see a trace of a grin under the mustache. In close-up, I found him even more handsome than from a distance: his thin face deeply etched and tan, his mustache ramshackle and black, the sandpaper of beard clearly evident since yesterday's morning shave, the strong and lean limbs, the flat, carpeted belly. He'd fully grown into himself, like the monument he said he didn't want to be, but alive. A testament to all that is masculine.

I wondered what he saw when he looked at me. Next to him, I felt inadequate, too pale and smooth and fair of complexion, too young and uncertain, like a lump of clay awaiting the expert hands of a potter. A lieutenant didn't deserve a general, hadn't earned the privilege yet, as if this whole situation weren't already too patently absurd. But he abruptly short-circuited my maze of thought by plumbing my mouth with his.

He pulled back a second later, as if he'd burnt himself, but he continued searching me, quizzical, unsure, as if fighting his own impulses, shaking his head and muttering, half to himself, "I'm a goddamned old fool." But we remained apart only long enough to gulp in air, and then we dived in again and swam straight down.

He tasted like sweet coffee and promise, as morning should. He rummaged in the bedside table drawer for pipe, tobacco, and matches. He tamped the rum-and-maple into the bowl—self-consciously, I might add, as I watched so closely you'd have thought I'd never seen him do it before—and lit it. After a moment, he slid between the sheets next to me and puffed contentedly. I rested my head on his chest, and he wrapped his free arm around me. From time to time, he chuckled, looking exceptionally pleased with himself. All I could do was look up and ask, "What's so funny?" but he only grinned and shook his head.

"Not a damn thing worth mentioning," he said.

He kept the pipe lit for a good half hour, a fragrant cloud above the bed. Memories associated with scents are some of the strongest I have, and the general's tobacco and his aftershave are forever lodged in that part of my head. When he finished, he set down the pipe and reached into the drawer again for one of his pinwheel red-and-white peppermints. He offered one to me, and I accepted. As we lay together, he nuzzled me like a puppy exploring a new home, and I responded in kind and at great length.

Some time later, I heard his stomach rumble. "Reality intrudes," he said. "I'm hungry. Aren't you?"

I was. We climbed out of bed and stretched. He offered a bear hug and shared his peppermint-flavored mouth with me again.

The air-conditioning felt chilly, and the general offered me a new bathrobe from his closet. "Got it for Christmas a few years back from my sister. But I won't part with my old one." His hung on a hook on the back of the bedroom door, and he shrugged into the ancient corduroy like an embrace from a close friend. Generous and long, deep brown with tan pockets and a tan collar and sash, it was well worn. The cuffs were frayed and the elbows had been patched neatly with some dark green fabric. The robe had been designed for someone as tall as himself but much broader.

"You could drown in that, sir," I said.

"Not a chance," he said. "My mother made it for me years ago. She always thought I'd fill out, so she made it large enough for me to grow into. Thirty years on, it's still doing its job." He found a pair of scuffed slippers under the bed, and we went downstairs to the kitchen.

"What can I fix you for breakfast? You like cereal?"

My shout of laughter mystified him. "Anything but cereal," I said.

"Eggs and toast?"

I nodded.

He poured orange juice, and I watched as he whisked eggs in a skillet, adding milk and grated parmesan cheese. When it was almost finished cooking, he made toast, an exacting process that he explained to me in detail. He began with whole grain sliced bread, fresh from a local bakery. The finished product had to be well but evenly browned, spread with salted butter all the way to the edges of the crust, and then cut on the diagonal into two isosceles triangles. I nodded, solemn. Ordinarily, one should fix only a single slice at a time so it could be consumed hot, he explained, and furthermore—

He stopped in mid-discourse. "You think I'm an idiot," he muttered. "Going on about toast."

I would not think him an idiot. "Good toast is one of the finest pleasures in life," I said. "You've figured out the secret."

"You," he said sternly, pointing the butter knife in my direction, "are a man after my own heart."

I certainly was, and I was pleased he knew it.

We ate in silence. Nothing needed to be said. We washed the dishes in silence, too, though I felt sure he would speak up when I reached over and untied his bathrobe. But he did not, just nodded, and when we had put the last plate in the cupboard, we silently climbed upstairs again. So much unexplored territory remained to be discovered, and if he wanted to trailblaze, he'd found a willing partner in me.

CHAPTER ELEVEN

Our Saturday was unseasonably cool for July, overcast and gloomy, with last night's rain continuing on and off. Decidedly an indoor day. I made several hesitant suggestions about departing, but the general would have none of it. "Do you have other plans?" he said. I did not, certainly none I would have traded in exchange for a day with him.

"Then stay. Unless you're tired of the company."

A rhetorical question, if ever one could be. "No, sir." He was, after all, still a general, though such rank pulling as this amused me.

"Sometimes it's good to spend the weekend with a like-minded companion."

"Yes, sir."

"Naked," he said, his mustache aquiver.

I agreed wholeheartedly.

We found little to say, but the afternoon wasn't uncomfortable, much to my surprise. Saturday passed into a wondrous night of thunder and rain outside and more pleasant storms in the bed we shared. Sunday morning dawned, still overcast and cool, and the general declared once again I would stay put. He left the bedroom and returned a few minutes later with the newspaper, coffee, and his pipe. Before we settled down, he sighed with some exasperation and left the room. He returned, clearly dissatisfied.

"What are you looking for?" I said.

"My glasses," he said, glowering, daring me to say anything.

I grinned. I'd seen them and went to fetch them from the coffee table in the living room. As I handed them to him, he growled, fierce, "Well?"

If I had any comments, this would not be the time to make them.

Little flaws such as the need for reading glasses make us human and endeared him to me even more. I told him so.

He stared at me.

"What now?" I said.

He cleared his throat. "Nothing." He climbed into bed with me, and we didn't stir from there until past noon. We even finished off the *New York Times* Sunday crossword puzzle, another hobby of his. On his bedside radio, the local classical station played tuneful baroque music, its brittle and luminous continuo a sparkling complement to our day.

Neither of us even mentioned the figurative rhinoceros in our military living room. What were we doing, a lieutenant and a general, and how would we ever extricate ourselves from the mire? Because we only sank deeper and deeper as the day passed.

❖

After supper, he asked if I had ever listened to Puccini's *Tosca.* I knew the work as well as the composer, as it happened to be one of my mother's favorites. I'd heard the music often, though I'd never really sat down and listened to it carefully, I told him.

That simply would not do. In the living room, he pulled out a boxed set from his record library. He handed me the booklet. "Skip the history. You can look at it later if you want, but it won't add anything to your appreciation of the music," he said. "Read the synopsis so you've got an idea of what's happening."

I read the outline of its three acts, a tragic and utterly improbable love story—but what is opera without such stuff? The general put Side 1 on the Magnavox, settled down next to me, and wrapped a protective arm around my shoulder. We followed the libretto, English on one side of the page and Italian on the other, and I took pleasure in his interest, watching him as carefully as I followed the story.

Before long, he was so caught up in the score that I doubt he even remembered my presence. He listened with his eyes closed, his head bobbing with the music. Now and then he hummed along, his voice rumbling deep, and any time I tried to speak, he shushed me until I just gave up and surrendered to the sound. To my surprise, the music proved more familiar than I expected, and at last I had some context for it.

When it was all done—six sides and two and a half hours later—I could certainly see why anyone might be attracted to the sweep, the spectacle, the obvious emotion. I didn't need to be fluent in Italian. I could translate the characters' joy, anger, and pain through the music. But the highlight for me was sitting next to General O'Neill and sharing his pleasure. We could have been listening to radio static, and I would have been satisfied.

"Good Lord," the general said when the needle lifted off the record at the end of the last side. "It's already dark outside."

My spirit sank as I realized our weekend was over. Monday was coming, and what would it bring?

"You want a snack or anything?"

"I'm not really very hungry, sir."

"Hmm. Neither am I," he said. We sat on the couch for a moment, looking at each other, and if I expected his grin to crack the tension, I was disappointed. "Back to work tomorrow," he said.

Yes. Work tomorrow. And Tuesday, and the rest of the week and month and year. I pondered these things as we dressed in an awkward hurry. I had nothing else to put on but my rumpled suit from Friday's event. The general offered me an apology, a promise for a new shirt, and a couple of safety pins for the old one. He climbed into blue jeans and a sweatshirt himself, and we went out through the back door into the garage and drove to the club in silence. The building was closed on Sunday nights, so we had the grounds to ourselves. He pulled his car next to mine in the parking lot and switched the engine off.

Cold drizzle continued to fall, as we sat in the dark for a few moments. I suspect he was as much at a loss for words as I. He could not see my face in the dark, nor could I see his, but I heard his breathing, and I knew he had something to say. He cleared his throat. At last, half to himself, he muttered, "Damn it." And then, "Stovepipe, I'm at a loss for words."

"I understand, sir."

He sighed and cleared his throat. "Stovepipe?" He cleared his throat again. "You have every right to throw the book at me. What happened is indefensible and unprofessional. What I'm trying to say..."

He breathed in and out, heavy, and I reached for his hand. He took hold as if it were a life preserver for a drowning man.

"Oh, hell," he said. "I don't know what I'm trying to say. The professional officer in me is ashamed I took advantage of another professional officer who has always had reason to trust me. Embarrassed that this officer may have felt he was doing my bidding because he might have perceived it as some kind of order, or that he—er, you—didn't have a choice. I would never use rank to reach such an end, and I hope he—*you*—didn't think…" He paused again and took another deep breath. "I knew better. I *knew* better. I should never—"

"Oh, be quiet," I said. "Please. You're talking nonsense."

"Am I?" He sighed and pulled his pipe and a crumpled tobacco pouch out of his jeans. In spite of the drizzle outside, he opened the window halfway to let out the smoke.

"This whole next week is going to be hell for me, and you, too, I reckon," he said. "I have to trust you to continue doing your job as if this weekend never happened. It's a big responsibility, one I have no right to place on your shoulders. I'll have to do the same, but I'm older. More experienced. I'd carry it myself if I could. But you—"

I had to ask one question. "Sir? This weekend—do you want it to happen again?" I dreaded the answer, but if we were at an end, I needed to know before I got out of the car.

"Do you?" he said, after a pause.

"I asked first," I said.

A longer pause, eternal, but this was at the end of it, and my heart leaped. "Yes," he muttered. "Yes, damn it."

"Thank you," I said. "I was afraid for a minute you were telling me it was over."

"You don't know what you're getting into," he said.

"I can take care of myself, sir. Nobody puts his hands on me if I don't want him to. And I can't remember ever telling you 'no.' "

"I didn't give you a chance."

"I was afraid that you wouldn't, not that you would."

"That's kind," he said.

"It's not kind. It's true."

"I wish you'd quit making this so easy," he said. "Even to suggest that we might have some kind of future is unfair, because I can't promise anything."

It dawned on me that if we were to continue, the attraction we shared would be the only uncomplicated part. We would have to be on guard every second. In no way could he change the relationship we had already firmly established at work. If anything, I'd probably feel as if he were coming down on me even harder, overcompensating like mad. Except for the nominal fact that two gay airmen could now share a public relationship, according to the Air Force, everything else about us was wrong, from fraternization to the impropriety of being personally involved with someone in your direct chain of command.

"I have no right to ask," he said. "But I'm such a selfish son of a bitch and a goddamned old fool that I'm going to ask anyway. Because I may never get another chance. It's easy for me to say it's worth the risk. I have nothing to lose. I could retire tomorrow and be comfortable for the rest of my life, and they can't take that away from me. But you're just beginning your career, and you're still young. Asking you to gamble your future against—"

"Are you asking?"

"I won't bother you again if you tell me to keep the hell out of your private life."

"Are you asking?"

"I could see to it that you're transferred to another unit with the highest recommendation from me. Any job you want. Immediately. Retraining into another career field, if you like."

"*Are you asking?*" I didn't mean to yell. I didn't mean to sound so angry, either, and he was taken aback for an instant. His temper reared like a horse seeing a snake, and he roared back.

"*Yes!*" At last, a glimmer of light charging through his doubt.

"Okay. Then let me give you an answer."

He put a gentle hand over my mouth. "Not yet," he said. "You've got a lot on your mind right now. I want you to think long and hard before you answer. Call me in a week," he said. "If you say yes, well, I don't rightly know what you can expect, but you will never find a man more grateful and more willing to show you how much."

Curiously, he never said a word about love or its possibility. Perhaps he believed men simply didn't speak of such things. I hardly expected him to offer his heart to me in a box, at least not yet. But, as articulate as he was, why couldn't he find the words to explain that he was brimming over? Perhaps I was being too harsh. Though we'd known each other for more than six months, in some significant ways, we had just met, and we had some first impressions to verify.

"What happened Friday night scared the hell out of me," he said. "But not so much that I stopped it on Saturday. Or today. Great God." He paused and shook his head. "What have I done?" He looked at me, long and searching. "Thank you for the best weekend I've ever had," he said.

Hope sprang. "You're welcome," I said.

His voice grew hoarse. "If you're smart, you'll say no, Harris."

Maybe I wasn't smart. In the shadows, he pressed his mouth softly against mine, and I pressed back. There was none of the all-consuming urgency of yesterday and last night and this morning. The intimacy of it unsettled me, but it felt exactly right, sitting there in his car with his arms around me in the dark. I reached my hand under his sweatshirt, and he murmured his approval with no trace of doubt. When we separated, reluctantly, I knew he was grinning in the dark. I could smell it.

"I can't promise you every weekend. We both know that's impossible," he said. "I will make time to share with you as often as you want. And you'll have my undivided attention. But it won't be easy. You know that." He stopped and sighed. "Listen to me. You haven't even said yes."

I opened my mouth to speak, but he stopped me again.

"Think it over," he said. "And be damn sure of your answer, because I'm going to hold you to it."

He rested his mustache against my cheek again. When he finally pulled himself away, he shook his head. "This can't be happening." Weary. "Good night, Longjohn, and I'll see you in the morning."

Tomorrow morning. Oh, yes. That.

I walked to my own car and climbed in, buckled my seat belt, adjusted the rearview mirror for the dark, fired up the engine, and switched on the lights. The general followed me out of the lot, turning right and heading inward, deeper into the confines and regulation of the base, while I turned left, toward the gate and the freedom that lay beyond the perimeter fence.

A week later, I called his number. Nothing in his answering machine message identified him by name, but I knew the voice. At the sound of the tone, I said, "Yes. Satisfied?" and hung up.

And sometime that weekend, he returned the call and left a simple "got your message" on my voice mail in response. And a second message saying "you won't regret it" followed by a pause. "Wait. Maybe you will. Son of a bitch," and laughing. And then a third, with a single word of thanks. And, improbably, a fourth, with his thanks repeated a dozen times.

CHAPTER TWELVE

At the NAF headquarters, a month followed during which I wondered repeatedly if I had dreamed a general for a lover. Apart from the phone messages he'd left on my answering machine, he gave no sign, no hint, as my morale sank lower and lower. Work became hell, with the general ranting daily for my perceived or petulantly real infractions. The staff was shocked at his venom, but at least I had a good idea why he raged so.

Julia and I continued our movie-and-dinner tradition. Even though she knew something was wrong, she graciously accepted my "I don't want to talk about it" and didn't press for details. The general's occasional distracted compliments when I'd exceeded expectations weren't much consolation, and my own anger matched his, even if I couldn't express it. I planned all sorts of traps and tricks to catch him and followed through on none of them.

At a business council breakfast in mid-August, he glared at me over his rubbery omelet and unacceptable toast, clearly upset about some mistake or perceived inadequacy. I had no idea what I'd done wrong, but I was just as willing to antagonize him in return. I selected the largest banana from a bowl of fruit on the table, and as he watched, I peeled it and ate the whole thing in two bites. He could have spat bullets in my direction.

It was an immature prank, and I hoped no one else was watching. I expected him to be furious. I thought it would at least scratch open an old wound if it didn't rekindle an old fire. I prepared myself for his fury, but to my astonishment, he said nothing about it during the drive back to the base afterward.

❖

At the end of the week, as the Friday doldrums sauntered in after lunch, I had little to do and was idly shuffling papers and procrastinating. The outer offices were empty except for me. Everyone else was gone on some pretext or other. I hadn't done anything more useful all day than track down the general's misplaced glasses twice.

When he summoned me mid-afternoon, I stood by his desk, expectant, as he sorted through some mail, waiting for him to notice me. He'd lit his pipe, which he rarely did in the office unless something was troubling him. He finally indicated for me to take a seat.

For some minutes I sat, stifling a yawn. I had little to anticipate beyond a quiet weekend at home, since Julia was out of town on leave. I'd probably see a movie by myself, wash the car, and do the laundry. This inconvenient general would be out of my sight, and I'd breathe easier.

Finally he looked up at me. He hesitated and then cleared his throat.

"Yes, sir?"

"Anything on the schedule, Downtown?"

"You're free for the rest of the afternoon, sir."

He glanced at the wall clock, about half past two. "You're dismissed. I have some work to finish, but there's no reason to keep you."

An unexpected surprise, but inwardly, I shrugged. Whatever. "Thank you, sir."

As I collected my things, he hollered for me again. I returned to his office and came to attention in front of his desk. He drew deeply on his pipe and exhaled. "A terrible habit," he said.

"Yes, sir."

"Rum-and-maple blend," he said. "Imported from Canada."

"Yes, sir. It has a very pleasant aroma."

"My granddad smoked a pipe," he said.

"Did he, sir?"

The general was stalling. Perhaps he needed a little courage. After a minute, he took a deep breath and asked, hesitant, his voice low, "Could you stand a visitor tonight?"

I whispered my response as well, though no one was around to hear us. "You might stop by?"

"I might."

"You're welcome anytime, sir. And you can stay as long as you like."

"Thanks, Knoxville. I...ah...might, later. I've got some...ah... work to finish first. I...ah...already told you that, didn't I?" I'd rarely seen him so flustered. "I hope to see you later, sir."

"Maybe," he said.

I didn't move. "Say yes," I said. "Please, sir?"

He sighed. "All right, damn it. Yes. Now will you get out of here?"

The pilot light of hope flamed into possibility. Satisfied, I turned to leave, but I paused by the door and turned to look at him again. After a minute, he looked up, over the top of his glasses. "Well? What?" he barked.

"Nothing, sir. Just being a tourist."

His glower melted, and his mustache bristled, almost imperceptible. Silent, he stood up and made an exaggerated full turn for my benefit. "Enough?"

"No, sir. May I buy another ticket?"

He pointed. "Damn it, go!"

"Yes, sir." I let him be.

For the first time since our weekend together a month earlier, he'd given me proof it hadn't all been a mirage. I might have floated out of the building. Such was my euphoria, at least until panic seized me. What should I serve for dinner? And, if I might be that lucky, breakfast? Before leaving the base, I stopped at the commissary and spent an agonizing hour browsing the well-stocked shelves. I went home with three sacks full of groceries, enough to serve half a dozen meals to any six guests.

At home, I dusted and vacuumed the whole place and scoured the bathroom. Changed the bedsheets. Washed the kitchen floor. Baked a pan of brownies. Early in the evening, I showered and stood in front of my open closet. Another crisis. What should I wear? A bathrobe might seem too eager, a little presumptuous. I didn't see any reason to dress formally, but neither would a T-shirt and blue jeans do. I settled for chinos and a polo shirt I changed three times, and sat down to wait, making a useless attempt to read.

When I still hadn't heard anything from him by nine o'clock, I assumed a false alarm. Perhaps his "later" meant Saturday or Sunday. After all, he'd asked rather non-specifically about the weekend. It wasn't as if I'd canceled any plans, I reminded myself. If nothing else, I had accomplished a week's worth of cleaning in one frenzied evening. But how dare he get my hopes up and then not show? I was still debating both sides of the issue when a brisk knock at the door interrupted me.

With exaggerated nonchalance, I went to the door, and there he stood. "Good evening," I said. "Come in, sir."

He stepped inside, and I shut the door behind him. He had traded his flight suit for khaki trousers and a sport jacket, casually elegant. We stood in the entry for a minute, staring at each other. I couldn't quite believe he was here. Perhaps he, too, felt some disbelief.

He handed me a cold bottle wrapped in a damp brown paper bag. "Chardonnay," he said. "Thought we might need it."

That sounded ominous. "Would you like a glass now?" I said.

He nodded. He looked around the living room, and he could hardly have been impressed with what he saw. My comfortable but worn furniture reflected an early Salvation Army decorating sensibility, a mix of acquisitions from family, friends, and secondhand stores. The most prominent features were shelves crammed with a thousand books and a tired plaid couch with a framed Toulouse-Lautrec poster reproduction hanging above it.

The latest addition to the inventory was a battered-but-operational console phonograph, about the same age as me, purchased at the local thrift store for twenty dollars, along with a batch of classical-music albums, including Tchaikovsky's Fifth Symphony and whatever opera had presented itself. I'd been listening faithfully, making an effort to expand my appreciation.

"Put on a record, if you'd like, sir. Make yourself at home," I said. He walked to the couch and sat down on the edge of it, as if he were afraid to settle in, radiating discomfort if not disapproval. I almost told him he wouldn't catch anything from it.

In the kitchen, after a couple of minutes' search, I located the corkscrew and then a pair of stemmed glasses. I'd never heard of the particular brand of wine he brought, but I was hardly a connoisseur. My sole criterion for judging a better vintage was a cork instead of a screw top. I found the receipt in the bag. He'd paid more for that bottle than I had for my phonograph.

As I poured two glasses, I heard the front door slam.

My heart and spirit sank. When I went into the living room, he was gone. I watched from the window as he backed his car out of the driveway and screeched away, the tires protesting loudly.

So. That was that. It occurred to me as I looked at the empty space where his car had been parked that he had quite possibly placed his personal core values at risk by coming to my apartment at all. I had yearned for such a visit but never convinced myself it could happen.

Until tonight, I'd been willing to believe I'd been fighting the desperate ache by myself. I hadn't considered what he had to lose by surrendering to desire.

What crossed his mind as he changed out of his Air Force uniform and into his civilian clothes and drove across the miles that separated us? At what cost did he make that journey? No wonder he felt so ill at ease, though this sudden awareness did not make his departure any easier for me. I went back to the kitchen and saw the bottle of wine perspiring on the counter, the two glasses poured.

I picked up one glass. "Cheers," I said, toasting my ill luck. It went down so smoothly that, after a minute, I gulped down the second glass. In the empty living room, I put a CD on the boom box—a little dance music from this century, thank you—and parked myself on the couch where the general had been only moments before. Anticipation, frustration, anger, bitterness, and dismay collided like a car crash in my head. I was keyed up and too tired to process any part of it, and the alcohol went to work. Before long, I was asleep, no doubt dreaming that the quickest way to a man's heart was through his chest with a sharp knife.

Perhaps an hour later, maybe more, I was awakened by urgent knocking. Groggy, I stumbled to the front door and found a general. Rather than let him in immediately, I stood with the screen door between us and glared at him, trying hard to be angry. It was justified, and I didn't want to cheat myself out of the pleasure. If he had made concessions to be with me, had I not done the same for him?

"What do you want?" I said.

He glanced around and sighed, exasperated. "I've been banging on the door for ten minutes."

"I might have gone out. Ever think of that?"

"You're car's right outside."

"I could have walked somewhere," I said. "You think I spend my whole life waiting around for you?"

"Let me in."

"I tried that once tonight already. It didn't take." But I stepped back anyway, and he let himself inside and shut the door. We faced each other again, and he crossed his arms in front of him to match mine, glowering at me.

"What?" I said. "What have *I* done?" I didn't have any patience left. "There's still some of that wine left if you need to get drunk before you can relax." I pointed toward the kitchen, and he headed in that direction. Let him find his own way, grope along the wall for the light switch by himself. I was staying put. At least he wouldn't be able to escape again without running past me.

He took his time. I finally went to the doorway of the kitchen. He stood at the sink, looking all around the room, scrutinizing everything, as if to decide whether or not he could tolerate such surroundings. My Formica-topped table was a relic but still in good shape, with solid matching chairs. The wallpaper, not of my choosing, featured salt and pepper shakers and a coffee mill, in stylized drawings and muted autumn colors. The pattern would have been popular around the time the table was new. It all fit, and, unapologetically, I liked it. Until that moment, I'd never been concerned about anyone else's opinion of it.

Did he feel about microwave ovens the same way he did about cell phones?

He discovered me watching from the doorway. "May I offer you a glass?" he said.

"I've already had two. I didn't like it." So there.

"Maybe I'll drink two so we're even." One eyebrow inched itself up a fraction as he looked at me, still glaring at him. "Or three."

"Suit yourself," I said. "But I'm not driving you home tonight. If you pass out, you'll wake up on the couch, because I'm not giving up my bed to a drunken general."

"Easy, there," he said, cocking his eyebrow even more.

I would not be easy. "You planning to make a run for it, or do you think you might stick around for a while?" I said.

"You asking me to?"

"Why should I?"

"Damned if I know, Paintbrush." Keeping an eye on me, he slowly took off his jacket and hung it on the back of a chair. When I still didn't crack, he said, "Maybe I should leave my coat on."

"Suit yourself," I said. "Go, if you want to. But see if I ever let you in here again."

We faced each other, defiant, our arms crossed defensively. But we could only scowl for so long before the absurdity of it overtook us. One or the other of us started grinning first, and he finally shook his head and said, "Get the hell over here."

I went, more willing than I'd intended to be.

Hesitant, he brushed his mustache against me, and I surrendered immediately. It was useless. I wanted the same thing. I put my hands on him. He covered my mouth with his and sampled me thoroughly.

Only when his breath became as ragged as mine did he push me away. The pounding in his chest and mine might have been Verdi's chorus of anvils.

Wondrously, he laughed. "I'm not finished," he said.

"I hope not, sir."

He let go of me as if he'd been burnt.

"Look," he snapped. "Surely you realize how inappropriate it is for you to call me 'sir' when you're practically feeling me up. It's damned ridiculous. Stop it, or I'm out of here."

His vehemence startled me, and my response was typically automatic. "Yes, sir."

"You just did it again!" he said.

I didn't know what else to call him. "It's not my fault. The Air Force has trained me well. What am I supposed to do? Call you Seamus? I don't know if I could even do that."

"Then find something else."

"Like what? I could use your middle name. Or I could shorten it to Edward, I guess."

"Don't like it, in the plural or the singular."

"There's Mr. O'Neill," I said, half joking.

He shook his head and sighed. "Of course not."

"A nickname of some sort?"

"Such as?" he said.

Nicknames are funny. A man can't choose his own. It has to spring naturally from some character trait or typical situation, though I knew he'd recoil if I suggested "Lefty" or "Smoky," two that came to mind immediately. I would never be able to come up with on-the-spot randomly generated nicknames as he did for me. I didn't even propose it.

"I don't know," I said. "We'll have to find something we're both comfortable with."

"But no more 'sir,' for God's sake. Agreed?"

"Yes, sir." Reflexes are hard to counteract.

"Damn it, Pitchfork. Don't be insubordinate," he said, exasperated. "From now on, every time we're out of uniform and you call me 'sir,' I will demand a penalty."

It was my turn to recoil. "Oh, no," I said. "I've had enough of that game. I won't pay you a single dime for a mistake like that."

His mustache started working. "Hmm...maybe we can work out some sort of penalty that doesn't involve a cash transaction."

Now, there was an idea. "What do you have in mind?"

"The punishment should fit the crime."

"You could call me 'sir' too," I said.

"That's hardly adequate compensation."

"Perhaps not."

"It took you so long to learn to be punctual," he said.

"And it was expensive," I reminded him.

"But unless the penalty is sufficient, you'll throw 'sir' at me all the time, just to wear me down."

"I wouldn't put it past me," I said.

"The penalty must adequately compensate me for that aggravation."

"Don't forget your pain and suffering."

"Of course. Perhaps some sort of service rendered."

"Hmm…what sort of service?" His crotch had been telegraphing his impatience for some minutes. "Can you think of some service I might render that would be of particular use to you at a time like this?" I reminded him he had pointed out to me on more than one occasion one might do better things with one's mouth than talk. He raised his left eyebrow a fraction of an inch, and his mustache quivered ever so slightly, A wicked laugh told me he had caught on.

"You're suggesting that I demand, if you'll excuse the vulgar vernacular, a cocksucking as a penalty every time you call me 'sir'?"

"Your vernacular is forgiven. What do you think?"

"You're shameless," he said.

"Is it a deal?"

His mustache bristled. "It's hardly fair. As much as I enjoy being on the receiving end, I also very much enjoy—oh, hell," he said. "I like sucking cock myself."

"They say it's better to give than to receive," I said. "If fairness is what you want, I would be happy to demand an even trade, one-for-one," I said. "Deal?"

He took a deep breath. "Deal." We shook hands. "Jesus," he said. "What am I getting myself into?"

"The best bargain you've ever made." He grinned. "I will make every effort to remove the offending 'sir' from my vocabulary as quickly as possible, sir," I said.

"You," he said, "are a liar. And I'm a goddamned fool."

"Yes, sir. You are, sir. I hope you've been counting. I've got at least five or six to pay off already tonight."

He picked up a note pad and pen from the kitchen counter, wrote

"SIR" across the top and made six *O*'s on the page. "I'll mark an *X* through each *O* as the debt is paid," he said. As he attached the sheet to the refrigerator with a magnet, he noticed the row of postcards, six of them by now. Temporarily distracted, he examined each one. "You kept them."

"I never told you how much I look forward to those postcards when you go," I said. "I miss you a little less when I know you're thinking about me, too."

He turned to look at me. "You mean that," he said.

I nodded.

"Tell me, Sharpshooter," he said. "What have I done to deserve you?"

"You're just lucky. Sir."

He made another mark on the paper. "You think I'm kidding."

My turn to smirk. "Not at all. Sir." Another mark. "Shall we begin crossing them off?" I said. "I'm ready if you are."

He reached out, hooked a finger in my waistband, and pulled me toward him. "I could wander around this Taj Mahal of yours until I find the bedroom, but if you lead me to it, we'll get there quicker," he said. "I'm going to wrestle you out of your shirt and trousers, and God knows what I might do after that."

"You'll think of something," I said. "As for me, I've got debts to pay. Sir."

He made another mark on the paper and then turned his attention to me, and who says a kitchen is just for cooking?

Afterward, our initial hunger satisfied, he retrieved a small suitcase from the car, as if I needed proof he would be content to stay the night with me. Back inside, I led him down the hall, and we undressed and climbed into bed. In the warm dark, I wanted only to explore him as if he were some Braille text. To learn him by heart: his strong arms, his flat fuzzy belly, the jut of his ribs as he breathed in. I ran my fingers across his dense mustache and sandpapered jaw, even his eyebrows. I moved slowly, deliberately, in no hurry. He responded, catlike, pressing himself against me and muttering under his breath, a combination of satisfaction and impatience. I didn't have to ask if I were doing the right thing. It brought on a slow, simmering kind of arousal that didn't require immediate release. Its theme was itself, pleasure taken in travel rather than the destination.

And he wasn't U.S. Air Force Brigadier General Seamus O'Neill. He wasn't my boss or the commander of Sixth Air Force, or a military pilot. He wasn't an airman at all, and neither was I at that moment. He was just a man, one I liked very much and who aroused me like none I'd ever known, and he was entirely under my power to persuade.

"Talk to me," I said.

"As you like," he murmured, a deep, throaty growl. "What can I say that would please you most?"

I'm not even sure what made me think to ask. "Tell me about your first time," I said.

He was puzzled. "What do you mean?"

"With a man. Your first experience."

I don't think he'd bargained for such a request. "Why?" he said.

"Just talk."

I could almost hear him frown in the dark. He was silent for a long time, and I wasn't sure if he didn't remember his first time or simply couldn't figure out how to put the experience into words. Once the general made up his mind to speak, he sat up in bed and brought me up next to him. He wrapped the sheet around us close, and slowly, navigating his tale with care, he told me about a captain in his late twenties who met one particular major, seven or eight years older. Captain O'Neill was captivated, and he fell pretty hard. The fact that the major admitted right away that he was gay and willing didn't help matters.

"I knew I was attracted to men and not to women, and it was only a matter of time before I would do something about it," the general said. "I'd never met a man who excited me the way he did. After a lot of agonizing on my part and none on his we ended up in bed one night, after sharing a six-pack of beer. Once we got that first time out of the way, we wound up in bed regularly, and we didn't need beer to get us started."

He was silent long enough that I figured he would tell me nothing more. But without prompting, he finally continued. "Didn't take me long to figure out he wasn't interested in anything long-term. 'No such thing as Mr. Right,' he used to say. 'Only Mr. Right Now.' And I liked him well enough to be his Mr. Right Now anytime he couldn't find someone he liked better. And I guess I was usually third or fourth in line. Sometimes he'd bang on my door at three o'clock in the morning, but I always let him in."

The major had been in the service for eleven or twelve years, and he'd been pretty careful. But eventually the rumors started, the wrong word in the right ear, and the talk finally caught up with him. He managed to resign before they could discharge him for conduct unbecoming an officer, the general told me.

"We'd been getting together on the sly for about a year by then. I was scared for both of us," the general said. "He asked if I'd quit the service with him, but I refused. If I had any confidence he was willing to settle down with me, I might have gone with him, but he wouldn't even promise next week, let alone next month. I stayed put."

After quitting the Air Force, the major didn't have any reason to be cautious, and AIDS caught up with him pretty quickly. "It scared the hell out of me," the general said. "I got myself tested immediately. When I found out I was negative, I vowed to stay that way."

They lost contact, though the general was careful to point out that the major had initiated the break. "Once he got really sick, he decided he didn't want anything to do with me," the general said. "I didn't hear from him again until he was near the end—this was nearly twenty years back. When I visited him in the hospital for the last time, I swore I wouldn't end up like he did.

"John Frederick Buchanan," he whispered. "I haven't even spoken his name in years." His voice hardened. "I never cried for anyone like I did for him. I felt guilty because I hadn't tried hard enough to make him settle down, as if that could have made any difference." He shook his head, as if to push away an unsettling memory.

"After Johnny's death, I lost myself in the service. I kept busy. It was easy. Didn't have much time to worry about being alone or being anything because I was flying so much," the general said. I remembered the patch on his flight suit with the "10,000 hours" tab above the major command insignia. How many takeoffs and landings equaled that much in-flight time?

"I was surprised to hear that you were married," I said.

"After Johnny got kicked out, I panicked—I knew I had to start dating women," he said, "but I didn't know the first thing about it. I knew she had to be attractive, someone my pilot buddies would approve of, but I didn't have any idea how to find a woman like that. Turns out I didn't have to. She found me instead. We were introduced at a dance at the officers' club. She was someone else's date, but she dumped him and came gunning for me. She had a lot more experience with the whole mating ritual than I did, and I guess she thought my naïveté was charming. When she proposed to me, I said yes. We got married not long before I was scheduled to meet the lieutenant-colonel promotion board. Just in time."

"I guess it worked," I said.

"It worked."

He felt sorry for her because she didn't know what she'd gotten herself into. "I don't like to admit it, but I was selfish," he said. "I figured my secret wouldn't matter, that I could keep that dog under the porch just by force of will, but it didn't work." He'd never conquered his yearning for male companionship and was ashamed of himself for blaming her.

"God knows she did her best," he said. "She was by my side for every ceremony, every official function, every formal dinner or dance, any event that demanded our presence as a couple. Always beautiful, always smiling, always gracious, but the whole thing became a charade."

He did not tell me her name, and I didn't ask for it. I didn't want to know, though I felt sorry for her, too. The role of a senior officer's wife may be prestigious and glamorous, but it can't be very fulfilling in private if the marriage is only rank and its privileges. Mrs. O'Neill hung on until he was selected for brigadier general, and when she told him she wanted a quiet divorce, he let her go without complaint.

"She was fed up with the act. I don't know if she ever figured out my secret. If she suspected, she never let on," he said. They'd been together for ten years, and the general had come to regard her more as a colleague than as a spouse. He'd treated her with utmost respect, he said, and he was proud of that.

"Surprised the hell out of everyone when we split up. No one had any idea we weren't perfectly happy," he said. "At least there were no kids to complicate things."

"You didn't want any?"

"She didn't. And I didn't argue."

He offered other details about which I was curious but reluctant to ask, primarily regarding the sexual aspect of their marriage. He'd fulfilled his obligations when he had to, he said, and he'd been relieved he could perform satisfactorily, but she'd never pressed him too much. Perhaps she, too, was relieved he seldom initiated it. He was always self-conscious about sex with her, as he'd learned the first time he took off his shirt in her presence that she found hairy chests distasteful. She'd even asked him to shave it, but he'd adamantly refused.

"It's damn lucky for me that you like furry men," he growled. I instinctively crept my fingers into the rug on his chest and found a warm welcome. Thus reassured, he continued his story. After the divorce, his ex-wife had remarried quickly enough that he assumed she'd been involved with him for some time. He'd been surprised but not particularly upset by it. He appreciated her discretion. She deserved whatever solace she could find, he said. He had no idea where she and her second husband had gone. The general himself had transferred bases twice since the divorce, and they hadn't any reason to keep in touch.

"I was faithful to her all the time we were married," he said. "Absolutely. When I make a commitment, I keep it."

"What about other guys?" I said. "After your divorce? I mean, I'm not the first one since your friend the major, am I?"

He shook his head. "Don't flatter yourself, Saltmine. And don't flatter me. I'm no saint." There had been other men, not only before the marriage but after the divorce, too, he said, though not many. "I've been careful because there have been a lot of good reasons these last twenty-five years to be careful. Too many men make the mistake of thinking with their cocks. I don't. It's damned hard sometimes, because nothing is as persuasive as cock. But I'm the boss."

Considering our own vigorous exploits so far, I wasn't sure I quite believed him, but the stance was commendable. I admired his self-control, just as I wondered how selective he was choosing to be about his sexual history. I hoped he wouldn't ask me about mine, because I had a few incidents in my past I would prefer to whitewash, too.

"It's *my* body," he insisted, "and I'm in charge, not the other way around. Lately, I've gotten out of the habit."

"Of what? Sex?"

"Yes. I mean, not entirely. I'm not the only general in the club, in case you're wondering, but I'm an old man, Dustpan, and I never expected anyone to come along and sweep me off my feet. You're mighty handy with a broom."

"Why did you hire me in the first place?" I'd never thought to ask such a question before.

"It does a general good to have a handsome sidekick," he said. "It's certainly done me good."

I persisted. "Because I was gay? Is that why?"

"Nope. It never even crossed my mind you might be interested in me," he said. "I never thought I'd get that lucky. Besides, I was convinced I had outgrown such foolish notions before you came along."

"I don't like being equated with anyone's foolish notions."

"There's no place else I'd rather be than right here," he said, firm. "You're damned handsome and damned sexy. You could certainly have your pick, and you seem to have picked me."

"You're damned handsome and damned sexy, too."

He laughed. "How did you acquire this fixation for senior citizens?"

"Being half a century old doesn't make you a senior citizen," I said.

He cocked an eyebrow. "Careful, now. You make me sound like an antique. Are you trying to undo all the warm feelings I've built up for you?"

"All I mean is that you've had the time to grow into yourself. You've been around."

"You don't know the half of it, Atlas," he said. "Last count, I've visited forty-three countries across the seven continents." He recited his list like a schoolyard braggart: England, Scandinavia, Germany, France, Italy, Switzerland, most of Europe, in fact, before and after the reorganization of the Soviet states, as well as Mexico, Brazil, Peru, Venezuela, Costa Rica, Japan, Korea, Thailand, the Philippines, Vietnam, Indonesia, Guam, American Samoa, Afghanistan, Kuwait, Saudi Arabia, even Antarctica. He'd traveled to all fifty states just because he wanted to say he'd done so, and all but two of Canada's provinces. He had every reason to be proud of himself.

"Aren't you the traveler," I said. It wasn't a question. The word just suited him, not only in tribute to his journeys around the globe but to the long and circuitous path he'd navigated in his career and his life. The road had been rocky, certainly, but somehow along the way, he'd been promoted to general and met me. Something about the word suggested his restlessness, too.

I tried it again. "Traveler."

"Yes."

"It's a good word, isn't it?"

"Very descriptive. You know, General Robert E. Lee's horse was named Traveler. I remember that from a Civil War history class I took in college."

"Tell me more."

"Some other time," he said. "Haven't we had enough talk for one night? It's late. You've got a lot of debt to work off tomorrow, and I've got to do my part and rise to the occasion. All I want right now is to wrap myself around you and get some sleep."

He'd get no argument from me. I settled down next to him and he pulled me in close. I would, as soon as the opportunity presented itself, request more details about his friend the major. So my restless traveler had actually considered settling down with another man at some point in the past. Had considered taking off his hat, folding up his maps, and unpacking his suitcase. Was there reason to hope he might consider it again?

CHAPTER THIRTEEN

We're supposed to wake up first in our own home. I did. When I realized I'd never fall back to sleep, I got out of bed carefully, so as not to disturb the general. The clock read seven, but the sun outlining the closed shade told me a beautiful morning was already in progress. I decided to fix breakfast for him and serve it in bed. Among my commissary purchases from the previous day were pancake mix and sausage, an easy choice, with coffee and juice. Such a spread would make a good impression, too, if he'd just sleep long enough for me to put it together.

Luck was on my side.

I assembled a neat tray—a steaming plateful of golden brown pancakes with melting butter, a pitcher of warm syrup, two sausage links, a glass of orange juice, and a mug of coffee made to his exact specifications—and then went in to wake him up. My turn to sit on the edge of the bed and whisper, "hey, you!" into his ear and watch him yawn and stretch. "You planning to sleep all day?"

"Wasn't planning to sleep," he said. "But I don't see any reason to get out of bed. Climb on in here."

"I'll join you right after breakfast," I said, "which, as you can see, I have already prepared for you." He sat up, leaning against the headboard, and I rested the tray on his lap, where it balanced precariously.

He examined the spread. "That looks wonderful, Stovetop."

Breakfast in bed may be a romantic cliché, but it isn't very practical. Still, he was game. He added syrup to the pancakes and then picked up his knife and fork. Gingerly, he sliced the stack into bite-sized pieces, careful not to tip the tray into the sheets. He tasted a bite and murmured his approval. I pulled a chair up close to the bed and settled down to watch.

"I'll do my best to entertain you," he said.

"Just eat. You can entertain me after breakfast."

When he realized I wasn't going to budge, he made a deliberate show of savoring every forkful, and sipping his juice and coffee. "Don't I get to watch *you* eat?" he asked finally.

"I've already eaten."

"Ah. So you're just waiting on me."

"Looks that way."

His mustache started its own landslide. He cleaned his plate quickly, leaving nothing but a half-full pitcher of syrup. He handed the tray back to me, and I set it aside. I don't know what made me look twice at that syrup, or what made me pick it up. But only a couple of seconds passed between my upturning the pitcher and the initial impact of the warm, sticky brown stuff as it spread over his chest, slowly making its way downward. In that couple of seconds, he yelped, "Hey! What's the big idea?"

I gave him no time to get over his astonishment as I climbed into bed with him. I do love the taste of warm maple syrup, and I wasn't going to let a drop of it go to waste. A quick flex of his eyebrows and a wicked laugh told me he approved. I was in no hurry. This was a meal I was determined to enjoy to the fullest. The stickiness added just enough friction, and the mingling of the rich maple against his tantalizing masculinity on my tongue was all the breakfast I needed.

When I was done, he pulled me up on top of him.

"Log Cabin, where above hell did you learn to do that?" he said.

Actually, I had never done anything like it before, but all I said was, "I guess you just make me hungry. You enjoy yourself?"

He sighed. "You can have me for breakfast anytime. And lunch and supper." He annexed my maple-flavored mouth to his.

Upon attempting to separate some time later, we discovered that dried syrup exhibits similar properties to airplane glue. The general got the worst of it, and my attempts to be sympathetic as we cautiously pulled apart didn't convince him. He might have been ripping strips of duct tape from his belly.

I stifled a chuckle, not very convincingly.

"It's not funny," he said.

Faced with his injured glare, I dissolved into helpless laughter.

Generals aren't accustomed to being on the receiving end of such treatment. And my particular general was furious. And when he realized he didn't have any honest reason to be furious with me, he became, well, furiouser, and I responded by laughing even harder. After we separated fully, I herded him into the shower and helped him scrub, but I knew he'd feel a little sticky all day. I was thoroughly proud of myself.

After our shower, as we toweled off, I wondered aloud how I could thank him for finding room in his weekend for me.

"You could call me 'sir' a few more times," he said. "Your debt will be paid before you know it."

I repeated my pronouncement from the night before, that he was a fool to have entered into such an agreement with me, because I'd see to it that he never got ahead of the game. He only grinned, lazy. "Who's the fool?" he said. "I'll see to it that you keep your end of the bargain. You'll be shackled to me for life."

He got no argument from me. "Promise?"

"Damn right I do. And you know I'm a man of my word."

That was sufficient. I opened the shade and the windows, too, and let the sun in. "Look at this magnificent day," I said. "What shall we do with it?"

"Close the shade and get back in bed," he said.

"You're overruled," I said. "We're not staying indoors on a day like this."

"You sound like your mom. I'll put money on it."

I did, in fact, but no matter. I watched the eager, overachieving breeze riffle through the trees lining my street and had an idea. "Let's fly a kite," I said.

"What?"

"And have a picnic. I can't think of a better way to spend a summer day."

He groaned. "I can think of a hundred better ways."

"Oh, come on. When was the last time you flew a kite?"

"That's easy," he said. "Never."

How, I asked him, was it possible for a man to reach fifty-one without even once enjoying the supreme pleasure of flying a kite?

"I fly planes," he said. "Why bother with kites?"

I shook my head. "You had a deprived childhood."

That settled it. He would learn to fly a kite today. I made a quick inventory for a picnic and decided we'd pick up some fried chicken and side dishes at the supermarket. I knew of a not-too-distant state park I'd never visited, and today we would remedy that situation.

We dressed identically, as I was able to match his blue jeans, white sneakers, and gray Air Force sweatshirt. We topped off with our softball team caps.

As we surveyed each other, I said, "May I grow a mustache like yours?"

"No," he said.

"You could protect me from the fallout."

He shook his head. "Nice try, Airmail, but I'm the only one around the NAF who can flout the regulations."

"And why is that?"

He cocked an eyebrow. "Because I'm a general."

That again. "Oh, right. I forgot," I said. "Sir." I unbuttoned his jeans and reached in through the denim and the white cotton of his shorts. He murmured his appreciation.

"I hate you," he muttered as I explored. "I hate you, because you're going to get me hot and bothered and then piss on the fire by insisting that we go fly a goddamn kite."

"Would I do a thing like that?"

Grumbling, the general backed away and buttoned his jeans himself.

As he sat at the kitchen table, pretending injury and nursing a third cup of coffee, I stirred up a jugful of lemonade with plenty of ice and not too much sugar. I mixed a pan of drop biscuits, too, and while they were baking, I chopped up raw carrots and celery and cucumber and packed everything into a cardboard box with napkins and plates and cups. Finally, I pulled a spare blanket from the bedroom closet to use as a tablecloth.

"You're awfully domestic all of a sudden," he said as I removed the biscuits from the oven.

"But don't they smell wonderful?"

He would not be pacified. But he helped me load the box and blanket and jug into the trunk of his car, and he climbed into the driver's seat. "You're sure I couldn't convince you to come back inside with me and work off a little more of your bad debt? What do you say?"

I admired his hopefulness, but I was dead set on flying a kite, in spite of other temptations. "I say turn left at the end of the block."

He sighed and put the car in gear. "Fine. Let's get this thing over with."

First I directed him to the local dollar store, where we picked up a ball of string and a traditional diamond-shape paper kite, rolled into a tight packet. The basic kite package hasn't changed since forever, I guess, and it's always like unwrapping a present. I'm somewhat amazed that kites are still available in the twenty-first century, but I'm convinced technology can't possibly improve this particular flying machine.

Next, I directed him to the grocery store. We parked, and I grabbed a basket on the way in. "I'll pick up a box of fried chicken from the delicatessen, and you scout around and see if there's anything else you want for our picnic," I said.

"Sir! Yes, sir!" He offered the most junior airman's automatic response to any given order, executed a smart about-face, and marched off.

The store was typically crowded for a Saturday morning. As I waited my turn at the deli, I was unpleasantly surprised to hear a familiar voice call me. "Lieutenant Mitchell!"

I turned and faced our executive officer, in civilian clothes, with a cart full of groceries. I'd never seen her at this market before, although I shopped here myself only on occasion, preferring the base commissary. Could I have chosen anyone else from our NAF to run into at the moment, I would have chosen *anyone* else.

"Good morning, Lieutenant Colonel Cartwright. How are you?"

"Fine. Yourself?"

"I'm fine, too. It's certainly a beautiful day."

"It is. Have you any plans?"

My plans were none of her business, but I could hardly say so. Perhaps, for once, she was simply trying to be sociable. I was stuck, still waiting my turn in line, and I couldn't walk away or pretend to be in a hurry. "Yes, ma'am. I'm taking full advantage of it. Going on a picnic, in fact."

"All by yourself?"

"No, ma'am, with a friend."

I hoped she wouldn't press for details. No one on the staff knew anything about my private life, and I was certainly not going to share with her. She might have been aware Julia was out of town, so I didn't want to be any more specific about my company for the day.

"Well, it was nice to see you, ma'am," I said, hoping she would take the hint. "Have a good afternoon."

She bade me good-bye, but I hadn't even finished breathing my relieved sigh when the general's voice cut through the din of the Saturday crowd. "Hey, Gunshot!" He was striding unmistakably toward me, triumphant, with two red apples, a package of chocolate cookies, and a bottle of Vermont's finest. His mustache managed a rumba as he dropped the stuff in my basket. "We don't want to run out of maple syrup, do we?" he said.

"Why, General O'Neill!"

I could see the look of consternation that crowded his face in that second. He recognized the voice without even looking around, but he pasted on a smile and faced her.

"How do, Jenny?"

"Fine, sir." I could almost hear her mind clicking away, calculating as she inventoried the general, unshaven in blue jeans and a sweatshirt. Clearly, he was here with me. And what would she possibly make of his concern for running out of syrup? Or of my referring to him as a friend? Our matching attire?

"How are you today, sir?" she said, a little uncertain.

I could see she desperately wanted to ask a question or two or three, but she knew she couldn't. She couldn't pump me for information in the general's presence, either, though I made a note to myself to prepare a good excuse for the following week, as I expected she would probably corner me as soon as she could, inquisitive as a town gossip. She would not be above pulling rank to insist upon a satisfactory answer or two.

"Fine, Jenny. You enjoy your weekend, now." He offered nothing more. Just stood with his arms crossed, looking at her, a faint and cryptic smile on his face. With a final puzzled glance at me, she wheeled her cart away.

"Great," the general muttered.

"Don't worry about it, sir," I said, attempting a weak joke. "It's a free country, and no one's going to tell us we can't shop off base on a Saturday morning."

"Somehow, I don't think that's what's troubling her." He shook his head, as if to clear away a bad memory. Then, unexpectedly, he chuckled. "She's going to wonder about the syrup all day long."

The deli clerk called my number, I collected my box of chicken, added some potato salad as an afterthought, paid for it all, and we hit the road. The general was uncharacteristically quiet, and I hoped our chance encounter with Jennifer Cartwright wouldn't spoil the rest of our day.

I would do my best to ensure it did not.

We drove far away from the base, a good hour and a half into the next county, and he seemed more relaxed with every mile. The farther we went, the less chance we'd be interrupted by inquisitive staff members. By the time we reached the park, his buoyant humor had returned.

The densely wooded park was sprawling and beautiful, like some great reward: a wooded, clear lake looped with a path for cyclists and runners, surrounded with acres of suitable picnic possibilities. Finding a quiet, private spot beneath the branches of an old shady tree proved easier than I had imagined. I'd expected competition for space on such a picture-book summer day, but we had plenty of options, and the merry breeze promised good things for kites.

We spread our blanket on the ground and unpacked chicken and biscuits, potato salad, cookies. I poured lemonade and set out plates and napkins and spoons, and we stood and surveyed as letter-perfect a picnic as one could find in fiction or film.

"Sunburn, you've done yourself proud. Couldn't ask for a better day, a better meal, or better company," the general said as he embraced me. "Forgive me for being such an old stick this morning."

"If you prove to me that you're truly sorry," I said, adding "sir" as an afterthought.

"Careful, Sunburn. I might tackle you right here."

"Go ahead and try, if you think you're man enough," I said. "Sir."

He wrestled me to the ground, his half-nelson catching me by surprise, but I was not one to take such a challenge lying down. I engaged fully into the spirit of the game, and we rolled and tumbled in the grass until he put a quick stop to it by situating his mouth against mine the instant he had the advantage. Then he pulled away, countering my protest with a lofty "You're the one who wanted to fly a kite instead."

Lunch awaited us first. I hadn't really had a proper breakfast, and I was suddenly ravenous. We sat down to eat, and over the course of a leisurely hour, gorged ourselves ridiculously full, one of the finest meals I'd eaten in my life, seasoned with salt and pepper and sun and easy laughter. I had never felt more certain of the future.

Putting the plates aside, in the heat of the early afternoon, I stretched out on the blanket, intending only to rest my eyes for a few minutes and woke up perhaps two hours later, my head in the general's lap and him with his pipe lit, looking as content as if all his dreams had improbably come true.

"Hey, you traveler," I said, yawning.

A grin as wide as sky stretched across his face.

I tried it again. "Traveler. That's it. That's you."

He nodded, satisfied. So I'd stumbled across something good and right because the name just suited him. We'd solved one problem, and maybe everything else in our world could reach a similarly fortuitous end.

"Sleep well?" he said. "You dreamed about me, of course."

I got up and stretched. "Awfully sure of yourself, aren't you?"

He nodded. He had every reason to be, and I guess he knew it.

"I didn't mean to fall asleep on you," I said. "Sorry."

"I'll be your pillow anytime. Besides, it's Saturday, and we have nothing on the agenda except us."

That reminded me. "And kite-flying!" I said. "Come on!"

I retrieved the kite and the string from the car. I unrolled the paper and flattened it out, crossed the sticks, and strung it properly, explaining each step as I went along. The general watched with interest. I was pleased to be teaching him a new skill that truly had some real-world applicability. Knowing how to fly a kite will serve a man well through all his days.

As I bent the stick to tie the bowstring, I remembered that we had nothing to use for the tail, a serious oversight on my part. "The tail keeps it upright," I explained. "It's ballast and balance. I should have thought to bring an old T-shirt. Do you have some rags in the car? An old towel, maybe?"

He shook his head. "But I've got an idea," he said. His mustache charged ahead of him, and I groaned.

"Okay, what is it?"

He whispered to me, and I burst out laughing. I had to admit it was ingenious, though, and it seemed to be our only option under the circumstances.

"I figured on getting you out of your drawers one way or another before the afternoon was over," the general said as we kicked off our shoes and socks and shucked our trousers in the back seat of the car. "You can stay as undressed as you want," he said, running his fingers up the inside of my leg. I smacked his hand away.

"Behave yourself, Traveler. Our next order of business is getting the kite in the air," I said.

"You're no fun," he said. As we pulled on our pants again, he said, "I'm still a little sticky from breakfast."

"Sorry, sir," I said.

"Liar. Just for that, I won't let you work off that 'sir' until next month."

"Now who's lying?" I said.

A few minutes later, I had fashioned a suitable tail from our undershorts and socks and attached it to the kite. I estimated that the weight would be just about right. The more wind there is, the more tail the kite needs, I told him. Finally, I fastened the bridle, the line connecting the kite to the ball of string.

We moved away from the trees into an open spot, relatively flat, and I gave the kite to the general to hold. "It's easier with two people," I said. "You'll be the launcher. I want the wind at my back, and you'll feel the breeze in your face." Years before, my dad had patiently clarified the science of it for me, and I shared what I knew. "The difference in air pressure from the face of the kite to the back surface of it will make it rise. That's lift, Traveler. See?" A flash of recognition crossed his face. "And the resistance of air to the forward motion of the kite is—"

"Drag," he said.

"And pulling it down, working against the lift is—"

"Gravity," he said with satisfaction.

"Very good. The angle of attack, the slant of the kite against the wind, has to provide enough lift to overcome gravity and drag," I said.

"You know what, Tightrope? That's what keeps a plane in the air, too. It's the same physics."

"Then you're already ahead of the game," I said. "I think we're ready for takeoff."

Into the wind, I backed away several dozen feet from him, unspooling string as I went and poising myself to run. I pulled the line so there was no slack. "Okay, Traveler, let go," I said. He offered our kite to the wind. I ran, and it rose, perfect.

It was a good day for up. Once confident that the kite was satisfied to continue heading in that direction, I called the general over and handed him the ball of string.

"What do I have to do?"

"Hang on. Let out more line when you need to."

"When? And how much?"

"The kite will let you know. Listen to what it says."

And the kite did tell him, tugging against the string, persuasive, as he let out more and more, a little at a time. The diamond grew smaller and smaller against the blue sky. The wind liked our kite, and I was pleased at how easily it climbed. The general was ecstatic, eager as I must have been, a boy of three or four, when my dad took me kite-flying for the first time. Air Force pilots make much of slipping the surly bonds of earth, and though I will never be a pilot, I believe if you attach your soul and imagination to a kite in a blue sunny sky, you can accomplish a similar result. A kite rising takes your spirit with it.

I reeled it in and switched places with the general, launching for him as he ran, and he was clearly proud of himself for a successful take-off. The wind that afternoon could not have been more ideal for a first-timer. Our kite bobbed and dipped occasionally, and I showed him how to let the line slacken until the kite regained its balance, but mostly it just aimed higher all by itself. We walked with it, introducing it to little currents and eddies in the air. Sometimes our diamond looped downward, caught itself and surged back upward, regaining lost altitude. The general wrapped himself around me and we held on to the string together, exultant, laughing and shouting enough to lift the sky.

It remains one of the finest days in my memory, the two of us with the kite on that afternoon, the kind of day you will always remember but never be able to rebuild, however carefully you scheme and plot.

Once the sun began its inevitable descent, we ended our adventure. The wind proved equally reluctant to let go of our kite. They'd become good friends. But slowly, the general reined it in. Silent, with a little sadness, we gathered our tablecloth and tidied up our picnic spot. The general set the kite gently on the back seat of his car. By the time we pulled into my driveway, a comfortable darkness had settled in. I unlocked the door to my apartment and we went inside.

He folded me into his arms. "Thank you, Blacksmith," he whispered. "I can't tell you how grateful I am for this day."

My cell phone, sitting on the coffee table, began vibrating to announce an incoming call.

"Don't answer it," he said. "Please?"

"Why not?"

"I don't want to share you with anyone tonight."

I let it ring.

❖

On Sunday morning, I awoke once again before he did. He stirred too, but I told him to stay put. I went to the kitchen to brew a pot of coffee and set the table for breakfast. When I returned to the room, I found him sprawled across the bed, asleep again, hanging tight to my old stuffed bear, which usually sat watch over me on the headboard. I grabbed my camera and spent the next half hour watching the general slumber, shifting now and then, holding the bear close. I shot nearly a whole roll of film of the pair of them in the available light from the bedside lamp, which cast some very provocative shadows.

Maybe the whir of the autofocus or the click of the shutter finally roused him, but he caught me in action, the camera viewfinder to my eye. "What fresh hell are you up to, Kodachrome?" he groaned.

"Just a little blackmail, Traveler."

"That's conduct unbecoming an officer."

"Give me a letter of reprimand," I said. "Or you could sentence me to a couple hours of hard labor. Sir."

That set his mustache afire.

After a sedate brunch in the kitchen, the general packed his overnight bag and took reluctant leave.

"I've got to," he said. "The lawn needs a mowing, and the garden wants a good weeding, and it has to be done this afternoon. A general can't let his yard go. Sets a bad example."

"I could help, Traveler. You'll get done faster, and then we could... well, who knows what we might come up with?"

He shook his head. "I'm tempted, but I won't have it said I'm taking advantage of my aide by deputizing him as a gardener, too." I protested, but he was right. Appearances counted. And for us, as general and lieutenant and as boss and employee, appearances counted twice or three times over.

Before he left, he dutifully marked an *X* across each *O* made good on the "sir" list posted on the fridge. I found excuses to call him sir a few more times, and we were back where we started.

"You'll never get ahead in this game," he said.

"Isn't that the whole point?" I asked.

After he'd gone, I discovered my bear was missing from the bedroom. In its place, I found a brand-new Arrow shirt, gleaming white. When the general called later to bid me good night, he explained.

"I owed you a shirt," he said. "I apologize for tearing your clothes off during our first night together, Hangman."

"Apology accepted," I said. "Now, what about my bear?"

"Sorry, Snapshot. Your bear's in my custody now. But rest assured, he'll be well taken care of. He'll sleep with me every night you're not available."

A week later, when I showed him the pictures of himself and the bear, he was very amused. He borrowed the negatives, and not long after that, he presented me with a wrapped package. I tore off the paper and found a photographic enlargement, matted and framed. The image he'd selected showed himself, the traveler at rest, holding tight to the bear, nestled intimately against fuzzy chest.

"Bear with me," the general said, grinning, as I scrutinized the photo.

"I can do that."

"Good."

I hung it on the wall in my bedroom.

To my indescribable relief, following our picnic-with-kite adventure, the general was markedly less reticent about sharing quality time with me outside of the uniformed confines of the base. Lieutenant Colonel Cartwright seemed to ease up a little after that weekend, too. I suspect the general had a "come to Jesus" meeting with her, though I never learned the details. He and I settled into a comfortable rhythm that never seemed at all routine. By day, I called him "sir" by necessity as he hollered at me with all the clap and boom he could command, and by night, weekends, and the occasional thrilling and unexpected drop-in on other days, I still called him "sir" with much more pleasant consequence. And neither of us dared to question the right or wrong of it.

CHAPTER FOURTEEN

At our final softball game of the season, late in the summer, a pop fly caught the general unprepared with his glove off, for some reason. When he reached for the ball, it clipped his ring finger so hard that he yelped. It immediately started to swell, and he spent the remainder of the game sidelined, with his hand jammed into a soda cup filled with ice.

I was fifth in the batting lineup, and we had two outs and two men on base by the time I was up. My heart sank, but I took my stance and gripped the bat, resolutely ignoring the catcalls and hoots of "easy out!" As I stood grimly at the plate, eyeing the pitcher, he tossed his first ball. A little wide, I thought. I didn't move.

"Steeeeeee-RIKE!" hollered the umpire.

Okay, I told myself. Relax. Keep your eye on the ball. Let it come to you. Swing level.

The next pitch was a ball, and so were the two after that. One more of the same, and I could walk, though I'd much prefer to land on base with an actual hit. Then the umpire called the next pitch a strike, too. I looked back at the general. I couldn't decipher everything he was yelling, but I caught the gist, and it wasn't complimentary. I faced the pitcher again, and on his sixth attempt, I stepped into it, swung hard, and connected with the ball. I heard the crack, and for a second, I watched it sail. Unbelievable.

"Run!" I could hear the general's voice louder than the rest, and when I rounded first, I could see the right-fielder had not only dropped the ball but had some trouble scooping it up, so I headed for second. The coach yelled at me to come to third, and I took his word for it. A fraction of a second after I leaped onto the bag, the baseman caught the ball.

"SAFE!" hollered the umpire. I'd brought home the runners who were on second and third, too. I couldn't believe my good fortune.

"Run on anything," the coach told me. "As soon as the ball leaves the pitcher's hand, step off the base and start inching toward home. If there's contact, run like hell."

There was contact. I ran like hell. The batter made it safely to first as I crossed home plate at a dead run and skidded into the backstop. My teammates were caught between disbelief and congratulations. Julia screamed and jumped up and down in the bleachers as if I'd just won the grand prize on some game show. The general gave me a crushing bear hug, and I thought for a minute he might kiss me in public. But all I needed was the ten seconds it took him to tell me, "Damn good play, Lou Gehrig. I knew you had it in you."

We managed to win the game by one run, which brought us to a respectable five wins to four losses for the season, apparently the first time the team had ever tipped the scale in that direction. "We're not tournament material yet, but we'll make it next year," the general said afterward, as we stood in the parking lot at the tailgate of someone's truck and drank a celebratory beer.

I insisted we take his swollen finger to the emergency room, volunteering to drive when he seemed reluctant. He claimed it was just a sprain and that he'd be fine in a day or two. But I marshaled him into the passenger seat of my car, and we headed to the base hospital.

He'd broken the finger, and he wasn't too pleased when the doctor refused to set the bone without getting the Academy ring out of the way first. The general winced and looked away as the doctor applied the cutters. I don't know if the pain or loss of the ring hurt worse. When the doctor handed the general the twisted metal, he examined it ruefully.

"That's white gold," he said.

"Sorry, sir," the doctor said. "You shouldn't wear any kind of jewelry when you play sports."

The general grunted and stuffed the ring into his pocket.

At least he hadn't been injured until the last game, he said to me as I drove him back to the ball diamond to pick up his car. That was a little compensation.

"I'm sorry about your ring, Traveler."

"No reason to be, Smokestack. It's just a damn college ring. Should have quit wearing it years ago, I reckon."

"Maybe you don't need to wear it anymore," I said.

"Hmm," he said. "Maybe." I knew he was downcast anyway.

Fortunately, the broken finger was on his right hand, so it wouldn't interfere with his ability to write. It would, however, add interesting décor to his sharp salute for a while. And the thickly wrapped neon-white cotton and tape against his tan skin served as a constant reminder, a souvenir of the season.

Julia had taken a team photo at one of the last games we played, late in the summer before it reluctantly gave way to autumn, and the picture showed sixteen regulars bunched together in the bleachers, mostly grinning, mostly optimistic in spite of ourselves. We all wore mitts, matching shirts and caps, and a couple shouldered bats or held balls. The general sat behind me, his gloved right hand resting on my shoulder. I hadn't been aware of it at the time, but I noticed it immediately when Julia gave me the print. It, too, joined my gallery.

The cast came off his finger after six weeks, and the doctor pronounced him fully mended. I knew the general had gotten his Academy ring fixed at no small expense. Curiously, he never put it back on.

CHAPTER FIFTEEN

As I picked up the midsize car at the airport's rental lot, I marveled a little at the course of events that had brought me this far. Yes, it was just another business trip, and I'd lost count of how many I'd been part of in the ten months I'd been the general's aide. I'd never understood why he insisted I participate in such events, but I didn't complain. Even though we rarely had any time to ourselves, he was close by.

On this particular occasion, we were completing a leadership conference at Wright-Patterson Air Force Base near Dayton. I should say, rather, that the general completed it. I'd hung around at the periphery with very little to do except listen to the bored complaints of the other generals' aides who were also accompanying their bosses. The conference ended Thursday morning, but instead of flying home afterward, we were at the airport picking up a rental car.

I was pleased he'd asked me along for this particular event because Wright-Patt is only a three-hour drive from my parents, and I loved visiting home in the fall. I'd turned in my request for leave before the trip. I could rent a car at the airport, be home by afternoon for a relaxing couple of days, and return the car to the airport in time for a flight on Sunday.

When I presented him with the leave-request form to sign, he motioned for me to shut the door. He got right to the point. "Let me come with you."

I was startled. "Home?"

He nodded and grinned.

My mother and father knew quite a bit about him already; my emails and phone calls were full of him, though I wondered sometimes if they noticed how my opinion of him had shifted since the early days.

I had never given them specific evidence to arouse their suspicion that my relationship with the general was anything other than professional, but they are smart people, and I would have been surprised if they hadn't started to suspect that I had a crush on him.

But taking the general home to meet Mom and Dad? One giant step forward. I hesitated for a minute.

"Ashamed to take me home to meet the folks, Buzzsaw?"

"No, sir," I said. Afraid, maybe, or at least apprehensive, but never ashamed. At least initially, then, I thought, why not, if he wants to?

"I'll phone them tonight and ask."

My mother was surprised at the nature of my call. "Why would your general want to come home with you?" she said.

"He just does," I said. "He wants to take a little break after the conference. He's a nice guy, Mom. You'll like him. Is it okay or not?"

"Of course, it's okay. But I don't know if our house is elegant enough for a general to visit."

"Oh, stop it. We'll be home in time for dinner Thursday, and we'll have to take off after breakfast on Sunday to catch an afternoon flight out of Columbus. Don't go to any trouble."

"But what will he do here for three days?"

"I don't know. Ask him to paint the master bedroom or weed the garden or something. And tell Dad he'd better take Friday off so he and I can go fishing."

"And you expect me to babysit your general while you and your father are out fishing?"

"G'night, Mom. Love you. Bye."

The general wore his blues—the Class A uniform with ribbons, tie, and coat, which he referred to as "the full horror"—when he traveled within the U.S., though civilian clothes were permitted as well. And if the general wanted to wear his uniform, I didn't have a choice when I accompanied him.

I would never put vanity past him. He knew as well as I did that he looked damn good in his blues. Once you noticed his uniform fit exceptionally well, you noticed the exceptional man wearing it. If anything could give the average citizen confidence in the country's military, the sight of General O'Neill striding purposefully along the boulevard in his Class A uniform could certainly do it. I could understand why he'd want to meet my parents thus attired. It showed him off to his best advantage and provided him a security blanket as well.

We had a beautiful day in an unseasonably warm October for traveling. The general was quiet for the first hour, smoking his pipe and contemplating. I kept looking over at him, and finally he'd catch my eye and glare, until I told him, "You can't fool me with that look, Traveler. This was your idea, remember. Besides, I know you're plotting all sorts of ways to embarrass me in front of my folks."

That wore him down.

"Will they like me?" he said.

"Why should they? They're fully expecting the worst."

He sighed. "Remind me again why I keep you around."

"Because someone has to make your coffee and find your glasses and scratch your belly every now and then."

"Ah," he said. "Now I remember."

When I announced we were about ten miles from home, he asked, "Do they know about you?"

I assumed he wondered if they knew about my being gay. "Yes. I told them when I was still in high school."

"How did they take the news?"

"They weren't exactly thrilled at first, but after they got used to the idea, they were okay with it. They've been very supportive. They were a little surprised when I joined the service, though," I said. They actually thought I was joking when I told them, my senior year of high school at dinner on Easter Sunday, that I intended to join the Air Force Reserve.

"And…" He hesitated. "Did you tell them about"—I wondered if he was going to say "us," but he didn't—"me?"

"Of course not, Traveler. I wouldn't presume to tell anyone your secrets, and you know it. As far as they're concerned, I'm bringing my boss home for the weekend because you wanted to take a break after the conference. That's all."

He was so visibly relieved it took some of the air out of me. I wondered if perhaps this weekend would prove more troublesome than it was worth. Did I really imagine I could introduce him to my mom and dad simply as my boss? Why would I ever bring any man home if there wasn't some personal aspect to our relationship? And how would they respond to *that* news? As I considered the set-up, I realized the visit was loaded with potential traps.

Too late now.

We pulled into the driveway and got out of the car. I'd forgotten to warn the general about the dogs, and they came tearing around the corner to meet us—Clement and Sixtus, Heinz 57 Varieties, both of them, rescued from the pound as pups, fully grown but retaining their puppy-like eagerness. Clement had joined the family at my insistence when I was in high school. He was easily a dozen years old and slowing down a bit but still as playful as ever in spite of the gray in his coat and muzzle. Sixtus had come after I'd graduated from the university, during my tenure teaching at the junior college before I rejoined the Air Force. When I brought him home, he was young enough that he aroused some sort of mothering instinct in Clement, and they became fierce allies.

I was grateful my parents agreed to keep my dogs when I went to Officer Training School, though I knew I would never be able to reclaim them. I am as devoted to the dogs as they are to me. They number among my finest companions, enthusiastically supportive and never judgmental. Every time I come home, I receive a welcome suitable for—well, for a general, maybe. And the general I brought with me would get one, too. The dogs actually are well-trained to sit and stay and come and fetch, but their natural exuberance upon the arrival of any guest overrides any command.

All I managed to say before the surge was "Look out, Traveler."

Clement and Sixtus nearly knocked him down because he stood between them and me. When they wagged their tails, their whole selves shook, joy on overdrive. I introduced the general. "Clement, sit! Sit!" He obliged, however briefly. "This is Traveler, but you have to salute him, because he's a general and he hates when you forget it. Traveler, this is Clement. Shake." The general bent down and laughed as Clement offered a paw and an enthusiastic face-licking. Sixtus wasn't to be left out, and he nosed his way into the circle as well.

"Sixtus, calm down. Sit." He did, long enough to let me know he'd heard me. "This is Traveler. Traveler, meet Sixtus." The general gave up and let the dogs bowl him over, giving him the maximum-strength welcome, too.

"I never knew you were a Catholic boy, too," the general said when he could get a breath.

"How'd you guess?"

"Only place I ever heard your dogs' names before is in the litany of the saints from that one prayer just before communion. What was it? That lineup I've never forgotten in forty-five years: Bartholomew, Matthew, Simon, Jude, Linus, Cletus, Clement, Sixtus..."

I started reciting along with him. "Cornelius, Cyprian, Lawrence, Crysogonus, John and Paul, Cosmas and Damian. And all the saints."

He grinned. "Altar boy?"

"From second grade until I graduated from high school," I said, over the dogs. They had turned back to me, complaining loudly because I wasn't showering them with sufficient affection. Into this din, my parents came to say hello.

They made a big fuss over me, too, as they always did. And which I always appreciated.

"Mom. Dad. This is Brigadier General Seamus O'Neill. Sir, meet my parents, Bruce and Jane Mitchell." They shook hands all around. I guess I had never mentioned how tall the general was. He had at least a foot on my mom. But I could tell they were favorably impressed. That, at least, was a relief.

My parents have never been ones to stand on ceremony, and the three of them were on a first-name basis instantly. I had never heard anyone call the general "Seamus" to his face before. We carried our suitcases inside. I could smell lasagna baking, a family favorite.

I moved right into my old room as usual. Within minutes, I swapped my uniform for jeans and an old sweatshirt and crossed the hall to the guest room, the general's temporary digs. My mother had left him fresh towels, an empty drawer in the dresser, and some hangers in the closet, and he moved right in. I sat on the bed as he unpacked.

I bounced. "The bed is pretty comfortable, Traveler," I said.

"I'm sure it is, Lonestar."

"It's going to be lonely, though," I said. "I'm afraid you'll have to sleep here all by yourself."

He grinned. "Lonely for you, maybe. I brought my own company." He pulled my stuffed bear from the suitcase and set him on the pillow.

"We've got some time before supper, though," I said.

"Have we?"

I hollered down the stairwell. "Mom! When's dinner?"

She hollered back from the kitchen. No decorum in our family, and we've all got healthy lungs. "Six fifteen!"

"See?" I told the general. "Almost an hour, and no appointments on your calendar. I can attest to that. You've got time to change into something more comfortable."

"You just want to get me out of my pants," he said.

"Sure," I said. "Undress all you want."

He shook his head. "Shameless. And then what?"

I shrugged. "I'll think of something. Sir." He hangered his blue shirt and put it in the closet. His undershirt came next. I didn't even have to ask. We faced each other. With one finger, I traced the furry patch that disappeared into his trousers, and he shivered. Was he cold? Aroused? Scared?

"You're going to get me in trouble one of these days, aren't you?" he said, soft.

That stopped me cold. For a second, sadness overwhelmed me, and I backed away with alarm. He noticed my dismay and was immediately contrite.

"Ah," he said. "Listen to me. Always saying stupid things. I'm sorry. I didn't mean that."

I wondered, not for the first time, if he blamed me somehow for our predicament. I may have fallen first, but he'd made the first move on that mid-July weekend. There was, however, plenty of blame to share if he were in the mood to accuse.

I looked at him.

He sighed. "You're making me self-conscious. Again."

"Why?"

He scowled. "Because I'm a skinny, hairy old man. There's nothing pretty about that."

"How many times do I have to tell you that I *like* skinny, hairy old men? It's one of the reasons I fell for you in the first place." Seeing him outside his shirt always charged me up, and he knew it. If I wanted to have a serious discussion and he didn't, all he had to do was start unbuttoning.

"Come here," he said, and when I hesitated, "Please?" I went and let him make up with me. We had a chance at last to drop guard and be ourselves. I was relieved to discover that he felt the same, fitted the same, and tasted the same as he had the last time we'd shared such closeness, and his warmth pressing against mine was all the testament either of us needed, proof that we merged very well indeed.

"I'm a goddamned old fool," he murmured into my ear.

"You won't get any argument from me, Traveler."

"Shh," he said, connecting his mouth to mine. He slid his hands from my shoulders down to my waist, and he insinuated his fingers inside my jeans. We separated only long enough to draw breath and then merged again. The rest of the world disappeared, at least until two voices interrupted us.

One, outraged, bellowed, "Harris!"

The other, shocked, contributed, "What is going *on* here?"

The general and I separated as if we had suddenly been poked with a cattle prod. I didn't know what to say. My mother and father stood in the doorway, open-mouthed, staring at the general, shirtless, clearly aroused, his hand inside my unbuttoned jeans.

CHAPTER SIXTEEN

Minutes later, we were seated in the living room, the general and I on opposite ends of the couch, both of us fully dressed, my mother in her rocker and my dad in his easy chair, and both of them glaring at us. I didn't know if I should feel penitent or triumphant. The general wouldn't even look at me, and of course, I've always had limited success in trying to read his mind.

"You think you might want to explain yourselves?" my father said, relatively calm under the circumstances. He wasn't in the mood for anything but facts, and I suspected he was not ready to like them.

"Okay," I said. I didn't, however, have any idea how to explain ourselves, and neither of them knew what to say either. I imagine it would take a while to sink in. Even after it sank, there would be some period of adjustment.

"It's not that we disapprove in general," my father said. He paused and thought about that for a moment and then blazed again. "But maybe we do in specific."

The general still hadn't said a word.

"And what do you have to say for yourself?" my mother asked him, accusing. "A grown man." He sat, stone-faced.

"Mom, I'm a grown man, too."

I half expected her to go into some sort of diatribe about dirty old men seducing the innocent young. Thankfully, she did not.

"Under our very roof!" my mother continued.

"Mom!"

"I'm sorry," she said. "I don't mean to sound so melodramatic. But did you think we wouldn't find out?"

"I was going to tell you." I glanced at the general, who might have taken a vow of silence for all he'd contributed so far. If anything, his reticence could be read as defiance. We weren't doing anything wrong, so why should we have to justify? "I mean, *we* were going to tell you." And then I wondered if I really meant "we." Would the general back me up or hang me out to dry?

Anger can be ice or fire. I felt both frigidity and heat from my parents. But our discussion didn't get very far before the shrieking blare of the smoke alarm in the kitchen drew our attention to the lasagna, burning in the oven. That emergency ended our abortive attempt to reestablish the status quo. Grateful for the distraction, I let my parents manage, and I pulled the general aside.

"Aren't you going to say *anything*?" I whispered, angry, but I felt like yelling. He shrugged, helpless. I'd never known him to be at a loss for words, but perhaps he'd never run into a situation where being a general would not get him out of jail free.

We sat down for a sullen meal, the lasagna blackened on top, tough and dry underneath. The sounds of the forks and knives against the plates seemed magnified by many decibels. Apart from an occasional "pass the bread," dinner was otherwise bereft of noise. None of us had an appetite, and the burnt casserole made the meal an effort.

My father cleared his throat at the end of the meal. "Seamus," he said. "We're going fishing tomorrow."

"Dad! That's *our* fishing trip!"

He glared at me. "Not this time!" he barked. He shook his finger at the general as if he were reprimanding an unruly child. "I'll call for you at five," he said. "It'll be chilly. I'll loan you a coat. Don't wear anything you don't want to get wet."

Did he plan to push the general overboard on pretext of some sort of fishing malfunction? I couldn't tell. Dad excused himself and went to the basement to ready the tackle. I knew he would get lost in the preparation, and I hoped he'd focus his single-mindedness on tomorrow's fishing and remain downstairs for the rest of the evening, preoccupied. Dealing with my parents one at a time might be easier.

Maybe.

I helped with the dishes. The general stood by, his arms crossed, watching.

"Good lasagna, Mom," I offered, after an eternal silence.

"It was not," she snapped. "It was ruined." More silence followed. She washed, and I dried. One plate. Two plates. Three. Salad bowls. Forks. Knives. She tackled the casserole dish, crusted with blackened cheese and tomato sauce. The only real secret the general and I had brought home was *us*, and that was out now. And since I couldn't imagine anything worse happening over the weekend, I decided to play the single ace I'd hidden up my sleeve for an emergency.

"You know, Mom, there's one thing you and General O'Neill have in common."

"Indeed?" She was still snapping. "And what might that be?"

"He likes opera, too."

Quite possibly, no other single thing I could have said would have piqued her interest. No one she knew shared her passion.

"I don't believe it," she said. Then, "Really?" She turned to look at the general, leaning against the counter. He nodded. "Who's your favorite?"

He didn't hesitate. "Puccini," he said.

"Which one?"

"*Tosca*, I reckon," he said. "But if you ask me another night, I might say *Manon Lescaut*."

My mother nodded slowly, full of wonder. Perhaps she truly sympathized with his dilemma. From my corner, I observed these were the most words the general had uttered all evening. Grateful for the success of this diversionary tactic, I handed the general the dish towel and went to find Clement and Sixtus and a tennis ball to throw while I thought about things. The dogs would cheer me up.

En route to bed a couple of hours later, I peeked unseen into the living room. My mother and the general were still deep into their discussion, sitting on the floor by the stereo speakers, surrounded by a pile of CDs. I stuck around long enough to hear the general say, "Jane, what about that aria at the beginning of Act II after Manon has left Don Grieux because his money ran out?"

I didn't even say good night.

I'm sure they were arguing the merits of *Madame Butterfly* versus *Turandot* long after I had fallen asleep. I left them to it. Once they'd satisfied their suspicion that each of them was as well-informed and committed as the other, I believe they cemented a bond no one else would be able to crack. I'm sure my father looked in on them before he retired, too, just as I'm certain he was truly mystified that a grown man and a grown woman could talk about such squalling as if it meant something.

❖

I was still asleep in the morning when my dad and the general hit the road, the skiff on a trailer behind the old pickup loaded with tackle boxes, my grandfather's creel, two rods, and a cooler filled with lunch courtesy of my mom—ham sandwiches on buttered wheat bread with thick-sliced cheddar and mustard, plus dill pickles, rippled potato chips, homemade cookies, crisp apples, and a large thermos of coffee. The menu never changed; it was as much a part of the ritual as the long drive to the lake and the celebratory cookout in the evening.

I would wonder most of the day about my dad and the general, whom I'd never reckoned to be a fisherman. He hadn't mentioned it, anyway. If he didn't have much experience, I hoped he could fake it, or at least that he was a quick study. Knowing my dad, there wouldn't be much talk. If the general proved unskilled, my dad would probably ignore him out of disgust and simply let him founder.

I had hoped to be fishing with Dad myself, leaving the general at home to drink coffee with my mom and spar some more about which Puccini aria was best. And while I suspect her estimation of the general had risen after last night's opera discussion, such knowledge would only go so far when placed against the fact that he'd been caught with his hand in my pants.

But morning found me at home instead, alone with my mother. I poured myself a cup of coffee and sat down at the kitchen table. I knew my mom had been waiting for me, and she didn't waste time starting her cross-examination.

"Harris, I'm kind of at a loss."

"I know, Mom. I'm sorry."

"Well, you don't need to be sorry, but we are a little surprised. We knew Seamus was your boss, but you never mentioned that you and he were otherwise involved."

I didn't blame her for feeling confused and even angry. If I had brought home Julia and my parents had caught us kissing, however, my mother and I would not be having this little talk.

"Did you think we wouldn't find out?" my mother said.

"No. I was going to tell you. I just wasn't sure how."

"I can see why. Just how old is he, Harris?"

"He's, um, fifty-one."

"Fifty-one! Harris, he's almost as old as I am!"

"This has nothing at all to do with age, Mom." I grabbed the single small straw that presented itself. "Dad's older than you are." A fact, true enough, but as my mother was quick to point out, not particularly relevant.

"Four years! That's all," she said. "At least we're part of the same generation. But you and this general... Good Lord! Harris, have you really given this whole thing very much thought?"

I sighed. "Mom, it's all I *do* think about."

She persisted. "How long have you two been—?"

I didn't wait for her to choose a word to describe what we'd been up to. "Since July." Immediately, I climbed on the defensive, declaring that the general had made the first move. I would never have done so, no matter how I felt about him. I explained that the Air Force didn't look kindly on any kind of relationship between officers of different ranks, with the exception of professional mentoring, an acceptable form of fraternization as long as boundaries were respected. I explained that the twenty-one years separating me from Seamus O'Neill included six levels of rank: first lieutenant, captain, major, lieutenant colonel, colonel, brigadier general.

Even if we ignored regulations, we still had to navigate the mine field of our own emotions. At least I did, anyway. Keeping the boss separate from the beloved was a challenge, Monday through Friday. Every minute sometimes. Daily, I had to pretend that General O'Neill was nothing more or less than the commander of Sixth Air Force, and I had to be the best general's aide I could be. If I made a stupid mistake and he yelled at me, I could not take it personally. He was angry at the lieutenant who screwed up, not at me.

I could feel myself beginning to perspire under my mother's gaze as I tried to explain. I sounded as if I were trying to sell her a used car, and she wasn't buying.

"I don't see how you can possibly stand it, Harris. From what you've told me, you don't have *any* good reason to pursue this relationship. What would happen if people found out?"

An easy question at last, and one I could answer with some certainty. "He'd take the blame and get the worst of it as the senior officer," I said. "No military court would ever believe a second lieutenant could persuade a general to get mixed up in something like this."

My mother took a sip of her coffee, by now gone cold. "Mixed up? I don't like the sound of that. Are you absolutely sure about him? It's only been a couple of months."

I shook my head. "No. I'm stuck, if he'll let me be stuck."

She shook her head. "There's still a part of me that hopes this is just a phase you're going through."

"Mom, wake up. I'm thirty years old. It's not a phase. I'm genuinely gay. You and Dad have known since I was in high school. It isn't going to change."

She could arch an eyebrow as well as any general. "You should know by now that I don't give a hoot about you being gay, Harris. I'm talking about this thing you seem to have for older men. Like that one professor of yours in college. Yes, we knew all about him. Just once, couldn't you fall for someone a little nearer to your own age?" she said. "I'm glad we've always been close. You know you can be open with us about anything. We just want you to be happy with the choices you make, and I'm referring specifically to your choice of a fifty-one-year-old boyfriend."

I changed her course. "Mom, how old were you when you got married?"

She thought about it for a second. "Twenty. Imagine."

"How did you know Dad was the one for you?"

She giggled. "I didn't, actually. I liked him a lot, and I enjoyed the time we spent together. We seemed to have a lot in common. He was so handsome. There were plenty of other girls who were interested in him, believe me." She paused to think, to remember. Perhaps no one had ever asked her such questions.

"When he asked me to marry him, I wondered if I would ever meet another man I liked as much," she said, choosing her words carefully. "I decided I wasn't willing to take that chance, so I said yes."

"At twenty."

"At twenty." She smiled. "It's amazing how smart we think we are at that age."

I was tactful enough not to point out I was now a decade older than she had been at the time she'd made her big decision. I'd had plenty of time to think, and I was sure. So I pushed my small advantage. "Were you sure Dad was in love with you?" As she thought about that, I asked the other half of the question. "Were you sure you were in love with him?"

She shook her head. "No. I don't think I was, at first. Not really. Not deeply, I mean. But I tried not to think about it. I couldn't. My girlfriends kept telling me how lucky I was to catch him, and I wanted to believe them. I was sure I would come to love him in time."

My grandmother, she said, insisted on a big wedding, and the planning started early. My mom may have felt she could back out at first, but she got caught up in the excitement, too. "I just pushed the doubts out of my mind and made myself not think about them," she said.

"Were you sure on your wedding day?"

She shook her head again. "That morning, I was so scared I locked myself in the bathroom and threw up. I was convinced I was making the biggest mistake of my life, but then it was time for me to get dressed, and Mother and my bridesmaids were so excited...well, I went through with it, and then it didn't seem so bad. Dad walked me down the aisle, and the ceremony was lovely. When we said 'I do,' I wasn't thinking about thirty years into the future. I wasn't even thinking about next week. Making the promise 'until death do us part' doesn't seem very real when you're so young."

I listened eagerly. I had never heard either her or my dad talk about their wedding, though I'd seen the photos in the album often enough to memorize them. Why had I never thought to ask before? What else remained hidden in our history?

"You learn," my mom continued. "We all do. And your dad and I learned as we went along. It wasn't easy at first, but we kept working at it because we really did like each other. And what do you know? Instead of falling in love, we grew into it. And here we are. Still married." She shook her head. "After all this time, I can tell you for certain I made the right choice. I'm happy. And satisfied. I know for certain we love each other now, deeply, and I believe we're friends, too. We've grown in our individual ways, and we've grown together. And I think there's still more for us to find out."

I wonder if my dad ever thinks about such things. I've become accustomed to his silences and never find them uncomfortable. He simply isn't in the habit of talking very much. My mother has adapted to his silence, too, although he communicates his feelings in dozens of nonverbal ways, opening doors for her, buying her flowers at unexpected times, never forgetting her birthday or their anniversary. He always kisses her good-bye when he leaves for work, and they still hold hands when they go walking together. Love, for my father, truly does go without saying.

"This is the first time you've ever brought someone home who's special to you," my mother said. "I'm glad you brought Seamus with you. He will always be welcome here if you love him. But how does he feel about you? I can't tell, and that concerns me."

It concerned me, too. I could read between my father's lines, but I clearly did not know the general well enough yet to translate him. "I think he feels the same," I said, wanting to be honest. "I hope so."

My mother poured another cup of coffee for both of us and gave me some time to think, distracting herself by preparing breakfast. I knew she had more questions than I had answers. And they were good questions. I'd become a master detective when it came to analyzing the clues and building a case, but the general had never spelled anything out for me or defined the rules of engagement for us. Until he actually did, I'd never know if I'd reached the right conclusion. I suspected that the general, faced with this new sensation, was afraid. I could not put him at ease when I felt uneasy myself.

My mother brought orange juice, English muffins, and oatmeal to the table, and I hadn't even poured the milk on my cereal before she resumed her inquisition. "So how much experience does he have with this kind of thing?"

Apart from his friend, the major who'd died from AIDS, I didn't know the depth of the general's experience. He'd admitted some connections since then for the purpose of sexual gratification, but I hadn't insisted on confession of how many or how often. I assumed I was, or would be, if I was lucky, his first and last serious, long-term relationship with another man. So, I merely explained he'd been married for about ten years and had gotten divorced a few years back.

"Because he's gay?"

"His wife asked for the divorce. It wasn't his idea."

"Did she know about him?"

"I don't know. Maybe. He didn't protest when she said she wanted to split up."

"What happened to his wife afterward?"

"She remarried. I don't know anything more." I hoped my mother didn't express interest in contacting her to get the real lowdown.

"Did they have any children? They'd probably be about your age."

"Thanks for pointing that out, Mom. No, there were no kids."

My mother persisted. "What about other men? While he was married? Or after the divorce?"

"Mom, why don't you ask him? I don't feel right telling tales about him when he's not here to defend himself."

She nodded, her resolve cemented. "All right, I will ask him." She would, too. "Has he come out, Harris? Publicly, I mean."

"Um…no."

"He hasn't?" She seemed genuinely surprised. "Why not?"

"Being romantically involved with another man—a junior officer, no less—is hardly a smart career move for a general, even if the Air Force allows gay people to serve openly," I said. "Coming out isn't exactly in his best interest, either."

She shook her head. "I don't get it. Why wouldn't he want to come out, since he can? Wouldn't that set a great example for the people in your unit?"

And everyone else in the Air Force, too, I thought. To my own surprise, I'd never thought to ask such a question. Had he ever considered coming out publicly? Would he, if I asked him to?

Time to shift tactics again. "Mom, do you like him?"

She sighed. "Well, I'd be lying if I said I didn't. But now I have to look at him in a different light, and I'm inclined to be more critical. I think he's too old for you. He's a little self-centered, if you ask me. He smokes. He's divorced. He's…well, I'm not going to tear him down in front of you. Because I really do like him." She gave me the first hint we might make peace when she giggled. "And by heavens, Harris, he's certainly a handsome man."

He certainly was, and when the man you fall in love with happens to be the sexiest man you've ever met, it's frosting for your favorite cake.

"And terribly charming, too. I can certainly see why you might fall for him." She grew reflective again, as if she'd suddenly reclaimed her proper "mom" decorum. "Harris, I'm a little worried about how all this will turn out."

"I know, Mom. I appreciate your concern."

She nodded. "You just be careful, Harris. Okay?"

"Okay."

We finished eating even though the oatmeal and toast had long since grown cold. We were content, and I helped her with the dishes afterward and even swept the floor, feeling slightly guilty about the dog hair. My mother surveyed my diligence with satisfaction. She'd taught me well.

"You and Seamus will keep a clean house," she said. "He's just as neat as you are. He even made his bed this morning, hospital corners and all."

I wondered how my traveler was adding up in my mother's mind.

The pieces probably didn't fit. His contradictions endeared him to me, but who else knew him as I did? The rest of the day passed uneventfully. My mother raised some good questions, and I had plenty to think about as I kept my ears tuned for the sound of my dad's pickup on the gravel driveway.

CHAPTER SEVENTEEN

The pickup pulled into the driveway in the early dusk. I could hear my father and the general talking, even laughing, as they brought their tackle and the cooler into the basement. They washed their hands at the utility sink and then came upstairs, both of them grinning. The creel was loaded with eight sleek, glistening rainbow trout. "How about that?" my dad said. "You ready for a feast tonight?"

I knew they were feeling good because of their luck, but something else had happened, and I wondered precisely what. They seemed to be the best of friends. And the general was wearing one of my dad's prized hats, a shapeless thing with lots of history, decorated with colorful flies he'd tied himself. I wonder if my dad hadn't surrendered it for the day because the general had caught five of the trout.

"What's your secret, Traveler?" I whispered to him.

He cupped his hand around my ear. "Use bait that works," he said. No help there. We trooped back outside to the driveway for victory photos, my father and the general standing by the skiff, holding up the string between them, heavy with the spoils.

When we had a minute to ourselves, I filed my complaint. "Thanks for skunking me out of my fishing trip with Dad," I said.

"I sympathize," he said, "but it wasn't my idea. Remember? How was your day?"

"Got the third degree from Mom. You don't need to tell me what kind of day *you* had. And you don't need to look so smug, either."

❖

The general cleaned the fish, earning bonus points with my mom, as my dad usually deferred this chore. Traveler dispatched them neatly and efficiently, slicing the bellies and removing the guts and bones. He chopped off the heads and tails and wrapped the scrap in newspaper as I watched, fascinated by his facility. For all my experience, I wasn't sure I could have done it with such precision. He'd obviously cleaned fish with some frequency.

My father fired up the charcoal grill out back, and the general volunteered to cook as well. He seasoned the trout with fresh lemon juice, sea salt, and coarsely ground black pepper and set them, sizzling, on the grate. Sparingly, he prodded the fish with a fork while he and my parents debated the merits of various other ways of preparing fresh fish—dipping in milk and cornmeal and pan-frying, for example, or broiling in the oven, or, God forbid, breading and deep-frying, which the general dubbed a sacrilege while my parents nodded, solemnly.

"You don't want to mask the flavor," the general said. "They're fresh-caught, damn it, and you ought to taste the lake." The discussion expanded to include appropriate sauces, from tartar to Hollandaise, but they agreed that good, fresh fish could stand on its own merits.

He asked if they'd yet learned the trick for freezing trout, gutted and cleaned and then frozen in some of the same water where you caught 'em. Just bring back a gallon or two, the general said. Clean the fish and freeze them in a cardboard milk carton filled with the lake water. "When you cook 'em, they taste fresh-caught." My mother fried potatoes with onions, as she always did with fish, and fixed some fresh coleslaw.

In spite of the good feeling radiating from the kitchen, my mom made sure the general and I remained separated at the table. So we sat across from each other, and I had to make do with his grin from a distance and once, when my parents were distracted, a slow, deliberate wink that made me feel as if he and I were in some kind of outlaw cahoots.

Dinner was delicious, and the general was quite modest under the extravagant praise we heaped on him. Somehow or other, everything seemed to be mended, and the cracks didn't even show. After dinner, he even offered to do the dishes. My mother protested. "You caught the fish and cleaned them and cooked them, too. The least I can do is wash up."

The general wouldn't hear of it. "Go relax. Both of you. Harris, I'll wash, and you'll dry."

"I'm on vacation," I said. "You can't order me around."

"Maybe not," he said. "But I can ask politely, and you'll do it. Please?"

I laughed. "All right, sir." That was one for the list. His eyebrows flexed, and he grinned.

"There," the general said to my mom. "I'm in charge. Now go." Reluctantly, my parents filed out. I know they didn't miss doing the dishes. They wanted to chaperone us, and I could hardly blame them. But I was eager for news about the fishing trip, and I wanted to be alone with Traveler, even for a few minutes.

In the kitchen, we stood side by side at the sink. He was elbow-deep in plates and suds, and he scooped up a handful of foam and deposited it on my nose. I wiped my face and scooped up more of the same and paid him back in kind.

"Keep out of my water."

"Sir. Yes, sir, sir."

"Behave, Dishrag, or I'll wash your mouth out with this soap."

"I'd like to see you try it, sir."

He maintained his decorum. "That's three," he said.

"Four," I said. "You need some help keeping track, sir?"

"Okay, five," he said. "You're mine for the rest of your days, or at least until next Tuesday."

"I couldn't be happier. In case you're counting, sir, I'm actually up to six, and that's just in the last ten minutes. Seven, if you include the one at the table."

"I will annotate my list accordingly," he said. "And being an honorable man yourself, you will pay your debt in full."

With one sudsy mitt, he pulled me close to him, his hand on my neck bringing me in, and he dropped his mustache to mine. He paused for a minute and whispered, "I don't care if we get caught this time, either," before trapping me again. The water dripped down my back, but it hardly mattered.

After finishing the dishes, we went to the front-porch swing so he could smoke his night pipe. Seated next to him, I listened to the quick scrape of match on box and watched as the flash illuminated his face. Carefully he puffed on the pipe, drawing fire into the tobacco, coaxing it to burn. When it was lit to his satisfaction, he moved even closer and put an arm around me. He took a long draw and exhaled. I don't think I ever heard a more satisfied sigh.

"You haven't told me anything about your fishing trip," I said.

I could feel his grin, even in the dark. "Some things a man has to keep to himself."

That was that. I knew I'd never get anything out of him. But I doubted, based on my own numerous fishing excursions with Dad, that they'd said much of anything. Fishing can be its own reward, its own conversation.

"Where did you learn to fish?" I said.

"My grandfather taught me years ago," he said. "We used to go fishing a lot when I was young. I loved it. Loved him. Every summer, all by myself, I'd get shipped up north for two months to his farm in Pennsylvania. That's where my mom grew up."

He seldom shared any details about his upbringing, and I listened with interest. "My old man might have been a father, but he sure wasn't a dad. He never wanted to play ball or go camping or fishing or hiking, and I was itching to do all those things. I'm fortunate my granddad shared those interests with me. He believed summers were made to be spent out of doors, and that's what we did. I lived for those times. Until today, I haven't gone fishing since he died, almost thirty years back, not long after my mother."

He sighed, and a moment later shook his head as if to shake off some ghost. "You're lucky your dad's like he is."

I agreed. "You're welcome to borrow my dad anytime you need one, Traveler."

"Thank you," he said. "You're very generous."

There was one caveat. "I'll have you know that my offer does *not* include future fishing trips. Those are mine."

He laughed. "I didn't mean to cheat you, but it was important for your dad and me to spend some time together, man to man. It didn't hurt that I was damned lucky today."

Clement and Sixtus roamed the porch, restless. I suspect we weren't active enough for them. The general reached for one of them and got both for his efforts. "One dog for each hand," he said. "Perfect." They could hardly contain their pleasure.

"Just try and stop."

"I don't mind," he said. "I always wanted a dog. My dad would never permit it. Said they were noisy and dirty and too much work and trouble."

"Well, they *are* noisy and dirty and too much work and trouble," I said. "But so are you, and that didn't stop me." He laughed. "A dog will be your friend forever. You couldn't ask for a more loyal companion."

Adding one to your life was not a responsibility to be taken lightly, however, I told him. A dog demanded attention and regular exercise every day. A dog meant commitment. A dog was yours to look after for the rest of its life.

"I don't care," he said. "I will have a dog. One of these days. *We* will have a dog."

"You can borrow Clement and Sixtus anytime, too, Traveler."

He nodded, satisfied. I would share anything with him. We sat in silence for a while, watching the dark and the stars, and I never felt luckier. When he was finished with his pipe, he knocked it against the porch railing to empty the ash. He unwrapped a peppermint for himself, and we stood up and faced each other. His mustache whispered against my neck and then my cheek until it tangled itself in mine. I would have stayed there all night, surrendered to his mint and rum-and-maple, but he pushed me away gently.

"Time to go in," he said. I protested, but he said, "I have to respect your folks. This thing can't be easy for them. Not that it's easy for me. You're quite tempting, you know."

Anger washed over me and put me in the mood to argue. "And just what is this 'thing' you're so worried about? I wish you'd tell me one of these days so I'd have a clue." Maybe I resented the fact that I'd spent the day worrying about him and defending his honor, and now that we finally had some time to ourselves, he wanted to cut it short.

I sat down on the porch step. He sat next to me and put an arm around my shoulder.

"Call it what you will, Sundown," he said. "I wonder myself sometimes. Maybe I don't know the destination, but I'm damn sure I want you to come along." He brushed his mustache against my cheek. "Trust me," he whispered. "Please?"

I wasn't ready to be placated, but he led me inside. He passed the rest of the evening with my parents watching television, one thing I'd never known him to have the patience to do. He was proving himself quite adaptable, but I was still upset, still impatient, and chose to retire to my room with a book and the dogs for companionship.

CHAPTER EIGHTEEN

I overslept the next morning. I'd done nothing the previous day to tire me out, unless it was the discussion with my mom, which had been exhausting in ways that had nothing to do with physical labor. Maybe I'd been keyed up because the general was out of my sight and with my father, a potentially volatile combination. Or maybe the whole situation simply frustrated me. At any rate, the clock read 9:09 when I woke up.

Dad would still be asleep, his tradition for a Saturday. We wouldn't see him until nearly noon, the only day of the week he indulged in such luxury, perhaps to catch up from the other days, when he arose at five a.m. My mom would already have laundry under way, and no doubt the general was on his second or third cup of coffee. I dressed quickly and headed downstairs, stopping short when I heard the general laughing, hearty. And one thing that truly shocked me: I could smell his tobacco.

A light, cool breeze in the hallway told me that the window was open, but my mother was actually letting him smoke his pipe in the house. In my memory, no one else had ever been granted such a privilege. Clearly, the general's stock had skyrocketed overnight.

I don't usually eavesdrop, but I couldn't help myself on this occasion. Quietly, I padded toward the kitchen entryway and stopped just outside. Though they could not see me, I had clear vision of the table, of my mother already dressed, and enough of the general to determine that he wore his shabby brown bathrobe. If he had tied the sash as carelessly as usual, my mother would have a good view of his furry chest. Clement and Sixtus prowled underfoot, restless, in case someone might drop a toast crust or a hamburger.

I backed up and chose my vantage point, well out of sight but well within earshot. "You have to understand our concerns," my mother was saying as I held my breath and tuned in. "Harris is really taken with you. You know that, don't you?"

A pause. "Is he?"

"Of course he is. Don't tell me you haven't figured that out. And he's scared to death of you, too. I don't know what you've done to him, but I don't quite understand how he can be in love with you and afraid of you at the same time."

The general was quiet.

"Seamus, I need some assurance from you," she said. "Harris is our only son. Our only child. We want what's best for him, and we want him to be happy, too. He came out to us when he was still in high school. He must've been about seventeen. Bruce and I were stunned. We had no idea. For a long time, we thought it might be just a phase he was going through, that he'd get over it and be just like other boys. But it didn't happen, and we've accepted that. I didn't know the first thing about the gay life, and believe me, I wanted to know. I wanted to understand. So I started reading and researching. I started talking to people and getting involved."

I, and probably my mother, too, expected some follow-on question or comment, but the general had none. For a minute, all I heard was the pouring of more coffee and clink of spoon against cup.

"You know, Seamus," my mother continued, "it may not have been my first choice for Harris to be gay, but he is. As long as he's content, I wouldn't wish him to be any different. If he wants to bring his boyfriend home, I'll support him all the way, and so will Bruce. That's what parents do. Harris intends to spend the rest of his life with you. Is that what you have in mind, too?"

Eternity passed.

I've never known my mother to have much patience and I silently blessed her for holding her temper on this occasion. She tried again, attacking from a different angle. "Seamus, what exactly *are* your intentions? I know that sounds old-fashioned. I'm sorry. But I'm a mom, and I'm allowed to be old-fashioned. And I'm certainly allowed to be concerned."

"You've no need to be," the general said.

"I'm not so sure," my mother said. "Harris told me you were married before." Here it comes, I thought.

"Ten years."

"And now you're divorced."

"Yes. Just after I was selected for promotion to full colonel, about five years back."

"Why?"

"The divorce wasn't my idea, Jane. My wife had enough by then, I reckon."

"Don't tell me you were running around on her, chasing boys on the side."

"Oh, no. No." The general sounded truly alarmed, even offended. "Never. I remained strictly faithful throughout the marriage."

"Well, that's admirable, at least. But when she asked for a divorce, I suppose you didn't argue."

"Nope. I never gave her any reason to suspect, but she may have guessed the truth anyway."

"And what truth would that be?" My mother would make a good district attorney.

"Jane—"

"Seamus."

He sighed. "All right." The direction of the conversation clearly unsettled him. "Career military officers are expected to get married. No exceptions. If you don't, it hurts your chances for promotion. Everyone wonders why you remained single, and they usually reach one conclusion, even if there's no evidence."

"And the conclusion they reach is that an unmarried officer is gay?" My mother wanted an answer. In the silence, I could hear her expectancy, and I suspect the general could, too.

He sighed, deep. "Yes. *Yes.* Gay. All right?"

My mother refused to let go. "Your poor wife. What a despicable thing to do to her."

"I'm sorry."

"You don't have to tell *me* you're sorry. I'm not the one you married," she said. "Isn't it easier now?"

"What do you mean?"

"For gay officers. With 'Don't Ask, Don't Tell' out of the picture."

He exhaled, long. "Well, it's a bit soon. The policy change is still relatively new."

"Harris came out at work as soon as he could. He told us. He sent us a copy of the article from the newspaper after the Pride Parade in June. Did you march, too?"

"Oh, no." He sounded truly alarmed.

"You didn't? Why not?"

"Well, I haven't actually, uh…"

"You mean you haven't even come out of the closet yet?"

"Well, a little."

"That's like being a little pregnant, Seamus. Either you are or you aren't. The closet door is open, or it's shut."

"Well, uh, Harris knows."

"Oh, he does? Isn't *that* a surprise?" Sarcasm dripped from her voice. "Don't you think you should let some other people know, too?"

"It's no one's business but my own. My private life should remain private."

"Don't you think you have a moral obligation to come out?" Her inflection suggested indignation, if not actual outrage. "That's what a leader is supposed to do. Set an example."

"I set an example every time I put on the uniform."

"That's not what I mean. You may look the part, but isn't it a little phony if you're keeping that secret? Whatever happened to 'be all that you can be'?"

"That was an Army slogan," he said. "They're not even using it anymore."

I could almost hear the general climbing on his high horse from my spot in the hall.

My mother continued. "That's not the point. How can you have any self-respect? And why should Harris risk his future on a man who—"

He interrupted, and I could hear the effort required for him to stay in control. "Harris isn't the only one taking a risk. Have you any idea what I've put on the line just to be sitting at this table? I'm the gambler here."

"Oh, you think so?" my mother countered. "Just exactly what kind of gamble is it if you choose to stay in the closet? The hardest thing you've had to do is keep a secret. What kind of risk is *that*?"

He cleared his throat. "As commander of Sixth Air Force, I oversee six air wings spread out across nine installations," he said. "That's over five thousand square miles of real estate."

I rolled my eyes. The general went through the entire speech he'd given me when I turned up for my interview, about the full extent of his domain and all of his responsibilities. He delivered this monologue flawlessly. My only thought was that my mother was exactly the wrong audience for such a speech, though she was extremely patient to let him get all the way to the end of it. Surely she recognized his remarks were as freeze-dried as the meals sold for backpackers at my father's store. When the general concluded with, "I have a lot on my plate," he paused to take a breath, and my mother pounced.

"You're just blowing smoke, Seamus. When you look at the big picture, of *course* you have a lot of responsibility. I get it. But nobody lives in the big picture. You live in a house on a street in a town, and you interact with people you meet every day. You say that it's too early to expect attitudes to change about gay people in the Air Force. Well, they won't *ever* change unless the people in charge make it happen. A general who's out can do more for those six thousand people than a dozen who are too scared to come out of the closet," she said. "You're supposed to be a leader. So lead!"

"I'm a general," he said. I could tell he was running out of patience, too. "I lead by default. Those stars on my shoulders should tell you everything you need to know about my qualifications and abilities."

"Don't you throw rank at me," she said. "I'm a civilian. I don't have to salute you or follow your orders. Those stars might make people jump at your Air Force base, but they don't mean a damn thing—excuse my French—in my kitchen. Generals may have the power to start wars, but it's mothers like me who make sure those wars come to an end."

In a debate, I'd want her to be on my side.

"As far as I'm concerned, you're just a man in a bathrobe with a cup of coffee, and I'm still waiting for you to give me even one good reason why you deserve my son!"

I held my breath.

My mother said, "I'm putting you on the spot, Seamus. I know. It's not hard to figure out what Harris sees in you, but I get the feeling that you're keeping him like a dirty secret, and I don't like it one bit."

My mother would not back down, and I suspect he knew it. Finally he cleared his throat. "Jane, I don't know what to say. I've never been caught up in anything like this before, and I'm scared as hell."

"What are you afraid of? Certainly not me. Not Bruce."

"No. Not you, and not Bruce. Y'all are wonderful people, and I'd be pleased to count you as my friends under any circumstances."

"Then why are you scared?"

The general sighed. "I've never known anyone like Harris. I can't believe he'd even give me the time of day except out of professional courtesy. But he seems genuinely fond of me. Maybe I'm afraid because I'm convinced it's all going to disappear, sooner or later. I'm not sure I deserve his attention," he said, "but I want it, all the same, and I won't let go of it. He actually likes me. *Me.*"

I could hear the wonder in his voice.

"I don't understand why he'd want a damn thing from me, Jane. But as long as he does, he'll get it. Whatever I can give him, and however long he's willing to let me provide it." I was startled to hear him put such sentiments into words. "Jane, he's teaching me that one man can be with another man, and it can be the right thing. The real thing. The *only* thing. When I'm around Harris, I want my hands on him all the time, and I want his hands on me."

From my spot in the hallway, I was beginning to get an erection. Not now, I told myself. Inappropriate.

"I'm sorry," the general said. "That's not what you want to hear about your son. But there's no one like Harris. *No* one. I've been in the Air Force for more than thirty years, and I've always resisted temptation to get seriously involved with anyone, especially with a…a man."

He told my mother about his single-mindedness, of which he was very proud. And he told my mother about the first time he saw me, how he felt as if he were shot through with electricity, how he had to go out of his way to hide from it, how perhaps, early on, after I'd started working for him, he went a little overboard, going too far in the other direction to prove to himself that he didn't really want me.

From my place in the hall, I was learning all kinds of things.

He concluded. "But the way I felt about Harris wouldn't stay hid. It had to come out, I reckon." A pause.

My mother sighed. "Harris was hardly even born when you joined the Air Force. Doesn't that bother you? Exactly how old are you, anyway?" She already knew. I guess she simply wanted him to admit it to her.

He sighed. "Age is just a number."

"And that's just a cliché."

"I'm fifty-one."

My mother shook her head. "Good God. Seamus, I'm fifty-three, and Bruce is fifty-seven. What am I supposed to think?"

The general didn't say anything. Was he embarrassed? Did my mother's common sense even dent him? I don't know what I wanted to be the truth. But I wanted him to spring to our defense—his and mine. My mother pressed her advantage. "What can you possibly offer Harris at your age?"

When he finally spoke, he'd clearly opted for a different tactic. I suspect he needed to come up for air. "He'll be well provided for," he said. "And I still have my own teeth and my own hair."

That did it. Both of them laughed.

"Don't be so modest," my mother said. "You're quite handsome, too, I must say."

I cringed. The general, however, took it in good spirit. "Thank you, ma'am. You're a fine figure of a woman yourself, speaking objectively, of course. But flattery will get you nowhere, because I'm already spoken for."

"Come to think of it, I am, too," she said. "Plus, don't you prefer guys?"

Another laugh between them.

Then he sighed. Stirred his coffee again. I could hear the spoon against the cup. "I want to be his electric blanket. His easy chair. His safe-deposit box. His knight in slightly tarnished armor. Anything he wants and everything he needs. Ridiculous, huh?" He laughed, short, nervous, harsh. "Jane, I'm a practical man. I'm a pilot, an Air Force officer, and fifty-one years old, for God's sake. I should have outgrown all this foolishness a long time ago."

My mother was curiously gentle. "Why? No one ever outgrows wanting to be loved. To be needed."

"I'm a general." As if that rendered him immune. I could hear the storm in him.

"Even generals, Seamus. Just like a mom, the heart doesn't recognize rank either."

"I feel like a damn fool, talking about this stuff. Harris and me. It's all so impractical, so—"

"Yes?"

"So...so wonderful." He was beaten but not vanquished, and he rallied. "Jane, what if he honestly, actually wants me in spite of the fact that I'm a general and fifty-one and a bullheaded, pompous ass? In spite of the fact that he could do so much better? Suppose he doesn't want to look any farther than me. Wouldn't it be all right for me to love him back?" He paused and took another deep breath. "Wouldn't I be a damn fool not to?"

My mother didn't say anything for a long while. I heard the general get up and pour himself more coffee and then sit down again. I heard the clink of the spoon in his cup again as he stirred in his sugar, and then he set the spoon into the saucer and waited.

"Yes," my mother said, finally. "You *would* be a fool. But after talking with Harris yesterday, I wonder if you've ever told him how you feel."

"I guess I really haven't. Not in so many words."

"Seamus, if you end up as our son-in-law, I don't care what your age is. You'll never be too old for me to give you a piece of my mind if I think you deserve it. And I'm going to tell you right now that you're a bigger damn fool than you *think* you are if you love him and don't tell him. Harris may have the patience of a marble saint up to a point, but you're going to lose him if you don't let him know."

"I didn't think of that."

My mother was exasperated. "Seamus, how can you be fifty-one and still be so stupid? Haven't you ever been in love before?"

I could almost hear him squirm.

"Great heavens, Seamus! How did you get to be a general when you don't know the first thing about people? If you want something, especially if it's something off the beaten path, you better go after it." She paused, then began a little more gently. "If you feel that way about Harris, tell him. *Show* him. I think one of the best ways to do that is to come out. Show him you're not ashamed of being gay. Because if you're ashamed to be gay, then you're ashamed of him, too."

The general let that one sink in.

"That's not a secret you can ask him to keep, Seamus. It's not fair, and you know it."

"Jane, I'm just not that brave."

I didn't like to hear him talk that way, probably any more than the general liked to admit weakness of any kind.

"Seamus, it's in there somewhere. I know it is. Dig deep. I think you'll find it." I could tell she wasn't finished with the subject, but I think she recognized the general needed a break from the inquest, and she changed the subject. "Tell me, Seamus. What is it he calls you? It's not your name."

"Traveler."

"Like someone who travels?"

"Yes."

"Why?"

"He wasn't comfortable using my first name, so we had to find a nickname. And one day—this was months ago—I was rattling off all the places I'd been in the last thirty years, and he said, 'Well, you certainly are the traveler.' And it just seemed to fit."

"Do you like it?"

He sighed. "Every time Harris says it, I get shook up. It's so different. *I'm* different because of him. It reminds me that what we have together is so special I can hardly put words to it." I'm sure this outpouring of emotion embarrassed him, but he continued anyway. "I haven't gotten used to it yet. Maybe I never want to. Maybe I always want him to take me by surprise. Every time he calls me Traveler, it's like coming home. I can finally take off the mask and just be myself. I don't know what I did to deserve someone like him."

I knew the general was perspiring under her barrage of questions. I was, too. The time had come for me to step in. Quietly, I backed myself down the hall and tiptoed upstairs. Then I took a deep breath and bounded, noisily, down again and into the kitchen.

"Morning, Mom." I kissed her on the forehead, and she gave me a quick hug.

"It's about time you got up, sleepyhead," she said.

That did it. "Mom, I'm not six years old anymore!" I was in the mood to get angry out of frustration as much as anything. "Dad's the one who sleeps until noon on Saturday. I've been up for a while. I just didn't come downstairs right away."

"A good thing," the general said. "Your mom's been making like Perry Mason in here. It hasn't been pretty."

I had to pretend I didn't know. "Have you been giving him the third degree, Mom?"

"Nothing of the sort. I'm just exercising the mother's Bill of Rights."

"And what might that include?" I said.

"When you're a mom yourself, you'll get the memo," she said, tart.

"I'll give you the short version," the general said. "She wants you to come to your senses and throw me over."

"Maybe after breakfast," I said. I sat down as the general excused himself from the table, fetched a cup and saucer from the pantry, and fixed coffee for me. Then he bent down and gave me a quick hug from behind my chair, a prelude to rubbing his two-days-unshaven chin against the back of my neck like a belt sander. I yelped.

"Wake up," he said.

I pushed him away, and he zeroed in for one more quick strike before taking his seat again, laughing. I stirred my coffee and sipped, trying to recover my dignity as my mother picked up the thread of her conversation again.

"Harris, I've been trying to get to know your…and just what is it I'm supposed to call you?" she said, addressing the general. "Boyfriend? Significant other? Partner? Or just his boss? Enlighten me."

The general quickly cut in. "Not his boss."

"Well," I said. "Technically, you are."

"But not at home," my mother said. "Harris outranks you here, no matter what he has to put up with at your Air Force base."

"Jane, I may be a general, but I can't do much about military tradition as far as rank is concerned."

I could see my mom's hackles start their ascent. I appreciated her concern, and I recognized she raised questions that needed answers. At the same time, I understood the general's apprehension. I felt a momentary stab of panic. They were both on my side, but could I make them see it? I needed eloquence. I needed brilliance and wit and panache to calm the waters and a steady hand to steer my ship.

As if such things would come to me.

"Mom, I know we've set ourselves up for some challenges. Maybe they seem insurmountable to you, but they're not. We'll find a way over them, somehow. I can't give you the particulars just now, but we will get there. Won't we, Traveler?"

He seemed startled to have been brought into the conversation at this point. He contributed nothing more than a nod.

Not my mom. "Challenges?" she said. "Ha! I don't know much about the Air Force or any of the services, but I know how they feel about gay men. I read the papers, and I watch the news."

"But gay people can serve openly now," I reminded her.

"Yes. Maybe the law has changed, but has anybody's mind changed? You said so yourself in that interview in the newspaper back in June. Remember? You can't tell me the cards aren't stacked against the both of you. And there are a lot of cards."

"Mom, I understand your concern, but everything will be fine." I sounded more confident than I felt. "We just need to work out a few minor details."

My mom snorted. "That's the understatement of the twenty-first century."

I was growing exasperated. No conclusion to our discussion would be satisfactory to all parties concerned, and suddenly I just wanted to end it, at least for now. "Mom, what can I say? I love you and Dad. I know you want what's best for me. I appreciate your concern, but I'm not a kid anymore. I know decisions have consequences. I choose to serve in the Air Force. I'm involved with this guy." I pointed at the general. "That's my choice, too."

"And mine, Jane," he said. I was surprised and silently grateful for his contribution.

She sighed. "My heart says you're right, but my head isn't so sure." She set down her coffee cup. "You two have some things to discuss. But you can't do it on an empty stomach. How about some pancakes?"

"Always a favorite," the general said. "Especially with lots of maple syrup." I bit my tongue to keep from laughing.

"Good. That's our usual Saturday breakfast," she said, thankfully oblivious to our inside joke. "Even if we don't get around to it until noon." She glanced at the clock. "And speaking of breakfast, it's time your father was up."

She excused herself, and the general and I eyed each other across the rims of our cups. The battle of Mom had ended in an uneasy truce, and I'm sure he was just as relieved as I was.

"We always do this," I said. "Cautiously make eye contact over a cup of coffee."

"Yup," he said.

"Good morning, Traveler," I said.

He grinned. "Good morning. How are you, Sundance?"

"Took me a long time to get to sleep last night," I said. "I was lonely, and you were so close I could almost taste you."

He nodded. "At least I had your bear."

The general set down his cup. I set mine down as well. We stood up.

"I'm waiting for you, Traveler," I said. "I'm always waiting for you. Don't blame me if I choose caution. You're still my boss. You're still a general, and I'm still a lieutenant. Until something changes, you're behind the wheel, and I'm just a passenger. I'm scared to make a move because I never know how you'll respond."

"What are you talking about? I like spontaneity."

"You like it when it's your idea," I said. "I *think* I know what you want, but your signals are all mixed up."

"What do I want?" He was humoring me, and I didn't like it. My frustration once again boiled over into anger. Whether or not he knew it, we were fast approaching some sort of flashpoint. We would need to define our terms and make some choices rather than skate around them, as he seemed to prefer.

"All this time, I thought you wanted me. Us."

I waited for him to respond, to verify for me what I'd overhead him tell my mom. He didn't.

He collected me in his arms. "Firestarter," he whispered. "Can't we just let things be for a while?"

I thought I'd been explaining why we couldn't. As I sputtered my reply, he put a finger across my lips. "Enough talk," he said.

I surrendered. I always did. Clement started barking and Sixtus joined in, and they made such a fuss that both of my parents were in the kitchen inside of a minute to see if the world were coming to an end. And it might have been, because they caught us once more.

"Seamus!" my mother wailed.

"Damn it, not again," my father contributed.

But it was not the cyclone it had been just two nights ago.

The rest of the day passed quietly in comparison. Breakfast was leisurely. The pancakes tasted wonderful, the general made too many jokes about syrup and conversation never flagged. But I couldn't help thinking he'd successfully managed to postpone a serious discussion again. By eavesdropping on him and my mother, I'd learned more about what made him tick than I had in the past six months combined, but I wished he would tell me directly. I needed to hear him call this love by name. I didn't think that was asking too much. I'd been camping in that particular field for months, and I had no intention of packing up my tent.

That evening, my father called the general and me into the living room. "Want to talk to you boys," he said.

Hmm. My father was not one to initiate conversation with anyone.

I sat down on the couch, and the general sat next to me. My father moved his chair in front of us. He got right to the point.

"Got some questions, Seamus," he said. "Harris, this concerns you, too." He paused for a moment, thoughtful, as if he were reviewing his agenda, and then started his inquiry.

"Seamus, you've been in the Air Force how long?"

"Thirty-three years, counting my time as a cadet."

"What's your MOS?" I knew enough about my dad's time in the Army to know the acronym meant Military Occupational Specialty. One's job, in other words.

"I'm a pilot."

"That's a damn long time to do the same thing. You retire when?"

"About four years from now."

"And you'll be how old?"

The general coughed. "Uh, fifty-five."

"Then what?"

"I'll be retired. Comfortably. I'll start drawing my pension immediately."

Retirement was not a word I'd ever heard my father utter. Indolence offended him. He liked being busy and always was. Though my mother would protest, my dad would probably be working at the sporting-goods store in some capacity until he died.

"But what will you do? Fly for a civilian airline or some corporation?"

"Probably not."

"Why?"

He cleared his throat. "Airlines tend to hire younger men."

"So what will you do?"

"Just relax, I suppose. I think I've earned it."

"And where will you settle down to do this relaxing?"

"Haven't thought about that yet." Hastily, he added. "I expect to find another job of some sort to keep busy."

"Mmm." My father thought about that for a minute. "What's your schooling?"

"Air Force Academy."

"Is that like college?"

"It *is* college. Four-year. I earned my bachelor's degree in American history."

"History. What good's that? Ever been a teacher or anything?"

"No, I'm just interested in the subject, kind of a hobby. After graduating, I went to pilot training at—"

"Harris, remind me. What's your schooling?"

"Come on, Dad." He didn't budge, so I played along. "Bachelor's degree from Ohio State and a master's from the University of Pittsburgh."

"Ever use them?"

These questions were for the general's benefit, but still. "Dad!"

He frowned.

I sighed. "Professor of English. Four years prior to rejoining the Air Force."

He redirected his attention to the general. "So you've been tied up with the service since you were how old?"

"Eighteen."

"Eighteen. Hmm. Ever owned a house?"

"Uh, I never had any need. The Air Force provides housing."

"Harris?"

"Of course, Dad. You know I have." I'd purchased my first house after graduate school when I'd started teaching.

"What do you do when your toilet backs up?" my dad asked the general.

"That's never happened to me." He thought about it for a moment. "Call a plumber, I guess."

"Harris?"

"Turn off the water flow to the toilet. Then contain the mess and try to clear the blockage with a plunger. Or a snake, if it's really clogged."

My dad nodded. "Seamus, have you ever had to live on a budget?"

"The Air Force has always paid me a fair salary," the general said. He was clearly uncomfortable with this line of questioning.

"So, you're saying no," my dad said. "Can you do your own taxes?"

"I don't. My accountant—"

"Change the air filter on your car? Patch a hole in drywall? Install a ceiling fan? Fix a leaky faucet?"

I could do all the things my dad mentioned and more. He'd taught me, in fact. The general didn't even answer. He stared at my father as he considered the pair of us. I knew what Dad was getting at. In my last decade, I had accumulated practical experience in living that the general had never acquired in his thirty-plus years in the Air Force. His full-time officer career had effectively shielded him from many everyday concerns.

I wondered how the general would manage the real world once he retired. If his entire sense of self was inextricably tied up with his rank, he'd be in for some unpleasant surprises after hanging up his uniform. Never again would he be treated with the deference he was afforded now, privilege doled out according to regulation. From my dad's perspective, Mr. Seamus O'Neill would be just another guy looking for a job with nothing on his resume but military service and a college degree in American history that he'd never used for anything.

My father dismissed the general, and he walked out, a thunderstorm brewing in his face. He probably felt as if he'd failed a critical exam.

My father looked at me. "That one's going to require a lot of care and feeding," he said.

"Yes, Dad."

"Just so you know," he said.

"I do," I said, "but can I keep him?"

He turned things over in his mind. Finally, he nodded. Grateful, and much to his surprise, I wrapped my arms around his neck and lightly kissed his forehead.

"Enough of that," he said, embarrassed. But pleased, I think.

I found the general on the porch, puffing savagely on his pipe. "Bruce hates me," he said.

I sat down next to him. "No, he doesn't," I said. "Even if you've never owned a house, you're a good fisherman, and you'd be surprised at the way my dad's calculator works. But you're lucky you found someone like me to look after you."

He wrapped an arm around my shoulder and sighed. "You're telling me."

CHAPTER NINETEEN

S unday Mass was part of the routine all the while I lived at home. When I left for college, I decided organized religion was old-fashioned, and I dropped my Catholic habits fairly quickly. My decision was prompted more by the church's stance on various issues such as homosexuality than anything else, however. I never told my parents about this crisis of faith and usually attended church with them during my visits, simply out of respect for them.

I always wear my blues when we attend Mass, since a military uniform is an uncommon sight around my hometown. I'm showing off a bit, but it puts my parents in the spotlight for a while, since none of their friends has a son or daughter in the military. It also serves as a reminder I'm my own man, making my own choices and my own living. I confess the attention doesn't bother me too much, either. It's rare that a lieutenant gets an opportunity to feel any sense of importance or pride in any kind of setting, military or otherwise.

Although I'd told my mother the general wouldn't be interested in attending church with us, I should have known she would ask him anyway, particularly after learning that he too had been raised a Catholic. He tried to decline her invitation.

"I haven't been to church in years," he said.

"Why?" my mother persisted.

"Kind of drifted away from it, I guess," he said. "I don't think I've ever lost faith. I just disagree with the church's position on some of the issues it cares a hell of a lot about. I couldn't see eye-to-eye. And it seems to me if you can't live according to the bylaws, you got no business being in the club," he said.

An interesting point of view, certainly, and it made me wonder how he regarded the military "club" and its sometimes-arcane bylaws, several of which he and I had been violating on a regular basis, but I would ask him about that later.

"Show Mom your dog tags," I said.

He laughed. He took the chain from around his neck and handed them to her.

"How'd you ever get them to stamp 'infidel' on there?" I said.

I knew what he would say, and I repeated the answer in tandem with him. "Because I'm a general."

"What a surprise to hear you say that," I said. "You're always pulling rank, Traveler. Good luck trying to sleep late tomorrow with two smart dogs around here."

Clement and Sixtus would figure out quickly the general was the only one in the house, and they'd come calling. If he kept his door shut, he might pull it off for a little while. First Mass was at eight, and we'd be home by nine-thirty or so. Mom would fix breakfast, and then we'd hit the road and be at the airport in plenty of time for our late-afternoon flight, I told him.

My mother had been examining the dog tags. Possibly, she'd never seen any up close. "Name, Social Security Number, blood type," she said, "and 'AF' would be Air Force. But what's supposed to be on the fourth line?"

"Religious preference," I said.

Infidel, indeed. She shook her head, and that settled the matter. "We'll call for you at seven, Seamus. Will that give you enough time? We leave at half past."

"Mom!" I said. "He said he didn't want to go."

"I'm not talking to you," she said.

I wasn't surprised when he caved in. "Well," he said. "I reckon it won't hurt, if you don't mind the company of an old sinner like me."

I groaned. As usual, he'd said the right thing. I guess it was all part of his renewal program, designed to build himself up. I appreciated his efforts but good Lord! My mom, victorious, just laughed, and so we were locked in for a date to church.

"This isn't fair," I said as I helped him with his tie at seven-twenty the next morning. "You're a guest. Just because I have to go to church doesn't mean you have to. You were supposed to say 'no, thanks' and sleep in. *Sir.*"

He was amused. "I reckon you'll survive, Switchblade. And mind who you're calling 'sir.' I'm still keeping track." His mustache shifted, restless again. I adjusted the knot on his tie and examined him. I had to admit he looked sharp, his blues perfectly creased. Everything about him suggested confidence and accomplishment. His military spit-and-polish easily outshone mine, as his acre-sized block of ribbons humbled the seven I'd earned.

"Pass muster?" he said.

"Of course, Traveler. You know your blues look good on you." I paused, just for a second, and offered a postscript. "But they'd look a lot better in a heap on the floor beside my bed."

"Damn," he said softly. "That's the best offer I've had in days."

"We could send Mom and Dad to church and make an excuse to stay here by ourselves."

For a moment I think he wavered. I could tell he liked the idea, but he recovered just as quickly and shook his head. "Shameless. And on a Sunday morning, no less. You're hellbound, mister." He fingered my mustache but went no further. We walked down the hallway and the stairs. He was behind me, and he leaned over and whispered into my ear, "Don't worry. I'll send you postcards."

There would be no need. He'd be right there beside me.

I'd like to have a snapshot of the four of us in a pew in the middle of the church. First, my father, who wore a non-customary tie and jacket for the occasion, then my mother, me, and finally, the general on the aisle, with everyone in the church staring at us, the center of distraction throughout the Mass. Nothing shy of torture would have gotten the general to admit how much he enjoyed being at the eye of this particular storm.

The sun electrified our church's stained glass windows, spilling deep ruby, indigo, gold, and green across us below, illuminating a little of the mystery and the wonder I used to feel at Mass. With Traveler next to me, under such light, our relationship didn't seem as much sinful as it did blessed.

Mass is a ritual. Once you've mastered it, you never forget, even if you're navigating by autopilot. The general didn't miss a beat. If he hadn't attended in years, he still remembered all the right responses because he'd learned them by heart. During the Eucharistic prayer, he elbowed me and grinned as the priest rattled off the litany of saints.

I remember his deep voice rumbling underneath, elemental, as we sang the old hymns. I'd never heard him sing out with his rich bass. I don't know why I was so surprised to discover that he was quite tuneful.

Such ability is hardly rare. I can do as much myself, but for a general, it seemed curious, even startling. Perhaps it was just because he sang loudly and confidently, which many Catholics refuse to do.

I remember the general's firm, no-nonsense handshake at the moment of the Mass when we shared a peaceful sign among ourselves. My mother kissed me on the forehead as she has done forever, and then, to my surprise, she kissed the general's forehead, too. Her gesture of familiarity struck me as telling in a way she could never have imagined, because she would not have greeted a stranger or even a casual friend in such a manner. Only family. Others behind and in front shook our hands too, welcoming me home, and even the monsignor came down to greet us and thank us for our military service. I appreciated the sincerity of his gesture.

After Mass, my father insisted we stay for coffee and doughnuts in the church hall. Usually my parents skipped the fellowship stuff, but I guess I couldn't blame them for wanting to prolong the moment of glory.

"Brace yourself," I told the general.

"You watch," he said. "I can take care of myself."

Of course he could. But I watched him anyway, a little jealous of the attention he attracted, since I felt mostly edged out. He had enough experience with community events where he was required to do little more than act general-like, making friendly small talk while balancing a cup and a plate of snacks. Still, I introduced him all around, and he remained gracious. When it was all over and we were on our way back home, he seemed extremely pleased with himself.

"Congratulations," I said. "Everyone at All Saints is now convinced that you run the U.S. Air Force single-handedly, with minimal assistance from your trusty sidekick, the Boy Lieutenant. For years to come, the congregation will retell the story of the day the general came to Mass, and you will pass into legend like all saints do."

He grinned, and my parents laughed, too.

"Well. Maybe not all," he said. "Suppose we say *some* saints and call it square. You reckon my soul will be saved?"

"On the strength of one Mass and two cups of coffee? It might take a little more than that. Sir," I concluded, insinuating.

"Careful, Stoplight. You're being insubordinate."

"So court-martial me. Sir."

"I'll figure out some kind of penalty."

Once we arrived home again, my parents changed from their

Sunday morning clothes into attire more suitable for the remainder of a restful day.

We hung back in the kitchen. "I hope I didn't steal your thunder today," the general said, contrite.

He had, but I didn't mind. "It's all right. Thanks for going. Mom and Dad won't say so, but it meant a lot to them. They're proud to show me off in my uniform," I said, "and I don't mind indulging them. It's as good for the soul as gospel now and then, I think."

I wondered, idly amused, about the future. If the general and I beat the odds and stayed together, we would surely have other occasions to attend Mass with my parents. Had they thought about that when they'd taken us to church this morning? I wonder if they weren't unconsciously beginning to treat him as a son-in-law already.

God bless them. They are fine people, as resilient as the morning come and just as hopeful.

"You know," I said, "you're making the most inconvenient good impression on them."

"Am I?"

"You know you are, Traveler. I've never seen anything so shamelessly calculated. Even the dogs like you. As if you're staking some kind of claim."

"Am I?"

Maybe we both wanted a future together after all. I wondered if he might at last be ready to talk about it, but after an uncertain moment, he chose to skate around the subject once again. "Damn," he growled. "Did I ever tell you how sexy you look in blue?"

He pulled me to him and coupled his mouth to mine, and then he pulled back. He looked at me in his arms, and I suspect he realized what had just occurred to me, too. He'd never expressed his feelings for me when we were both in uniform, as if he'd made some conscious effort to separate us from the Air Force and the uniform that marked it. But this time, deliberately, he wrapped his arms around me and pulled me against himself, tightly, as if he would squeeze the life from me. Perhaps he truly was staking a claim.

Pressing into me, the hardware on his shirt might have left a permanent imprint on my chest, but it would have been nothing like the permanent mark he'd already made in my heart. And when his mouth instinctively found mine, I knew he was as hungry as I was. If not here and now in this kitchen on a fall Sunday morning in the house where I grew up, then somewhere and soon, he would be called to settle his account. An answer would be demanded of him. Such an appetite as his was not without consequence.

Neither of us heard my parents come back into the kitchen until my father groaned, "Oh, not again."

"Boys!" my mother said, stern.

Guilty, we separated.

"Y'all need to make a little more noise," the general said. "Well, get your eyes full." We'd never kissed for an audience, but even if modesty should have dictated otherwise, I forgot everything but the man connected to me.

When we separated, I felt my face flush, but he wore defiance instead, underneath a triumphant grin, as if he'd won some victory. And though my mother and father tried to appear disapproving, I couldn't quite buy it this time. My father shook his head, resigned, muttering under his breath. Faced with the awkward grace of our courting, my mother could only giggle. I wondered if Dad could ever have behaved the same way.

She shooed us out of the kitchen so she and my father could attend to breakfast.

The general and I escaped to the backyard for a walk with Clement and Sixtus. We have plenty of trees and a couple of acres to wander. And wander we did, but we weren't exploring the grounds once we were out of sight of the house, under the sun and the wide blue sky. And maybe the dogs raised a fuss and maybe not. Quite possibly, we wouldn't have heard bombs dropping.

❖

Before noon, we loaded our suitcases into the car. We had plenty of time to reach the airport, return the rental, and get to our gate. We'd probably sit for an hour, but the general never complained. I had long since adapted myself to that habit, at least, and always carried a paperback book with me, as he did himself, for such occasions.

My father scowled. "I expect you to do right by our son," he told the general. "But I'll kick your ass across three states if I find out from Harris that you're behaving like a prick."

I was mortified, and the general was suitably embarrassed, too, but he said, "You've got a deal, Bruce. I couldn't ask for more than that."

My mother gave him a hug and a quick kiss on the cheek. "Seamus, we look forward to your next visit."

Solemnly, the general shook hands with each of them and, in the process, handed each of them one of his embossed brass coins, colorfully imprinted with our Sixth Air Force emblem. Mystified, they examined these tokens carefully.

"Wow," I said. "You're lucky. He doesn't give those away too often."

"It's lovely," my mother said, "but what is it?"

"It's the general's coin," I said. "His personal souvenir as the commander of Sixth Air Force. See? It has our patch on one side and the one-star flag on the other, and it says 'commander' underneath."

"What's it for?" my dad said.

"Excellence, usually," I said. "Going above and beyond the call of duty. It's kind of a good-luck charm."

My mother shook her head. "What did we do to deserve this honor?"

"You welcomed me into your family," the general said. "That's enough. But you're willing to share Harris with me, too. That's a meritorious achievement that deserves more than a coin, but it's all I've got right now. Call it my marker, gratefully given, for a debt I can never repay."

I felt myself blush. Imagine someone talking that way about me. My parents didn't know what to say.

After a quick farewell pat for the dogs, who always seem sorrowful when anyone departs, we climbed into the car. I headed down the driveway with a couple of honks of the horn and a wave out the window.

We drove most of the route in comfortable silence. Only when we got closer to the city did we start talking.

"Now you've met my folks," I said.

"They're fine people. I'm grateful for their hospitality."

"I hope you'll get a chance to visit with them again soon."

"I intend to."

"I'm sorry."

"For what?"

"For how things went."

"What the hell are you talking about? Maybe we didn't file a flight plan before we took off, but we arrived at our intended destination."

"We did?"

He grinned. "Why do you think I wanted to come home with you, Harris?"

"You mean—?"

He nodded. "I had every intention of telling them about us. How could we spend three days together and *not* talk about it?"

After all that. "I hate you, Traveler."

"Liar," he said, still grinning.

"How did you know everything would work out all right?"

"I'm a general," he said. That cinched it. I couldn't help but laugh.

As we neared the exit that would put us on the bypass to Interstate 70 toward Dayton, he told me to keep going straight into Columbus instead.

"Why?"

"Just drive," he said. "I'll tell you when to turn off."

"I know this area pretty well, Traveler, and if we don't take the bypass, we'll have to go through downtown, and you never know what that's going to be like, even on a weekend. We don't have too much extra time to get to the airport as it is, and we have to return the car first."

He pressed a gentle hand over my mouth and grinned. All right, then. I would humor him. A few miles farther, we were close to downtown, and he pointed out an exit. I took it. He directed me to turn left at the next traffic light. I did. Not long after that, he directed me to turn into the parking lot of an upscale hotel.

"What's the idea?"

"We have a reservation," he said.

"We do?"

"We do. One night. I wish we could stay for two or three," he said. "I swapped our flight this evening for tomorrow afternoon instead. I made the arrangements by phone yesterday. See? I don't need a sitter all the time. Your folks are wonderful people," he said, "but we need some one-on-one time with no audience. Barking dogs included."

He got out of the car and waited by the trunk expectantly as I released the catch. He removed his bag and was heading for the door when he realized I was still sitting in the front seat, too surprised to move. He came back to the car and leaned down to my open window, his face level with mine. "Hey, Shirttail. You coming?" he said. Then he realized his double entendre and grinned. "You will be soon. I guarantee it."

CHAPTER TWENTY

We managed to keep our composure through the lobby and to the desk. The general gave his name, and the clerk looked it up on the computer. "A single with two double beds," he said. "You're on the twelfth floor. Nice view from the balcony."

The general and I filled out the registration forms, and he passed over a credit card to pay for the room. The clerk gave each of us a key and told us that checkout was at noon the next day. We thanked him and headed across the lobby toward the elevator.

"Why two beds instead of one?" I said, once we were inside the elevator and gliding upward to our floor.

He wagged his eyebrows. "Two places to play."

We set down our suitcases inside the room. It was furnished with a pair of easy chairs, a reading lamp, a coffee table with the daily newspaper folded on it, a large flat-screen television, and a coffee bar in addition to the beds. A sliding glass door led to a balcony with a pleasant view of the city skyline as promised. I wasn't surprised the general had sprung for the best, and I was pleased he'd done it all by himself.

The general hooked the "do not disturb" sign on the door, slid the deadbolt into place, and hooked the security chain. He drew the drapes across the window and the door to the balcony, letting in just enough afternoon sun around the edges to put the room in comfortable half-light, more than enough to see the glint in his eyes as he faced me, his mustache set on "charge." He started unbuttoning his shirt.

"You waiting for an engraved invitation?" he said.

Nothing so formal. We didn't even pull back the spread before tumbling into the bed like dice rolling lucky seven. The three days spent with my parents might have been the longest foreplay we'd ever managed. We were fully primed and ready, with no two- or four-legged interference or interruption. Our swords drawn, we had nothing but the most pleasurable dueling left to do, and the rest of the day for it. We settled into our *en garde* with a lusty abandon that would have made any swashbuckler proud.

❖

Early in the evening, we showered and dressed and shared a quiet dinner in the restaurant at the hotel. As we walked back to our room, I had an inspiration. "Let's go out tonight."

"Where?"

"A bar I know. It's not too far from here." He hesitated. "Come on, Traveler. When was the last time you went to a gay bar?"

"That's easy. Never."

"You're kidding."

"Of course not."

"You don't know what you're missing."

"I think I do."

I conceded. "All right. Maybe you do, but humor me this once. I went to school in this city, and I want to visit my old stomping ground for a nostalgia trip. Okay?"

He sighed. "All right, Shotglass. We'll go. But I don't think I have anything suitable to wear."

"How about your blues? That would generate significant interest among the clientele, I imagine."

"Ha," he said. "I'd rather stay here with you instead. Clothing is optional, and you can call me 'sir' a few more times."

I stood firm. I didn't know when we might get another opportunity to visit such a bar. It was reasonably close by, and it would be good to get out of the hotel for a while. We could take a taxi so we wouldn't have to worry about parking. We'd stay long enough to have one drink and then return to the hotel. Besides, we couldn't make up for weeks of frustrated intimacy in one day.

As I counted off my reasons, he groaned and covered his ears. "Enough. I surrender."

We settled for casual attire, khaki trousers and sport shirts, understated and suggestive of nothing particularly queer. Though we might be slightly out of place in the bar, we would attract no attention elsewhere, and he declared himself satisfied.

It was just half past eight.

"A little early, but not too early," I said. "Come on. I promise to behave myself, at least until we're inside the bar."

I grabbed him around the neck and brought his mouth to mine. When we separated, he sighed. "Let's get this thing over with," he said. We grabbed our jackets and headed downstairs.

CHAPTER TWENTY-ONE

We caught a taxi outside the hotel, and I directed the driver to let us out about two blocks from the bar. I knew the general would be self-conscious, so I wanted to be as inconspicuous as possible. As we walked toward the entrance, he glanced around nervously. "Are you sure about this?" he said.

"Yes," I said. "We're not violating any law. We're both adults. We're just going into a bar to have a beer." He still seemed reluctant, but I pushed him from behind. "Go in. I know you're curious."

We stepped inside, our eyes adjusting to the dim lights as we stood in the doorway. I'd counted on a small crowd, partly because we were early and partly because Sunday nights usually attracted fewer customers. Nonetheless, perhaps two dozen men were inside, and I was aware all eyes turned our way as soon as we entered. Though this wasn't unusual, I also knew the general wouldn't be aware of such a thing. He took the scrutiny personally, and I could feel his hackles rise, like a backyard dog challenged by a trespasser.

"Easy, Traveler," I said. I took his hand and led him to a seat at the bar, a large square island surrounded with high stools. We took off our jackets and made ourselves comfortable.

The bartender, standing inside the square, came over to us as we sat down. "What'll it be, guys?" Noncommittal. He didn't care. We were two more customers.

"A beer, I guess," the general said. "Whatever you've got on tap."

"The same for me, please," I said.

"Gotta see some ID first, pal."

I was amused but the general was mortified as I handed over my driver's license. Satisfied, the bartender pulled two icy mugs from a cooler, drew the beer, and set the glasses in front of us. Optimistic, I asked him to start a tab, and he left us alone.

"See?" I said. "That wasn't so bad, was it?"

The general didn't answer. He gulped half of his glass of beer, still anxious, still self-conscious, brooding a little.

"Now everyone thinks I'm some kind of chicken hawk," he grumbled. "As if I'd bring a minor into a bar."

I sighed. "Look, Traveler, it's just a precaution. It didn't mean anything. The bartender is required to ask for ID."

"He didn't ask me," he said, dark.

"I'd say there's no doubt that you're over twenty-one. What of it?"

He hid his mustache in the mug and concentrated on the contents.

I looked around the place. Little had changed since my college days, though the place did seem smaller and perhaps a little more weary than I recalled. The unassuming interior was dimly lit, with a couple of pool tables and a jukebox. On Fridays and Saturdays, the bar offered a DJ, and they had a small space for dancing if anyone felt like doing so, but on other nights, a jukebox provided the soundtrack for whatever casual cruising took place. The same neon signs on the walls advertised various brands of beer. A large television behind the bar aired a baseball game with the sound off. Nothing would seem particularly gay to an outsider.

Before getting involved with my English professor during junior year, I'd been a very "out" undergraduate. I and similarly gay friends had spent a lot of evenings and weekends in the place, and we'd found a warm welcome. At one time, such a place seemed bright and full of potential. Now? Inwardly, I shrugged.

I glanced at the clientele, mixed in age as well as attire, and assumed the general and I wouldn't be out of place, even with our conspicuous age difference. I felt no antagonism from the others, just friendly curiosity. One man in particular gave me the eye, though I got the distinct impression he liked me as much as he heartily disapproved of my companion.

I didn't expect to see anyone familiar, so I was quite startled to discover a portly, balding man in a bright orange shirt with a blue cravat, inspecting us with eager intent. I remembered his name instantly: Terry Barksdale. Clearly, he remembered me, too. His eyes lit up. He leaped from his seat and rushed over to us.

"Harris Mitchell! Imagine seeing you here again!" He crushed me against him in a bear hug and kissed me full on the lips. "You darling boy! How long has it been?"

Who could forget Terry? He was probably in his fifties when my friends and I used to see him here a decade ago, when we'd bookmarked him as the stereotypical, sad old queen, a catalogue of every gay cliché. He had them all: an absurdly flamboyant fashion sense, mincing gestures, a girlish giggle, even a faint lisp. We poked fun at his terminally hopeful outlook as he eagerly made passes at everyone. He was always good for a round or two of drinks, and thus always surrounded by hangers-on who gladly took advantage of his generosity. I couldn't remember visiting the bar even once when he wasn't holding court.

I had less compassion then. Now I felt sorry for him and wished I could make up for my rude dismissals of his harmless flirtations with me. But if he remembered, he didn't seem to mind, or else he'd long since forgiven me.

"It's so good to see someone from the old crowd again," he said. "Most of those girls are *so* long gone."

"Do you still come here every night, Terry?" I said.

"But of course! What would they do without me? I keep this place in business single-handedly!"

The bartender laughed. "You got that right, Terry," he said.

"Don't you get tired of the same old scene?" I said.

"You know me. Hope springs eternal." In a stage whisper, he added, "I wish I could say the same for my dick. Thank God for that magical blue pill!"

I laughed with him. The general was thoroughly dismayed. More so when Terry turned his eager attention to my companion. Clearly, Terry liked what he saw.

"And what have we *here*?" he said.

"Terry, this is—"

The general cut in. "Seamus O'Neill." He offered Terry a short, businesslike handshake.

"Ooh, Irish! And so strong! Where did you ever find this sexy hunk, Harris? Oh, my. I'd ride that mustache of his *any*time. He's just too damn *hot*."

I certainly agreed. I'd told the general as much on many occasions, but the compliment sounded strange coming from another man, and a relative stranger at that. When Terry took the unexpected liberty of squeezing the general on his backside, he jumped and sloshed beer down the front of his shirt.

He protested. "Hey!"

Terry noticed his discomfort, too. "Don't you mind me, Seamus," he said. "I just can't keep my hands to myself when there's a sexy ass within reach."

The general coughed, and even in the dim light, I could tell he'd turned red. He was out of his element, and I think he knew it. Sans uniform, in a world far away from a military base, he was certainly at a disadvantage. Generals have no power in places like this, where rank holds no currency. Nothing can cover lack of experience in the practical aspects of navigating a gay bar.

Terry chattered on, filling me in about others from the old days, some of whom I recalled and most whose names meant nothing. At the end of his monologue, he began grilling me. How long since I'd been home? Where was I living now? What was I doing with myself these days?

Without hesitation, I gave him a quick rundown of my life since he'd seen me last. I stopped short of explaining that I was now the aide-de-camp of the man standing right next to me. That information, I decided, would be the general's to reveal if he chose.

At the end of my brief recitation, Terry asked the question I'd been dreading. "So, what line of work are you in, Seamus?"

Would he offer the truth, however awkward, or an outright lie?

The general cleared his throat. I could almost see his mind working, frantically, trying to devise the best response. Finally, he said, "I'm a pilot."

"Ooh! You're a lucky man, Harris. Seamus could fly me around the world or anyplace else he wanted to go."

Terry didn't ask any more questions. I was surprised he didn't inquire about the airline the general worked for. But I was thankful that Terry prodded no more deeply into the relationship between the general and me.

At last, with nothing more to discuss, Terry said, "Well, I'll let you two lovebirds enjoy yourselves," he said. "I'm working my magic on that young fellow over there, and I must get back. He'll think I've abandoned him, and he'll go home with somebody else tonight." I looked across the bar where a bored young man sat by with three empty cocktail glasses in front of him. I suspected the success of Terry's abracadabra would be proportional to the quantity of alcohol consumed by his intended.

He kissed me good-bye on the lips, and the general, too. "Harris, if you ever get tired of this man, you just give me a call, and I'll take him off your hands in a heartbeat," Terry said.

As he scurried back to his seat, the general muttered under his breath, "The hell you will." He wiped his mouth with a napkin as if he were removing some unpleasant taste.

"Be nice," I said. "He's just being sociable. Every time I came here with my friends, Terry was sitting in that same seat. I'd forgotten all about him. I certainly never expected to bump into him again."

"Your lucky night," the general said. I knew he was displeased. "I'm all wet, and I smell like a brewery," he said. "My shirt is probably ruined."

"It's beer, not paint, Traveler. Besides," I said, "you spilled it yourself."

"Right," he said. "How clumsy of me. Where's the men's room? I'll see if I can rinse it out."

I pointed, and off he went. He'd find out soon enough that the restroom featured a trough urinal, and he'd likely attract an observer or two while he was in there. I feared it would only fuel his sour mood.

As soon as the general was out of sight, the man who'd been giving me the eye slipped into the seat next to mine. He put an arm around my shoulder, familiarly. "So what are your plans for the evening?"

"I've already got company," I said, "in case you haven't noticed."

"Yeah, I noticed," he said. "Suppose you ditch Grandpa and come with me?"

I removed his arm from my shoulder. "I choose my own friends, thank you."

"Oh, come on." He groped himself suggestively. "I got ten inches, rock hard, and I could give you the ride of your life. You'll be begging for more."

I doubted each aspect of his claims.

He persisted. "If you're a top man, that's okay, too. I'm versatile, whichever you want."

"Actually," I said, "what I want is for you to leave me alone. If I wasn't so afraid of offending you, I'd tell you to go to hell, but since I was raised to be polite, I'll just say no, thanks."

The smile drained from his face immediately. "Bitch," he said. He left me to my thoughts, and I wondered again how smart this whole idea had been. I wasn't sure what I expected to gain from the general's first visit to a gay bar. I'd hoped, I guess, that we could relax for once in a safe public place.

The jukebox faded from a Motown oldie into Bruce Springsteen. I watched Terry, his arm around the waist of his quarry, who seemed monumentally bored but perhaps a little too inebriated to do much about it. I sighed and emptied my glass, the beer warm and sour.

"Two more?" The bartender.

"I guess so," I said, immediately wondering why I should want to extend our stay.

As the bartender set the frosty mugs in front of me, the general came storming from the men's room, seething. His shirt front was soggy, and the water had dripped to the front of his trousers. Uh-oh, I thought. I hoped he hadn't gotten a good look at the results, as he appeared to have had a slight accident.

"What's wrong, Traveler?"

He grabbed his glass and drank half of it in one gulp, his throat pumping furiously.

"Goddamned little punk," he said, too loud. Others turned to look at us.

"Be more specific," I said. "And perhaps a little quieter. What happened?"

He lowered his tone, but his anger continued at a rolling boil. "I'm at the sink trying to clean my shirt, and this damn kid comes at me and offers to suck me off. Right there in the men's room!"

"Traveler…"

"He's so damned insistent about it. I tell him *hell*, no, and he doesn't even listen. He starts unzipping my pants, for Christ's sake, and that's when I got the hell out of there. Is everybody in this place some kind of goddamned freak?"

"Easy, Traveler. Please just sit down, okay?"

He caught his breath and parked himself on the stool. Bruce Springsteen finished his paean to the working man, and a few seconds later, some contemporary dance pop blared out of the jukebox speakers, an itchy electronic beat underneath washes of synthesizer, a simple bass line and an even simpler melody. An anonymous female voice moaned over the top: "Be my loverboy, be my lover." A couple of patrons gravitated to the dance floor and started gyrating suggestively.

It was a long shot, but I asked anyway. "You want to dance?"

"To *that*?" the general snorted. "That's not music."

He didn't seem inclined to talk, and I was starting to feel a bit uncomfortable. Under the glare of the man with ten inches, I moved my bar stool closer to the general's.

"What's wrong?" he said.

"Nothing," I said. "I just want to make sure everyone knows we're together."

"You don't have to sit in my lap," he said. But at least his anger had subsided.

I cupped a hand around his ear. "You're the sexiest man here. I wouldn't want anyone to steal you away from me."

"No chance of that," he whispered back, "regardless of the offers that have come my way of late." I slid my hand around to the back of his neck, and brushed my fingers gently against the short hairs. I could feel him crackle. He liked it, and I did, too.

"Hey," I said. "I like to ride your mustache myself. And you like to ride mine, as I recall. Suppose we finish our beer and beat it back to the hotel?"

"That's the best idea you've had tonight."

After two glasses of beer, I needed to hit the men's room myself. I completed my business unmolested and returned to the bar. The general had picked up the summer issue of a Midwestern glossy gay magazine lying on the bar and was paging through it. The cover featured a pouting, well-muscled, hairless, blond youth, his genitals coyly obscured by an inflatable pool toy. I took my seat and watched as the general paused to inspect some of the ads, many of which promised services you might not be able to explain to a straight man without blushing.

I scrutinized the general as he took in the images, most in lurid color, splashed across the pages. In the gay community, we brag about our rainbow, our diversity, but how could my general even imagine settling anywhere into the continuum? We could search through magazines from Provincetown to San Francisco without finding pictures of people like him, everyday men with everyday lives, narrow, fuzzy middle-aged men who were still trying to figure out where or if they fit. Could there be such a thing as gay pride for a gay general? Even in our recently liberated military, we were mired in the detritus of not asking and especially not telling.

On the military side, we had six ranks separating us, and in that respect, the scale tipped his way. On the personal side—the practical necessity of living publicly as a gay man—could we ever bridge the gap between his innocence and my experience?

Would he want to?

He finally tossed the magazine aside and swallowed the last of his beer.

"Let's go," I said. He didn't belong here. If I wanted to be with him, neither did I, and I was content. As I paid the bartender, Mr. Ten Inches sidled up to the general and whispered into his ear. The color drained from his face, and I thought for a second he would take a swing at the guy. But the general maintained his composure, cupped a hand around the guy's ear, and delivered a terse remark that obviously pleased him even less than mine had a little earlier.

Then the general steered me toward the door. Before we stepped out into the night, I wrapped my arm around his neck and pulled his mouth down to mine. For a second, he struggled against my embrace. "Not here," he whispered, fierce.

I responded with the same ferocity. "Yes, here, damn it. If we can kiss anywhere in public, it's inside a place like this. Now's your chance, so would you just humor me for once?"

He sighed and complied like a sullen child.

"You can do better than that, Traveler," I said when he pushed me away.

After another sigh, he proved as much, and I hung on to him until I was satisfied he remembered why people did such things in the first place. Someone—Terry, perhaps?—hooted, "You *go*, girls!" And though the general tried hard to keep a straight face, he even grinned when we finally finished. A handful of people in the bar clapped and whistled when we separated, and the general turned and offered a rakish salute.

CHAPTER TWENTY-TWO

We walked out of the bar with my hand in his. We stood next to a rainbow flag in the flashing neon light of the bar sign, and he breathed in and out, heavy, as if he'd just finished a workout. Perhaps he had. As we stood on the sidewalk, a pack of drunken college boys stumbled past us. One of them, catching sight of the general's hand in mine, hooted, "Guys! Check out the faggots!"

The general let go of me as if I were a jolt of electricity. His fingers curled into fists. Thankfully, the boys were too well lubricated to make much of an issue of us, and when they sized up the general and saw he was in the mood to engage, they backed away and left us alone, to my unrestrained relief. We did not need such confrontation.

"Okay," I said finally. "I admit this was a bad idea. I'm sorry. Do you want me to call a taxi?"

"Let's walk. It's only a couple of miles, isn't it?" the general said. "I could use some fresh air after that place."

I nodded, and we walked, side by side but still apart. His angry silence was a canyon, a chasm, with us on opposite sides.

I ached for him, wanted to comfort him but wasn't sure how. Perhaps he'd been strafed with too much information over the past several days. Regardless of what he'd insisted earlier, he could never have anticipated my parents' welcoming him into our family with such honest conviction. There was our lusty afternoon in the hotel room, a first for us, which he had initiated with no prompting from me. And my brainstorm, his first visit to a gay bar, provided the perfect disastrous end to our perfect adventure.

I hadn't realized the bar might seem like an unforgiving place to a stranger, even a hostile place with an atmosphere of desperation. Because I had always gone to gay bars with a group of like-minded friends, I'd never thought about the challenge such an establishment might present to a fighting man like the general.

But couldn't he have made more of an effort to play along? To follow my lead for a change? He might never be comfortable showing his affection fully in a public place, but he would have to learn to trust me and unbend a little. I am by no means an exhibitionist, but I see no problem with holding hands or even embracing in public as a natural response to being in love. If such expression shocks anyone looking on, I care very little. The surest way to get me to do something is to tell me I couldn't or shouldn't. Kissing a handsome man on Main Street. Joining the military and falling for a general.

The general takes his honor seriously, and he was waging his own war inside. I knew it. In the business world, such a relationship as ours is not without its ethical dilemmas. The boss-and-employee romance may be the stuff of novels, but the reality is much less likely to result in a happy ending. In our case, the Air Force complicated things considerably.

My certainty that love could somehow conquer all was ridiculously naïve. Military law had something to say about it. Between two officers, close friendship, to say nothing of a sexual relationship, is forbidden. Between two men, it would be ruinous, in spite of the presumptive gay-friendliness of the military these days. We had already violated several key statutes of the Uniform Code of Military Justice, and if we stayed together, we would continue to do so.

I knew as well as he did that no general officer in the Air Force had ever been convicted by court-martial for engaging in an unprofessional sexual relationship. Freedom from such censure seems to be another privilege of rank. But even so, he had a lot more to lose than I did. His retirement benefits were at stake. Maybe the general didn't have to worry about a court martial, but a serious fraternization charge might result in his being reduced in rank by one or even two grades, which could cost him hundreds of thousands of dollars in retirement pay. And the gay angle would only increase the ugly publicity. The *Air Force Times*, our national independent newspaper and barometer, would certainly cover the story in gleeful, painstaking detail. The scandal would overshadow whatever good the general had accomplished in three decades of service. How could we weather such a storm?

My retirement wasn't in jeopardy and possibly never would be, since I hadn't decided yet whether I'd put in the requisite twenty years of active duty. But I was smart enough to realize a discharge by court-martial would do me no good. It would follow me for life. I'd never be able to quit having to explain it.

No wonder we'd so carefully avoided discussing our relationship at any length, tap-danced around it, frantically, beautifully, as if technique and style alone could cover our vulnerability. But we would not be able to ignore it much longer. Our crossroads were fast approaching, and one of us must make a decision.

My mother had asked the general a question I'd never thought to pose myself: why *not* come out? He had an opportunity to make history as the first Air Force general to come out as a gay man while still serving. There were several high-ranking officers who'd come out after they retired, and even an Army one-star who'd come out as a lesbian while still on active service, but so far, no one had taken such a risk in the Air Force. But I suspected he would not be interested in making that kind of history.

Where did that leave us? I had to know.

"Traveler?"

I waited for him to respond, and when he didn't, I repeated myself.

"*What?*" he barked.

"Have you ever considered coming out?"

"Coming out of what?"

He didn't have to play dumb. It wasn't becoming. I explained anyway. "Out of the closet. Letting people know you're gay instead of pretending to be straight."

"Why would I want to do a fool thing like that?"

I knew he was irate and upset, but his thoughtlessness angered me. "What's foolish about it? Everyone on and off base knows *I'm* gay, after that article in the *Times* about the pride parade. I come out almost every day. Am I a fool?"

He cleared his throat.

"It's part of who I am, Traveler. Why wouldn't I want people to know? I told my mom and dad as soon as I was sure. All my friends knew, and it wasn't a big deal. I didn't have to keep it a secret until I enlisted in the Reserve after high school. I had to remember not to tell anyone. It wasn't easy, but I managed.

"I *like* who I am, Traveler. I've never bought into the notion that being gay was something to be ashamed of. I think being gay has made me more aware of the world around me. More tolerant of people who are different. More likely to question, and less likely to accept the status quo just because that's how it's always been done."

An organization like the military, which too often accepts such slender premises as gospel, is really no place for me. But I suppose I've always been an optimist, too, confident I can remake the world to fit me rather than conform. The general's faintly disparaging "hmmph" suggested that he did not agree.

"To me, the Air Force is a job," I said. "I take it very seriously, and I serve with pride. In uniform, I give the best I can. But my officer's oath didn't say anything about sacrificing my private life. At the end of the day, I have to be able to leave the NAF behind and pick up the rest of me. 'Don't Ask, Don't Tell' is history. Now I can serve my country and not feel as if I'm betraying myself or my oath.

"When I accepted my commission, I knew I'd be able to come out at work eventually. And I hoped I would find someone to love, maybe even a guy who happened to be in the service, too. And I thought I had," I said. "That's you, in case you're wondering. Do you feel the same?"

I had in mind to make him admit it, or at least confess otherwise. When he did not reply, I pressed, borrowing a point from my mom.

"Good leaders lead by example, Traveler. Actions speak louder and faster than words. You've proven that to me over and over, from the first day I started working for you. Remember our discussion about the Air Force Core Values?"

He nodded.

"What's the first one?"

He rolled his eyes and sighed.

"What is it?"

"Integrity." I could barely hear him.

"Which means?"

"Honor. Truthfulness. Reliability." He paused and swallowed. "Honesty."

"There's a reason integrity comes first, Traveler. It's the foundation for the others. So I'm asking again. Will you come out?"

He didn't hesitate. "No."

"Why?"

"You can quit asking." He sighed. "Life was so much less complicated under 'Don't Ask, Don't Tell.'"

I was incensed. "How can you even say that? It was humiliating, not to mention unfair. It was the only prejudice officially sanctioned by the Uniform Code of Military Justice."

"Even so," he grumbled. "You knew where you stood. Black and white, with no gray areas. Everyone kept his mouth shut. In the old days, we wouldn't even be having this conversation."

"In the old days, we would never have known each other," I said. "I would never have joined the service again if I had to stay in the closet. The only way I can put on my uniform in the morning and come to work is because I'm satisfied that there's room for me in this Air Force as a gay man. These are the new days! Being gay isn't a dirty little secret. I can't think of one good reason why you would *want* to keep it a secret."

"I can think of a dozen," he said, flat.

"Such as?"

He considered for a minute. "If I came out, people would rethink everything they ever knew or thought about me. Everything I ever did or said would be cut apart by people looking for clues so they could say 'Ha! I knew it all along!' Every good thing I've tried to do for Sixth Air Force and every damn unit I've commanded would go right down the sewer. I'd be the laughingstock of the whole force. I wouldn't have a snowball's chance in hell of getting that second star. I'd have no legacy left, apart from being the faggot general."

He'd adopted his "company" voice, the same he used to berate me at the office when others were present. I didn't like it. His tone suggested but one thing: how could I be so ignorant as to advocate his coming out? Given that we had no audience at the moment, I had to believe for once he wasn't putting me on. As he talked, he quickened and lengthened his stride, as if to distance himself from this discussion, or perhaps distance himself from me entirely.

I had a hard time keeping up, and not just with the pace of his feet.

"Traveler, being gay isn't the only thing you are. You're tall and skinny and left-handed. You have brown eyes and a black mustache. You're a Southern gentleman. And Irish. You're an airman. A pilot. A leader. An opera lover. A dancer. You're all kinds of things. A complicated, multifaceted person, a padlock with a fifteen-digit combination. None of those things by itself defines you. All the pieces fit together to make you Seamus Edwards O'Neill."

He shook his head. "If I come out, nobody will give a goddamn about anything else. I won't."

"Ever?"

He set his jaw. "Ever."

"Even after you retire?"

"Even then. End of discussion."

"So, in other words, if we want to stay together, it's always got to be a secret."

"Looks that way."

"How could we ever make any kind of life together? You'd be scared all the time I'd say or do something that would expose you," I said. "You're scared now."

"There's no reason anyone would have to know."

"I disagree," I said. "Do you see us sharing a home at some point?" He nodded.

"How will you explain it to the neighbors? Or your dad and sister?"

"I don't know, damn it. We'll cross that bridge when, or if, we come to it."

Could I live with that? It's always been hard for me to hide my enthusiasm. Our vow of silence now was torturous for me. I knew I could never keep our relationship under wraps indefinitely. I didn't want to spend my future in such a protective posture. Early on, I was confident, or perhaps simple-minded enough to believe we could be together without sacrificing our honor, our integrity, or our service. Now I wondered if he'd catch me if I tumbled or step back and watch me fall.

"There's no point in doing anything if you don't aim high," he said. "Being out won't get you promoted to general. Or even colonel," he said.

"So why did I bother? Is that what you're trying to say? Maybe I don't want to be a general or a colonel."

"You don't have a thing to worry about," he said. "If you wanted to get past lieutenant colonel, you should have stayed in the closet yourself. Kept your mouth shut and married a woman instead of announcing from the rooftops that you're queer."

"I see how well that worked out for you."

"Check the shoulderboards, Harris."

I felt insulted. "You aren't wearing any. If you want to be General O'Neill twenty-four hours a day—"

He cut in, even angrier. "I *am* General O'Neill twenty-four hours a day. It's a full-time job, seven days a week, twelve months a year."

"So there's no room at all for you to be plain old Traveler?"

If I thought such a pronouncement would stop him short, make him rethink his intractable position, I was wrong. His face remained stone. "Maybe not," he said.

He took his pipe from his pocket and clamped it into his mouth. I wished he would stop for a minute and light it. The ritual of packing in the tobacco and lighting it always seemed to calm him, slow him down. But he kept up his purposeful stride.

If he wouldn't give an inch, why should I? "What I was trying to get at before you interrupted me is this. If you're so dead-set on following the letter of the military law all of a sudden, then we're finished. We don't have a choice."

He said nothing.

"No more nights or weekends together. Strictly professional from here on in," I said. "Do you want me? Or do you want the Air Force? You can't serve two masters equally without compromising each one."

His sullen response did not surprise me. I'd heard it too many times. "I'm a general. I can do whatever I damn well please," he said.

Such logic might be unassailable if you're a general. But I was a second lieutenant.

We're taught at an early age to respect the symbols of rank and to recognize our place in the hierarchy. For a new military recruit, the understanding of rank is paramount. From the minute he steps off the bus at basic training and an angry sergeant starts yelling at him to do what he's told and do it *now*, he learns quickly. Anyone who outranks him can give an order, and if it isn't illegal or immoral, he's obligated to obey, no questions asked. Every branch of the military depends on the structured system of rank—people who are smart enough to keep their mouths shut, or who would never think to open theirs in the first place.

Getting promoted depends on a variety of factors, including performance, politics, and luck. Exemplary achievement isn't as critical as one might think or hope. Of course, competition gets stiffer as one moves up. Some good men and women achieve rank commensurate with their exceptional talents and abilities. But in spite of the system, some detestable people manage to attain senior leadership positions too, having clawed their way to the top at the expense of other, more qualified candidates. Is rank really the measure of a human being? We're the same skin and bone under the costume. Some choose to wear rank on their sleeves. Others wear their hearts. I'm not sure it's possible to wear both, to walk the fine line straight down the middle.

I choose the heart. But I'm only a second lieutenant.

"Okay, so you're a general," I said. "But you haven't exactly been celibate these last thirty years. You told me once you aren't the only general in the 'club,' as you called it. So you're part of an elite group inside another elite group. But when you're sucking some other general's cock, are you worried about violating military policy? Do you think you pose some kind of threat to national security? How about when he's sucking yours?"

I'd never seen him look at me that way, as if all of hell burned inside him, and he would singe me with a glance.

I couldn't help myself. I had to laugh, though the situation was entirely without humor. "Since we're lovers, unless you consider us nothing more than fuck buddies, I believe I'm within my rights to ask you about my competition."

"It's none of your goddamned business!"

He was right. It wasn't. "But it's my business if you want *me* to suck your cock, Traveler. Do you?"

He took two steps ahead and stopped, his back to me. He muttered under his breath.

"Did you say something?"

He repeated himself, louder. "Damn right I do!"

By this time, I was surprised we were still on speaking terms, but I continued to pile fuel upon his rage. I moved to face him, but he refused to look in my eyes. "In spite of any Air Force regulation. In spite of the Uniform Code of Military Justice," I said. "Yes?"

His strangled "yes" was the cry of a tortured man. I had to slit him, bleed him of his infernal indifference, even if I tore my own heart in two. He had to know himself before he could know me. Before he could know and understand and accept us.

I wondered if what we had could stand a tempering in fire. Perhaps it was foolish to think we could be sure of anything as we surveyed this new territory. Perhaps we could do nothing but stake our claim, a little piece of ground for ourselves, and then work to fortify and protect it with measures yet to be determined.

"I love you, Traveler, or General O'Neill or whatever the hell you want me to call you now. If you feel the same way, too, maybe one of these days, you'll tell me. We can't change the rules. But if we want any future together, we have to figure out a way to live with those rules, even if it means bending them so we can fit. I think we can. You remind people that you're a general a hundred times a day, and you always get what you want. But there's a time coming when you won't be able to hide behind that excuse anymore. Drunken frat boys will call you a faggot, and you won't be able to do a damn thing about it, unless you want to fight every single one of them. But in spite of them, in spite of this whole world, I still believe it's possible. Do you? Do you even want to believe it?"

A beaten man faced me, his eyes reflecting a life of sorrowful surprise. I realized then that even if he could have admitted he loved me too, his confession would be worthless under the duress required to extract it from him.

Still. "Traveler?"

We came to an intersection. As if propelled by his own impatience, he stepped into the street, not even looking both ways for traffic, and crossed against the light. A car screeched to a halt. The driver laid on the horn and angrily flipped him off, but he ignored it and kept walking. I stopped at the corner. I had to capture and hold his attention somehow. "Seamus!"

I yelled it, angry, authoritative, a warning, and everyone within a block turned to look at us. We froze, a still life of a small but defining moment in a landscape for two figures. I'd never used his first name to his face, as if it had been some sacred oath. His nickname might be a suitable substitute on most occasions, but desperate times demanded desperate measures. The sound of his name stopped him cold. He wheeled around and glared at me.

"Now that I have your attention, Seamus," I hollered across the street, "I'll ask you again. Do you believe it's possible?"

He hurled his "*yes!*" at me with such violence that his reply didn't register for a second. When it did, I felt overwhelmed. My eyes spilled over, and I had to turn away from him. I would not let him see me cry. A moment later, he'd covered the distance from his side of the street to mine and wrapped his arms around me protectively. His mustache brushed my ear. "I'm sorry, Harris," he whispered. "I'm not angry with you. Everything's just happening so fast. I want the same things as you. I really do."

Desperate times. He gripped me more tightly. "Say you believe me," he said.

At least he'd said yes. For that, I was grateful. But still. "How can I?"

He sighed. "That's a fair question."

He apparently had no answer. We separated, and he turned me to face him.

"You have a real talent for tangling up my life, Harris Mitchell.

You're making me think. Hard. And I don't like it because I'm a goddamned coward."

He'd said the same thing to my mother, but I refused to recast my ideal. We continued our walk, lapsing into an oddly uncomfortable silence. I could think of nothing to fill it except to ask what had transpired between himself and the guy in the bar just before we left. The general only spat on the sidewalk, clearly disgusted.

"He said, 'Hey, Grandpa, what's your secret? Hypnotism? How else are you hanging on to that cute piece of ass?' I think that's what he called you." His voice hardened. "I'm new to this scene. Is that what you are?"

He might be my senior by twenty-plus years, but his petulance suited a surly teenager. My patience had worn thin after the circuitous, tortuous path we'd walked this night. Had he already forgotten his pledge to our future? This was not the sort of evidence that would sway my jury in his favor.

"Of course," I fired back. "A drunken, jealous queen will tell you the truth every time."

"Calm down," he said, although he was working his own soap into a lather again, too. "I saw how he was looking at you. If you wanted to go with him, I wouldn't have stopped you."

I was livid. Did he honestly, truly not know me at all?

"Traveler, if I wanted to leave the bar with him, there's nothing you *could* have done to stop me. I left with you because I wanted to. Why won't you believe it? Quit analyzing everything, and take my word for it. Are you trying to prove to yourself that you don't deserve my attention? Some kind of self-fulfilling prophecy? How stupid is that?"

He sighed. "I'm too old for this."

I pushed the general up against a store window so we could see ourselves reflected, side by side, in the glass. He dropped his head as if he were afraid of what he'd find staring back at him, but I put my fingers under his chin and raised it.

"No," I said. "Traveler, look at us. Together. Side by side. Quit trying to be a superhero. You're no use to me unless you're life-size. That skinny old mustached guy in the window is everything I want, all in one place, and I shouldn't have to apologize every time I tell him so. If he's too stubborn to believe what I'm saying, that's his problem." I addressed the summary of my complaint to his face, not his reflection.

"I'm tired of having to repeat myself! You cross-examine me as if you think I'm lying to you. If your word is your bond, why won't you give me that same courtesy?"

He scowled, cross. I was crosser, however.

"Traveler, I have nothing else to offer. If it's not enough for you, then I'll find someone else."

He shot back. "I guess you can pick up a skinny old mustached guy like me anywhere."

I'd begun to suspect he would never learn, and I was ready to scream, curse, throw china plates at his head. "You bet. A dime a dozen. On every corner of every street in every town, so why should you kid yourself there's anything special about you?" But he continued staring at the pair of us in the window as if we were strangers, and I finally backed away, discouraged. "You really are a goddamned fool," I said. "At least we can agree on that."

Unexpectedly, he laughed, sincere and hearty.

"I'm not kidding, Traveler. Don't you dare make this into a joke, you sorry son of a bitch." Like a pressure cooker on a hot stove, I hissed at his reflection, as if it might somehow be more reasonable than the human version. "Understand this, you selfish prick. Falling in love wasn't my idea. Remember? You started it back in January when you stood in front of my desk and asked me to come and work for you. And now it's too late to change my mind. I'm not playing hard to get. All you have to do is ask."

He faced me again, his mustache galloping and his eyes bright and moist. As I continued sputtering at him, he quietly but firmly placed a hand over my mouth. "Whoa, Cowboy," he said, gentle. I'm sure he hadn't expected such vehemence. "Quiet down," he said. "Quiet down, now." He squeezed my shoulder. "I'm asking," he said. "You hear?"

"I hear. And I'm accepting."

He nodded. "Let's go. We've still got some ground to cover."

And not just to reach the hotel, still a half mile or more away. "Have we resolved anything?" I said, utterly downcast.

"I'm yours if you want me," he said. "If that's anything."

"It is," I said. "The same goes for me."

We started walking, closer together, and a block later, he draped his arm around my shoulder and pulled me to him until self-consciousness won out. To cover his awkwardness, he stopped under a streetlamp and filled and lit his pipe, relieved.

"Traveler? What did you tell the guy back there, after he asked about your impressive hypnotic powers?"

He chuckled. "I told him to go fuck himself, since it was obvious no one else was interested."

That was more like it. We continued our walk to our hotel as he puffed contentedly, and the silence was peaceful and comfortable again. When we got to the entrance, I waited with him as he took a final drag from the pipe and knocked the ashes into the gutter. The clock in the lobby chimed eleven as we passed.

We said little to each other once we arrived at the room. I felt suddenly shy, as if we'd never been alone together before, and he seemed to feel the same. We busied ourselves with packing, though we would have plenty of time to take care of such things in the morning. Our rescheduled flight didn't take off until nearly three in the afternoon.

The romance that had begun our stay in this room with such possibility and promise, however, had evaporated. I cursed inwardly for thinking a visit to the bar would be a worthwhile field trip. The walk home and my off-the-cuff rant hadn't fully cleared the air, but I could do little to change the outcome.

Sometimes I am surprised at what and how and where I continue to learn. The general mentored me all the time, whether he knew it or not. I learned simply by watching how he reacted in public and in private. When a man trains himself his entire adult life to be discreet about a part of himself he secretly believes is shameful, would it not take the same lifetime to unlearn it, not merely to whitewash the stain but bleach it out entirely? The general had a long way to go. I wondered if he truly wanted to get there, if I—we—were enough incentive for him to set out on the journey. We desperately needed to hash out these things together. I got nowhere with them in my head.

I had time to brood, as he chose to shower alone. I had raised the issues, but no actual discussion had ensued, only agreement that such talk was needed. No appointment had been set. When he finished in the bathroom, I took my turn and took my time and was not surprised when I emerged to find him already under the covers of the bed we hadn't used earlier, the clean sheets drawn to his neck as he pretended sleep. After weighing the options, I climbed into the empty bed and turned off the lamp.

After a couple of hours, I was awakened from fitful sleep by a lanky, naked figure climbing into bed with me, muttering under his breath about being a goddamned old fool until I gave him something else to do with his mouth. He'd come over to my side, defecting from the fort of his own construction on his own high ground. What compromise was hammered out and what it cost by way of concession I could hardly guess, but he seemed to have made his choice, too.

We would have to solve our equation, and the answer would have to include him and me inside the same parentheses. If he needed more time, I would give him time. If he would not be rushed, I would not insist on speed, but I would demand progress. On that unresolved chord, I drifted into sleep, folded against him, feeling warm, safe, absurdly confident.

❖

Optimism is easy in the morning. Daylight is a strong persuader, and yesterday seems farther away and less troublesome from a distance. I was awakened by the general's cheerful whistling from the bathroom. The tune sounded vaguely familiar, and I lay in bed for a minute trying to place it, because the catchy, simplistic melody seemed so foreign coming from him. He repeated it several times before the words came back to me: Be my loverboy, be my lover. From the bar last night.

Before I arose, I could smell the coffee brewing. He had already poured a cup for me, still steaming, the cream already added. He continued to whistle the fragment of song, and I wondered if he could place it himself. When I poked my head around the door and said good morning, he reached out and pulled me into his embrace as if he'd been expecting me.

As we stood skin to skin, he rubbed his bristled face against my neck. I realized how much I loved this particularly masculine display of his affection. But still, I had a part to play in the game, too, and I pushed him away in simulated protest.

"You'll wear me down to nothing with that sandpaper of yours, Traveler," I said.

He laughed again. "I'd better scrape it off, then." As I watched, he filled the sink with warm water, applying a generous mound of mentholated foam to his face and spreading it around. He raised his chin and eyed himself in the mirror, razor poised. Then he stopped and fixed his gaze to me. "Being a tourist again?"

"I like the view. You should sell postcards."

He raised his eyebrows. "There you go again."

"It's sad. So many unlucky people will never get to observe your splendid naked self."

He gave me a long look. "You mean that, don't you?"

"Have you already forgotten what I told you last night?" I said.

"I have not," he said. "As you rightfully pointed out to me, your word is your bond, and henceforth, I will respect your opinions even if I might privately disagree with them."

"Thank you. So, I won't have to tell you again?"

"Well," he said, "don't be hasty. You might remind me now and then for old time's sake. I promise I won't argue the point."

Ah, vanity. "I don't mind accommodating the sexiest man I've ever known, et cetera, et cetera," I said.

He wrapped his arms around me and rubbed his bristled chin into my neck once again with full vigor, transferring most of his Barbasol to me in the process. It was my turn to laugh, and he tossed me a towel after he finally pulled away. He smeared lather over his chin again and applied the razor.

Who does not like to watch a man shave? It's an art learned by trial and error. For a man with a heavy beard like his, it was not to be hurried. My watching amused him, but after one careful scrape, leaving a cleared inch-and-a-quarter wide patch like a snow shovel against a winter's driveway, he set down the razor.

"What?" I said. He arched an eyebrow. "Give me a break, Traveler. I hardly ever get the chance to watch you shave." He sighed and picked up the razor again, but his naked belly was too close, and I never could resist it. I stepped closer, reached and made contact. He stood patiently as I raked through his deep shag until my enthusiasm got the better of me, and he finally yelped. "Damn it, Lawnmower! That stuff is still attached."

"Sorry," I said.

"Are not," he growled. "If you insist on staying, you'll have to behave yourself. And keep your hands off me."

"Sir. Yes, sir."

He sighed again. "That's two. Get *away* from me."

But I couldn't let go of mischief just yet. I squirted a generous mound of shaving cream into my hand and, without warning or permission, pressed it against his chest and began spreading it around, slowly. He cocked his head and scowled.

"You're not getting near my belly with a razor," he said.

"Shh," I said. "You know I'd never do that. I just wanted to illustrate that shaving cream has other uses." I massaged the cool, luxurious foam into his chest, and he discovered he liked the sensation. He pressed himself against my hands as they slid across the terrain, and I pressed back.

"I'll have to shower again," he said.

"Guess you will," I said. In the meantime, though, he gamely continued shaving, carefully navigating the blade across his face, rinsing the razor in the sink, repeating. I worked my way down his front, lathering the rug. I paused to add yet another dollop of cream from the can and shifted my attention farther down. Only when my languid massage aroused him to the point that he sliced his cheek with the razor did he lose patience. He winced and sighed, beaten. As the blood trickled down the white foam, he ordered me out of his sight. "You're trying to kill me. Now, *git!*"

Reluctantly, I got.

A couple of minutes later, I heard the water drain from the sink. I heard him turn on the shower and pull back the curtain and step inside, and a minute after that, I heard his voice, impatient over the rush and steam of the water. "What the hell are you waiting for, Burma Shave? An engraved invitation?"

I am embarrassed to admit we exhausted his entire can of shaving cream and wasted many gallons of water in the shower afterward. But what great fun we had.

He would wear evidence of the razor-edge cut for nearly a week, which only made him look more like a pirate. He needed no cutlass or eye patch, and his treasure chest was mine for the looting.

CHAPTER TWENTY-THREE

The days blurred for me after the general and I returned from Ohio and threw ourselves back into work. The general had a NAF to run; I had a general to look after. At the office, we established a rhythm. I grew more efficient until I could frequently anticipate what he wanted even before he asked for it, and more than once, he'd simply shake his head and ask for the millionth time what he'd done to deserve me.

I wanted to give him a million more reasons to ask.

Of course, we had appearances to keep up. The general still howled at me like a pack of coyotes and kept me jumping. His acting could have netted him an Academy Award. Linda often mentioned privately she thought the general was too hard on me. To my surprise, several members of the NAF staff echoed her concern and even thanked me for ensuring that the general remained fully mission-capable in spite of the maintenance required. They continued to worry I would be replaced any day, as my predecessors had been.

I played along.

The time we had to ourselves was burnished gold. An afternoon at the county historical museum. A night at the carnival when it came to town, riding the Tilt-a-Whirl and sharing cotton candy, my marksmanship skills winning him a stuffed bear of his own at the rifle shoot on the midway. Falling asleep on my living-room couch with his head in my lap watching an antique Gary Cooper western on television. Browsing secondhand record stores for rare jazz albums. Playing Scrabble until four in the morning. A disastrous attempt to replicate his mother's buttermilk doughnut recipe. My surprisingly successful efforts, under his instruction, to learn the foxtrot and the cha-cha, and his promise to teach me every dance he knew.

I lived for such times. But we were no closer to hammering out a solution to our predicament. I kept pushing it to the back of my mind. A question unasked can never be answered "no."

❖

The general's flight had arrived a few minutes early. He'd returned from yet another conference, one I couldn't attend because of various other duties. I had dropped him off at the airport on his way out and had come to fetch him upon his return, though the hour was late and he could just as easily have gotten a taxi.

Impatient, he waited near the baggage claim, in his blues, just the shirt and tie, no jacket against the November chill. His suitcase and carry-on bag rested at his feet, the stem of his unlit pipe secure in his teeth and his fingers wrapped around the belly of my bear. From the admiring glances of passersby, I knew he cut quite a figure. Just as I knew he didn't care what people might have thought about the bear.

When he caught sight of me, he grinned, like sun cracking open the purple sky at morning. I wasn't in uniform, as we were after hours, so I greeted him with a masculine, businesslike hug. I felt his surprise, but I also felt him snake and spark when we touched.

"How was the conference, Traveler?"

"Useless," he said. "Great God, I missed having coffee with you in the morning. This thing"—and he shook the bear at me—"isn't worth a damn anymore. I can't even get a good night's sleep without you."

On the way home in the car, I kept my right hand on the car's gearshift and he kept his left hand clasped on top of mine. I could tell he wanted to talk, and I kept quiet as he selected his plan of attack and chose his words.

"I had my first argument about you," he said finally.

This surprised me. "You did? With whom?"

"Friend of mine. A casual friend. Maybe not even that. A fellow officer. You don't know him," he said. "When we happened to be TDY together, we got in the habit of hooking up for a little...uh...discreet extracurricular activity, if you know what I mean."

I did, and immediately a pang of jealousy shot through me. I kept my voice as calm as I could manage. "Do you see him often?" I certainly wanted to know how many times in the past they'd hooked up for a little of that discreet activity.

"A couple of times a year at conferences and so on," he said.

"Another general?"

He nodded. "A two-star. I passed on his invite this time, and he had to know why. Of course, I didn't go into specifics. He assumed you're another officer and junior to me. I wouldn't give him any more details, but he was mighty curious. He also said you'd never know if I picked up a little action on the side."

"Well, he's right about that," I said. Anger crept inside my voice. "I wouldn't find out unless you told me. Or unless I caught you."

"Simmer down, Boilerplate. You won't," he said. "I told him no, and that's that. He was pretty steamed."

"Could he cause you any trouble?" I said.

"I doubt it. He'd be in a worse fix because he's married for the second or third time with a couple of kids still at home, besides being senior to me."

"How long have you known him?"

"Eight, ten years. But we didn't...get involved until after my divorce."

I bit back the jealousy as best I could, but I wanted to know everything about my presumed rival. What did the general find attractive about him? Was he handsome? Slender or stout? Furry or smooth? Was he well-hung? Did he render services to the general he'd been hesitant to ask of me? And who propositioned the other first?

Who were the other members in this little secret society, and what competition did they offer?

I took a deep breath. "So tell me about this general. What's his name?"

The general stepped cautiously into this minefield. "What difference does it make? I told you before—"

"Yes. I know. You told me you're not the only general in the 'club.' But that's an abstraction. Not a specific general at a specific conference asking you to share his bed. What kind of things did you like to do with him?"

I'd never asked such a question. His talents in the bedroom suggested more practice than he may have liked to admit, but he'd always been particularly close-mouthed about where he'd learned his lessons. I suspect it was not from library books or instructional videos.

He let go of my hand and shifted in his seat.

"Harris, look. You know I've had other partners. You've had other partners, too. I suspect you've got more experience than I do. But let's not compare notes. I don't want to know where you picked up that experience or who with," he said. "I guess I want to think that I'm the first one…well, that this is like the first time—"

I felt his frustration as he quit speaking. I felt the same, and maybe I'd asked about the other general just to get that assurance, that what Traveler and I had was different, as if we had both started from scratch.

"I can say you're the first, Traveler, because I've never known anyone like you. And you're the last, too, because you're all I want. And I'm not going to change my mind."

"Promise?" he said.

"I do," I said. "I'm sorry. I didn't think I was the jealous type."

"I'm mighty flattered you'd get that way over me, Shadowbox. I never thought I'd give you any cause. But I confess I felt the same way about your boyfriend."

"What boyfriend?"

"The one you mentioned in the *Times* article. Remember?"

Oh, that. "I didn't actually have a boyfriend. I just said that because I thought it would make good copy for the reporter."

"The day the story appeared in the paper, I drove over to the office to look for that picture on your desk."

"You didn't find one."

"But I continued to check regularly."

"You won't find a picture unless you let me put yours there."

His next question came so quickly that I knew he hadn't heard me. "Why did you join the Air Force?"

"Do you wish I hadn't?" I said.

His eyes narrowed. Had I offended him? I filled the awkward pause with the truth. "I had a serious crush on my trigonometry teacher during my senior year in high school. He was in the Air Force Reserve, and I thought it might give us something in common."

"Did it?"

"Only the fact that we were both in the Reserve. When I got back from basic training that summer after graduation, he wouldn't even meet me for coffee."

"That was a long way to go for damn little."

"Not really. Maybe the reason I enlisted was stupid, but it worked out," I said. "I broadened my horizons. I met people unlike any I'd ever known. I made some good friends. And I got to spend four years as a journeyman photographer." It was my turn for a question. "Why did you pick me to be your aide? You didn't even know me. I'd only ever seen you once, at the newcomer's briefing when you made your speech. I was impressed. But you didn't actually speak to me until our interview last January," I said. "You didn't know me at all."

He seemed reluctant to tell me until I coaxed a response from him. "All right," he said. "I didn't know you, but I remember clearly when I spotted you for the first time in that auditorium. I said to myself, 'There's an intelligent man. A thoughtful man. What's he doing here?' I liked what I saw. I kept an eye out for you. I was certain I'd run into you again somewhere. When Julia recommended you for the aide position, I made some inquiries. When I discovered it was you, I couldn't believe my luck. Satisfied?"

Perhaps he believed that generals weren't supposed to behave in such a manner, that they were exempt from such vulgar matters as physical attraction and passion by virtue of rank alone. When he hired me, I suspect he'd never anticipated we'd become lovers even if he might have wondered about the possibility. Love has no clearly defined shape, and it surely perplexes a man like the general who prefers his scales to balance.

I found myself curious about those who had preceded me in the aide position. Had he chosen them for the same reason, for the same attraction he felt to me? Had he ever expressed interest in being intimate with them? Sent signals, conscious or unconscious? Had any of them have accepted his advances? It was certainly possible. I also knew he wouldn't want to discuss it, which deterred me not at all.

"Traveler, you had five other aides in the two years before me. Were they…I mean, were you involved with any of them?"

"*Jesus Christ, of course not!*" he said with such vehemence that I slammed on the brakes by reflex and the tires squealed. Fortunately, no other vehicle was behind me. "Do you think I make a habit of seducing lieutenants? What kind of officer—what kind of *man*—do you take me for?" I could feel his anger as I eased the car forward again, and after a couple of blocks of his offended silence, I apologized, and we continued our drive in awkward silence until we reached the intersection in town where we had to make a choice.

"My place or yours, Traveler?" Ordinarily, such a question would have been rhetorical, since Friday night stretched before us and the weekend beyond, but we had taken some strange turns en route to this junction, and I would not second-guess him.

"Take me home, Steamboat."

His weary reply suggested I'd get nothing more from him this night but an abrupt thank-you for the ride to his door. He'd been so energized to see me at the airport that I felt let down as I steered the car toward the base. Maybe I should have kept my mouth shut. Perhaps I could blame the mystery general who'd expected Traveler to share his bed.

Life is messy. My willingness to embrace General O'Neill's being queer must shake his bolts loose every time he realizes it. I suspect he still had difficulty defining himself in those terms, but he'd have to make peace with it if we wanted to share a future.

I remained quiet during the several miles to the base gate and then to his house. I pulled the car into the driveway and helped him with his bags. I stood by, awaiting dismissal as he unlocked the door. To my surprise, he asked if I wanted a cup of coffee. The offer felt like an afterthought, but I was hungry for his company and hoping for a truce.

"It'll keep me up all night," I said, "if that's the idea."

He didn't even chuckle. But make coffee he did, following the same recipe we used at the office. Since he'd eaten no dinner, he made toast for himself as well, four slices, one at a time, prepared to his exacting standards. I enjoyed watching him at these rituals. Like smoking his pipe, they defined him as distinctively as a fingerprint. But this night, he was in the mood to grouse and quick to take injury. He asked why I watched so intently and why I seemed so amused.

"You get more pleasure from a toaster than anyone I know," I said.

"What's funny about that?"

I protested. I'd intended a compliment, but he grew defensive. "I've been alone for a long time," he said. "Long after you're gone, I'll still be making toast the way I want. It won't let me down."

His remark shocked me. I thought at first he might be kidding, but his humorless countenance proved otherwise.

"Have I let you down?" I said.

He merely shrugged.

"Have I, Traveler?" I said with some alarm. "How? And what makes you think I'm going anywhere?" I held my breath. His answer could be a knife that cut deep, but he offered nothing. Desperate, I forced a light tone. "Don't you remember you're stuck with me for the rest of your life?"

Apparently, this assurance provided no consolation. "What about the rest of *your* life?" he said.

"That's for you to say, Traveler."

"It's not that simple, Sagebrush."

"It is, too. You commit first. And then everything else comes together." That commitment was critical, I told him, and it had to be wholehearted, unreserved. A long time ago, he'd asked me to think about himself and me and us for a week and then call him on the phone and let him know my decision, I reminded him. That same night, I'd been certain of my answer. But, as he requested, I thought about it for a week before calling him.

"I didn't say yes to flatter you. I meant it. Besides," I said, still hoping a little humor might pull him from his black mood, "who wouldn't want to fall in love with a general?"

My attempt proved futile. Darkness only settled in a little more deeply. "Trust me," he said, flat. "The novelty will wear off the first time I can't get it up when you want it."

His observation shocked me, as much for its crudeness as for its unexpectedness. We'd never spoken of such things before, possibly because we hadn't yet encountered such a problem. If we did, we would work out an appropriate solution. This line of conversation made me impatient because it struck me as pointless. He could not truly believe the success of our relationship rested so heavily or so exclusively on sexual performance. The coffee, this late in the day, was making me bounce inside, and I didn't like that either.

"What about the novelty of being in love with a second lieutenant?" I'd worked myself into a fighting mood. "Some young guy you can brag about to the other generals in your exclusive club? Your rank is hardly an aphrodisiac, Traveler," I said. "I know you're a general. You remind me all the time, but my heart doesn't give a damn. I want *you*, not your insignia."

"When you're my age, I'll be seventy, if I'm not dead by then. And *you'll* be looking for a man who's thirty, if you even stick around that long." He'd spun into a proper rage himself, and it matched mine.

"And you know this how?" I said. "The Magic 8 Ball? Did you read it in your horoscope today? You told me you don't think with your cock, but you're wrong. I think you do, and it scares you, because what if it lets you down? You won't have anything. If you honestly believe there's nothing between us but sex, then we're already done, as far as I'm concerned."

"Quit being so dramatic," he said. "Don't tell me sex isn't important."

"Of course it is. But it's not the only thing. Don't you want more?" I said. "There's intimacy that has nothing to do with sex and everything to do with friendship. Fidelity. Communication. Trust. Honesty."

He rolled his eyes. "No wonder you've never met Mr. Right."

"I thought I had," I said. "Maybe you don't want the responsibility."

"How do you know you won't meet someone tomorrow who fits your specifications better than me?"

"*Why would you want to give me any reason to look?*"

That stopped him cold. I rarely thundered so. Perhaps I'd learned its occasional usefulness from him. "I thought our happily-ever-after had already started. Maybe I miscalculated."

I reminded him that my parents had been married for thirty-one years, but it hadn't necessarily been easy. They'd worked through some rough patches because they decided that their union was worthwhile. But they'd never grown so confident that they quit trying. I remembered a few times growing up when they'd been so angry at each other, I thought they might spontaneously combust. They didn't. They hung on and the storms blew past and left them a little stronger, a little more resilient than before. Perhaps some antagonism now and then obliges a long-term relationship.

"You can't give up, Traveler," I said. "If you ever get complacent, you set yourself up for failure. When I'm fifty, you better believe I'll still be around. And you better be sending me postcards if we have to be apart. When I'm seventy and you're ninety, you're still going to be complaining about my fingers exploring under your shirt because I'll never quit reaching up there to scratch. You like it too much."

"I do not," he said.

"If I kept it up long enough, you'd sign over your life insurance policy to me."

A ghost of a smile propped itself under his mustache.

"Our age difference isn't going away. It's a constant, but so is this: you can yell at me all day long, if that amuses you. I'll yell right back, but all night long you're going to be my blanket, wrapped around me in bed. I intend to wake up every morning with your sandpaper rubbing against the back of my neck because I know how much you like torturing me with it. And because you know I secretly love it, even though I'm a fool to say so."

That lifted the dark a little. I knew he wanted to apologize, but his stubborn pride wouldn't permit it yet. He poured us a second cup of coffee. I didn't want it, but I drank it anyway. Afterward, we washed the dishes together. I put on my jacket and picked up my keys, and he followed me to the front door. We stood there, ill at ease. This night's uncomfortable symphony was unfinished and needed resolution.

"That coffee's going to rattle your bones tonight, isn't it?" he said. I nodded. I knew better than to drink it this late.

"Mine, too," he said. It was an invitation, the best he could do at the moment, but it was sufficient. I set down my keys, and he wrapped his arms around me with near desperation. We both needed the shelter, and he was grateful when I welcomed him. When I reached inside his shirt, he growled, "You're wasting your time. I already named you the beneficiary on my life insurance."

"Keep it," I said as he muttered his contentment. "This is all I want."

We weren't in the mood to end up in bed. Perhaps the drift of our conversation made us a little self-conscious, but we needed to spend some time together nonetheless. At my insistence, he changed out of his uniform and we hit the road again, aimless and a little restless. We found ourselves at the mall. The only place still open was the multiplex, offering a lone midnight movie.

"What do you say?" I said.

He shrugged. "What's it about?"

"No clue. Does it matter?" I said.

"If you promise to distract me, I won't watch anyway."

His sense of humor had returned, a good sign. We bought a box of Junior Mints and headed upstairs to the balcony—occupied only by several other couples unlikely to watch the film either. Our potluck proved to be a horror movie. Such films rate the bottom of my list of useful time-fillers, but we would be alone in the dark for a couple of hours, and I was content. Once the lights went down, he put an arm around me.

"If you get scared," he whispered, "you can throw yourself at me."

"Only if I get scared?" I whispered back.

His mustache tickled my ear. "I'm easy. Throw yourself at me anytime you like."

CHAPTER TWENTY-FOUR

Novemember skidded into December.
My thirty-first birthday arrived, and the general baked a respectable chocolate cake at home and brought it into the office for me. Julia and Linda expressed pleasant astonishment at his culinary skills, and he modestly basked in their enthusiasm. I spent a quiet Thanksgiving at home with my parents, and the general went reluctantly to visit his sister in Virginia while his dad joined them from Tennessee. The general phoned me briefly every day just because he missed hearing me call him Traveler, he said.

Otherwise, we continued to spend evenings and weekends together whenever we could. I knew we hadn't won our battle. Instead, we'd declared a truce and steered clear of the danger, as if it might simply go away of its own accord if we vigilantly ignored it.

❖

The general's Christmas party on the first Friday of December, I discovered, was a tradition, this being his third in as many years. He took a day of leave to prepare for it, which surprised me until I saw the scope and detail of it.

Julia and I attended together. Our friendship had continued to hold fast, and we still met for Friday movie-and-dinner dates, though not as often. More than once, she voiced her suspicion that I'd found a boyfriend, and I'm sure my mysterious smile and vague replies reinforced her opinion. But I could not bring myself to tell her about the general and me, and she deferred to my privacy.

On the wintry night of the party, I picked her up at her place, which smelled of warm chocolate from a session of fudge-making. The previous year, she told me, she'd discovered the general's fondness for it, which she subsidized on occasion. At her insistence, I dressed up more than I would have otherwise, in my best suit and tie. I felt overdone, but she too wore a formal and lovely outfit, so we were well-matched. I also followed her advice and skipped dinner, as she warned me there would be an extravagant buffet. The street in front of his house was already parked with a dozen cars when we arrived.

When we knocked, the general answered the door himself. I was pleased to see how elegantly he was attired: a black wool suit, a gleaming white shirt, and a bright green tie with a single red ribbon pinned to it. I'm sure he wore it for its significance as a symbol of AIDS awareness, though I wondered how many others would recall that connection.

And great heavens, but he looked sexy. Effortlessly so. My insides melted. Again.

"Glad you could make it, Julia. You, too, Shotgun."

"Wouldn't have missed it for the world, sir," Julia said.

He shook my hand firmly and gave Julia a brief, businesslike pat on the back and peck on the cheek. "Mistletoe," he said when I raised my eyebrows. I looked, and sure enough, he had fastened a sprig of the berries to the ceiling light in the foyer.

"What?" he said when I rolled my eyes. "You want one, too?"

Julia giggled as the general seized me by the shoulders and gave me a noisy, exaggerated buss on the forehead.

"Satisfied?" he said.

"People will talk," I said.

He shook his head. "Not about me. I'm a general," he said. "Besides, you should know that sort of thing is legal now." He gave me a sly, secret smile.

Julia handed the general a pan of chocolate fudge, still warm, its surface adorned with red and green candy sprinkles. "I slaved for hours over a hot stove, just for you. How many other public affairs officers would do such a thing for their boss?"

He grinned. "I only need one." He sniffed appreciatively. "Mmm. Thank you, Julia. Shotgun, this is the best fudge on the planet, but you'll have to take my word for it, because I won't share a single piece."

He hung up our coats in the cavernous hall closet and ushered us inside. Julia headed for the kitchen with the fudge, but I stopped to take in the interior. As familiar as it was to me, on this night he had transformed it from its usual cool utility into a scene both seasonal and inviting. A little light and warmth and color can do magic for a room.

He'd built a robust, merry fire and decorated with solemn grace. Fragrant pine boughs and red ribbons crowded the mantelpiece, framed by a string of colored lights, blinking on and off. Tasteful holiday carols filtered from the Magnavox. His dining room table wore a festive tablecloth nearly hidden by heaping platters and bowls, neatly arranged, fragrant cheeses and gourmet crackers and thin-sliced breads, carved ham and salami, fresh fruit-and-vegetable plates, assorted dips, even chunks of fruitcake and neon-sugar-sprinkled holiday cookies.

He'd put out the china plates and cloth napkins and silverware, gleaming in the light from six candles set in a pine wreath at the center of the table. A crystal bowl on the sideboard contained sparkling red punch with a green ring of ice floating in it. Bottles of wine stood by stemmed glasses. He'd dimmed the lights, and everyone looked charming and attractive, himself most of all.

"It looks like a Christmas card in here," I said. "I never would have guessed you had such talents."

"There's a lot you don't know yet about your old Traveler," he said, low.

That caught me up short. So I was his. "Teach me," I whispered back.

"I was hoping you would ask."

Julia chose that moment to come back, and she caught the general with his mustache against my ear. "No secrets, you two," she said. "What conspiracy are you plotting now?"

"We're going to kidnap Santa Claus and hijack Christmas," I said. "You want to help? We need a glamorous assistant."

She laughed. We surveyed the perfect table. "Everything looks too beautiful to eat," she said.

"None of that," the general said. "Fill your plate. And try the sugar cookies—my mother's recipe. Excuse me while I encourage my guests to come to the table."

A familiar voice called my name. I turned to find Mark, and we shared a warm hug.

"I was hoping you'd be here, Harris," he said. "Let me introduce Lou."

An extraordinarily handsome man with curly hair, a precise black mustache, and a radiant, sinful smile extended his hand. He was slim, compact, dashing, sharply dressed, and in all ways appealing.

"Luis Antonio Dámaso de Alonso, to be exact," he said, extending his hand.

"What a beautiful name. It's like music," I said, returning the handshake. "I'm Harris Alfred Langdon Mitchell myself."

"That's rather magnificent, too. But Mark, here, insists on shortchanging me to a single syllable. I think he's just jealous because his name is so colorless by comparison."

"If you really want me to call you Luis Antonio Dámaso, I'll be happy to accommodate you. I'll just have to get up a half hour earlier in the morning," Mark said.

Lou put an arm around his shoulder and pulled him close. I suspected this was a game they played often. "My great-grandfather was a bullfighter in Juarez," he said. "I was named in his honor in the hope that I'd follow in his footsteps. But I decided to become a vegetarian instead." His laughter was contagious.

"Hi, Lou," Julia said. "Good to see you again."

"Hey, gorgeous. Likewise." They exchanged a hug as well. "What have you been up to? Keeping the NAF out of the papers?"

"No, I've been trying to get the NAF *into* the papers," she said. "We could use a couple of good-news stories to generate some positive publicity."

"You'd have no trouble featuring this little soiree on the society page," Lou said. "Did you bring your camera?"

"Somehow I don't think General O'Neill would be interested in appearing on the society page."

"He should think about it. He looks like he's stepped out of the pages of *Gentleman's Quarterly* tonight," Lou said. "And just look at this splendid table!"

"Dig in, by the way," I said. "General's orders." We each took a plate and helped ourselves. After a little small talk over the snacks, Julia excused herself.

"I'm going to make the rounds just to be polite," she said. "Shouldn't take me long."

"Have fun," I said. She rolled her eyes.

"So, Harris," Mark said. "How are you doing? We haven't sat down to chat for a while. Have things calmed down any?"

"The general is still impossible. It's his greatest talent."

"I know. But you seem to be coping pretty well. And let me thank you on behalf of the staff for keeping him in line."

"You're welcome. Just doing my job."

"It's always a blast to socialize with the boss when you're off duty, isn't it?" Mark said.

"Ordinarily, but I wouldn't have missed this for the world," I said. "Who knew the general could be such a congenial host? Or such a talented decorator?"

Lou nudged me and winked. "I think Seamus may be hiding a few other talents in his *closet*, too."

Mark laughed. "You think General O'Neill might be one of the family, Harris?"

"We've discussed the matter at length," Lou said, "and we are of the opinion that he is, without a doubt. Further evidence might include the red ribbon on his tie."

"I think it's just intended as a splash of color," I said. "Red and green for Christmas."

"Uh-huh," Lou said. "And he just randomly decided to pin it on exactly like the AIDS awareness ribbon and just in time for World AIDS Day. I think he's sending us a message in code."

"Suppose we go ask him," I said.

All three of us laughed. Fortunately, my remark ended that particular conversational thread, and we turned to other subjects. Lou asked about my job and I asked about his. I recalled that he ran the Chamber of Commerce and had never served in the military. He was outgoing and warmly familiar in a manner that put me at ease immediately. Had he not been with Mark and had I not already committed to a certain gent wearing a green tie with red accent elsewhere in the room, I would certainly have wanted to know him more intimately.

"How'd you two meet?"

"I was a real-estate agent in Tucson," Lou said. "Back in the late eighties."

"And I was newly stationed at Davis-Monthan Air Force Base as a captain, living in temporary housing. I wanted a place of my own," Mark said. "So I picked a real-estate agency out of the phone book and called for an appointment."

Lou took over. "When he came into the office, I took one good look at him, and that's all she wrote. When he asked to see some houses, I said—"

"'Let me show you mine, for starters.'" Mark chuckled.

"He moved in two weeks later," Lou said. "Luckily, a real-estate agent has portable skills, so when he was transferred to his next duty station in godforsaken backwoods Indiana, I pulled up stakes, too."

"And I haven't been able to shake him since," Mark said. Lou gave him a playful poke. "To my everlasting good fortune, I might add."

"Thank you. The worst time was his remote tour to South Korea back in 1997," Lou told me. "I couldn't go with him, obviously. It was the hardest two years of my life. We only got to see each other every six months, and I dropped half of my income on phone bills. It was a relief when he finally retired. I was tired of being the lover undercover."

"You put up with a hell of a lot for a hell of a long time, Lou," Mark said.

"I did. You can thank me again later tonight, Casanova. It's my turn to be on top, by the way."

I took thorough joy in watching them together. Outwardly, they seemed very different, and they certainly came from different backgrounds, but they had found common ground and built a home there. I envied their closeness, their ease with each other, the casual banter and inside jokes, their complete lack of self-consciousness. Even a stranger could tell that they were committed partners in love. That they were utterly comfortable being themselves in the general's home, in front of Mark's military and civilian coworkers, spoke more of hopefulness for the future than anything I could imagine. Maybe we truly were heading for a new world.

I wished the general could have been with us. I wanted him to see close up, two men who loved each other. I wanted him and me to be Mark and Lou, now and twenty-five years from now.

Mark interrupted my reverie. "So what's the scoop, Harris?"

"Huh? Oh, sorry. About what?"

"I just wondered if you were seeing anyone special these days," Mark said.

"Bet he's mooning over some hot stud right now," Lou said. "Eh, Harris?"

I wondered how much, if any, I could tell them about my relationship with the general. I was aching for someone to know. I missed having a friend to listen when I felt the need to praise or damn the man I loved. I might never be able to confide fully in Mark and Lou, but I couldn't resist nodding.

"Good for you," Mark said. "When can we meet him?"

I hesitated. "It's a little complicated right now."

"Ah," Mark said. "Military?"

"Mmm-hmm."

"And he hasn't come out, right?"

"Mmm-hmm."

Lou shook his head. "I don't get it. You guys don't have to stay in the closet anymore. Why would anybody want to?"

"Everyone's different," Mark said. "I'm sure if he's made the choice not to come out, there must be a good reason."

"I guess," I said. "I've asked him, but no luck."

"Maybe he'll see the light one of these days," Lou said.

"Maybe," I said. "He's pretty stubborn."

"We'd love to have you join us for dinner," Mark said. "Ask him if he'd be interested. It would be very low-key, just the four of us. You can certainly trust us to keep any confidence required."

"Thanks. I don't think he'll be interested, though."

Julia rejoined our group, and our lively conversation continued as we swapped stories and traded gossip. The general, for his part, never had ten minutes to himself. But since charm is a habit with him, even an art form, he played the role of the gracious host to the last degree. He moved effortlessly from one group of guests to another, putting them at ease with talk and easy laughter, urging them to eat and drink. I admired him for it, although I wondered why he put himself to the trouble. He'd certainly be unlikely to receive few, if any, return invitations. But such is a general's lot. Even if he might accept an invitation, who would be so bold as to ask? He had few close friends, another casualty of rank. At his level, friendship becomes almost political, and it shouldn't require that much work. His circle was mostly limited to other generals and senior-ranked civilians, and my experience indicated they weren't a very interesting lot.

I'd certainly been lucky to find Traveler, considering the odds against us. At the party, I felt the longing cut more sharply. I found myself envious even of his pleasantries toward others. I felt left out, realizing I knew nothing about a giant-sized portion of his life. I wondered if he and I would ever be able to host a holiday party together, greeting guests and making witty conversation, pouring burgundy and serving crackers and brie. I wanted it as much as I doubted it could ever be, though I tried hard to crowd those misgivings from my head.

Two hours slipped by, and I wished everyone were far away so that I could have the general to myself. He must have sensed my frustration, because he kept signaling, discreetly. Even across the room in the subdued light, his brown eyes shone brightly, and he'd wink, deliberate. I couldn't keep from grinning, though when Julia asked me why, I couldn't answer.

"You want to get going?" she said. She looked at her watch. "I've had enough, and we've certainly filled the square. We might earn ourselves some brownie points if we start the ball rolling. I'm sure the general doesn't want to entertain this dull crowd all night."

Most of the others didn't seem to be in any particular hurry, and who could blame them? The winter chill lurked beyond the door, and food and drink and conversation were plentiful inside. She had a point, however. The sooner I left, the sooner I could come back. When she excused herself to use the bathroom, I cornered the general in the kitchen alone for a moment.

"Julia wants to go," I said.

"Good," he said. And then, low, into my ear, he said, "Be back here at ten."

"I'll have to come up with some excuse," I said. "It's early yet, and Julia will probably want to go to the club or something."

"You're very resourceful," he said. "You'll figure something out."

I glanced at the kitchen wall clock. It read 8:45. "Will everyone be gone before ten?"

He grinned again. "Trust me. I'm a general, remember." How could I forget? He squeezed my shoulder and was still whispering in my ear when Julia came into the room. He straightened up, guilty, but she gave no sign anything was amiss.

"There you are," she said. "Still conspiring against the rest of us?"

"Always," I said.

"Well, General O'Neill, we're going to be the trendsetters and hit the road. Maybe the rest will get the same idea and leave you in peace."

He laughed. "Last one out gets to do the dishes," he said. "That'll be a good incentive."

"We'll bid you good night then, sir, with thanks for the finest Christmas party I've ever attended," I said.

"You're very welcome. Thanks again for the fudge, Julia."

"Anytime, sir."

The general fetched our coats, and we bundled up. We exchanged good-byes and holiday wishes with the rest of the party. Mark and Lou took their cue from us, and the general retrieved their coats as well.

"You're a lucky man, Mark," I told him as we embraced in the foyer.

"I'm the lucky one, amigo," Lou said. He pointed to the mistletoe. "Who's first?"

"I'll take the plunge," I said. I didn't expect him to kiss me full on the mouth, but he did, and did he ever. It was more than a little arousing, though I don't know which was more titillating—the kiss itself or the fact that the general was watching while Lou kissed me.

When we separated, I couldn't help grinning.

"You enjoyed that," Julia said.

"I did," I said. "Thoroughly. I'm ready to convert. Let me know when you're available, Lou, and I'm all yours."

"I'm tempted," Lou said, "but I'll have to see if I can jettison this guy first." He jerked his thumb at Mark.

"Step aside, homewrecker," Mark said to me. "Let's see if I can make him forget all about you." He and Lou showed everyone how it should be done with a lusty and lengthy exchange.

We applauded. To my shock, the general said, "Hey, what about me?"

"Keep your shirt on," Lou said. "I'm saving the best for last."

"Not while I'm around," Mark said. "It's too risky. You'll convert everyone in the place. I can't take you anywhere, Luis Antonio Dámaso."

Lou extended a hand to the general. "Good night, Seamus, and a merry holiday to you. Thanks for a wonderful party," he said. "Come for dinner after Christmas?"

"Of course," the general said. "Call me, and we'll set the date."

Mark and Lou walked off to their car, holding hands. I was sorry to see them go.

"Thanks for coming," the general said to Julia and me. "Y'all behave yourselves."

"Will you need me for anything tomorrow or Sunday, sir?" I asked.

He shook his head. "No, thanks, Bonfire. Relax. We've got a busy week coming up."

He waited at the door until we were safely in our car, and he waved a farewell as we drove off.

"Well," I said. "That was a fascinating party for any number of reasons. Mark told me about Lou, and I've been wanting to meet him. What a hot guy!"

"I agree," Julia said. "Lou is a prince, and he and Mark make a great couple. I'm glad General O'Neill feels comfortable around them. Not everybody does."

I didn't doubt it.

Julia and I weren't hungry, of course, but she suggested that we check out the DJ at the club. We looked in, but I didn't feel like dancing. I didn't want to perspire and get myself rumpled. I wanted to be presentable when I went back over to the general's. Anxiously watching the clock, I told her I wasn't really feeling too well, and I wanted to make it an early night.

She sighed. "You're no fun sometimes." We drove back to her place in silence. I knew she was puzzled and a little annoyed with my quick leave-taking. I'd certainly given her no indication that I'd felt ill or uncomfortable earlier.

I walked her to the door and we shared a dutiful kiss.

"I'm not even going to invite you in for a drink," she said. Abruptly, she switched gears. "You want to do anything this weekend? A movie or something? There's a Christmas concert at the community center that might be entertaining."

I didn't know. It would depend on the general's availability, though I could hardly tell her so. "I'll call you," I said.

With an admonishment to get a good night's sleep and take care of myself, she went inside. I forced myself to walk, not run, back to my car, and I even remembered to head off in the direction that would suggest I was leaving the base rather than returning to the general's.

I parked a few blocks away from his house and made my way on foot, as it would arouse less suspicion. The walk to the general's was perhaps a quarter of a mile, and the chill of the dark provided extra incentive for speed if I needed any.

I went around to the back door. Tonight would be an exception, as I virtually never stayed over at his house. Afternoon visits made more sense on Saturday or Sunday. No one would think twice about the general's aide stopping by his house on the weekend, as long as I left within a reasonable time. Whenever possible, we spent our time together at my apartment, located far enough away from the base that we remained anonymous.

The trade-off, of course, was that I missed him most at night, missed his angles and lines against me in bed. The deception was getting easier, and though we both knew we could never afford to become lazy, the risk was nothing compared to the sheer pleasure of nights together, equal parts sandstorm and calm sea. With his flint against my steel, we didn't need darkness to see sparks.

I knocked, just at ten o'clock. He came to the door immediately, held it open for me, and I stepped inside. He had loosened his tie and put on an old butcher's apron to wash the dishes from the party. He grinned and pressed his mustache to mine. When we separated, breathless, he still wore the same grin, colored with anticipation.

We didn't speak. I don't think either of us intended to be silent, it just worked out that way. After a couple of minutes, we both recognized that conversation was unnecessary, and then neither of us wanted to break the spell. The stereo played contemplative Gregorian chant for Christmas, ancient and beautiful, and we needed no other noise.

Wordlessly, I picked up the towel and began to dry the dishes as he washed. When we finished, he fixed two mugs of cocoa, and we retired to the living room. He was in his element, and I wanted to let him show off. He poked up the fire. Turned off the lamp so that only the colored Christmas lights blinked in neon semaphore. Sat next to me on the couch with a deep, comfortable sigh, as if he'd finally had a burden lifted from him. A second later, he stood up, sudden, as if he'd forgotten something, and I guess he had. He removed his tie and unbuttoned his shirt for me.

That I no longer had to ask him amused me. He took it as a matter of course that I would want to revisit his furry belly (could I homestead in the territory, I would do so). We were building habits. He settled down into a corner of the couch, and I curled up next to him like a languid cat. He growled, content.

I believe the world could have ended that night and we would have been happy.

As the fire cracked and popped, I fell asleep there, my face pillowed on his chest, his arm wrapped around me. He stayed awake, on guard. When I roused myself a couple hours later, he said, "Hey, Snowshoe. About time you woke up." His first words since I'd returned to his house.

"Mmm-hmm," I said. The fire had died, and the room grown chilly. We stood, and he stretched, carefully. He must have felt a little cramped, but he didn't say a word. He coaxed the fire back to life, added a couple of logs, turned over the record on the stereo, disappeared from the room for a minute and came back with an old wool blanket, thick and warm. He tossed it to me, and when he sat next to me again, I wrapped it around us and we sank into the couch again to watch the fire dance.

"You think you might stay awake for a while?" he said, his voice a warm buzz in my ear.

I considered. "Probably not." And, regretfully, I meant it.

"What am I? Just a sleeping bag?" he said, gruff.

"Sorry, Traveler," I murmured. He pulled me closer, and I don't remember much after that. The gray dawn found us there, the fire long dead, the colored lights still blinking on, off, on, off, nestled together under the blanket and stretched as well as two men can across a single couch.

I awoke first. His arms as usual were wrapped protectively around me, and I kept my eyes closed and listened to his satisfied breathing, feeling the rise and fall of his chest, measured, regular, comfortable. It only took him a few minutes to awaken himself. The first thing he saw when he opened his eyes was me, and the pleasure in his face made me smile.

"Hey, Bedspread," he said. "You kept me warm all night long." I tried to apologize for wasting the whole night sleeping, but he would have none of it. "You were here," he said. "That's enough. I was afraid you wouldn't come back. I thought maybe you'd run off with Lou."

"And leave you here to fend for yourself? How could I?"

"I admit I was jealous as hell. But you came back to me, and you're here now, and we have a whole weekend to spend together."

And spend it we did, every cent, and borrowed against the days to come.

CHAPTER TWENTY-FIVE

Christmas was a week and a half away. I had already told my parents I wouldn't be coming home, and they understood. The general never spent that particular holiday with his family, and we were trying to decide how to maximize our time together, as we would have a four-day weekend to ourselves. I was in favor of a new experience like a ski trip or a train ride to Chicago to check out some blues and jazz clubs. He was open to suggestions.

Julia came over to my apartment on Friday evening. We'd planned our regular movie-and-dinner, but she surprised me by saying she wanted to cook in. We rummaged in the refrigerator and pantry and put together a respectable meal of spaghetti, garlic toast, and salad. After we finished the dishes, Julia sat me down on the couch and parked herself next to me.

"Okay, Harris," she said, no-nonsense and getting right to her point. "Please tell me you and the general aren't personally involved. Please tell me you're smarter than that."

I couldn't say a word.

"Oh, Lord," Julia groaned.

"How did you know?"

"Oh, come on, Harris," she snapped. "You think I'm blind? All those secret signals between you two at the Christmas party got me thinking. I'll bet you went right back to his house after dumping me. Everyone else would have been gone by the time you got there, of course. I tried your phone half a dozen times over the weekend, and you never returned my calls. I got worried, so I came by on Sunday. You weren't here, of course. I don't even have to snoop around to find the evidence, because it's in plain sight."

She counted on her fingers what she'd discovered just this evening, thanks to her unexpected request to eat in: one of his flight suits in the laundry basket in the bathroom, the postcards on the fridge and the package of tobacco *in* the fridge, not to mention the faint scent of pipe smoke in the apartment, the opera records, the reading glasses on the coffee table. The most damning exhibit? "I don't even want to *know* how you got the general to pose for that picture in bed with the teddy bear."

"I can explain everything," I said, when she concluded her list and fixed me with her triumphant glare of disapproval. But I couldn't, actually, and she knew it.

"Well?"

I finally said, "Since July."

"What are you even *thinking?*" she said.

"I don't know." For a second, I wondered what proof of me might be found at the general's house. I knew I had left clues.

She shook her head and sighed. "You hid it pretty well if it took me this long to catch on. But I'm the public affairs officer. Remember? If this thing blows up, I have to deal with the fallout. It could be almost as bad as a plane crash in terms of the negative publicity. It'll make a big noise and a big mess and get you both into a world of trouble," she said. "The potential for catastrophe boggles the mind."

She reiterated what I'd already gone over in my head a hundred times. We'd both be humiliated, he'd retire in shame and probably be demoted in the bargain, and my officer career would be over before it had barely begun.

I knew. "What do you suggest?"

"Dump him," she said promptly.

I shook my head. "Can't."

"Then resign your commission. Immediately. And General O'Neill can retire immediately. And go have your fairy-tale ending far away from Sixth Air Force."

I was willing. Since the beginning, I'd known we would reach a crisis point that would require some action if we were truly sincere about a happily-ever-after for our story. Julia persisted. I wasn't sure if she was upset because of the impropriety of a lieutenant and a general being involved, particularly since both parties were male, or simply because such folly was happening on her watch, and she'd have to deal with the backlash if the story ever broke. I suspected it was the latter, complicated by the fact that we were such close friends.

"Look, Harris. You're a great catch," she said. "You're young and good-looking and fun and interesting, and you've got a great future ahead of you. Why throw yourself away on an old guy like General O'Neill?"

I protested. "He's a great catch, too."

"Whatever," she said, tart. "I don't imagine you have much competition." She shook her head and groaned. "Harris, what am I going to do with you? I can't say I'm surprised to find out that the general is gay, and it doesn't change my opinion of him one bit. I'm glad to hear he actually has a personal life, but what are you two even *thinking*? I have half a mind to ask him the same thing."

"Don't you dare!" I said. "Can't you just pretend you don't know?"

She shook her head. "That's impossible. I'm glad I figured it out. At least I can be prepared. But you've got to promise me you'll be extra careful, even if you think you're being as secretive as you can possibly be. Double your effort. I mean it. I don't want this to erupt. I don't think I could bear it. You mean too much to me. Both of you."

We embraced, and I whispered my thanks.

"Will you at least think about breaking it off?" she said.

"I can't."

"Why not?"

"It's too late."

She sighed again. "I know he's your type. How do you know it's not just a physical thing?"

"Well, there isn't a checklist in any Air Force regulation," I said.

"Ha ha," she said, flat. "Real funny."

How did I know? A very good question. I found myself trying to pin him down, relieved at the opportunity to say his name aloud to someone else who knew him, to brag about him a little, how suggestive his deep voice could be when he'd tell me a secret. How just one look into his chocolate-colored eyes could tell me he was all lit up from the inside.

How he hardly ever called me by name, but whatever he called me was exactly right. How particular he was about his coffee and toast. How he used just the proper amount of aftershave, so it didn't overpower. Just a hint, so that when he gave me a bear hug, I'd catch a whiff of it on my shirt afterward. The welcome mat on his belly. His pushbroom mustache and how he rubbed his beard against the back of my neck in the morning before shaving. About his getting lost in a fifty-year-old opera record, just humming along, in tears when the heroine died at the end. The tick of his pocket watch. The postcards he sent me whenever he left town alone. That he hated *Moby Dick*. How he knew the difference between the samba and the mambo just by listening to the beat. And could dance both. How he slept with my bear when we were apart, and more importantly, how we slept together, like the rhythm and surety of breathing. His pipe and peppermints, and his mouth tasting like the perfect blend of the two.

Any one of these details might sound insignificant by itself. Together, they seemed contradictory, improbable, absurd if not impossible. How could one explain the intangibility of the beloved?

"Harris?"

"He's not perfect," I said. "He's certainly got a temper, and a streak of mischief running through him that would get anyone else into trouble but not him, because he's a general. He's going to be a cantankerous old man if I don't keep him in line. And he's insecure about being over fifty because he's as vain as a prima donna, though he'll deny it to the death. His heart is always showing."

"Harris."

"How he's scared he's going to lose me, and how he hasn't figured out that it will never happen. How naïve he is about so many things. Practical things, like life outside the military. Like being gay. I want him to think he's the one taking care of me, but it's really the other way around, and I want it to stay that way. I never want him to know."

"Harris!"

"What?"

"Enough, already. You've convinced me," she said.

"About what?"

"Have you been listening to yourself? All I asked was a simple question, and you've been yakking for ten minutes. And not one word about how handsome he is. Saying you like a guy for his personality sounds like you're going on the defensive because he's fat or bald or ugly."

I admit that physical characteristics hadn't even crossed my mind when Julia asked her simple question. All these months later, I knew there was so much more to him than that. We shared an intellectual and maybe even some kind of spiritual bond that transcended the merely physical.

"I don't need to point out the obvious," I said.

Improbably, Julia giggled. "Remember when I told you last year that he was your type? Of course, I never realized you'd seduce him."

"Hey! I can't take credit for that," I said. "I didn't have any idea how to proceed, even if I wanted to. He made the first move."

"Probably because he's a general," she said. "They always know what to do."

"No doubt," I said. At least her sense of humor had returned, a good thing. She wrapped her arms around me in a comforting hug.

"If you've come this far, maybe you really *can* make it the rest of the way," she said. And neither of us could think of anything more to say.

❖

The sudden snowstorm just before the holidays caught everyone off guard. Monday was overcast and damp, with temperatures in the upper thirties. A slow, monotonous drizzle started in the afternoon, but then the temperature began dropping a couple of degrees at a time. By early afternoon, the thermometer read twenty-six degrees, and the rain had turned to snow.

The rain froze, icing the roads and making driving difficult. Before dark, the snow began falling with purpose. By next morning, we had nearly a foot, though the roads were passable after the attention of the plows on base and off. The general put the NAF on a two-hour delay. Most of the civilians called in and took the day off.

The chore of extracting the staff car from the snow and ice fell to me, of course, and I told the general I'd be outside for half the day, probably, digging it out of the drifts and scraping the windows clear in case we needed the transportation. Actually, it was even more work than I'd anticipated. The shoveling was the least of it, as I separated the vehicle from the banked snow and cleared a path so it could be backed out of the parking lot. The car had a glaze of ice on it nearly half an inch thick. I fired up the engine and turned on the defrosters full blast, but the going was slow nonetheless.

As I hammered away, impatient at the monotony of it, I came to life instantly when a snowball clipped me neatly on the back of my neck, a soft explosion of crystal cold. It didn't hurt, but it was unexpected. As soon as it hit, it started to melt and slide down my collar. I yelled "Son of a bitch!" and dropped the scraper. I scooped up a handful of snow myself and turned to face my assailant, who was the general, of course, laughing out loud.

My first missile landed wide of its target, but I took proper aim with my second, cocked my arm, pitched, and connected with his mustache, much to his surprise and mine as well.

Then came the war. We were all over the parking lot, ducking and weaving behind the cars and squealing like two sets of bad brakes. I knocked off his blue flight cover several times, but no snowball could remove my wool watch cap.

By the time we quit some twenty minutes later, we were both gasping for breath, gulping in the sharp, ice-blue air and howling so hard we couldn't stop. His mustache looked like a frosted shredded-wheat biscuit, and his flight suit looked as if he'd been caught under a waterfall. My combat-fatigue pants and field jacket were just as soggy but offered more protection. Still, both of us shivered.

"You got a couple of good shots in, Snowman," he said. "I'll grant you a truce, maybe, but no surrender."

"I didn't earn my Small Arms Expert Marksmanship ribbon for nothing, sir."

The car completed the job by itself. I hadn't turned off the defroster when our battle commenced, and in the meantime, the warmth of the engine running had melted most of the ice.

"That's good enough," the general said. "I'm not driving today if I can help it. Let's go inside and thaw out. I reckon that coffee will taste pretty good."

"My shorts are going to be wet all day," I said. I examined his wet flight suit. "I see you solved that little problem by not wearing any yourself."

He grinned, wicked. "Commando-style. Just for you."

I certainly didn't need that kind of distraction. "People will notice every time you bend over."

He grinned. "They won't. Who's going to be staring at a fifty-one-year-old man's ass? Apart from you, I mean."

He had me there. I felt damp and chilled for most of the day, in fact, but the general claimed the spare flight suit from the armoire in my office and thus passed the day warm and pleased with himself. And naked underneath, which would now cross my mind inconveniently every time I saw him in the olive-green "bag."

❖

Traveler, not the general, passed a quiet, lazy Christmas Eve and Christmas Day with me in my apartment. I prepared a traditional meal of turkey and dressing, potatoes and gravy, green bean casserole, cranberry sauce, and candied yams. We spent most of the day working a thousand-piece jigsaw puzzle on the living room floor, sipping hot cocoa and humming along to the old Christmas records I'd purchased at the Goodwill store. He presented me with a spring-wound pocket watch of my own, not quite as stately as his grandfather's but beautiful nonetheless, with its own unique tick. In return, I gave him a black cowboy hat, in part to satisfy my own curiosity, and he wore it as naturally as any gaucho.

We'd even attended midnight Mass together, at his suggestion. He would only admit that he enjoyed hearing traditional Yuletide carols sung by a choir, though I wonder if my mother had extracted a promise from him that we would go. Regardless, the service had been celebratory, full of joy-to-the-worldliness, candlelight, and the exotic mystery of incense. The general squirmed like any impatient five-year-old during the lengthy sermon. I firmly declined his whispered invitation to join him in the restroom at the back of the church so he could give me my Christmas present early.

But I confess I was tempted.

If we found ourselves under the same roof one day, I knew in some way I would always be the dad, even if he was the one wrapping himself around me in bed in the dark. I would be the practical one, paying bills on time and making sure we ate enough fruit and vegetables. Him? He'd be the one whispering in my ear at church that we should duck into the restroom for a service call before Communion. And I knew, sometimes, I would allow myself to be persuaded, like an indulgent parent humoring a favorite child.

When we promise a lifetime to another person, we tend to forget that time is made up of the passing days, one by one. He and I expressed our passion for each other when we could, as lusty and demanding and satisfying as it is supposed to be, but we got to know each other best filling in all the cracks of a day with snowball fights and Christmas lights and paper kites that linked one minute to the next.

CHAPTER TWENTY-SIX

The general would pin on that second star at the end of January. I hit my eighteen-month point as a second lieutenant a bit sooner, at the end of December, which meant I was eligible for promotion to first lieutenant a month before him. Briefly, we would be five ranks apart instead of six.

The promotion list had appeared on schedule late in the year. The general's name was on it, to no one's astonishment, but I liked seeing it in print just the same. The *Air Force Times* ran a teaser on the cover—"eight general officers selected for second star"—and put the list inside, with brief biographical sketches of the selectees.

The NAF, of course, wanted to make a big deal of the general's promotion. Lieutenant Colonel Cartwright, with the vice commander's approval, planned to borrow the base theater, engage the honor guard to post the colors and an Air Force band to play the National Anthem, and invite local civic leaders as well as the entire Sixth Air Force staff and all assigned personnel. It would be quite an occasion.

She put quite a lot of effort into the plan before presenting her grand scheme to the general. And he said *hell*, no. Good for him, though I was at the center of the storm. Finally, I worked quietly with Julia and the protocol office to build a proper ceremony on a much smaller scale.

A second star! It was a vote of confidence, and it meant three more years of service, his last three, after a lifetime of Air Force. He'd be looking at retirement at fifty-four, and I suspected he'd be ready. It would mean huge changes for him and for us. I knew he could hang on for three years. I was hopeful we could hang on as well, though I knew the likelihood of a permanent change-of-station before then for him as well as for me. He'd been at the NAF for more three years already. I didn't know what plans they had for him. He would probably be hauled up to the headquarters as deputy commander or something.

Neither of us mentioned the future, as if we could somehow stave it off by ignoring it.

The general decided to hold his promotion ceremony in the NAF headquarters conference room, which had plenty of seats for the staff, his family, and invited friends. He selected a Friday when the commanding general of our parent unit, Air Mobility Command, could fit the ceremony into his schedule. I coordinated with his staff to work out the preliminary logistics. General O'Neill's father and sister would attend, and I would meet them at last.

They would have the honor of pinning on star Number Two. I half hoped the general would let me, but such a thing would have been unthinkable. In fact, he apologized even before I could ask. "I'm sorry, Landslide. It can't be done. I can only buck so much protocol. I'm already on thin ice for downsizing the ceremony. You've been eligible for pinning on first lieutenant since the end of December. If you don't mind waiting a little longer, we can have your ceremony at the same time as mine. Your folks can come, and they can meet my dad and sister, too. What do you say?"

I consented. I wasn't about to make a big deal out of promotion to first lieutenant. Barring a murder conviction, every second lieutenant gets promoted. There are no boards to meet and no professional military education involved, just eighteen months of time-in-grade. I guess the Air Force wants us to concentrate on learning how to be officers before teaching us to lead troops and manage air assets. The *Air Force Times* would not be running a list of second lieutenants who were eligible for promotion.

Publicly, of course, the general commented he'd decided to promote me at the same ceremony to save time and expense. We'd miss but a single afternoon of work, and he'd have to spring for only one reception. Lieutenant Colonel Cartwright objected, but he overruled her with a raised eyebrow, and she kept quiet after that.

He also proclaimed rather loudly to all that the ceremony would also mark the end of my sentence. I'd hit the one-year point and would be paroled. As he'd pointed out to me before, aide-de-camp is not a career field, only a career-broadening tour.

"I won't be accused of hindering anyone's chance for promotion to captain," he announced to me several times when he had sufficient witnesses. "Not even yours."

Exhortations from the staff about extending my term met deaf ears. The general claimed he had already begun the search for his next victim. He felt he deserved a captain after all he'd put up with from me, particularly with that second star imminent.

"I'm ready for some fresh meat," he said. "Lieutenant Mitchell is already a couple of weeks past his sell-by date. You can smell him a mile off."

That usually generated a laugh, however desultory.

I discovered that the general's favorite recording of *Tosca*, released on LP in the late 1950s, had finally been released on compact disc, and I bought it for him as a promotion gift. I wrapped the set in deep blue tissue paper and pressed on two silver gummed stars, the kind your second-grade teacher used to dole out sparingly as a reward for excellence. I hid it in a dresser drawer and tried to forget about it.

Julia kept a sharp eye on us, looking for any sign that we might betray ourselves, any hint of dangerous complacency. Since Christmas, however, she didn't have much to observe. The general and I hadn't spent any significant time alone together, not even New Year's Eve. He was preoccupied, a world on his mind, and how much was us, I could not guess.

I grew frustrated, particularly as he grew more demanding and short-tempered in the days before the promotion ceremony. One afternoon, as he barked at me repeatedly, firing one complaint after another at me like bursts of M-16 fire, I could do nothing but stand in front of his desk and repeat, "Yes, sir. Yes, sir." After the sixth or seventh one, I'd had enough. I slipped in one of these, softly: "Yes, Traveler."

Mid-rant, he screeched to a halt. Swallowed a deep breath, took off his glasses, and looked at me. Softly, he said, "Thanks for the reminder, Old Scout. I needed that." The rest of the afternoon passed at a lower volume. At the end of the day, he insisted I stop by his house so he could properly apologize.

I hardly expected the penance he had in mind. After a long and necessary embrace upon my arrival, he fixed me a chocolate ice cream soda, the traditional way, with syrup and seltzer water, complete with whipped cream and cherry, in a tall glass with a straw and long spoon. Solemnly, I sat at the kitchen table to eat, and I enjoyed it so thoroughly that he made a second one for me and one for himself as well.

"Satisfied?" he said as I slurped the last of the chocolate syrup from the bottom of my glass.

I nodded. As far as I was concerned, he was forgiven.

"Good. Now get out of here. Don't you think I have better things to do than soda-jerking?"

"Actually, no," I said.

He grinned. "Maybe I should open a malt shop after I retire from the Air Force. You think your dad would approve?"

❖

My folks came to town for the big event, of course. My dad took a week's vacation, boarded the dogs with a neighbor, and they drove out. My apartment was a little cramped for the three of us but not too uncomfortable. I sacked out on the couch and gave them the bedroom. Fortunately, they were far removed and well away from the hysteria at the NAF as the pending ceremony drew closer. I took a couple days of leave so we could spend some time together. I felt I deserved a break, too.

I knew the general thought all the fuss was ludicrous. If they'd let him, he would simply have started wearing the second star on the appropriate day, but ceremony is part of a general's game, and the rules must be followed.

The general's dad, sister Kathleen, and brother-in-law David came to town a few days before the ceremony. Though the house had plenty of room, I knew the general wasn't terribly excited about having them underfoot. He liked his privacy. And, of course, I couldn't visit him as long as they were on hand.

In the months since my first dinner date with the general, I had learned little about his dad and sister. He rarely mentioned them. I assumed he would tell me when he was ready, or perhaps they would speak for themselves. I'd already established that the general and Kathleen were not particularly close, though they were but a few years apart in age. I concluded the general and his dad, Charlie O'Neill, weren't on the most intimate terms either.

I did discover that Mr. O'Neill was in his late seventies and quite active for his age. He was an avid golfer, a sport the general truly loathed. On the rare occasions when Mr. O'Neill visited, he brought his clubs and spent most of his time on the course. A retired broker, he'd never served in the military himself. I had no expectations we'd forge any kind of bond, but I was anxious to meet him nonetheless.

Maybe I was only looking for clues to the general's past, trying to discover what made him the man he'd become. He'd grown up in a time when being gay was a secret most people kept. I wonder if the general joined the Air Force at least in part to prove to himself and everyone that he could be so much like the "regular" boys that no one would ever question. How much, if any, did his family guess?

My parents were eager to see the general again, and he felt the same. As busy as he was, he took the entire afternoon on Thursday, the day before the ceremony, and invited my mom and dad to the base for a private tour of a C-5, which they'd never seen up close. I met them at the base's front gate and escorted them to our headquarters building, and the general took over from there. He'd called the maintenance operations center and instructed the crew to ready a static plane for him, with an external power cart so we'd have electricity for the aircraft systems. A few minutes later, in his staff car, we drove out to the flightline and he led us aboard to begin his show-and-tell.

A young staff sergeant had been dispatched to hook up the power cart. He was nervous, given the circumstances, but he managed his duties with speed and efficiency and then promptly ducked out of sight. We forgot all about him as the general settled effortlessly into the uncharacteristic role of tour guide. I'd never seen him in such guise before, but it suited him perfectly.

He's an expert, even if his affection for the C-5 Galaxy is nonexistent. He was still pining for the old C-141 Starlifter, which had been retired from the Air Force inventory some years back. He had threatened to retire rather than learn to fly a new airframe, according to Mark, but no one really believed it, particularly given the lure of a star on the shoulderboards. He was telling everyone "This old dog doesn't want to learn any new tricks" until he climbed on the plane that took him to Lackland Air Force Base for the C-5 pilot course. By a wide margin, he was the oldest student in his class.

I'd flown with the general often enough that the plane was familiar to me, but my mom and dad proved a captive audience. The general was a terrific salesman, and he didn't miss a single attribute of the Air Force's largest cargo hauler, the backbone of its transportation mission for over four decades. My parents, fascinated, asked dozens of questions and the general knew all the answers. The statistics were second nature to him. He put my parents in the pilot seats and showed them how they might fire up the engines, take off, and communicate by radio. They were impressed, and I was, too.

A couple of times in the past I'd heard him comment when he had an appreciative audience that his wife had left him because she couldn't stand his mistress. "My ex wanted to put the C-5 down as the correspondent in the divorce," he would say. It never failed to produce a laugh. He had no reason to say such a thing to my parents, but I could see how his love for flight might have made anyone jealous.

While my mother and father were scrutinizing the engineer's panel, with its million switches, dials, gauges, and monitors, the general brushed his mustache against my ear and whispered, "Do they still like me?"

I nodded. "You made the most inconvenient good impression on them at home, and you're only making matters worse now," I said.

"Good," he said, and I could hear his relief. He squeezed my shoulder. Our tour continued through the bunk rooms with their compact beds and into the rear upper deck, which seated seventy-plus passengers and two loadmasters. He showed off the gleaming galleys designed for food preparation, and even the latrines. He explained the compartments were fully pressurized in flight, just like a commercial jet plane.

He directed my parents downstairs to the lower deck, but as I moved to follow, he took hold of my shirttail. "Hey, you," he whispered. "Not so fast." He folded me into his arms. "Did I ever tell you how damned sexy you are?"

"I don't recall."

"Liar," he said. He pressed his mustache against mine, quickly and persuasively.

"Why you don't wise up and tell me to get the hell gone from your life?" he said when we separated.

"You couldn't stand it," I said.

"You've got that right," he said. "Thank you, Flightline. I mean that." Under his grin, my heart melted all over again. He fingered the nape of my neck, and who knows what he would have done next if we hadn't been interrupted by a stranger's voice?

"Um, excuse me, sir?"

The general let go of me as if I'd given him an electric shock, and color rose in his face. I froze, wishing I could disappear. The general turned toward the voice and found the maintenance sergeant peering in at us.

"Well?" the general said, sharp. "What is it?" When the sergeant didn't answer quickly enough to suit the general's satisfaction, he asked again with more impatience. "What do you *want*, damn it?"

The unfortunate sergeant flinched, no doubt wondering what he'd done wrong. His voice tremulous, he said, "I-I'm sorry, sir. I wanted to find out if you need anything else before I head back to the shop."

The general sighed, calmed himself down, and his professionalism returned. "No. You're dismissed," he said. "Thank you, Sergeant."

"You're welcome, sir. Thank you, sir." He disappeared in an instant, and I didn't blame him, but the general turned his attention back to me, his face a dark cloud. We were, I'm sure, both wondering how long the sergeant had been watching us. What had he seen?

Would he tell?

"Good Christ," the general whispered. "I thought he left a long time ago."

"Me, too."

"We've got to be more careful," he said at last. I neglected to point out that he'd initiated the contact, not me. My reminder would have served no purpose. His consternation was interrupted by my dad's voice from below.

"Son? Are you still up there?"

"Coming, Dad."

I hopped down the ladder and the general followed, and if our close call preoccupied him, he nonetheless assumed his tour-guide duties with grace and ease. The massive cargo compartment presented new wonders for my parents to explore. The general opened both ends of the aircraft to show off the upward-hinged nose and outward-opening "clamshell" doors in the rear, an impressive spectacle. As my parents expressed their amazement, the general roundly dismissed the claims made by his fighter-pilot buddies who claimed that they had the more glamorous job.

"We're providing the combat support anywhere in the world. If the troops need it, we can deliver it to them. We're carrying humanitarian aid. Blankets. Food. Water. Life itself!" He said he wasn't sure he could have flown a bomber or a fighter because of the possibility of endangering civilians. But cargo and passengers? "There's no damn better job in the whole Air Force," he said. "I've been flying cargo planes my entire career, and it's been a privilege."

I'd never known him to conduct a private tour for anyone else, and I was pleased that my mom and dad were in appropriate awe. We spent almost three hours on the airplane altogether, and by the time we were done, he seemed to have forgotten all about our close call with the sergeant. My parents' unhesitant goodwill was powerfully persuasive, and he responded in kind. Had he been auditioning for a part in our family, he couldn't have performed better.

❖

We had dinner at my apartment that night. My mother and the general cooked, listening to his new *Tosca* on a portable CD player in the kitchen while my dad and I traded sections of the newspaper in the living room. I didn't know what excuse the general had given his own family for being absent that night. I didn't care. We enjoyed ourselves thoroughly, and by the time he and I said good night at the front door—my parents having discreetly retired first to give us a few minutes of privacy—midnight had come and gone and we were into the early morning of the big day.

"Maybe one of these days, we'll be able to say good night and never have to say good-bye afterward," I said as he wrapped himself around me.

"It'll come. We're getting a little closer each day, Network." He cleared his throat. "We have to be a bit more careful at work, however."

"You can't blame me for that, Traveler. If you had kept your hands to yourself—"

He shut me up by affixing his mouth to mine. Twenty minutes later, we were still good-bye-ing, reluctant to let go of each other. "The two of us can fit on your couch," he said. "We've proved it before. And there are no staff sergeants around to interrupt us."

"I'm positive I could persuade you to stick around," I told him. "You'd better get out of here before I decide to prove it."

He laughed. "Are you sure? Bring it on, Double Dog. I dare you."

I slid my hand inside his shirt as he mumbled his approval. But as much as he would have enjoyed himself tonight, I knew he would be angry tomorrow for his weakness and the lack of sleep. I extracted my hand from his shirt, even as he protested. "Go," I said. "What would your family think if you didn't come home tonight?"

He sighed, full of disappointment, regret, longing. His departure didn't make sleep any easier for me, but day came soon enough.

CHAPTER TWENTY-SEVEN

The promotion ceremony demanded the "full horror" version of our blues, of course. In the general's office, before the ceremony, I helped him with the finishing touches, fixing his tie and giving him a quick brushing-down. He looked as sharp and sexy as ever in blue, with his silver stars, badges, and colorful ribbon rack. A few minutes before the ceremony was scheduled to begin, he closed his office door and faced me.

"Come here," he said. "There's something I want to show you."

I came over. "What is it?"

His answer surprised me. "How much you mean to me," he said. His mouth met mine but then he pushed me away. "Harris," he said. "There's one thing I've never said to you, and I'm kind of ashamed of myself."

He'd aroused my curiosity.

"Harris, we've been down some rough road these last couple of months. Gotten into trouble because we ignored some things I've been trying damn hard not to think about." He took a deep breath as I looked at him expectantly. "I think you know how I feel about you. I've tried to show you because I'm not so good about putting it into words, but here goes. I love you, Harris Mitchell."

It was the closest I had ever felt to the sensation of an erupting volcano.

He pressed ahead. "I know it sounds like some damn romance-novel cliché, but I reckon it's true. I love you, Harris. You hear?"

Like music, I heard. How long had I been waiting for him say it? A grin spread across his face as wide as the horizon line. He wrapped his arms around me, and we stood there together, the silence punctuated only by the resonant tick of his pocket watch like a heartbeat. Reluctantly we pulled apart, and he held me out at arms' length.

"In case you have any doubt, I love you, too, Traveler."

"I don't have any doubt," he said. He arched an eyebrow. "I just said I loved you, didn't I?"

"You did. Thank you for verifying my suspicions."

"I've never said that to a man before," he said. "I love you, Harris. I'm a goddamned fool, and you're entirely to blame."

"I accept full responsibility, and I won't apologize."

"I'm the one who should apologize for not telling you sooner. I've known it since you were late for your first day of work last January."

"So you *were* flirting with me during our interview."

"Like mad."

"I knew it."

He embraced me again. I was elated, floating. In the back of my mind, I wondered what we would do about it.

"Let's get this damn thing over with, all right?" he said.

The guests gathered in the conference room where we were holding the ceremony. Lieutenant Colonel Cartwright had assumed control of the pared-down event, and she corralled a couple of unfortunate airmen to help her ensure everything was just so. They bustled about as she snapped orders in a petulant whisper. I introduced my parents to Linda as the general's secretary and my co-conspirator in managing him. And I was finally able to introduce Julia.

"I feel as if we already know you," my mom said, embracing her as if she were some long-lost daughter. "We've heard so much about you. Harris even sent us your picture." Julia and my mother hit it off instantly without any encouragement from me. I was ordered to leave them alone so they could compare notes.

"About what?"

"Go!" my mother said. "You too, Bruce."

We went. Mark and Lou joined us in exile, offering me congratulatory hugs.

"Thanks for coming, guys. Great to see you again, Lou," I said.

"Couldn't miss your big day," Lou said. "This handsome gent must be your dad."

"Handsome Dad, meet my friend Lou Alonso. He runs the local chamber of commerce, and he's also the most insincere guy you'll ever meet."

My dad laughed.

"Thanks for blowing my cover, Harris," Lou said.

"I'll take the compliment anyway," my dad said. "I'm Bruce Mitchell." He offered his hand.

"And this is my friend Mark Sinclair, our budget officer," I said. "Mark and Lou have been partners for twenty-five years."

"Congratulations," my dad said. "That's a real milestone."

Lou grinned, big, and elbowed me in the ribs. "He didn't bat an eyelash," he said. "I knew I'd like your dad. Did I mention how handsome he is?"

"You did. You'll like my mom, too," I said. "That's her over there, talking to Julia and Linda. I'm sure my ears should be burning."

"You think?" my dad said.

General O'Neill interrupted us. "May I borrow your son for a minute, Bruce?"

"You're the boss," my dad said.

The general pulled me away and steered me toward his own dad, who seemed to eye me with a combination of suspicion and disdain. Perhaps he was just nearsighted.

"Lieutenant, meet my dad, Charlie O'Neill. Pop, this is Harris Mitchell, my aide. He's indispensible. I wouldn't accomplish a damn thing without him."

This encomium impressed the old man not in the least. He offered a limp handshake and murmured my last name, sizing me up and finding nothing to interest him. I returned the favor. He was several inches shorter than the general, gaunt and clean-shaven with a prominent nose and watery blue eyes, unsmiling and not at all handsome, although I could certainly see some family resemblance. I tried to engage him in conversation, but he met my attempts with mostly monosyllabic replies and no encouragement for me to continue.

So much for the general's father, I thought, though I immediately chided myself for making such a quick, harsh judgment. I wanted to like him for the general's sake. He stood by us, hopeful, but Mr. O'Neill clearly had nothing to say to me.

"Y'all can visit later on," the general said, optimistic. His dad checked his wristwatch. "Be patient, Pop. We'll start the ceremony in a couple minutes."

Next, I faced the sister, Kathleen, and brother-in-law, David, who had given the general four nephews and one niece he hardly knew and rarely saw. They ranged in age from mid-teens to early twenties and were not in attendance. None of them, he said, had expressed any interest in military service.

I assumed from Kathleen's appearance that she favored her mother rather than her father. She was attractive and well-dressed, but I wondered why she seemed so dissatisfied and why she wasn't smiling. She carried herself with studied elegance, but it seemed put on. Soft-spoken, her Southern accent much more prominent than the general's and slightly sugar-coated, she took her brother's rank very seriously, as if it somehow rubbed off on her and rendered her equally important.

My first impression was that I didn't like her very much either. David, at least, was much friendlier; like me, he'd put four years into the Reserve after high school, he told me, and he'd also grown bored with it and didn't reenlist after his first term. Having no other conversational topic at hand, I inquired about his military experience, but Kathleen stood close, as if to keep an eye on him, and she kept interrupting him with questions and comments that had nothing to do with our attempted discussion.

Mr. O'Neill joined us, and he and Kathleen edged me out, monopolizing the general's attention and ignoring me entirely, so I stepped out of the circle and returned to my own parents. I didn't see any hurry to introduce them to Mr. O'Neill or to Kathleen, though I did want them to meet at some point. I wondered what they would think of each other. Instead, I merely pointed them out across the room. I'd let the general handle the rest in his own good time.

Abruptly, the general left his family and headed my way again, pulling me away from my parents with an apologetic shrug. "So you've met my dad and sister," he said.

"Yes," I said. "Do you think they'll be more friendly after they know me a little better?"

He shook his head. "I doubt it. I wish you could have known my mother, though. She was beautiful inside and out. So warm and outgoing. You would have liked her. She would have liked you, too." He aroused my curiosity. He'd told me so little about her that I wondered what kind of relationship they had. I hoped they'd been close, that he'd found some understanding in her his father probably lacked. Next, the general parked me in front of his boss, the four-star from the command headquarters, whom I'd never met. He shook hands with me.

"So you're the one," he said after learning my name. "General O'Neill credits you with keeping his whole life in order. That's quite an accomplishment for a lieutenant."

"Thank you, sir."

"Good work. And congratulations on your promotion." That was all he had for me, and it was enough. He turned his attention to the general. "Seamus, when will you trim that damned renegade mustache and bring it within regulation? You look like a bandit."

I backed away with a polite "excuse me" and went back to my own side of the room. My dad was sharing a story with Colonel Blankenship, the vice commander. Linda and my mom were still comparing notes. I arrived just in time to hear Linda confide that I was the best aide the general ever had, and the longest-lasting, too. I extracted Julia, and we retreated to the corner with Mark and Lou, commiserating in low tones about the pomposity of these occasions and trading observations about the assembled crowd. Four o'clock finally caught up with us.

The ceremony itself wasn't very complicated. Everyone came to attention, and Colonel Blankenship narrated, reading the official promotion order. For the eighth time in his career, the general repeated the oath at the prompting of his boss.

"I, Seamus Edwards O'Neill, having been appointed a major general in the United States Air Force, do solemnly swear that I will support and defend the constitution of the United States against all enemies, foreign and domestic, that I will bear true faith and allegiance to the same, that I take this obligation freely, without any mental reservation or purpose of evasion, and that I will well and faithfully discharge the duties of the office upon which I am about to enter, so help me God."

His dad and sister pinned the new stars on the epaulets of his service coat. Camera flashes accompanied the action, as Julia and I and a base photographer documented the whole thing. The general was given an opportunity to speak afterward, and he did, briefly.

"I'd like to thank my family and friends and colleagues for attending," he said. "I'd like to thank all the folks in the Numbered Air Force for their support, especially the staff I work with every day. I learned a long time ago that the secret of good leadership is to surround yourself with experts. This promotion is a tribute to y'all's hard work." That earned an appreciative laugh. "Honestly, I couldn't have done it alone. I can't believe it myself. Who would've thought a skinny kid from east Tennessee could get this far?"

A skinny *gay* kid, no less…

And that was it. Some applause, a couple more photos, and we were invited for cake and champagne punch that packed a pretty lethal kick for an afternoon function. I wondered if Lieutenant Colonel Cartwright was overcompensating, or if her helpers had made the punch extra strong as a joke. The general gulped down a cupful as I watched and immediately ladled himself a second.

"Save some for the rest of us, sir," I said. He merely wagged his eyebrows my way before emptying the second cup as well.

After a suitable twenty minutes of socializing, the four-star excused himself. He had to catch a plane. He shook hands all around and departed. Then the general turned to me. "You ready for this, Roadmap?"

"Yes, sir."

He nodded and patted his pockets. Before he could ask, "Where the hell are my glasses?" I passed them to him. He grinned and stepped to the front of the room to make his announcement. "If I could have y'all's attention. We have an equally momentous occasion to celebrate this afternoon. In fact, it's nearly a month past due. Lieutenant Mitchell, front and center." I stepped into my place and came to attention. At the general's cue, the vice commander read the official order: By direction of the President, Second Lieutenant Harris Mitchell was hereby promoted to the rank of first lieutenant, effective as of 15 December.

"Raise your right hand," the general said.

I raised.

He read from a sheet that Linda had typed out for him. "Repeat after me. I, Harris Alfred Langdon Mitchell—" And he paused, pretending unfamiliarity with my full name. "That's a hell of a moniker for a lieutenant. Maybe we'll just call you 'Hal' to save time." He was already feeling his punch, I could tell. He looked around, expecting polite laughter, but when none came, he cleared his throat and continued with the oath. Mine was identical to his, and I declaimed it for the second time in my career.

"Congratulations, First Lieutenant Mitchell," he said. I saluted, sharp, and the general shook my hand. My parents stepped up and removed the gold bars from my blue coat and pinned the single silver ones in their place. More photos, during and after. My parents and me. The general, who removed his glasses, and me. The four of us. Julia and me.

"We're the same rank at last!" she whispered. "Oh, Harris! Now we can announce our engagement!" Everyone wondered why we were laughing so hard.

Charlie O'Neill and Kathleen watched impassively. I meant nothing to them, but I guess the general had let them know my participation was a nonnegotiable part of the afternoon's schedule, and they would have to endure it. I'm sure they wondered why a major general would tarnish his own promotion ceremony by sharing it with a first lieutenant.

Once it was over, most of the crowd disappeared. Mark and Lou bowed out as well, leaving the general and his family, Julia, my parents, and me. We quickly ran out of conversation. I was looking forward to concluding the festivities and getting away for the weekend, even though it would be a quiet one with my parents, but the general had other ideas.

"We need to celebrate this occasion properly," he said, gulping another glass of punch. I knew he could hold his champagne well, but even he had a limit. I'd counted at least four, and no cake, and I knew his nuts and bolts were loosening a bit. "What about supper? My treat."

My parents liked the idea, so I felt obligated to agree as well. Julia begged off, pleading a previous engagement, but I knew she didn't like Kathleen or the general's dad any more than I did. Before we left the conference room, I collected the general's eyeglasses from the lectern, where he'd placed them after the ceremony. He'd probably want them later. I surveyed the room. Someone had dropped a piece of cake, and it had gotten ground into the carpet. The half-full punch bowl and used cups and plates would still be there on Monday morning unless someone tidied the room beforehand.

I'd come back and clean up the mess after dinner, I told myself.

CHAPTER TWENTY-EIGHT

We went to the officers' club, of course, as the general was guaranteed a pleasant dining experience as well as attentive service. He hadn't called ahead for a reservation, however, so we had a few minutes to stand in the lobby while the flustered maître d' rushed about to prepare a suitable table.

"Oh! Seamus!" my mother said. "I almost forgot. I've got some pictures for you." She took an envelope from her purse and handed it to the general.

"What's this?" he said.

"From your visit. We had an extra set of prints made for you and one for Harris."

Kathleen appeared to be scandalized. General O'Neill actually had consecrated our home with his presence? But though curiosity might be smothering her, she refused to ask for any details and pretended no interest in the pictures. The general's dad ignored us all. As quiet and detached as he was, we could almost have forgotten he was present.

As I looked over the general's shoulder, he shuffled through the dozen or so prints, and the whole of our three-day visit came back to me. There were several shots of my father and the general grinning insanely for the camera, holding a string of trout between them. There was the general in my father's checkered apron, grilling the fish in the backyard. The general sitting next to me on the couch and with his arm around my mom on the front porch swing. With Clement and Sixtus.

At the bottom of the stack was a shot of the general and me, taken by my mom or dad without our knowledge that Sunday, after we'd returned from church, when we'd left the house to wander in the backyard with the dogs. I remembered the likely moment. We'd been walking, holding hands, and when the general pulled me to him, I didn't resist. And, in fact, we'd stood there for some time, just tasting each other under the blinking sun, oblivious to the big world. We'd grown so accustomed to the dogs barking at us that we paid them no heed.

I never thought my folks might come looking for us, but clearly, they had and clearly, they'd found us. In the photo, the general and I are locked in an embrace, his mouth aligned with mine. And while my face is mostly hidden, his is unmistakable—the mustache, the haircut, the pipe in his hand. Seamus O'Neill kissing another man. Exhibit A, the photo finish, undeniable proof of sedition, and in uniform, no less. Proof of what he is. What I am.

How we are.

In some quarters, the snapshot might be the visual equivalent of a taunt, evidence that could be used against him in particular and me only if I chose to identify myself as the other party involved. Looking at such a photo put the general face-to-face with—what? The future? Destiny? Truth, caught by the harsh camera eye? Or perhaps nothing so dire, simply the reality of two men, mouth on mouth, enjoying.

My first thought as I stared at the print was relief that no one else could see it, and thankfulness it hadn't surfaced at the reception when others might have asked for a look. And though the general kept his composure, he stiffened, and the color drained from his face. He quickly buried it in the stack, wrapped the pictures in the envelope and slipped it into the inside pocket of his service coat.

"Bet you didn't know you were on *Candid Camera*, did you, Seamus?"

"Can't say I did, Jane."

My mother was so pleased that she paid no attention to his tight-lipped response. I knew she didn't include the one troublesome shot to be mean-spirited or funny. She'd proven herself more than willing to accept him into the family, regardless of her own preferences about whom I should love. I think she simply assumed the general would appreciate having such a photo of the pair of us. Under other circumstances, he might have, but not here, not tonight.

The general excused himself to go to the restroom. I wondered if he was seeking an escape hatch. Perhaps all the excitement had hit the general a little harder than he expected. Perhaps he was second-guessing his idea to throw all of us together for dinner. Perhaps it was the photograph, which I suspect pierced him to his core, and he sought the closest trench. Perhaps, he didn't trust my parents, believing they might choose this opportunity to out him in the presence of his family.

Perhaps he didn't trust himself. After all, he had told me he loved me, but second thoughts and doubt might lurk around his edges.

Perhaps he didn't trust me.

I was particularly concerned because we wouldn't have any time alone to defuse this potential bomb for at least a couple of days.

I wondered when the disapproval Kathleen wore on her face would catch up with her mouth. It did as soon as the general headed to the restroom. She fixed a dour gaze on my parents. "Really," she said. "You shouldn't call him Seamus, especially when he's in uniform."

"Why not?" my mother said, mystified. "It's his name, isn't it?"

"It's just not appropriate, given his position," Kathleen said. "You should call him General O'Neill. Or 'sir.'"

"Oh, come on, Kathleen," David said. "Relax. This is supposed to be a party." She glared at him and he shrugged.

"*You* call him Seamus," my dad pointed out.

"He's my brother. It's obviously different for the immediate family," she said, clearly injured. I wished she wouldn't presume that my parents were thick. She certainly spoke to them as if she thought they might not understand unless she enunciated carefully and spoke slowly, rather like an arrogant American trying to make a foreigner comprehend English.

"Seamus and Bruce are old fishing buddies," my mom said. "You can't get much closer than that." Kathleen appeared skeptical. "Ask Seamus—General O'Neill, I mean—ask him to show you the pictures when he comes back," my mom said. I tried to signal to her but she missed the hint. "We got some great shots. He's quite the trout fisherman."

My dad, aware of my distress, whispered into her ear. Her eyes got big. "Oops!" she said. "Never mind."

"I'm a little rusty on military customs and courtesy," my dad said to Kathleen. "But I'll try to remember." I doubted his sincerity, but his remark seemed to placate Kathleen. The general returned from the restroom, unaware of the controversy that had arisen during his absence.

My thoughts were interrupted by our waiter, a young man neatly dressed in a ruffled tuxedo shirt, red bow tie, and a manner perhaps a little too flamboyant for my comfort. I saw that Kathleen noticed as well. He offered abject apologies for the delay as he escorted us to a large round table in the corner of the dining room.

The general assigned our seats, putting me directly on his right, then my mom, my dad, Mr. O'Neill, David, and Kathleen on the general's left. He was perspiring a bit, his color up, and he took his service-dress coat off and hung it on the back of his chair. I smelled whiskey on his breath and assumed he had detoured by the bar for a quick one on his way to the restroom. I was perspiring, too, though for different reasons.

Once we were seated, our waiter fussed and flitted about, distributing menus, setting out warm bread and butter and a basket of crackers, filling water glasses, and reciting the day's specials, soups, and vegetables from memory. "Oh!" he said afterward. "I'm Jeffrey, by the way."

"We'll have a bottle of champagne first, Jeffrey," the general told him. "The good stuff."

"Yes, *sir*!" He hustled away.

I could see he had an eye for the general, and why not? Jeffrey had good taste. I only hoped the general wouldn't do or say anything to embarrass the young man. But it was Kathleen who stuck her foot in first.

"Really," she said. "I don't know why they hire people like that to work here."

"People like what?" my dad said.

"*You* know," Kathleen said.

"I don't," my dad said. "Really."

She dropped her voice to a stage whisper. "Homosexuals."

"How do you know he's people like that?" my dad said.

"Oh, please," Kathleen said, rolling her eyes and offering a limp-wristed wave.

"We all have to work somewhere," my dad said. David snickered. Kathleen glared at him, at my dad, everyone.

"But why would they hire them to work *here*?" She persisted. "Waiting on high-ranking officers and distinguished visitors and such."

"Maybe because most people don't care about their waiter's private life as long as the service is good?" my dad said. "Or maybe because they aren't prejudiced?"

"I am *not* prejudiced."

"And some of your best friends are gay," David volunteered with a grin.

"Shut up, David. I'm pretty sure I know some homosexuals."

"You might be surprised," my dad said.

The general cleared his throat and said, "That'll do, Bruce."

Jeffrey provided a welcome interruption, reappearing with a bottle of champagne on ice and seven stemmed glasses on a tray. He popped the cork and poured with a practiced flourish, offering a glass to each of us. "I'll be back to take your order in a few minutes," he said. "If there's anything at all I can do for you, sir, just give me the high sign." If he sought the general's approval, none was offered.

I felt a little sorry for Jeffrey as he backed away, and was immediately angry at my condescension. At least he was being himself, no less and no more. I could not say the same for either the general or myself at the moment.

Kathleen lifted her glass and said, "To *Major* General O'Neill."

My mother added, "And to *First* Lieutenant Mitchell." Kathleen didn't like that addendum, but we all touched glasses anyway and sipped. The general swallowed his and immediately poured himself a second, emptying the bottle.

Champagne had figured prominently in our coming together in the first place. I'm not sure the general would have let his guard down if it hadn't been for his impromptu dance recital at the retirement party and that bottle he'd received as a reward. Since there was no way tonight could end as satisfactorily as that night had, however, I wished the general would go easy. I didn't want him to let down too much guard here.

He caught my eye as he downed the second glass. Could he read my mind? I picked up no signal from him. We opened the menus. The general held his out at arm's length and frowned, clearly dissatisfied. Silently, I passed his eyeglasses to him, but if I expected him to make a joke about his nearsightedness as he customarily did, he disappointed me.

He pushed his chair back. "I'll have a word with the *sommelier* about a bottle of wine that might be suitable for our celebration," he said, excusing himself quickly. Great, I thought. More alcohol.

Kathleen wasn't ready to let go of the conversational topic she'd brought up moments before. "Now they let openly homosexual people serve in the military. They don't even have to keep it a secret."

"Yes," my mother said. "Isn't it wonderful? 'Don't Ask, Don't Tell' is finally on the scrap heap where it belongs. That's one campaign promise the President kept."

"And even the damned Republican majority in Congress couldn't stop him," my dad said, with evident satisfaction.

I didn't want to get into politics either, particularly since I suspected everyone at the table except for us counted themselves among the damned Republicans. Wasn't there some inconsequential or at least noncommittal subject we could discuss? And could we please steer the conversation in that direction?

The awkward pause was filled by Mr. O'Neill, of all people, who seized the moment to share his thoughts on the matter. "The Air Force made a big mistake when they started letting in the faggots," he said. "The Army, too. Whole military's going to hell in a handbasket. Mark my words."

He'd been so quiet all afternoon that everyone, astonished, turned to look at him. These were the most words he'd spoken since the reception, and so spectacularly inappropriate I couldn't believe he'd actually said them aloud. But if he knew he'd distinguished himself, he gave no sign. He reached for the basket of crackers and busied himself with the saltines. No one knew how to respond, and quiet settled upon us as we waited for the general to return.

"What are y'all discussing so intently?" he asked as he took his seat again, a curious remark, as we were all studiously silent.

But Kathleen still could not let go. "We were discussing whether or not avowed homosexuals should be permitted to serve in the military," she said.

The general coughed and cleared his throat.

David spoke up. "Charlie is not in favor of it. Neither is your sister. Bruce and Jane, however—" was as far as he got before Kathleen ordered him to shut up. He snickered but did as requested. Mr. O'Neill seemed oblivious to the storm he'd caused. He munched his crackers, unconcerned.

In the awkward gap that followed, I could see my mom was readying her own response. Had she gotten the chance to deliver it, Mr. O'Neill would have regretted ever bringing up the subject. But my dad broke in first.

"Were you in the service, O'Neill?" My dad, customarily polite, was not in the habit of referring to anyone by his last name alone, but I sensed his anger as well as the control required to keep it in check.

"No. Thank God," Mr. O'Neill muttered.

"*What?*" My mother was outraged. My dad placed a gentle hand on her arm and turned again to Mr. O'Neill.

"You're lucky. I was drafted just out of high school. I spent two years in Vietnam back in '69 and '70," my dad said. "Some of the guys in my platoon were gay. Everybody knew it and nobody gave a damn. With enemy fire coming in, you got enough to worry about, like surviving. You pray that your rifle won't jam, and you hope to hell your buddy has got your back. Trust me. The last thing on your mind is what he likes to do in bed."

I had never heard my dad share this observation. I was surprised and grateful he volunteered to do so now. Mr. O'Neill brushed cracker crumbs onto the floor and declined to make eye contact.

"The gay soldiers were scared to death just like the rest of us, and they bled and died like there was no difference at all. And that's enough about that. Seamus," he said, "would you pass the bread, please?"

The general handed over the basket. I think Kathleen was too taken aback to notice that my dad had ignored her stern request about using the general's first name. But she was irritated.

"Why should you care?" Kathleen asked my dad. "You're not a homosexual."

My mother, waiting for her chance, jumped into the fight. "We're not. But our son is gay, thank you very much."

Ten years ago, my mom would never have made such a confession. Early on, my parents would have been too shy, if not embarrassed, to admit their son was gay for fear that such a declaration would reflect poorly on them. But I encouraged them repeatedly to speak up and spread the good word. *Every* family has a son or daughter or parent or aunt or uncle or cousin who is gay. My persistence paid off. They overcame their reluctance and took the lessons to heart. They, too, were now out and proud, as I had taught and then insisted. But while I had become accustomed to coming out every day, I preferred to do it on my own terms.

Kathleen's mouth made a capital *O*, and her eyes widened. She stared at me as if I were a lab specimen or an alien. "You are?" she breathed. Perhaps she believed she'd never actually seen one up close.

"Is that a problem?" I said.

David stifled a giggle. I wondered if Kathleen would dress him down later. He certainly didn't appear to be on her side in many respects. Mr. O'Neill curled his lip and seemed to withdraw even farther into himself. I suspected I would have no more words with him this evening, and I was content with that.

Kathleen turned to the general. "Seamus! I can't believe you would have a—a—homosexual as your aide!"

"Why not?" David said. "Obviously he does."

"Did you know?" Kathleen asked the general.

"Of course not," the general fired back.

My mouth made a capital *O*. My mom, thankfully, chose to take it as a joke. "Seamus, you're such a kidder sometimes."

I waited for him to confirm or deny or at least make a witty remark. As long as the subject had been brought out into the open, why not acknowledge it? He did nothing but examine the champagne bottle, which was still empty. Kathleen didn't even notice. She was too busy climbing her pedestal. "*I* have *four* sons," she said, "and *not one* of them is a homosexual," she said, smugness dripping from her mouth.

My mother bristled. "How do you know?" she said. "Maybe they're just afraid to tell you, which wouldn't surprise me a bit."

"Believe me," Kathleen said. "I know."

"Well," David said. "We don't, actually. With four sons, it's certainly possible—statistically, I mean."

"David!" Kathleen said. "I can't believe you would even say such a thing!"

"It's always possible," he said. "They say it runs in families."

"We don't have anyone like that in our family," she said.

"Oh, yeah?" David said. "What about that one uncle of yours?" He turned to us. "Her mom's brother," he explained. The general had never shared this family lore with me. "Apparently, he wasn't even allowed in the house when Seamus and Kathleen were growing up."

I half expected my mother or dad to mention that someone else in Kathleen's family was most certainly gay, and there was a photo in a handy coat pocket that could provide corroborating evidence. I looked at the general, but his face was stone. He was confident I would never out him, that I would honor his decision to remain in the closet even though I did not agree with it or respect it. The choice to come out would have to be his, not mine, but his arrogant certainty that I would keep the secret galled me even more than his behavior.

Mr. O'Neill suddenly sputtered to life again. "I got a joke for you, Seamus," he said. Once again, his interjection stopped the conversation dead, and everyone turned to look—wondering, perhaps, what stunningly incongruous contribution he would make this time.

But surely no one expected him to say, "These two fags go into a bar, see."

Collectively, the members of our group recoiled. Even Kathleen choked on her buttered bread.

"Maybe not right now, Charlie," David said.

"Maybe never," my dad said. "You got the wrong crowd for that bullshit."

With no encouragement to continue, Mr. O'Neill snorted once and shut up. I wondered if the general's dad was perhaps senile or simply mean-spirited. I waited for the general to rebuke his father for his prejudice, or at least his monumental lack of situational awareness. A simple "that'll do, Pop" would have been better than the nothing he offered, though everyone at the table looked to him for guidance.

That's what generals provide. Historically, anyway.

I believe everyone at the table had determined by then that our having dinner together was a mistake. And we were a long, long way from dessert.

"Ready to order?" Jeffrey's cheerful voice was a welcome respite. He looked expectantly at the general.

"Yes, Jerry," he said. Jeffrey's grin dimmed a little. I could see his disappointment, and I wondered for a moment if he would offer a correction. He did not.

Gratefully, we picked up our menus and made our selections. I chose the rib-eye steak, as did my dad and the general's dad. My mom and David opted for lemon-peppered breast of chicken, and Kathleen ordered baked salmon. The general selected spaghetti with meatballs and garlic breadsticks. Salads arrived in quick order, and that, at least, gave us some work to do. Besides, the general needed to get some food into his stomach, particularly since Jeffrey—whom the general next referred to as Johnny—brought a bottle of merlot immediately afterward.

The general tasted a mouthful and declared it suitable. I didn't want a glass, but after a sullen glare from him when I tried to refuse, I accepted one anyway, although I didn't drink it. David and I tried to initiate some non-controversial conversation to kill time as we waited for our dinner. My mom and dad offered a remark or two, but the bewildering awkwardness of the whole affair seemed to stun them into silence. Kathleen was ice, the general distracted and somewhat left of sober, their father miles away. I was weary and talked out by the time Jeffrey arrived again.

He delivered each plate to its rightful place. The meals were beautifully presented, savory, and pleasing in all ways, and everyone perked up. Dad's steak and mine were lean and broiled to perfection, the potatoes and gravy plentiful and aromatic. The general's plate, heaped with pasta, a generous helping of tomato sauce and meatballs, included two plump breadsticks.

The general picked up one of the breadsticks and examined it. His eyes met mine and his mustache bristled slightly. His wheels were in motion, no doubt greased by a little too much alcohol.

"Remind you of anything, Harris?" he said. He grinned, but there was no humor in it.

I suspected where he was headed, but I would not go there. "Looks just like a breadstick to me, sir," I said.

"You have no imagination, Harris," he said, a little too carefully, as if speech required tremendous concentration. I had a brief, horrifying flashback to the community-council breakfast the previous summer when I'd pulled a little stunt with a banana, and for a moment I was afraid he'd duplicate it with the breadstick.

"Is there anything more I can get for you, General O'Neill?" I could tell Jeffrey still hoped for some friendly acknowledgment that he had carried out his duties with poise, efficiency, and enthusiasm.

"No, Jimmy," the general said, dismissing him with a wave of his hand. "We'll let you know if we need anything else."

"His name is Jeffrey, sir," I whispered, after the waiter departed.

"Jimmy. Jeffrey. I'll call him whatever the hell I want," the general said thickly. "If he doesn't like it, there's not a damn thing he can do about it. He's a waiter. I'm a general."

"That's no reason to be an asshole, Seamus," David said. "Just use the guy's right name." I was surprised to hear his criticism, as timely as it was. Kathleen said nothing. The general merely grunted.

I had never seen him treat anyone with such rudeness, least of all waiters, clerks, or others who served him. He had always been unfailingly polite, even compassionate, believing impeccable manners to be a hallmark of high rank. Like discourtesy, losing control of oneself in public was a mortal sin. Between the punch, champagne, and wine, I'd lost count of how many drinks the general had consumed, with nothing to eat but a few bites of salad, though blaming alcohol or any other weakness for ill behavior was the refuge of a coward.

The general hated apologies and mostly avoided them, but how would he view this evening's performance from the vantage point of a hung-over tomorrow? And how would he explain himself to me on Monday morning?

At least he dropped his line of inquiry regarding the breadstick, and for the next fifteen minutes, hunger took over and we were content just to eat, the attention that well-prepared food deserves. Jeffrey came by once and caught my eye, but I shook my head, and he did not interrupt, merely tiptoed away. The general didn't notice.

My parents and I seemed to be of the same mind. If we could only eat quickly and excuse ourselves, this whole wretched event would be over. The three of us set down our forks and folded our napkins by our plates in record time. My dad checked his watch. I knew, in the interest of politeness, we could not leave the table while the general's family was still eating, however.

Mr. O'Neill kept his eyes on his plate, though he did little besides push the food around with his knife, taking an occasional halfhearted bite and chewing with agonizing slowness. David enjoyed his meal at a most leisurely pace. Between bites, Kathleen carried on an earnest whispered conversation with her brother, but he seemed irritated as well as inattentive. He filled his wineglass again, slopping the red liquid over the side and onto the white tablecloth. I also noticed spots of tomato sauce on his blue shirt and tie, which shocked me. Though we might studiously ignore it, the effect of his alcohol consumption was apparent.

Kathleen placed a restraining hand on his arm. "Maybe you've had enough, Seamus," she said. He jerked his arm away and nearly knocked over the glass.

"Fuck off, Kathleen," he said, angry and loud enough to draw the attention of diners at a nearby table. Our party, meanwhile, froze in place. Even the general became aware of the awkwardness, and he attempted to laugh it off. "That slipped," he said.

My estimation of him had slipped as well. I hardly knew this man. As much as I disliked Kathleen, the general had no excuse to be vulgar toward her, and I felt a momentary flash of sympathy. My parents exchanged puzzled glances. I could guess their thoughts. Only yesterday, he'd been their tour guide aboard the C-5, no doubt assuring them that our future together was as solid and as full of potential as the airframe. At the table now he was a stranger, utterly foreign. I could not understand why he chose this night, of all nights, for such mischief, when it couldn't have been more inappropriate, and the consequences couldn't have been more potentially disastrous.

In defiance, the general emptied his glass in a single swallow.

"What were we talking about before dinner?" he said hazily. "Oh, yes, I remember. Homosexuality and its relative compatibility with military service." It was a mouthful of tricky words for one in his state of inebriation, and he stumbled over them. But everyone understood, and precisely no one wanted to pick up the topic again.

Jeffrey chose that opportune moment to return to our table. "How was everything?" I'm sure by this time he was as anxious for our meal to be over as I was. Though he didn't address the question to me, I chose to answer, as the general clearly had no intention of responding. "Everything was delicious. Thank you, Jeffrey." My mom and dad echoed the message.

"I'll just get these plates out of your way," he said. Without incident, he removed my parents' dishes, mine, David's, Kathleen's.

"Are we all finished, sir?" Jeffrey asked Mr. O'Neill. In response, he shoved his plate away and Jeffrey took it. Lastly, he approached the general, who had eaten all of his spaghetti and meatballs. There was half of a breadstick left, but he'd set down his knife and fork and crumpled his napkin. Jeffrey looked to me again, panic in his face. I shrugged and nodded. Gingerly, he removed the last plate.

The general waited until Jeffrey had hoisted the tray of dirty dishes to his shoulder before speaking up. "I wasn't done with that breadstick, Jackie," he said.

Mr. O'Neill snickered, and Jeffrey turned crimson. "Oh, sir! I am so very sorry! *So* sorry. Please forgive me. I'll just run to the kitchen and get you some fresh ones. I'll bring them right out, sir. Just give me a moment." As quickly as he could, under his load of dishes and mortification, he slunk away and returned a moment later with a basket covered with a clean napkin, apologizing again for being hasty.

This time, my dad took it upon himself to speak for my boss. "Thank you, Jeffrey. We're sorry for the misunderstanding."

Jeffrey left us once again. The general lifted the napkin from the basket to reveal steaming and fragrant breadsticks, enough for all of us.

"Have one," the general said, gruff. He thrust the basket toward my parents, who politely declined. "Pop? David? Kathleen? Can't eat all these damn things myself."

I could tell Kathleen had formulated a suitable retort, but perhaps wisely, she held her tongue.

"Lieutenant. Have one."

"No, thank you, sir. I'm full. Couldn't eat another bite."

He picked a breadstick from the basket and handed it to me. "I said have one."

"Really, sir. I'm stuffed. But thanks just the same."

He glared and dropped the breadstick on the table in front of me. I knew awfulness would follow as well as I knew I could not stop it. His mustache bristled. "*Eat it,*" he said. Then, hard, "That's an order."

"*No, sir!*"

The rest of our table sat mesmerized by the whole surreal performance. The general's voice lulled as it wheedled. "Show us one of the many talents you bring to the United States Air Force as a brand-new first lieutenant," he said. "Not just a brand-new first lieutenant, but as a card-carrying, Grade-A, government-inspected ho-mo-*sex*-ual first lieutenant," the general said. The words were slushy, but everyone caught the gist. He dangled the breadstick in front of me again. "Look at that, Lieutenant. Beautiful, isn't it? I'll bet you could swallow it whole," he said, insinuating. "Pretend it's—"

That snapped me out of the trance. I shoved my chair back from the table at the same time as my father, who looked as if he could dispatch the general with his steak knife. Dad walked around the table and pulled the general out of his chair. With his face three inches from the general's, my father managed to keep his voice low in spite of his seething anger. "I don't care how much rank you wear, you drunken bastard. You may be an officer, but you're no gentleman."

The general seemed bewildered for a moment, as if he too had just been awakened. He stared at my father and then at me as if he were trying to locate some object lost but possibly retrievable. Or simply prove to himself, once and for all, that he didn't really want it to begin with.

The starch went out of him. He slumped down into his seat again, perhaps weary of the whole outrageous game, his mustache finally stilled. We'd reached the climax of this day, with nothing left to do but turn away from each other, embarrassed by things said at the moment of passionate release, of dirtying the sheets. Had he really spoken of love three hours before this?

I remained frozen, speechless, but in those same seconds, my mother was neither still nor quiet. She gasped. "Seamus! How could you?" Tears filled her eyes and overflowed. My dad helped her out of her chair.

His "Come on, son. Let's go," reminded me to move, and I stood up slowly, shrugged into my jacket and buttoned it. I wasn't even aware of the general's family, who were no doubt just as horrified at the appalling turn of events. We turned to walk out and were almost to the door when my father pulled out his wallet, returned to the table, threw two twenties in front of the general, and then rejoined my mother and me. We hurried to the car.

Moments later, as we drove past the entrance to the club, the general hurtled through the door as if he'd been shot from the other side, hatless and coatless and napkin still in hand, right into the path of the car. My dad slammed on the brakes and screeched to a stop not a second too soon. The general was talking, pleading. I could see the heat of his voice in the chilled night air, as if his words were solids, suspended, but I could not decipher them. My dad hurled invective at him through the closed windows and leaned on the horn until the general stepped back. As we pulled out of the parking lot, I turned to look at him, standing defeated, framed in the Panavision of the back window of the car, watching us as we drove away, his mouth open in a soundless howl.

Chapter Twenty-nine

On the drive back to the apartment, my father raged in silence. My mother was still in tears. I felt my humiliation had been complete.

"Harris, what was that all about?" she said.

"I don't know, Mom." I suspected the whole affair was simply an unfortunate collusion of the wrong elements at the right time, too much alcohol and too much pressure, which made me feel no better.

"What must his father think of him?" she continued.

"What must his father think of *me*?" I said. "To say nothing of Kathleen, the bitch."

My mother was too upset even to chastise me for such language.

"I didn't know he was such a heavy drinker," she said.

"He's not," I said. "I've never seen him like this." But perhaps I had at the retirement party the previous summer.

I felt immobile. What would happen next? I could not even think about tomorrow, let alone the next week and the whole wide-open future I had so boldly and fearlessly plotted for Traveler and me. I needed some time alone to think. Once back at my apartment and out of uniform, I put on a good front and convinced my parents that I would be fine. Though they had their misgivings, they agreed to give me some space.

They hit the road early the next morning. For once, I could return a frequent favor by packing them a hearty lunch for the long trip home, even if the temperature was such that they wouldn't be able to enjoy a picnic outdoors. It also kept me busy, though my mom fussed anxiously around me, still bewildered by the course of events.

"You come home as soon as you can get a couple of days off," my father said. "You hear me?"

I heard.

My mother gave me a warm hug and a kiss. "We're proud of you, Harris. Congratulations on your promotion. You earned it," she said.

Thankfully, I was spared an obvious question that I couldn't begin to answer just yet: what next? The whole day seemed unreal. I promised to come home soon, thankful for their tact. More likely, they didn't know what to say. What could cauterize such wounds?

❖

Julia called mid-morning Saturday and asked how the dinner went.

"Remember when you asked me if I would break up with General O'Neill? I think I have an answer that will make you much happier," I said, aiming for a little levity.

"Uh-oh. I don't like the sound of that at all. Come on. Spill. Everything."

My brave face evaporated as soon as I started telling her about it. Within the hour, she was at my house bearing groceries and an overnight bag.

"I'm staying with you all weekend," she said. "No arguments. Somebody's got to see to it that you eat and sleep and don't do anything drastic."

There was no fear of that, but I was grateful for her company. She did her best to keep me entertained, to take my mind off the situation, and to let me rant and whine and curse as necessary. It helped immensely, and by Sunday evening, I felt much more in command of my emotions, even if I had no idea where the general and I were to go next. I persuaded Julia to head back to her own apartment that night because we both had to be at the office Monday morning.

"How will you ever face him?" she said. "More to the point, how will he ever face you?"

"He won't even come in tomorrow. Just you watch," I said. "Scratch the paint, and you'll find a coward underneath. And when he does come in, Tuesday or Wednesday, I'll manage. My one-year stint as his aide is over, and you know how he says he never keeps anyone longer than that. I'll go back to the personnel office for the time being."

"Then what?"

"I don't know yet. I could resign my commission next year if I decide I've had enough of the Air Force," I said.

"You could always file sexual harassment charges against him if you want," Julia said. "From what you told me, he's the one who pressured you into this relationship."

"That would haul him out of the closet, wouldn't it?"

"He'd deserve it, even if it would put me in the firing line, too," she said. "The press would be all over it."

"It was stupid to get tangled up with him in the first place. He's as homophobic as any straight guy I've ever met, and he's too old to change. If he wants to beat himself up, that's his business, but I'm not going to let him beat me up, too."

Julia congratulated me for my perspective. I wished I'd felt as confident as I sounded. Evidence of Traveler was everywhere in my life, not merely in the artifacts readily identifiable in my apartment but also in my practical head and impractical heart. What would I do without him? I couldn't think about that now. With my assurance that I would call her in the morning before work, she left reluctantly, and I settled down for a sleepless night. After thrashing around in bed for about two hours, I finally turned the light on. I tried reading and watching television but didn't have the patience for either. Restless, I did a load of laundry and ironed my blue shirts. I tidied up the apartment, dusted, washed the kitchen floor, scrubbed the bathtub.

All the while, my mind galloped, accusing. How could he have done such a thing, even if he was drunk? I could not fathom the casual carelessness of his betrayal, as if he had suddenly become a stranger, as if the past year had not existed at all, as if our entire relationship had been built on some delusion. Until a day or two ago, I'd believed we were so solid nothing could come between us. I knew we'd have challenges ahead, but I thought we'd be left standing together, though hurricanes threatened destruction.

He told me he loved me! He was a smart man, a man of his word, and he would never have said such a thing without considering the consequences. If alcohol was the catalyst, it seemed to have worked in reverse. I would have expected a drunken confession of love to come first because it could be so easily retracted, but the general had stormed those particular gates with a clear head.

The cliché says there is truth in wine, however. His injudicious consumption on Friday night may have been the match that lit the fuse, but no explosion would have been possible without a charge having been set in advance. He might be able to laugh off the image of himself asleep with a stuffed bear—he'd come up with a clever explanation, and no one would even think to ask who'd been behind the camera—

but what could he say in his defense about a photo of himself locked in an intimate embrace with another man, another officer? Maybe the image brought something into sharp relief for him and he panicked. When a man is cornered and afraid, there is always a risk that he will lash out.

What hounded him, and how could I have been so unaware of it? Did the threat of the Uniform Code of Military Justice suddenly loom even larger? Was the weight of a second star just too much to bear? Did it tip the scales in the wrong direction when placed opposite the single silver bar of a new first lieutenant? These questions bothered me even more than the general's insulting remark about the breadstick.

When I fell for the general, I neglected to pack a parachute. Perhaps he had. I could not forget how neat and squared-away his house was, and how regulated his life had become under three decades of military supervision. Human beings are not supposed to be so straight. That's why we have some rounded corners. The angles and the lines give us outlines for our existence, but we live most comfortably inside the curves.

He was a great actor if he could make me believe an entire novel-length fiction about us. But why would he take the trouble to bond with my parents if he weren't serious about laying some groundwork for a future?

He'd finally succeeded at one thing I didn't believe he could ever accomplish: changing my mind about my feelings for him. The dinner incident had been a small thing, even forgivable if he were truly penitent, but it broke the dam nonetheless and unleashed the flood of doubt I'd been ignoring all along, a maelstrom indeed for two o'clock on a dismal Monday morning. Hours ticked by as my head spun, with no conclusions reached when the cold dawn crept in.

❖

Daylight puts everything into perspective. However dark Sunday night might be, Monday morning comes, with a new week to face. I showered and shaved and dressed and fixed breakfast and drove to the base. Habits make things easy. When necessary, we can hit autopilot and accomplish the minimum.

As I'd predicted, the general didn't come into the office. Only my certainty that he would be absent gave me the courage to show up myself. He called Linda and pleaded sick. I cleaned up the conference room to remove all evidence of Friday's special event, dumping the leftover punch down the restroom sink and vacuuming cake crumbs off the carpet. Otherwise, I puttered around with little to do, spending much of the day talking with Julia in her office. Lieutenant Colonel Cartwright remained surly, perhaps still angry about the promotion ceremony, but she left me alone. Friday's debacle at the club seemed to have escaped her radar, and Linda's, too. I was grateful for the reprieve.

On Tuesday, the general called and told Linda he'd decided to stay home yet another day, still feeling out of sorts. I could only imagine the thoughts that coursed through his mind. I only hoped they were as torturous and cataclysmic as mine.

I got out of bed on Wednesday morning with good intentions, but I knew he couldn't stretch his absence to another day. Knowing I'd have to face him made me a little queasy. It was my turn to call in sick. Truthfully, I reported an upset stomach to Linda and told her I would be staying home myself. She sympathized and said she would inform the general.

I made good use of the time, spending the first half of the day thinking the matter through. The general and I would have to discuss the situation, but what did I want from him? Did I seek an explanation or admission of guilt? An apology? A promise to change? A reconciliation or a formal breakup? Was there some wild card he might play that I couldn't foresee?

Our lives are shaped by the choices we make. If we opt out of making those choices through laziness or fear or carelessness, others will make them for us. If I squandered my life helping others accomplish their dreams, I'd never achieve my own. I had to accept the consequences, including the possibility of a Traveler-less future.

Thursday came, and I couldn't put off the reckoning any longer. We had to face each other, and I simply wanted to get past it. As usual, he was already in his office by the time I hung up my hat at seven fifteen. Linda warned me to step cautiously.

"He was in an ugly mood all day yesterday, Lieutenant Mitchell. I thought he might still be sick, but he spent most of the time locked in his office, smoking that stinky old pipe of his," she said. "I don't know what's gotten into his shorts, but I don't like it. He's already started in again today, so look out."

Hmm. I thanked her for the information.

I made coffee as usual, only this time, I tampered with the recipe, eliminating the French roast and doubling the Maxwell House to see if he could really tell the difference. If he was already in bad humor, why not antagonize him more? When the coffee finished brewing, I poured a cup for him and for myself, and walked into his office. I set the mug on his desk, on the leather coaster where it belonged. In accordance with our routine for the past year, I sat down in the chair across from him, wondering how he would begin this day.

He'd worn his blues, open-collared shirt neatly pressed, name tag and silver pilot wings but no ribbons, each shoulderboard bearing two stars, the very model of a modern major general. He sat at the computer, checking his email, probably still wading through the messages that had piled up since the previous Friday. The system seemed to be running slowly, and after a couple of minutes he lost patience, yelling "goddamn it" to the universe and abruptly yanking the power strip's plug out of the wall.

He finally turned to face me. He took off his glasses, but he would not look in my eyes. "Good morning, Satellite." So he still hadn't run out of nicknames for me, or else it was a habit too ingrained to correct. Or it was as meaningless as it sounded. On the surface, today might have been no different from any other day, but this morning, he looked as if the weight of two more stars had added eons to his age. He looked haggard from worry or lack of sleep or half a century catching up with him, tapping him on the shoulder and saying "Hey, you. Pay attention." An angry red gash, still fresh and damp, marked where the morning's razor had bitten into his cheek.

"Someone distracting you again while you were shaving?" I said.

Involuntarily, he touched the cut and winced. My question hit home. I expected him to react with some anger, disgust, at least one of his famous glares, but he seemed instead almost shocked I would have the nerve to ask such a thing, scratching open an old wound. The hurt surprise on his face twisted into me deeper than his sarcasm or anger could have, and his humble, honest answer suggested a beaten man.

"No. No, Harris. Just carelessness." He cradled the mug in his hands and took a swallow of coffee a minute too soon and burned his mouth on the scalding liquid. "Damn it," he said. On the heels of everything else, this little thing seemed cruel, as if even the usual banal comforts of morning had turned against him. He set the mug down a little abruptly, and the coffee sloshed over the side, leaving a small puddle on his desk.

He shook his head and muttered "damn it" again. "Are your folks still in town?"

"They left on Saturday."

"Mine, too," he said. "I thought my dad might stick around for a couple of days, but he didn't want to. There's no reason why he should, I guess. It's not as if we'll ever become friends. I'm surprised he came at all. And I can only abide Kathleen for so long." He sighed. "She means well."

He blew across the surface of his coffee until it cooled enough for him to take a proper swallow. He frowned. Sipped again, suspicious, opened his mouth to complain and then closed it. So he actually could taste the difference in the recipe. Gotcha, I thought to myself, and felt immediately ashamed. Such petty victories offer small comfort.

The phone rang then, and the general took the call. Its message or its messenger reminded him that he had a NAF to run, first and foremost, in spite of our personal differences and whatever hell we'd manufactured for ourselves. Immediately distracted and perhaps gratefully so, he shooed me away.

I went to my desk and busied myself by updating various policy letters and other official communications to reflect the general's new rank, but it was tiresome work. The general proved testy for the rest of the morning, and he found plenty of opportunities to fuss and yell. In retaliation, I manufactured some excuse to skip our regularly scheduled run, to his surprise. He set out alone while I spent an hour commiserating with Julia.

His solitary exercise cheered him up not in the least. No one escaped censure during the afternoon's lengthy staff meeting, the most uncomfortable I'd ever attended. Clearly, he was dissatisfied about every single thing, and he vented his anger at top volume. Later, pressed by coworkers for my opinion as to the cause, I pleaded ignorance and admitted to being as mystified as everyone else.

Late in the afternoon, as I refilled his coffee cup with the renegade brew, I realized we could not go on like this even one more day. This was no place for such skirmishes. The general could do as he pleased, but I took too much pride in my own professionalism. Our showdown could not wait. The sooner I extricated myself from his proximity, the better for us both and for the NAF. After Linda had gone home for the day, I marched back into his office, closed the door behind me, and parked myself in front of his desk.

"We need to talk," I said.

He sighed, a sad, careful, let's-get-this-over-with sigh. "We do need to talk," he said.

Thus given permission, I said, "Last year, you told me if I wanted to take another position elsewhere, you would find me a suitable one and give me the highest recommendation. I'm ready to go, as soon as possible."

He shook his head. "I can't let you go, Doghouse. Not like this."

"When you hired me, you told me if I would be straight with you, you would return the favor. You know as well as I do that I have to go."

"You're the best aide I've ever had, and I'm not going to lose you," he said. "End of discussion."

"Oh, yeah?" My embers could still blaze. Minus the glamour of being close to a man I loved, I could easily find fault with the position. "What's in it for me?" I said. "I get to be your lackey? Your valet? Your chauffeur? Your waiter, all the time bringing you coffee and lunch? Your whipping boy? Your possession, like your boots or your ball mitt? You hold me hostage to a job description that doesn't even exist so you can make me do anything you want, and then publicly humiliate me because I don't measure up. It's a great job, all right, as long as you don't need any self-respect. Who wouldn't jump at the chance to be General O'Neill's aide?"

I watched the color rise in his face, but he kept his temper. "Where do you get such notions?" he said when I'd finished my tirade. "I'm not your owner. I'm your boss. You're my aide. You're supposed to help me, whatever kind of help I need. That's what an aide does. I may be noisy. I know I demand a lot from my staff. From you. I'm a general, and that's what *we* do. But have I ever *ever* treated you like a servant?"

I had to admit he never had.

"Thank you," he said gruffly. He'd earned the right to feel insulted, I suspect, and under other circumstances, he would never have dropped the matter. Given his disadvantage at the moment, however, such a detour would have been particularly unfortunate. I remained standing in front of his desk, my arms crossed. After an awkward pause, he asked me to sit. "You're making me nervous."

I sat. He looked at me expectantly. I took in another deep breath and jumped in. "I've spent the last five days trying to reconcile what you told me last Friday afternoon with what you did at the restaurant later, in front of my parents and your family."

He looked away and hung his head.

"I've been giving you the benefit of the doubt ever since you put me in this job," I said. "I was convinced there would be a worthwhile payoff. When I fell in love with you, I thought I'd hit the jackpot, especially when you said you loved me, too. Maybe it means something different for you. Or maybe I assumed too much."

I congratulated myself for remaining calm. A few days ago, I would have been yelling, cursing, throwing bricks if I'd gotten my hands on them. He took a swallow of coffee and set the mug down. Pulled his pipe from his pocket and clamped down on the stem. He shifted things around on his desk. He sighed. Finally, he looked at me, unflinching,

"I certainly deserve all hell and damnation," he said. "And a court-martial first for conduct unbecoming an officer but also," he lowered his voice, although there was no one around to overhear, "a man in love. I'm deeply sorry, Harris. How could I be that stupid? Obviously, I had too much to drink, but that's a poor excuse. Maybe I was afraid. A man does some desperate things when he's cornered."

"Afraid of what?" I said. "Afraid of me? Of being in love? I don't get it. Are you trying to prove to yourself that you're just not worth it? Or are you telling me that *I'm* not worth it?"

He did not answer.

"How can you think so little of yourself? Of me? Of us? Haven't you figured out yet that happiness is an option? Why are you stuck in some useless past that won't let you enjoy being a gay man, Traveler?" Instantly I retracted. "Sorry. I guess I should stick with 'General O'Neill' from now on."

He looked at me, and his eyes were damp. "No," he said, hoarse. "Not that. Please, Harris. I couldn't bear it. What can I do to prove that I'm worth one more chance? Please? I can retire in three years. That's not such a long time to wait."

"What am I supposed to do in the meantime?" I shot back. "Look at your picture and jerk off?"

"Okay, okay," he said, hasty. "We don't have to wait. I could retire right now."

"Would you?"

"If you ask me to."

"But you're hoping I won't ask."

After a minute, he nodded. "I'm sorry. Maybe I'm just a selfish bastard, but I still think I can do some good for the Air Force. I'd like to try," he said, and then took a deep breath and looked me square in the eyes. "Still, it's not as important to me right now as a second chance. If retirement is what you want, then I'll retire."

Perhaps he would, but forcing him to retire sooner than he

anticipated would not be firm ground upon which to build a second chance. How did I know he wouldn't resent me later if not sooner, wouldn't throw it at me every time we had an argument? And, of course, there was the other matter that had been troubling me...

I made up my mind.

"I've got a better idea," I said. "Come out," I said. "You don't have to worry about another promotion. You said so yourself. Why not come out and still serve your last three years?"

He dropped his gaze, as if he were being scolded.

We had hiked this trail before, and I reiterated my old arguments, how it would set a great example of leadership in action, show the Air Force's core values in action. Make a strong statement. Make history.

Silence.

"Suppose I make that the condition you asked for. It would convince me you mean what you say."

Slowly he shook his head. "I can't," he whispered. "Please don't ask."

I should have known. "And, whatever you do, don't tell," I said. "I'm sorry. You wanted a second chance. That's what I want in exchange. Do you need a week to think about it?"

I wondered if he recalled our first meeting the previous July, when he'd demanded I take a week to decide if I wanted to pursue our relationship. However, in this case, I couldn't see his being any less intractable in a week or a month or a year. We couldn't compromise. One of us would have to forfeit his position completely for us to move forward together.

It would not be him. He didn't even need to say no. What he didn't realize was that it could not be me.

I needed a break, a rest. He would be very hard to give up. I had so much invested, and I'd foolishly assumed our market would never crash. Damn him and his sorrowful eyes. My heart would run away with me again, and I would forgive him for all his sins. Would beg him to take *me* back, as if somehow our quandary were solely of my own making, as if his crippling doubt had been entirely my fault. I would give in. And I would be lost.

"About that transfer to another unit," I said.

"Yes." His voice frosted over. "You'll find the personnel field a refreshing change of pace after your year of drudgery with me."

I'd had all the excitement I wanted. "I'll do some checking tomorrow. I'm sure there's a vacancy someplace. I'll initiate the transfer paperwork for your signature." It would do for the interim. In the aftermath of our apparently imminent breakup, I'd need time away to recoup my losses and decide if a career in the Air Force was really in the cards for me.

"So that's that," he said, harsh. "Satisfied now, Lieutenant Mitchell?"

There was one more thing. "I'll need to get my bear."

Was divorce like this? The division of significant property? He said nothing, neither confirmed nor denied, but it was one more knife under the ribs. Finally, he nodded, slowly, and I wondered how we would effect such an exchange of hostages. My bear for his heart.

"Is there anything else you want?" he said without inflection. "You're welcome to it." He stood before me, stripped to his bones, his eyes piercing me to my core. "Oh," he said. "Here's an idea."

He'd piqued my curiosity. As I watched, he rummaged through his desk drawers for a pair of scissors and then a white envelope. Purposefully, he pulled his blue shirt out of his pants and his white undershirt too, exposing his furry chest. Without a word, he clipped a generous fistful of the coarse hair, dropped it into the envelope, and sealed it.

He tucked in his shirt and handed me the envelope.

I hardly trusted myself to speak. "What's this for?"

"A souvenir," he said, hard. "You like it so damned much, and I've got plenty."

My eyes began to smart and sting and spill, and I wiped them with the back of my hand. I turned to go. I wasn't sure exactly where I was going or what I'd do for the rest of the day. In spite of my brave words, I wasn't so sure we had settled anything, and I was of half a mind to march directly to the personnel office and resign my commission, to hell with a transfer.

"Lieutenant, you're not dismissed yet," he said, stern if not exactly angry.

I paused, my hand on the doorknob.

"*Lieutenant Mitchell!*" he barked.

I turned to face him. He was a major general, after all, and he could certainly issue an order to a first lieutenant.

"Come here," he said. I did as I was told. "I can't argue with a single word you said, but I'm damned if I'm going to let you go that easily. You have every right to be angry, but that's the worst time to make any important decision. I won't let you make this one until you think it through carefully. All right, I'm one sorry son of a bitch in addition to being a goddamned old fool."

He'd get no argument from me.

"I'll be twice goddamned if I know why you should give me a second chance, Harris," he said, "but I'm asking for one anyway. I've done wrong, but if you don't think I could be reconstructed, why would you bother telling me what I have to fix? All right. You've given me your terms. I don't like them, but they're your terms. We've both got some thinking to do, and we'll leave it at that for the time being.

"I know I stole your fishing trip when we visited your folks. Take tomorrow and all next week and go home. Go fishing with your dad. Leave now," he said. "That *is* an order, and if you think carefully, you might realize it's the first genuine order I've ever given you." He may have been right. "*Now* you're dismissed, Harris." As I turned to go, he gripped my shoulder and turned me around to face him again, and he said, fierce, "We'll pick up this discussion when you come back. Understood?"

He would not let go of my shoulder until I nodded. Clutching the white envelope, I made my way out, grabbed my hat and coat and keys, headed for the parking lot, and didn't look back for fear I would turn myself into salt.

CHAPTER THIRTY

After the general's dismissal, I hit the road that same afternoon and drove straight through. My parents were surprised and pleased to see me, and a week stretched before me with no responsibilities but a fishing trip with Dad and some quality time with the dogs.

I explained the bargain I'd made with the general, that I'd give him a second chance if he came out. Mom and Dad seemed relieved I'd set the bar so high. They shared my skepticism he'd ever make the jump, in spite of the apparent sincerity of his apology and declaration of love. For my part, I wondered if he'd simply try to sneak under or go around.

After I'd been home for a few days, the postcards started arriving, several at a time. I was surprised at the variety, not just scenic vistas from around the world, but puppies, state flags, hotels across the U.S.A., military aircraft, recipes, antique trucks and more, each image backed with its own act of contrition. In the message box, each contained a new nickname and a brief message in his untidy scrawl: "I love you. Come back. Your Traveler."

My mother gave me a hug as she handed me three more. "He doesn't give up, does he?" she said.

"He certainly never seems to run out of postcards."

"Words on paper," she said. "Not very imaginative words, either, if you ask me."

She showed me a letter the general had sent to them a few days after our visit in the fall. He'd never told me that he'd written to them, and I was a little surprised. It was brief and direct, drafted on his old manual typewriter and signed in his bold slant, communicating his resolve. The note was primarily a thank-you, but its marshmallow center revealed something about him I didn't think anyone else knew:

Dear Bruce and Jane,

   First, let me say thanks for your hospitality during our visit last week. I know it wasn't easy for you, and I certainly am grateful that you handled our news so well. It meant a lot to Harris. Meant a lot to me, too. You're fine people, and I would be honored if you counted me among your friends.

   Second, let me assure you that the time I get to spend with Harris means more to me than anything I can name— even our workdays are special. I know he gets frustrated. I do too, although I have more practice keeping it in check. We're facing some hard choices, but we'll meet them head-on. We'll get by the obstacles and be stronger afterward.

   I still can't believe I've found him. I feel bulletproof when he's with me. There's nothing we can't accomplish together if we set our minds to it.

   This whole damn thing is new to me. I reckon I will make mistakes along the way, but I will make them right one way or another. Thanks for giving me a chance. As I get to know you better, you will also get to know me better, and I hope you will find some things in me to like.

   Sincerely,

   Seamus O'Neill

"He expected to make mistakes," my mother said after I'd read it. "But just because he warned us doesn't make everything all right. I still can't understand how the man who wrote this could have behaved so dreadfully at dinner that night."

Maybe we all make foolish blunders when we're figuring out the steps to a new dance. I'd told the general once that mistakes were sometimes more instructive than doing things right. Something he said to me before I left replayed in my head, like a record needle stuck in a scratch. If you didn't think I could be reconstructed, why would you tell me what I have to fix?

I was surprised she'd kept the letter. Maybe we were both just a couple of hopeless optimists.

"Mom, don't you think people deserve a second chance?"

"It depends on what they did to mess up their first chance," she said, tart. "You're never going to get me to admit he deserves one after what he did."

"He needed a wake-up call," I said. "Maybe that was it."

"Are you ready to hold up your end of the bargain if he does come out?"

"I gave my word, Mom. I'll have to give him one more chance, but it will be the only one."

❖

Our afternoon passed uneventfully. Dad was at the store. Mom and I were baking oatmeal cookies with *Rigoletto* playing on the stereo when my cell phone rang and startled both of us. Julia's name showed on the display. At the base, it was about eleven o'clock, and the weekly staff meeting would have just concluded.

"Hi, Julia."

"Harris!" I could hear excitement in her voice.

"What's up? Aren't you at work?"

"We just got out of the staff meeting a minute ago. Harris, I wish you had been here. You won't believe it!"

"What?"

"You'll never guess!" she said. "It was incredible. I still can't believe it myself!"

"*What?* Tell me!"

Julia caught her breath. "At the staff meeting," she said. "In front of everyone. It was amazing."

I grew annoyed. "Julia! *Tell me!*"

"Harris, General O'Neill came out."

The phone slipped from my fingers and I scrambled to pick it up.

"Harris?" Julia sounded concerned. "Did you hear what I said?"

"Sorry. I dropped the phone. Tell me again, just so I can be sure I heard right."

She spoke distinctly. "General O'Neill came out, Harris. Right at the beginning of the staff meeting. And then he went ahead and held the meeting as if nothing was different. I've never seen anything like it."

My mind cartwheeled. He came out? I couldn't imagine any circumstance that would have led the general to do such a thing, given his vehement refusal when I'd practically begged him to consider it.

I sat down. "Tell me everything. And I mean *every single thing.*"

In detail, Julia outlined the previous hour. As usual, the staff had filed into the conference room ten minutes before the start of the meeting. Lieutenant Colonel Beemis, the security forces commander, was talking to the medical officer, Major Lee. Julia hadn't been paying attention until she heard my name come up in their conversation, and she tuned in. Major Lee said, "Isn't he a first lieutenant now?" and Lieutenant Colonel Beemis said, "He's still a fag." Julia couldn't believe her ears. And just as he said it, loud enough for everyone to hear the contempt in his voice, the general entered the room.

"Who's still a fag?" he said.

"No one, sir," Lieutenant Colonel Beemis said. "It was a slip of the tongue. It won't happen again, sir."

And the general said, "Answer me. Who's still a fag?" And Lieutenant Colonel Beemis admitted he was talking about me. He said he didn't mean any harm by it.

"Why did you say that Lieutenant Mitchell is still a fag?"

Silence.

Then came the earthquake, Julia said, a real 9.5-on-the-Richter-scale house-shaker as the general let loose. He slammed his coffee mug on the table hard enough that it broke. Coffee splashed everywhere, but nobody moved. He raged for a good ten minutes, his volume turned up to eleven, according to Julia. He said he had zero tolerance for that kind of language, that it created a toxic atmosphere for a professional workplace, he said. That the NAF had the responsibility for six-thousand-plus airmen and civilians who looked to him for guidance and leadership and expected him to set high standards, not reinforce hurtful stereotypes.

He promised to file a complaint against Beemis as soon as the meeting was over. If it ended his career, he would deserve it, because he ought to know better, and if he didn't, he had no business being in the service. And the general went on about "Don't Ask, Don't Tell" and how pointless it was, and that it took too long for the military to get rid of the damn thing, and how, as far as he was concerned, the United States Air Force had no room for such small-minded attitudes and prejudice. If people didn't start speaking up when it happened, the disease would spread. Didn't gay airmen already have a hard enough time?

He went on at great length about the core values, too, Julia said.

And he concluded his rant by saying, "If y'all are wondering why I'm raising such holy hell, maybe it's because I'm a 'fag' myself. You heard me. And if there's one word that makes my blood boil, it's 'fag.' I don't want to hear any of y'all use it in this headquarters again, or anywhere in Sixth Air Force, for that matter. Have I made myself crystal clear?"

He made eye contact with everyone at the table, one at a time, as if he dared anyone to contradict. No one did anything but nod. The general sent the cringing Beemis to get some paper towels to mop up the spilled coffee and clean up the broken mug while everyone watched. Then the general asked Linda to fetch him another cup of coffee, and he started the staff meeting as if nothing unusual had happened.

When Julia finished telling her tale, she was nearly breathless. "I can't remember everything he said, but that's the gist of it," she said. "It was so awesome, Harris. I wish you'd been here. Can you even believe it?"

I couldn't and said so.

"It gives you something more to consider, though, doesn't it?" she said. "About your future with the general?"

"If I didn't know better, I'd say you actually *wanted* us to be together. I thought you were totally against the idea."

"Well, sue me. Who couldn't help but root for the most improbable romance of the century?"

"You're nuts."

She giggled. "Anyway, Harris, I know you've got a lot on your mind, but I really felt this was a news flash you needed to hear. It's probably all over the NAF by now."

"Thanks for calling, Julia," I said. "I love you. You know that?"

"Go on," she said. "I knew it all the time."

As soon as I disconnected the call, the phone rang again. This time it was Mark.

"Harris?"

"Hi, Mark."

"Have you heard?"

"Julia called a few minutes ago."

"So you got the whole story."

"Her version of it, anyway. I'm still not sure I believe it."

"Trust me, Harris. I'm as surprised as you are. Who'd have thought? When that dipshit Beemis made his stupid crack, it shook up General O'Neill but good, and he blew his top. It must have been bottled up inside him for a long time. I don't think he could help himself. It was a spectacular eruption, let me tell you. I wish you'd been here."

"Me, too. He told me time and again that he'd never come out—"
Too late, I stopped myself. There was a moment of silence. Mark coughed.

"Lou figured it out before I did. When he suggested to me you might be involved, I didn't even want to believe it. You're a brave man, Harris."

"Ha! You mean a stupid one."

"Don't say that. I don't know how you managed. It's hard to carry on a relationship like you're under Threat Condition Delta."

"Our relationship, or whatever you want to call it, is not exactly common knowledge," I said. "I don't even know if we *have* a relationship anymore."

"You can trust Lou and me to keep mum."

"I know. Thanks. Does anyone think it's suspicious that I'm on leave right now?"

"I don't think so. General O'Neill said you took some time off to celebrate your promotion, and that's a perfectly legitimate excuse. Certainly no one has made any connection between your absence and the general's announcement. Everyone will be in shock for a while, I suspect. And I must say the two of you have been *very* discreet. He's put on a convincing act this past year, making everyone think the two of you hardly get along."

"Is there any gossip going around about what happened after the promotion ceremony?"

"All I know is that you went out to dinner at the club," Mark said. "Julia mentioned to me privately that it was pretty unpleasant for you, but she didn't share any of the details. No one else seems to be aware of it. Not even Linda, which is surprising."

I was relieved. "It was awful. He drank too much, and he embarrassed both of us in front of my parents and his family, too. That's the main reason why I took leave. It was General O'Neill's idea, actually. He insisted. I've got some things to sort out."

"I'm sorry it didn't go well, Harris. But I think the fact that he came out is a good thing."

"It sure is a surprise. Thanks for calling, Mark. I'll see you next Monday when I come back to work, but you might as well know that I won't be the general's aide for much longer. Especially now."

"It's probably for the best, under the circumstances. Speaking for the rest of the staff, we're going to miss you terribly."

"Thanks."

"Be good to yourself, Harris. I don't envy you one bit. I suspect he's put you through a lot."

"Yeah."

"If you ever need a friend to listen, you know I'm here."

"I know. I appreciate it."

"Take care. See you soon."

"Thanks for calling. Bye, Mark."

I disconnected and tossed the phone onto the counter.

"Harris," my mom said. "What's going on?"

"You'll never guess," I said. "And you probably won't even believe it. General O'Neill came out at the staff meeting this afternoon. In front of everyone."

Her eyes widened, and her mouth dropped open. "What?"

I repeated myself. "He might just as well have dropped a bomb."

"I think he did," my mother said.

"I wonder what changed his mind."

My mother gave me another hug. "I'm sure you had something to do with it."

I'd been expecting something to happen, but I'd never thought it would be this approximate shape and stripe. He's been so adamant in his insistence on remaining in the closet.

My mom and I returned to the kitchen. The cookies gave us something to do, and as *Rigoletto* approached its climax, the fervent opinions expressed by father and daughter in the story made conversation impossible. It was just as well. I couldn't find a word to say, and I suspect my mom felt the same.

The music ended. We stood by the oven and watched the last pan of cookies bake.

"Harris," my mom said, finally, "do you think Seamus would've come out at all if it hadn't been for his conduct at dinner last week?"

"Probably not. What do you think?"

"I agree with you," she said.

"So, what he did at the club—does that make it a good thing or a bad thing?"

It certainly had been an insult. Had we been by ourselves, the general and I might have made similarly lewd fun of the breadstick and laughed about it.

"You mean does the end justify the means?" she said. "It's a puzzle, isn't it?"

I nodded. He'd come out, so I got what I really wanted. Hadn't I?
"I would have picked other means," I said. "And maybe a different
end, too." Since he couldn't shut the closet door again and hope no one
had noticed, I too would have to keep my part of the pact and give him
the second chance he'd demanded.

What I needed most at that moment was another hug, and my
mom proved as generous as ever.

❖

That evening, after the workday and supper, with its intense and
emotional but unresolved discussion about the general's coming out,
my dad disappeared into the basement and spent a couple of hours
readying himself for our fishing trip the next morning. The day
would be cold, and our prospects for catching anything at all weren't
particularly good, but he knew we needed to go in spite of the weather.
We might reel in a smallmouth bass or two if we were lucky. It wasn't
unheard of in late January, and our favorite lake had been friendly
in winters past. My dad had brought home some live minnows from
the store, a good bait choice for bass, and we'd try several different
spinners and lures and see what luck we might have. As usual, I let my
dad handle the preparation alone.

I went to bed early and slept better than I had in days. Dad came
to wake me before dawn. Silently, we fixed our own breakfast, but my
mom got out of bed anyway to pack lunch for us and brew a quart of
steaming coffee for the old thermal jug. We would be grateful for it
later, on the water. We dressed warmly, union suits under our coveralls,
in anticipation of the cold. Fog filled the morning, and Dad steered the
truck through it cautiously.

He kept a box of old cassettes kept under the front seat of the
truck, and he pulled it out and handed it to me with instructions to
find Hank. I rummaged through the box for a scuffed "greatest hits"
collection and popped it into the deck. Hank Williams is to my father
what Puccini is to my mother. And just as I'd never really heard *Tosca*
until the general roped me into it, I'd never really paid much attention
to ol' Hank. I could identify his sound, backwoods flavored and rough-
hewn as Lincoln's rail fence, but I'd never listened closely to his stories
before.

His soaring voice, a naked and honest howl, is anchored by his
earthbound guitar strumming three or four chords, seasoned with some

pedal steel guitar, fiddle, and upright bass. The painfully direct lyrics tell of universal sorrow, and the aptness of the songs suggested that he'd somehow managed to eavesdrop on my life for his inspiration. He sang of the blues that came around every evening, long gone and lonesome. He wondered why you didn't love him like you used to do. Swore he'd be a bachelor until he died. He sang of the misery of love's ball and chain, of the vain wish to turn back the years to a time before love became indifference. He seemed to know firsthand of the brief but unfulfilling respite found in a bottle.

I remember reading somewhere that Hank Williams was dead at twenty-nine, his demise hastened by drugs and alcohol and a bad heart. I'd already outlived him, but I'm convinced he's not actually gone. He was there in the truck with us, prophesying like some sage, the wisest man in the world. He kept us good company. My dad hummed along as we rolled down the back roads in the darkness and early morning fog. The general might scoff, but I found more solace in Hank Williams that morning than I could ever have found in *Tosca*.

Our January was slightly warmer than usual. At the lake, we parked, unloaded the skiff, and carried it to the launch. There was no ice in the water, fortunately, so we would be able to motor without difficulty. Next, we brought down our tackle and lunch and coffee and climbed in the boat. As the rising sun began to puncture the fog, we pushed away from shore, confident.

Bass don't hibernate, so they're a good bet for the die-hard fisherman in the Ohio winter, but they aren't easy to catch at that time of year. They like the warmest part of the water at the center of the lake. Bass avoid strong currents and look for submerged logs and big rocks for hiding. My dad knew the lake intimately, and he'd developed strategies based on years of experience.

The fog reluctantly gave way to sun, shy at first but coming in full at last, and it warmed us outside and in. Pessimism is hard under such heat. We stopped our boat in a likely spot and paused for a cup of coffee. Even in summer, this was part of our custom. I would not call my father superstitious, but we always followed the same steps—for luck, perhaps. We did not talk, again a custom, but words were not needed. I'd never had a sense that he chose to be uncommunicative. He just needed few words.

We selected a favorite rod and reel, strong line with plenty of the give necessary for bass fishing and hooked minnows to start. In opposite ends of the skiff, we cast to opposite sides. Slowly, I reeled in, dragging the bait through the water at a deliberate leisurely pace. Any bass in the lake would be a bit sluggish and not tempted by a fast-moving meal. After half a dozen casts, I settled into a gentle groove. The quick forward movement of my shoulder felt smooth and natural, a little like throwing a softball overhand.

The scent of the lake in the sun provided its own intoxicant, as pleasant as the warm buzz spreading through one's midsection after a glass of brandy. Add the quiet, rhythmic slap of lake water against the skiff; the sun shining on the surface so blindingly bright, like a flashbulb reflected in a mirror; and the high and piercing call of the birds, urgent and far off, and I was nearly lulled into peaceful sleep. More than once, I was startled to find myself still casting and reeling in, like some windup toy unattended. In vain, I attempted to focus my mind on the issue of Traveler, but I got nowhere. The lake and the cool beauty of the day easily coaxed me away from any attempt to untangle the snarled line of it.

My dad moved the skiff several times, but we had no better luck. Even if we caught nothing, however, there was no place I would have preferred to be. I was surprised when my dad reeled in, placed his rod in the boat, and reached for the lunch bucket. Had so much time passed already? The sun had settled high in the sky. It wasn't noon yet but it was close, and the temperature had probably hit the low forties.

He passed me a sandwich and poured me another cup of coffee, still steaming. It felt good to cradle the cup in my hands.

"Dad?"

He looked up. "What's on your mind, son?"

"Giving Traveler another chance," I said. "I know I have to. Those were my terms. But I'm still not excited about it."

"Well," he said, "he's out now, like he should be. Better sooner than never, don't you think?"

I nodded.

"That's a big secret to keep bottled up. Not too surprising he popped his cork. His timing was lousy, but done's done." My dad thought about it for a minute. "He's got a long row to hoe. He's on his way, but he still owes everyone an apology for being such an asshole at the officers' club the other night."

"He apologized to me already," I said. "You and Mom will hear from him, too. He's a little apprehensive of how you might react."

My dad chuckled. "He deserves to be."

"I was positive he would never come out and I wouldn't have to worry about giving him another chance. Now I'm getting cold feet."

He poured more coffee for himself and warmed his hands against the mug. "It's your privilege to change your mind," he said, finally, "but how would you feel if you backed out?"

"I wouldn't like myself very much," I said.

"Well, there you go," my dad said.

I sighed. There I went.

"You'll do the right thing," my dad said.

I appreciated his confidence, though I didn't share it.

We weren't ready to give up the possibility of fresh fish for dinner yet. After lunch, Dad motored the skiff to another likely spot in the lake. Having had no luck with minnows, I decided to try a lure for a while. I was pleased with the nod of satisfaction my dad offered when I selected a red teardrop—the best color if you're after bass, as he'd taught me. He also selected a lure quite different from mine. I suspect he knew it was not the best option under these conditions, but if the fish were down there, we would give them a choice.

Lunch lowered my resistance even more. Relaxed, my belly full, I felt drowsy, and I cast my line and reeled it in so slowly that the lure hardly moved in the water. But maybe that was the ultimate persuader. A quick nibble, followed by a more urgent tug, yanked me from my reverie. My dad watched to see if I'd hooked one, ready to assist if necessary.

Smallmouth bass are fighters. Part of the satisfaction of landing one is that it puts up such a protest. As soon as I felt the strike, I jerked the rod upward to lodge the hook inside its mouth. If the fish felt sluggish, my action woke it up and set the hook, and the tussle began. I let out line, reeled some of it back, then let out more, intent on tiring it out so that I could bring it in for good. Given its size—perhaps fifteen inches long, and four or five pounds on average—the bass is strong. I have great respect for it, combative until the end.

I reeled in the line and verified I had indeed hooked a fine speckled bass, writhing as if it somehow knew life depended upon shaking loose of the hook, now deeply embedded in its mouth. I shifted the pole to one hand, and my father passed me the net. Carefully (I'd lost more than one fish by being too eager at this stage), I dipped into the water and scooped it up with one deliberate movement.

As a boy, I'd always loathed what came next. The erratic flopping of a trapped fish used to scare me. My father, oblivious, would put the fish out of its misery with a quick strike of the pliers against its head. Then he'd carefully remove the hook, but I couldn't face the accusing dead eye. Where was the sport? I believed the contest was nothing more than a grossly unequal match between a superior force with all the advantages of technology and intelligence and a dumb creature with only instinct to guide it. But I have grown up since then and gained a great respect for the sporting nature of fishing, not only the art of it but the craft as well.

I stared at the bass entangled in my net, flipping, twisting, gasping, desperate. I knew what needed to be done next, and ordinarily, I had no qualms. But on this warm winter day, having won, I could not follow through.

"Dad," I said. "I don't know if—"

He recognized my hesitation. "It's okay, son."

I dipped my hands in the water first and then gripped the fish at the gills, carefully digging the hook from its mouth with the pliers. Vigorously, the bass continued its tussle, its tail smacking my arm like a scolding. The hook retrieved, I dropped the fish in the water. It darted off instantly, apparently none the worse for its close call.

"I'm sorry, Dad."

He put a hand on my shoulder. "No reason to be, Harris."

Occasionally, we went fishing to catch and release on purpose. Certain times of year, certain locales, and certain types of fish demanded it. We didn't mind, for we took satisfaction in the competition and the victory. But this was different. I was grateful for his understanding.

We dumped the rest of the minnows too, having no immediate need for them. I hoped my bass would find a couple of them, a reward for the ordeal it had been through. We stowed our gear and puttered back to the launch, loaded the skiff onto the trailer, packed our gear, and headed for home, with Hank Williams accompanying us once again.

There was summer trout still in the freezer, and my mother thawed it out. We had seafood for dinner anyway, seasoned with salt and dill and lemon, and we savored the meal as much as if we'd caught it fresh that afternoon. We'd had our fishing excursion, my father and I, and I felt as if I'd been properly reintegrated into the family and the world again.

I decided I needed a day or two alone to regroup and prepare to resume battle in whatever form it might take on Monday, so I chose to leave home early Friday.

"What's next?" my mom asked me at breakfast.

"I'll keep you posted," I said.

The general had met my minimum criteria for moving us forward, and he'd done it with a vengeance. My part came next, giving him the second chance. What form would that take? I had no inkling how we could reach a truce, reestablish equilibrium, engineer the perfect compromise, the cautiously optimistic blueprint for our future together. Given the sudden change of circumstance, I would not be able to continue as his aide, and I was thankful for the extra incentive for him to remove me from the position. If we were meant to be together, we would find a way, even if I had to transfer to another base. If not, I would let him be.

I knew I'd never extricate myself from him entirely. He meant too much to me. Even if we did nothing more than exchange greetings at Christmas, I'd want to keep track of Seamus O'Neill. On the long ride back, I had plenty of time to think, but my state of mind was not the agonizing twist-and-blame it had been before. I no longer felt like a bass hooked and trapped in a net. I felt calm enough to face the general again and to establish some new ground rules. If he made good on the second chance or if he didn't, I had become stronger, and I could manage. If our journey were fire, I had been tempered.

Sitting on the porch of my apartment was a package wrapped neatly in brown paper and clear tape, stamped and postmarked from the base. There was no return address, but I knew from the slanted handwriting who'd sent it and what it contained, and my courage failed. In the kitchen, I set the box on the table and sat down and wept as if all rivers depended on me for sustenance.

Unwrapped, there was my old bear, as I'd requested, none the worse for half a year in the general's custody except that it was scented unmistakably with the fragrant, bitter mystery of his aftershave. I put the bear back where he belonged, in the center of my bed, and slept with him wrapped tightly against me that night, while some five or six miles away, the general slept alone.

CHAPTER THIRTY-ONE

On Saturday morning, early, the pager went off. The general hadn't used it in so long that I'd nearly forgotten about it. I hadn't even taken it home with me, and for a minute, I could not place its curious buzzing. And buzz it did, urgent, until I located it. He was calling from his house, and, reluctantly, I called back.

"Where are you?" he barked. Not even hello.

"My apartment. I got back from Ohio last night." Then, defensive: "I'm on leave until Monday."

"I know," he said, impatient. "How could I forget? It's been a hell of a week, but I'm entirely to blame. In case you're wondering, I can't manage a damn thing for myself. My whole life is crumbling to pieces. That should make you feel better."

It didn't. I said nothing, and he continued. "You going anywhere this morning?"

"Hadn't planned on it."

"Stay put. I'm on my way."

Could I tell him no? He didn't give me a chance to argue. The phone went dead.

Surprisingly, I wasn't upset or even anxious. For once, I didn't feel as if I had to rush around throwing clutter into closets, wiping down the bathroom, putting out fresh towels, changing my shirt. I sat calmly on the couch with a fresh cup of coffee, relieved that our first meeting would take place on my home turf instead of his—or worse, the office.

When I answered an urgent knock, I opened the door to a man wearing blue jeans, sneakers, a dark green sweatshirt, and a ball cap. In his arms, he held a beautiful puppy, short-haired, mostly black with some oddly positioned white and gray patches suggesting a mixed heritage. It wore a neon red collar, a little too large, although the size of the puppy's paws suggested it would grow into the collar with ease. The animal was inquisitive and a little anxious, probably not more than nine or ten weeks old, but already a handful. I guessed it didn't like to be held. Perhaps it didn't like the general. Perhaps it realized there was a big world out there and time spent not exploring was time wasted.

I looked beyond the dog to the man holding it, all tallness and bristle, impatience and growl. Even dressed as casually as he was, he would stand out in a crowd. His mustache jutted out aggressively, untamed as always. I could feel the serrated edge of his unshaven jaw just by looking. He bit on the stem of his empty pipe as if he would shear it clean off. And he scowled, bothered by something or everything.

"General O'Neill," I said.

He winced. Sighed. Adjusted his cargo of puppy. "You have my permission to call me anything but that," he said.

I crossed my arms and met his gaze.

"Please, Harris?" he said. Then, "Oh, damn it!" as the puppy squirmed in his arms, yapped urgently and licked his nose, struggling to get free. He set it down and it raced into my apartment, toenails clicking as it skidded on the wooden floor of the living room, sniffing out this whole new world.

"He or she?" I said.

"She," he said. "I told you once—stupidly, I might add—that you needed a woman in your life if you wanted to get anywhere in the Air Force. Well, this here's the only gal I won't fight for your attention."

"What's her name?"

"Hasn't got one yet. That's your department. Think about it. Get acquainted with her. You'll pick the right one."

"So is she mine?"

He shook his head and looked at me square. "Nope. Ours."

I was speechless. He expected as much, I warrant. I watched as the puppy inspected the couch, the easy chair, the rug.

"My landlord doesn't allow pets," I said when I found a voice. "There's no way I could hide a puppy here."

"She'll live at my house," he said. "The backyard's fenced, remember."

"You've never trained a puppy."

He nodded. "I reckon that'll have to be your responsibility, too, since you've got the experience. But I'll help. You can teach me how. You like her? I recollect your fondness for dark and furry stuff." He placed a hand under his sweatshirt, insinuating. I ignored his not-so-subtle reference, and he labored on. "Visited four different animal shelters to find the right one. I picked up a sack of Puppy Chow, a dish, a couple of rubber chew toys, a leash, even a bed full of cedar chips. Smells wonderful, just like a sawmill."

I met his blithe confidence with a list of potential problems. "How will you keep her with all the traveling you do? Even when you're here, you're at work most of the time, and she'll be all alone. That's not good for a puppy. She needs people around her. She'll chew everything she can sink her teeth into because that's what puppies do. And you can't lock her in a cage all day. It's not fair," I said. "Besides, once you start the training, you've got to work with her every day if you want it to stick. How would you explain to the neighbors why I'm at your house all the time training your dog?"

"*Our* dog, Harris. Will you quit being so technical?" he said. "We'll work out the details later, but today we're going to the park and getting to know each other." He looked at me, expectant, as if his pronouncement settled the matter. I sighed. I'd never thought he'd bring reinforcements to buttress his position. He knew how I felt about dogs, and I was ready to cave in, but practicality and fairness to the animal made me reluctant.

He continued his sales pitch. "I'll bring her with me to the office every day. There's no law against that. We can work with her during lunch. The NAF can use a mascot, and as long as she's well-behaved, who's to complain?"

Particularly if she's the general's dog. Maybe it would work out after all, but there were some gigantic "ifs" to traverse before I would even think about taking on such a project. Besides, why was he acting so sure of himself? I followed the puppy as she nosed her way into the kitchen, and the general followed me.

"You're coming back, aren't you?" he said.

"Don't you think people will talk? An openly gay general with an openly gay aide?"

"So, you've heard my little news."

"Your little news has made its way around the world twice by now, I'll bet."

"I'd been meaning to come out. Ever since you established the condition, Harris. Honest. The staff meeting wasn't exactly my forum of choice. But when I heard that son of a bitch Beemis make that crack about you, something snapped inside me. I couldn't stop myself. But as soon as I said it, I knew it was the right thing to do."

"I'm proud of you."

"Does it still count?" he said. "Even if it was an accident, I did what you wanted."

"Of course it counts," I said. "I didn't spell out the circumstances. I just said you had to do it. You'll have a hard time shutting the closet door again once you've broken it down."

He let out a relieved sign. "Thank you. I was afraid…well, never mind. Thank you." He cleared his throat. "Now, about your part of the bargain—"

I interrupted. "Has there been any significant fallout?"

"I've kept it pretty low-key. I'm trying to, anyway. There will be no press conference, but I reckon everyone in the NAF knows by now," he said. "I spent a pretty uncomfortable hour on the phone with the four-star, but I brought him around." He chuckled. "Yesterday, in the commissary, a young airman came up to me. Couldn't have been more than eighteen or nineteen. He was quaking in his boots, but he looked me square in the eye and said thank you for coming out, sir, and shook my hand. It made my day."

"Now you can put a picture of your boyfriend on your desk, too."

"Do I *have* a boyfriend?"

I bypassed the question. "Have you told your dad and Kathleen yet?"

"No. Jesus! One thing at a time. I'm more concerned about your parents and what they must think of me after my little performance at the club."

"You lost a lot of points," I said. "It was a critical error. Whether it's fatal or not depends on you."

He nodded. "I put a letter in the mail yesterday. It was a hard one to write. I'll call them in a few days, too, but I wanted to write first and apologize. Will they ever want to see me again?"

"You can still expect a cool reception for a while," I said. "Coming out helped a lot, but you'll have a lot of work to do to get back in their good graces."

"I'm ready."

The puppy circled around me, sniffing my shoes and endearing herself, tail wagging furiously. She chose that moment to squat and relieve herself on the rag carpet in front of the kitchen sink, distracting us for a minute. I wasn't as upset as the general seemed to think I might be, and he grabbed some paper towels and blotted the damp stain.

"Don't worry," I said. "It's an old rug. But it's not too early to start paper-training her."

Listen to me. What was I getting myself into?

"She's got it easy. She's still young and open-minded. Doesn't know any better and hasn't got any bad habits yet," the general said. He paused to collect his thoughts. "I reckon I don't have to tell you I could use a little obedience training myself."

Hmm…interestingly put, I thought.

He continued. "I'm an old dog, and you know what they say about us."

"I do."

"If anyone can teach me anything in the way of new tricks, it's you. And you have my permission to whack me with a rolled-up newspaper whenever you think I deserve it. I'm a stubborn old man, but eventually, I'll get it through my thick skull," he said. "I'm not willing to settle for a souvenir. I need you more than any other thing in my life, Harris Alfred Langdon Mitchell. There's too damn much of you to put into an envelope." He took a deep breath. "I love you. With everything in me, I do. That's a true statement, and I give you my sorry word on it," he said.

"Will you put that in writing?"

He shook his head. "You have my word. I'm not sure of the consequences," he said, "but you have my word. About that second chance—you did promise, Hacksaw."

"I did?"

"You did. Just say yes. Nod your head." And then he glared at me. "I'll settle for a 'maybe' right now."

He waited, expectant, eager, nervous, a little uncertain. As if for a fraction of a second I wouldn't give in. As if he thought for a moment that I really had any other choice. Or wanted one. Under my scrutiny, his brown eyes watered and overflowed, and I was a beaten man. With less unwillingness than I intended to show him, I stepped inside his embrace. After a hesitant second, he attached his mouth to mine.

"I've never been so scared," he said when we separated. "If I have any excuse for my miserable behavior, that's the best I can offer. I can't say you'll never regret it. You probably will sometimes, because you know I can be a real—"

"Prick," I said.

"Prick," he said. "I sleep better when I can wake up next to you in the morning. If you like to watch me shaving, I'll cut myself to ribbons anytime you want to distract me." I gave him, he said, courage to fight his doubt. Love, he said, could change what you want, and it could change your tactics, techniques, and procedures as well.

He was learning.

I had my own fears to face. "You asked me once how I could be sure that you were the one for me. How do you know *you* won't change your mind?"

He raised his eyebrows. "It won't happen in your lifetime," he said. "That's as long as I can promise. Done?"

I nodded.

He wagged his eyebrows. "So I do have a boyfriend?"

"Don't you think that sounds kind of high-schoolish?"

"I feel kind of high-schoolish right now. As for the photo on my desk, it's already there," he said. "Has been for months, in fact."

"No."

"Yes," he said. "It's the softball team photo from the summer, but we're both in it side by side, and I've got my arm around your shoulder."

"I remember. Why didn't I think of that?"

"It will have to do for the time being. And now that we've got all that settled," he said, "there's one more little thing."

He excused himself, went out to his car, and returned with a packet that he handed to me without ceremony. It was a single red rose, a little tired but valiant, wrapped in what looked like official correspondence on Air Force letterhead, with the blue seal in the left corner.

He was a bit embarrassed. "I'm not in the habit of doing such things," he muttered. "I never gave a man a rose before." He clamped his jaw on the pipe stem and glowered as if he dared me to say a word.

"Thank you."

"You're welcome." He was still scowling, as if he were angry at himself for succumbing to a cliché.

Curious, I unwrapped the paper and read its words. Succinct to the point of abruptness, the letter contained only a couple of lines addressed to his boss, the four-star. Briefly, it stated that, effective immediately,

Major General Seamus E. O'Neill was resigning his commission and retiring from service in the U.S. Air Force. It had been an honor to serve, and thank you very much.

"I don't get it," I said.

"Well," he said, "until my mouth got away from me at the staff meeting, this was my Plan A. I was going to retire, like it says in the letter. And I was going to rent a hall and hire a brass band to announce to the world that I was queer and planning to retire so I could enjoy it. I didn't know how else to show what you, and us, meant to me," he said.

"And then you devised Plan B."

He nodded. "On the fly, you might say. But I can't retire now."

"You could if you wanted to."

"No. I've thrown down the gauntlet. I can't walk away."

I could hear the pride in his voice, and I knew he was actually looking forward to the fight. He'd tackle it, as he had every other barrier in his life, with lusty conviction and energetic spirit. The greatest hurdle had been cleared, and nothing would be as difficult afterward.

"Guess you're right," I said. "I could resign my commission instead. We could wait a respectable month or two, and then we could move in together."

"That's a possibility." He didn't sound convinced. "Do you want to resign?"

I realized I didn't. "I can't think of anything I'd rather do right now than serve in the Air Force."

"I was hoping you would say that. I want us to have that experience in common. So we're agreed we'll both continue wearing the uniform, at least for the time being?"

"Agreed."

He sounded relieved. "I like it better this way, even if it means we have to wait a couple of years before we can settle down. You're still going to have to sneak around and knock on my door in the middle of the night and hope no one sees you."

"So are you."

"I'm willing."

"Me, too." He winked. "I'd hate to lose that two-star pension. It will come in handy when we go homesteading."

"Don't look so pleased, Traveler," I said. "You've got a rocky road ahead. You don't know how hard it's going to be for the next couple of weeks, let alone the next three years. How do I know you won't start blaming me for putting you up to it? You'll hate me."

"I won't. End of discussion." He took me into his arms again. "I offer you a dog and a rose and my sorry ass, and you're willing to give me a second chance," he said. "You're more generous than I deserve. I can't tell you how much—"

"You don't have to tell me," I said. "You have to show me."

"I know. Every day. Mending a broken promise is a lifetime's work, and even then, you might still see the cracks. But I'm ready. It's more important to me than anything, even if we still have this Air Force business to get through. It's a mine field," he said, "but I think we can get across." He looked at me, stern. "You'll be back to work on Monday. Correct?"

I sighed and nodded.

He seemed relieved. The puppy started chewing the shoestrings of his sneakers, and he got down on the floor with her. She transferred her attentions to his fingers, gnawing with needle-sharp teeth. "It's just temporary, you know," he said as they tussled. "You're transferring to another base, away from my bad influence. I can find you a position at one of the units in the NAF. That way, I'll still see you sometimes, and you can catch a hop back here on a C-5 to visit me. Do you want to go back into personnel?"

"Not if I can help it," I said. "Maybe something a little more invigorating? Although nothing could top this past year."

He grinned. "You'd be a good candidate for pilot training."

"Not on your life. One egomaniacal flyer in the family is enough. I could never compete."

He laughed. "Maintenance officer? Communications? Civil engineer? Cop?"

"How about the Military Equal Opportunity office? I could do some good there, I think."

He nodded. "A sane and practical choice. I'll make the necessary arrangements Monday morning. I'll start the search for a new aide immediately, but you'll have to stay on until your school starts."

That worked for me. Three years apart would be a long stretch, but we'd manage. We'd be able to exchange calls and emails, and I'd insist he continue to send me postcards regularly. Perhaps I could even convince him to get a cell phone.

"It won't be easy, but it will be worth it," he said.

I agreed.

"I don't know how the rest of the staff will take the news. They seem to think you do a good job keeping me in line."

Maybe so. But the transition wouldn't be difficult, I told him. "Everyone in the headquarters thinks you hate me."

He seemed surprised. "They do?"

"Sure. You're so demanding, and you always seem to be angry at me. Always hollering, especially when you have an audience. Didn't you ever notice? And you never call me by name. Linda is convinced you only do it because you want to embarrass me."

"Hmm," he said, thoughtful. "They think I actually hate you?"

"Yup."

"But you know this guy better than that, right?"

I did. "I figured out a long time ago he was mostly bluff."

He paused for a long time and then sighed. "Remind me why you would stake your future on a guy like him."

Because underneath his mask, he's a complicated package of conviction and wonder, mischief and fear, spirit and surprise, equal parts malice-with-intent and heaven-and-nature singing? That must be it. But I gave him three words. "I love him."

He stood, and we faced each other. "That's enough," he said simply. "He loves you, too." He drew me to him, and I angled my head to take his mouth once more. He built a good fire, and we actually could teach conflagration a thing or two about heat and smoke and urgency. When we came up for air, he let out a low whistle and chuckled. "You pack a hell of a kick, Muleskinner," he said. Then, as if I might all of a sudden be offended he quickly apologized. "I'm sorry. Harris. It's just another stupid habit I should quit."

"Oh, hush, Traveler. If you start calling me 'Harris' all the time, I'll think you're mad at me. I can hear you, no matter what ridiculous thing you call me." I suspected his nickname generator would never run out of ingenious ways to fetch me, and I didn't mind. "I don't know who will be unlucky enough to be your next aide," I said. "And God help him, because he's going to need it. But if I ever catch you calling him anything but his name, I'll throw you to the dogs."

The puppy, as if to prove she'd heard me and would fully cooperate, took hold of the general's pants leg and tugged, furious. And as we stood there, the three of us, I decided this was how our family should look. He drew me to him and folded me into his arms, strong and warm and familiar. When he sanded my neck with his unshaven jaw, any protest from me would have been pointless.

"I don't mind telling you, for the first time in my life, I'm a little uncertain about the consequences of giving my word," he said. "This is unfamiliar territory." Like a proverb, he muttered, "I'm a goddamned old fool."

"You certainly are," I said. And foolishness in hard times is the heart of wisdom.

"And for my part, you're my compass. I need your north," he said. "And, well…" His mustache loped on ahead of him.

"What?"

"My belly misses your hands." He paused and shook his head. "That sounds dumb. I'm sorry."

It didn't sound dumb at all. I didn't know what to say, but I knew what to do. I reached underneath his sweatshirt, and inside of a minute, he was making the hungry sounds I loved. Nothing I could put in an envelope would ever match his contented sigh.

"That's it," he whispered. "We're home."

About the Author

Richard Compson Sater retired from the U.S. Air Force Reserve after twenty-four years of service, having attained the rank of lieutenant colonel. He spent most of his career as a photojournalist and public affairs officer under the "Don't Ask, Don't Tell" directive that kept gay service members in the closet. He is a veteran of both Operation Enduring Freedom (Afghanistan) and Operation Iraqi Freedom. *Rank* is his first novel.

Sater earned a bachelor's degree in creative writing from the University of Pittsburgh, a master's in creative writing from Purdue University, and a Ph.D. in fine arts from Ohio University. In addition to his military service, he has at various times been a college professor, classical music radio host, bookkeeper, bartender, and window shade salesman. He lives in Seattle with his handsome spouse and their dog.

Books Available From Bold Strokes Books

Rank by Richard Compson Sater. Rank means nothing to the heart, but the Air Force isn't as impartial. Every airman learns that rank has its privileges. What about love? (978-1-62639-845-0)

The Grim Reaper's Calling Card by Donald Webb. When Katsuro Tanaka begins investigating the disappearance of a young nurse, he discovers more missing persons, and they all have one thing in common: The Grim Reaper Tarot Card. (978-1-62639-748-4)

Smoldering Desires by C.E. Knipes. Evan McGarrity has found the man of his dreams in Sebastian Tantalos. When an old boyfriend from Sebastian's past enters the picture, Evan must fight for the man he loves. (978-1-62639-714-9)

Tallulah Bankhead Slept Here by Sam Lollar. A coming of age/coming out story, set in El Paso of 1967, that tells of Aaron's adventures with movie stars, cool cars, and topless bars. (978-1-62639-710-1)

The City of Seven Gods by Andrew J. Peters. In an ancient city of aerie temples, a young priest and a barbarian mercenary struggle to refashion their lives after their worlds are torn apart by betrayal. (978-1-62639-775-0)

Lysistrata Cove by Dena Hankins. Jack and Eve navigate the maelstrom of their darkest desires and find love by transgressing gender, dominance, submission, and the law on the crystal blue Caribbean Sea. (978-1-62639-821-4)

Garden District Gothic by Greg Herren. Scotty Bradley has to solve a notorious thirty-year-old unsolved murder that has terrible repercussions in the present. (978-1-62639-667-8)

The Man on Top of the World by Vanessa Clark. Jonathan Maxwell falling in love with Izzy Rich, the world's hottest glam rock superstar, is not only unpredictable but complicated when a bold teenage fan-girl changes everything. (978-1-62639-699-9)

The Orchard of Flesh by Christian Baines. With two hotheaded men under his roof including his werewolf lover, a vampire tries to solve an increasingly lethal mystery while keeping Sydney's supernatural factions from the brink of war. (978-1-62639-649-4)

Funny Bone by Daniel W. Kelly. Sometimes sex feels so good you just gotta giggle! (978-1-62639-683-8)

The Thassos Confabulation by Sam Sommer. With the inheritance of a great deal of money, David and Chris also inherit a nondescript brown paper parcel and a strange and perplexing letter that sends David on a quest to understand its meaning. (978-1-62639-665-4)

The Photographer's Truth by Ralph Josiah Bardsley. Silicon Valley tech geek Ian Baines gets more than he bargained for on an unexpected journey of self-discovery through the lustrous nightlife of Paris. (978-1-62639-637-1)

Crimson Souls by William Holden. A scorned shadow demon brings a centuries-old vendetta to a bloody end as he assembles the last of the descendants of Harvard's Secret Court. (978-1-62639-628-9)

The Long Season by Michael Vance Gurley. When Brett Bennett enters the professional hockey world of 1926 Chicago, will he meet his match in either handsome goalie Jean-Paul or in the man who may destroy everything? (978-1-62639-655-5)

Triad Blood by 'Nathan Burgoine. Cheating tradition, Luc, Anders, and Curtis—vampire, demon, and wizard—form a bond to gain their freedom, but will surviving those they cheated be beyond their combined power? (978-1-62639-587-9)

Death Comes Darkly by David S. Pederson. Can dashing detective Heath Barrington solve the murder of an eccentric millionaire and find love with policeman Alan Keyes, who, despite his lust, harbors feelings of guilt and shame? (978-1-62639-625-8)

Slaves of Greenworld by David Holly. On the planet Greenworld, the amnesiac Dove must cope with intrigues, alien monsters, and a growing slave revolt, while reveling in homoerotic sexual intimacy with his own slave Raret. (978-1-62639-623-4)

Men in Love: M/M Romance, edited by Jerry L. Wheeler. Love stories between men, from first blush to wedding bells and beyond. (978-1-62639-7361)

Love on the Jersey Shore by Richard Natale. Two working-class cousins help one another navigate the choppy waters of sexual chemistry and true love. (978-1-62639-550-3)

Final Departure by Steve Pickens. What do you do when an unexpected body interrupts the worst day of your life? (978-1-62639-536-7)

Night Sweats by Tom Cardamone. These stories are as gripping as the hand on your throat. (978-1-62639-572-5)

Soul's Blood by Stephen Graham King. After receiving a summons from a love long past, Keene and his associates, Lexa-Blue and the sentient ship Maverick Heart, are plunged into turmoil on a planet poised for war. (978-1-62639-508-4)

Corpus Calvin by David Swatling. Cloverkist Inn may be haunted, but a ghost materializes from Jason Dekker's past and Calvin's canine instinct kicks in to protect a young boy from mortal danger. (978-1-62639-428-5)

Brothers by Ralph Josiah Bardsley. Blood is thicker than water, but you can drown in either. Jamus Cork and Sean Malloy struggle against tradition to find love in the Irish enclave of South Boston. (978-1-62639-538-1)

Every Unworthy Thing by Jon Wilson. Gang wars, racial tensions, a kidnapped girl, and a lone PI! What could go wrong? (978-1-62639-514-5)

Puppet Boy by Christian Baines. Budding filmmaker Eric can't stop thinking about the handsome young actor that's transferred to his class. Could Julien be his muse? Even his first boyfriend? Or something far more sinister? (978-1-62639-510-7)

The Prophecy by Jerry Rabushka. Religion and revolution threaten to bring an ancient civilization to its knees...unless love does it first. (978-1-62639-440-7)